THE DAY AFTER GETTYSBURG

Baen Books
by Robert Conroy

★

Himmler's War
Rising Sun
1920: America's Great War
Liberty: 1784
1882: Custer in Chains
Germanica
Stormfront
The Day After Gettysburg (with J.R. Dunn)

Baen Books
by J.R. Dunn

★

Days of Cain
This Side of Judgment
Full Tide of Night

To purchase these and other Baen titles in e-book format,
please go to www.baen.com

THE DAY AFTER GETTYSBURG

★

ROBERT CONROY
J. R. DUNN

THE DAY AFTER GETTYSBURG

Copyright © 2017 by the Estate of Robert Conroy and J.R. Dunn

A Baen Books Original

Baen Publishing Enterprises
P.O. Box 1403
Riverdale, NY 10471
www.baen.com

ISBN: 978-1-4814-8251-6

Cover art by Kurt Miller
Map by Randy Asplund

First Baen hardcover printing, June 2017

Distributed by Simon & Schuster
1230 Avenue of the Americas
New York, NY 10020

Printed in the United States of America

10 9 8 7 6 5 4 3 2 1

A huge thank you to the readers of Robert's work.
He has written about many battles over the years,
but this book represents his last battle.

Thank you Robert.
As you look down upon all you have accomplished,
we remember your knowledge and enthusiasm
for history and your need to ask "what if . . ."
We wish you were still here to share the success
and joy that was your passion, and that lives on
through the works you have left behind.

Diane, Maura, Quinn and Brennan

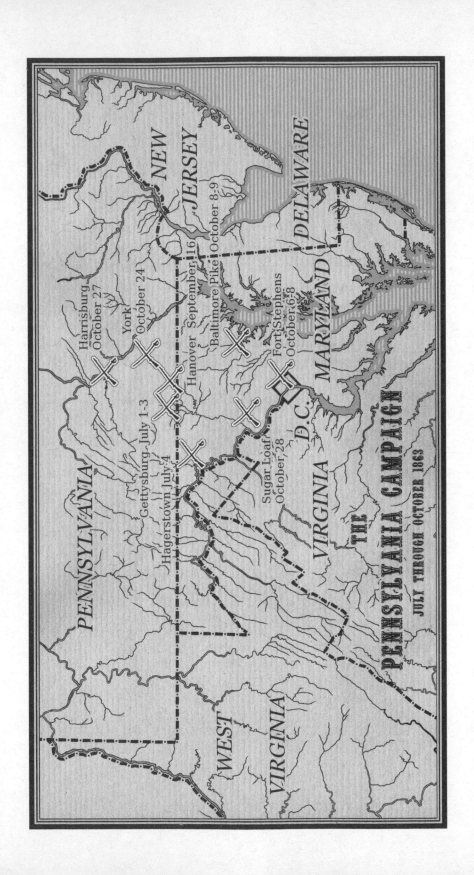

THE PENNSYLVANIA CAMPAIGN

JULY THROUGH OCTOBER 1863

Harrisburg
October 27

York
October 24

Hanover September 16

Baltimore Pike October 8-9

Fort Stephens
October 6-8

Gettysburg July 1-3

Hagerstown July 4

Sugar Loaf
October 28

PENNSYLVANIA

NEW JERSEY

DELAWARE

MARYLAND

D.C.

VIRGINIA

WEST VIRGINIA

THE DAY AFTER GETTYSBURG

★ INTRODUCTION ★

After three agonizing and incredibly bloody days of fighting in the scorching heat of July, 1863, the Battle of Gettysburg limped to a close. Both Union and Confederate armies were exhausted and had been mauled almost beyond recognition. Those three days had resulted in the costliest battle in the history of the United States. The Union had been victorious but had paid a brutal price. The Confederacy, with her smaller army and population base, had suffered even more severely. Estimates of the dead and wounded varied, but could have reached fifty thousand, split almost equally between the two armies.

As Confederate General Robert E. Lee watched his defeated Army of Northern Virginia withdraw from the field, he is said to have proclaimed that the defeat was all his fault and most historians will not dispute that sad fact. Those same historians will say that he overreached. He'd attacked a larger and well-trained Union Army that held the high ground as well as having the advantage of interior lines, and was led by a general, George Gordon Meade, who understood what he had to do to stave off defeat. Historians also fault Lee for thinking that the soldiers in his army could accomplish the impossible. They couldn't. They were superb soldiers but they were mortal.

Still, it was a close victory for the North and most Union soldiers were glad to see the Confederates go on their way back across the Potomac and into Virginia. But Abraham Lincoln did not hold that view. He fully understood that the Rebel army had to be destroyed,

1

not defeated, before the terrible war could be concluded. He prodded Meade into following Lee and drawing him into a climactic battle before he could escape across the Potomac. Meade followed, but not aggressively. He knew that his army had suffered grievous casualties and was exhausted and hungry. In short, Meade's army was a fragile thing to send on a chase.

In real history, Lee successfully crosses the Potomac and escapes Meade's slowly closing clutches. Both armies take the next few months to regroup and prepare for the next round of fighting. Lincoln recognizes that Meade is not the aggressive spirit who can demolish Lee's army. A few months later, Grant takes over. Two bloody years later, Lee surrenders to Grant at Appomattox Court House.

But what if Lee had been unable to cross the Potomac and, gambler that he was, decided to launch an all or nothing attack against the plodding Union army? And what if he had won an enormous and totally unexpected victory for the Confederacy? How would that have changed the course of the war? What impact would it have had on the presidency itself?

There was no Fourth Day of Gettysburg. It is simply my term for that critical time following the actual three days of fighting at that now immortal Pennsylvania town. And while there might have been a Sixth Indiana Mounted Infantry, I cannot find when and where it actually took the field. Therefore, it and the personnel associated with it are figments of my imagination.

And finally, a word about sexual assaults: They have occurred in every war and the Civil War was no exception. There did seem to be a degree of restraint and the assaults appeared to be fewer in number and nothing like what occurred in European or Asian wars. This was due perhaps to the fact that people on both sides were basically of the same stock, spoke the same language, wore the same clothing, and were pretty much all Christians and Americans. Although attacks on female slaves and former slaves were more common than attacks on white women, they did occur. Historians rarely talked about them and one can only speculate as to why. Despite the apparent restraint, women were always in jeopardy, especially those in the countryside and atrocities did occur.

—Robert Conroy

★ CHAPTER 1 ★

Robert E. Lee tried to rub the exhaustion from his eyes but failed. It was difficult for him to focus his vision. He felt like he was about to slip from his horse. That would never do, he chided himself as he patted the large and faithful grey horse, Traveler. He was almost as well known as Lee himself.

What was confounding his plans was the fact that the waters of the Potomac were rain-swollen and high and moving quickly to the sea. *But not quickly enough*, he thought bitterly. One pontoon bridge had already been swept away and there were serious doubts as to whether others would hold. His soldiers were entrenching, building defenses in anticipation of an attack by a Union army that greatly outnumbered them. If he could not get his men across the Potomac, this could easily spell the end of the Army of Northern Virginia and the Confederate States of America. If his army was destroyed, there would be nothing between Meade's Army of the Potomac and Richmond.

Many weeks earlier, he had said that Meade would make no mistakes, and the Union general hadn't. Meade had skillfully defended the hills near Gettysburg. And now he was chasing Lee and would soon catch him. Lee almost smiled. He thought he had the measure of the man. Defense was what Meade did best, and now he was on the offensive with an army that had just suffered somewhere around twenty thousand casualties. So too had Lee's smaller Confederate army, and the loss of all those fine young men deeply saddened him. But while Lincoln could replace his losses, Lee could not. Jefferson Davis would try to get more troops and supplies to him, but it wouldn't matter worth a damn if Lee couldn't get his army back across the Potomac and into Virginia.

Now Lee did smile. He knew exactly what he had to do.

"Captain Thorne—you wouldn't happen to have any fresh food or clean water or maybe some good southern tobacco on you, would you? I wouldn't mind a chance to change my underwear or possibly converse with a good-looking woman, either."

Steven Thorne was so tired it took almost all of his strength to smile and respond to his good friend Archie Willis. "Since I have no idea or memory of what any of those things are, I cannot answer you, Captain."

"But sir, are you not the acting commander of this regiment? And as such, aren't you supposed to know everything?"

"As I am now your commanding officer, if I told you to go to hell, would you comply?"

Willis laughed, but it quickly became a cough. The roads from the killing fields of Gettysburg were alternatively chokingly dusty and muddy. Today, each step taken by man or horse raised a cloud of dust to clog the air and make breathing difficult. The men were cold, tired, hungry, and emotionally whipped. Everyone said they had won the battle, and that might be true as far as it went. But at what cost?

"Well then, Steven, do you think we will catch Bobby Lee?"

"I think it's entirely possible, but what happens then? Did you ever see a dog chase a carriage? And what does the dog do when the carriage halts and the dog thinks he has caught it? Most of the time the dog has no idea what to do with his prize and I wonder if General Meade knows what to do if and when he catches Lee. I for one do not look forward to any such development."

Both men, along with the two hundred soldiers who comprised the rest of their regiment, needed at least a month's rest. They had won a gigantic battle but would have nightmares for the rest of their lives. At least the air was cleaner. Gone was the stench of thousands of obscenely bloated bodies rotting in the blazing sun, and gone too were the screams of the wounded as they lay in endless rows waiting for someone, anyone, to help them. Or maybe to put them out of their misery with a prayer to God to forgive them for doing so. Unfortunately, God was conspicuously absent from the battlefields around the previously unknown town of Gettysburg.

The two men were riding side by side. The rest of the mounted infantry rode behind them. Several dozen walked, having lost their horses in the battle. Reporters would say they were "marching", but they were in truth walking, and barely walking at that. Shuffling might be a better word. Their bodies pleaded for rest.

"Just think, Archie. If it wasn't for the fact that I had two weeks more time in grade as a captain than you, the regiment would be yours."

"And an empty honor it is."

They stopped and looked at each other. Units everywhere were doing the same thing. Thorne's regiment, the Sixth Indiana Mounted Infantry, was near the front of the long, winding Union column, but far enough back so that they could not see the head of the snake. It did not escape them that their unit was mixed up with others. They knew they weren't supposed to be in this position, but just where the hell was the rest of the division, the corps?

Suddenly, they heard gunfire. The rumble and crackle were in the distance and were not an immediate threat, but one thing had just become abundantly clear. They had found Robert E. Lee.

"General Lee, sir, would you mind telling me just why the hell are we standing here staring at this sorry little creek?"

Lee smiled. General James Longstreet had arrived and perhaps the rift that had come between them could be closed, or at least eased. Hindsight had shown that Longstreet's plans for the battle at Gettysburg had been correct. A frontal assault, carried out by Pickett or anyone else, had been doomed to bloody failure. The Army of Northern Virginia should have either tried to turn the Union flanks or simply called it a day and withdrawn. From a different position, perhaps, he could have taunted Meade into attacking him on ground favorable to his army. *Likely not*, he thought. Meade was a defender, not an attacker.

Lee had assumed too much and the burden of failure was on him. He had to redeem himself and the Army of Northern Virginia or the Confederacy was a lost cause.

"General Longstreet," he said genially, "I'll have you know that this is a most important river. It separates us from our homes and will be our downfall if we do not find a way to resolve the problem of crossing it. While it is certainly not as wide as the Tennessee or as lovely as the Seine is reputed to be, right now it is the most important river in the world to us. If we cannot solve the issue before us, we might be destroyed."

"May I assume you have a plan," said Longstreet.

Lee turned and acknowledged the presence of his commanders. Along with Longstreet were generals Ewell and Anderson. He longed to see truculent but trustworthy Stonewall Jackson in the group, but that good man had been killed at Chancellorsville and no one of his caliber had been found to replace him. Longstreet tried, and he was good, but he wasn't Stonewall. The others, Richard Ewell and Richard Anderson, had performed spottily at Gettysburg. Perhaps, he thought, he wasn't specific enough or demanding enough in the way he gave his orders. He understood that they weren't used to his methods and it was something he would have to correct. Maybe they just weren't used to each other at all just yet.

Jeb Stuart was not present either. His cavalrymen were harrying the Union advance and sending frequent reports. This is what they should have been during the great battle, instead of dancing across the Union rear in a quest for glory. He'd chided Stuart for his failure and demanded that it never happen again. Apparently, it would not happen again. Lee was getting inundated with reports.

Lee continued. "Gentlemen, as you know, we are between Hagerstown and the river and, barring a miracle, a vastly larger Union army will soon be descending upon us. Therefore, we must make some very painful decisions."

Lee looked at their faces. Only Longstreet seemed confident as he continued. "Have you ever seen a small animal trapped by a larger predator? There are only two things the smaller prey can do. First, and I find this truly amazing, an animal will sometimes curl up and await death, allowing the predator to chew on him while he yet breathes. Second, there are other small animals who will fight and claw for their very existence, and sometimes will win their way free by virtue of their ferocity."

Longstreet nodded solemnly and said, "I recall getting bit by an angry rabbit once."

"And what did you do, Pete?" asked Ewell, laughing. Even though Longstreet's first name was James, he was commonly called Pete.

Longstreet grinned at the memory. "Since I was but a little one, I ran home to Momma. General Lee, do you think we can get General Meade to run home to Momma, or, in this case, Uncle Abraham?"

Lee nodded. It was time to get serious. "I don't know, but we can certainly try. Meade expects us to sit here in our trenches and wait for his artillery to pound us to pieces so that his infantry can storm over us. I do not wish to be that prey that simply waits to die. I wish to cast the dice and launch one ferocious attack against an enemy that is as exhausted as we are, disorganized, and strung out in long columns. We may not win the war, but we might just give us time for the river to go down and for us to cross it in safety."

"When do you wish this to happen?" asked Ewell.

Lee looked skyward at the position of the sun. "There is still plenty of daylight and our cavalry has provided us with an effective screen. They must know we are out here, but they do not know in what numbers or precisely where, while we know a good deal about them. In two hours, they will be close enough for us to fall on them. In two hours, we will attack."

The first indication Thorne had that something was terribly wrong was when the Rebel cavalry chased in their pickets. The enemy horsemen had been especially aggressive and Thorne had put it down to their trying to protect the carcass of their army. He hadn't given the Confederates much thought—he was too tired for that. What Lee did was out of his control. Instead, he concentrated on organizing what was left of the Sixth Indiana into something that made sense and doing so while on the march. He decided on two small battalions of about a hundred men each divided into three companies in each. He didn't have enough officers left to cover that so he gave command of several companies to NCOs. It might not be what their lordships in Washington thought was correct, but they could all go to hell. They weren't at the front, and the Sixth Indiana was.

Then they heard it. That screech that made the hair on the back of their necks stand up. The Rebel yell, howling defiance from thousands of throats. The Rebels were attacking.

Guns weren't just popping and crackling. Now the sound of

fighting became a roar as cannon joined in. A low hill hid what was happening from Thorne. He wanted to put his men somewhere, but he couldn't form a coherent line. He satisfied himself by placing one of the two small battalions on either side of the dirt path that somebody called a road. He had them dismount and told them to await orders.

A few moments later, they didn't have to wait for anything. A host of fear-crazed Union soldiers was running towards them, ignoring their officers and throwing away their equipment. To Thorne's horror, many were surrendering, just standing awaiting the enemy with their arms in the air. A wave of Rebels crested the hill and headed towards his position. There seemed to be thousands of them. He had but two hundred men.

"Fall back and maintain your formation," he ordered, praying silently. A retreat under fire was difficult under any circumstances and his truncated regiment hadn't yet worked together as a new unit.

The Rebels were close enough to open fire on them. Bullets began striking his men. The retreating Union soldiers hit his line, running and clawing their way to the rear.

Then it was over. His men broke and joined the mob. Some got their horses while others ran after them. "Son of a bitch," Thorne shouted. A terrified young private handed him the reins to his horse and ran away. Thorne mounted and joined the race to the rear. He saw Willis trying to stop some men from fleeing and being knocked to the ground for his troubles. Getting up, Willis saw Thorne, waved, and mounted. Then he too ran away.

"Do you surrender?"

Thorne was shocked. A Rebel soldier was only a few yards away and had a musket pointed at him. He was about to say he did surrender when the Rebel's head disappeared in a cloud of red mist and bone. Someone was still fighting and had just saved him. Before he could move, he felt a bullet whiz by him. He pulled his Colt and fired at the Rebel who'd shot at him. The man screamed and spun, clutching his shoulder.

Rebel soldiers were all around him. He spurred his horse and drove it mercilessly. He didn't want to die and he didn't want to be made prisoner, which would likely result in death if the tales of life in Confederate prisons were even half true. He was only twenty-six years old and had a life ahead of him. All he had to do was survive this damn war, a task which had suddenly gotten very difficult.

He rode to the top of a hill and, sensing a lack of pressure, paused and looked behind him. Confederate units were advancing in fairly good order while huge groups of Union soldiers were being swept up and captured.

Incredibly, Archie Willis found him. "I'm headed to New York, how about you?"

"Where's the regiment?"

"What regiment? You and I may be the whole damn thing. At least the Rebels won't be advancing much farther."

Thorne agreed. In the distance, the Rebel advance had just about stopped, possibly from exhaustion. There seemed to be as many prisoners as there were Rebel soldiers, all being sorted and led off in columns.

"I've been in the Army of the Potomac for a year," Thorne said, "and I've never seen it break and run. I've known it to be defeated too many times, but nothing like this."

Willis grabbed his arm and shook it to get Thorne's attention. "Unless you want to wait here until Jeb Stuart's cavalry show up again, I suggest we do our own breaking and running. If you haven't noticed, we're just about alone out here."

Thorne looked around. Willis was right. The two of them were the rear guard of the Army of the Potomac. They spurred their mounts and rode north through the shocked population of Hagerstown.

★ CHAPTER 2 ★

Abraham Lincoln wanted to hold his head in his hands and weep, but it would not do. The others gathered around his office in the second floor of the President's House, or, as some people preferred, the White House, might have felt the same way, but they too hid their emotions. Stoicism was all part of the game they played. Of course, neither Secretary of War Edwin Stanton nor Commanding General Henry Halleck bore any responsibility for the disaster that was unfolding: the unravelling of the Union's great victory at Gettysburg.

"It is my fault, all my fault," Lincoln finally said, his voice little more than a whisper. "I ordered General Meade and the army to do something that was beyond them. I should have known. I should have known that Lee would turn and fight like a wildcat. I also should have known that General Meade was not the man to take on Lee in open battle. Meade has proven himself excellent when others are attacking him, but less so when he is doing the attacking. I knew he was reluctant to chase Lee and I should have honored that reluctance."

"And who would replace him?" That was Halleck. "Shall we go with Hooker or Burnside again, or perhaps McDowell—if we can get him away from his love of food? Or would you suggest McClellan, the man who would like to replace you as President?"

The secretary turned to Halleck. "General, all of those men have lost battles and I can only pray that the President is not considering any one of them. Or perhaps you would like to take the field against General Lee?"

Halleck flushed at the jibe. He had entered the war with the reputation of a brilliant military scholar, but events had proven him to be a mediocre field commander at best.

Lincoln stretched his long legs and tried to fight off the headache that was threatening to consume him. *Not now*, he thought. He could not give in to the feelings of depression that occasionally overwhelmed him and rendered him unable to function properly. "General Meade will remain in command if for no other reason than that we have nobody better to replace him, at least not at this time."

"Neither Congress nor the press will like that," Stanton said.

"Then let them come up with somebody else," Lincoln said tersely. He just wanted to sleep. How could it have happened that the glorious victory at Gettysburg had been simply thrown away? *Because I asked a man to fly when all he could do was walk.*

"What about Grant?" asked Stanton. Word of Ulysses Grant's great victory at Vicksburg had only recently arrived. The Confederacy was cut in half and the Union controlled the Mississippi all the way from New Orleans up to its northern headwaters.

Halleck flushed angrily. "Impossible. He has never held a large command like the Army of the Potomac. And then there is the question of his drinking."

"Nor had any of the other worthies we just named," snapped Stanton. "And I'm damn certain most of them drank as well. God only knows that Hooker did."

As the evening wore on, they discussed other possibilities. Rosecrans was at Chattanooga, Buell at Nashville, and they, along with others, inspired no confidence whatsoever. Other names were tossed into the hat, Sedgwick and MacPherson among them. Lincoln recalled having offered command of the Army of the Potomac to John Reynolds, only to have that man refuse because he wanted a free hand, which no one in the room would give him. He'd been killed at Gettysburg. *Too bad*, thought Lincoln. Now maybe they would have complied with his wishes. They were that desperate.

Lincoln watched Halleck. The commanding general, he concluded, was afraid of Grant. Halleck had tried to have Grant removed from command on the charge that the man drank too much. Maybe he did, but he also fought, which he had told Halleck and others, and the Union needed fighters like Grant, not thinkers like Halleck.

Lincoln rose. The others did as well. "I am to bed. I do not think that General Lee will do anything this evening or, for that matter, for a number of evenings. We will leave General Meade in command with the instructions that he is to reorganize and reconstitute his army, but that he is not to seek out a battle with Lee's army." Lincoln permitted himself a wry smile. "After what has transpired, I don't think Meade will argue with that directive."

The Army of the Potomac was beginning to pull itself together. Once it became clear that the Rebels were not going to chase them any farther, units began finding their men and men began finding their units. The chaos and confusion of the retreat was being put behind them.

Thorne slept on the ground in a field that night. He and Willis had again become separated in the confusion, but he was far from alone. The number of men lying nearby reminded him of the killing fields he'd left at Gettysburg. Images he simply couldn't shake: all those corpses, lying amid the stones and the peach trees, that would never move again. Only the men now surrounding him got up at dawn, stretched, farted, and relieved themselves. Thorne saw that he wasn't the only officer who'd been separated from his men. He was gratified to see his horse standing close by, munching on grass.

It was well after noon when he rode onto a large field that had once been planted with crops and now grew thousands of men standing around in ankle-deep churned-up mud. Banners and unit flags were waved and voices called for soldiers to come home to their respective regiments. It sounded like a mob of auctioneers and peddlers trying to hawk their wares. Groups of soldiers, along with individual lost soldiers, searched among the pennants for their units, not always finding them. There were tales of whole regiments being swallowed up by the overwhelming Confederate assault. Finally, and somewhat to his surprise, he spotted the pennant of the Sixth Indiana Mounted Infantry and Captain Archie Willis singing out in a loud voice that the lost soldiers should come home.

The two men embraced, again surprised and pleased that each had survived the unsuspected ordeal. "How many have you found, or have found us?" Thorne asked.

"At last count, our mighty regiment is up to sixty-one soldiers, many of whom are thoroughly embarrassed at having run like sheep. I've assured them that I ran like a scared cat myself, which is only marginally better than running like a sheep. What really matters, I told them, is that they made it and that they've come back. I told them everyone was scared."

"I wasn't," said Thorne, "Not me. No sir. I was damn well terrified." He then told of his close encounter with the two Rebels. "I'd still like to thank the man who killed the man who wanted to take me prisoner."

Willis shrugged. "Maybe it wasn't even an aimed shot. Maybe it was just some damned fluke. There was a lot of sharp and deadly crap flying around that battlefield. Regardless, I'm certainly glad you're back to take command. By the way, word is that we'll be marching back towards Gettysburg and setting up a defensive line somewhere."

"And then what? Do we sit on our hindquarters and wait for Bobby Lee to decide he's strong enough to take us on again?"

"Lord, I hope not, Steve. We just too damn close to getting our rumps whipped at Gettysburg and then we did get whipped at Hagerstown. I don't want to go through that again."

"Well, unless somebody decides to surrender, we might not have a choice."

A handful of their soldiers rode in and sheepishly said they were reporting for duty. That they had kept their mounts was a bonus. Both officers made them as welcome as possible and told them not to let their comrades ride them too hard since most of them had run as well. Thorne was confident that it would all work out, but there would be some interesting discussions and recriminations before it was over.

"Is Meade still in charge?" Thorne asked.

"Last I heard, yes. But nobody's talking much to me about grand strategy. By the way, I heard that a levy of fifty recruits was coming down from Indiana to join us."

Thorne whistled. "That would be a big help, but why wouldn't they be sent to help form a new regiment?"

Policy to date had regiments that had been reduced to almost nothing kept on the rolls while new recruits were used to form new regiments, which led to a lot of confusion regarding which regiments had enough men to actually be functional. Thorne didn't want to be in command of a regiment that was merely squad sized.

"I guess it helped that our badly wounded colonel is a relative of

Governor Morton's," Thorne said. "I wonder if he knows that the good colonel is totally out of the war."

The last time Thorne had seen Colonel Josiah Baird, the man was dazed and looking for his left leg, which had been blown off below the knee. "Let's not tell him. He might want his men back."

"Even better, the ranking man is a militia captain who is junior to you. You're going to be brevetted to the rank of major. Congratulations on surviving long enough to become a field-grade officer."

That comment was made without rancor. In wartime, promotions often came because men senior to you were killed or wounded. If Baird was still in a hospital and was within reach, he would pay his respects.

That said, he had another truly vexing problem that needed solving. "Archie, I am cold, wet, filthy, and would kill for a beer. However, that is not all that important right now. But does anybody around here have anything to eat?"

The train ride from Indianapolis had been long, slow, and arduous. Cassandra Baird and her mother Rachel were travelling in the comfort of their own railroad car, which made life a little more bearable and was one of the benefits of being major investors in the railroad. But the weather was hot and sticky and the temperature inside the car almost unbearable. Opening windows only brought in humid air along with black smoke and ashes from the engine. Still, privacy was one of the privileges of wealth. They could sweat and suffer by themselves without having to share their misery with the scores of unwashed people jammed into other cars. The Bairds were not snobs, far from it, but it made no sense not to use at least some of their money on themselves at this painful time.

They were headed to Washington to see their father and husband, Colonel Josiah Baird. The telegram they'd received only said that he'd been badly wounded in the leg but had survived. Unsaid was for how long would he be surviving. They wished they could somehow make the train go faster, but that would not happen. Not only were speeding trains dangerous to all concerned, as the high number of crashes attested, but there were numerous stoppages and delays to allow higher-priority military trains go past them.

Ultimately, their ride ended and, along with their half-Negro servant, Mariah, they left the train. They sent Mariah and their luggage on ahead to the Hay-Adams Hotel while they took a cab to the Cosgrove Hospital, a private facility only a few blocks from the President's House.

The Cosgrove was well appointed and reserved for more senior officers. Like a good hotel, it was currently fully booked. Each officer had a private room and there appeared to be more than enough nurses and attendants. Cassie wondered if some of the medical personnel could be better utilized at a hospital where there were more wounded. Still, she didn't think she was greedy by wanting her father to have the best of care.

They were mildly surprised to find that Colonel Baird was the senior ranking wounded officer currently being treated. A stern-faced doctor prepared them for what they would see, but it didn't totally help. They couldn't stifle gasps when they saw him lying on his back, covered by a sheet that clearly showed that his left leg was missing below the knee.

The colonel glared at them. "If you cry, I will ship you both back home. I don't want tears; I want to get the hell out of this bed. The doctors say I can start to walk with crutches, and after that I want the best artificial leg our money can buy."

"You'll have it, my dear," said Rachel as she kissed him on the forehead.

"And, my dear, I want to get you in bed as soon as possible to prove to both of us that I'm still a man."

"Josiah!" said Rachel, as Cassandra turned away to hide her embarrassment and her smile. She envied them their married life. It seemed so warm and intimate, and sometimes even rowdy. She wished she could find that kind of life for herself. However, she was twenty-three, plain, thin, and by everyone's definition, a spinster. All she had going for her was her father's money and she'd been approached by a number of sharks who wanted nothing more than to marry her to get it.

She thought she'd found happiness with one young man named Richard Dean, but he'd heeded his country's call and gotten killed charging up Marye's Heights at Fredericksburg. She'd even allowed him a few physical privileges before he left for the army. Since then, she'd considered herself in mourning, in large part because she'd shamed and coerced the shy young man into enlisting. And now he was dead.

"How long are you going to stay here in Washington?" the colonel asked hopefully.

"We could all go home almost immediately," Rachel said. "I rather think we can get you on the train and, with a nurse or a doctor along, take you back home."

"No," he said firmly. "For one thing, they have a fine supply of artificial limbs in this town. Can't imagine why—you'd think there was a war on. Also, I want to remain here close to my political cronies. I want them to stay firm. The damned battle that we just lost might cause them to weaken their resolve and I cannot have that. There's too much Copperhead activity in Indiana, along with people who simply want the war to end at all costs. We must win. We must keep the country united and we must free the slaves!"

Cassandra smiled. She and her family were as staunch in their abolitionism as anyone alive. To them, slavery was an outright abomination, an insult both to humanity and the Creator. To her, the Copperheads and others who wanted peace were traitors. At least the Confederates were fighting for their principles, while the Copperheads were betraying their nation.

Josiah sighed. "And I must see to the recovery of my regiment. We fought only one major battle and were all but destroyed. There had been a few skirmishes, but nothing like the horrors of Gettysburg. Have you seen the lists?"

"We have," said Cassandra. There had been too many names she'd known. She would make an effort to visit as many of the others who were in local hospitals as was possible. She promised herself that she would write letters to the families of the dead.

Josiah continued. "Captain, I mean Major, Thorne now commands what amounts to a couple of hundred survivors. Do you recall him?"

Cassandra didn't, but her mother did. "He is a good man. I'm sure he'll do well."

"He'd damned well better. I'm getting tired. Why don't you two leave me in peace and come back tomorrow? And Cassie, how much longer are you going to wear mourning clothes?"

"Until I feel they are no longer appropriate," she said firmly.

"They never were appropriate. Richard Dean was a complete booby."

The women kissed him on the forehead and left the hospital. They hailed a cab and went back to the hotel.

"Cassandra, I believe it is time to get back to have a glass of sherry. I don't know if the hotel will serve unattended women, but, if they don't we can always arrange something through room service."

"I already had Mariah check, Mother. We'll be served in our room. The hotel is very concerned that a pair of unattended women could be mistaken for ladies of the pavement and that some ugly misunderstandings could arise."

Her mother's eyes widened. "They wouldn't *dare*."

Cassie smiled. "Come along, Mother."

★ CHAPTER 3 ★

The Army of the Potomac settled around the Pennsylvania city of Hanover. There was irony in their choice. Just before the battle of Gettysburg, Union cavalry had fought Jeb Stuart's cavalry in the town and delayed its return to Lee's main army.

The Union army's position in Pennsylvania meant that they had effectively surrendered the town and battlefield of Gettysburg, which displeased the troops. Even though the land still stank of the rotting dead, it was something that they and their comrades had fought and bled over. They did not like the idea of giving up something that had cost so much. The Union troops were not mollified by being told that the move was temporary. Hanover was closer to Washington and that made it easier to reinforce and resupply the army.

On the other hand, Lee had made no effort to take the bloodied battlefield and town either. Thorne thought that maybe both sides might well leave it as a memorial to human bravery and human folly. Scouts reported that Lee had not retreated south of the Potomac into the safety of Virginia. Instead, he was firmly ensconced in Pennsylvania, somewhere around Chambersburg or Shippensburg, which were slightly to the north and west of Hanover.

Thorne and the other officers amused themselves by poring over maps and trying to guess what Lee would do next. It wasn't lost on them that nobody was trying to guess what Meade would do. That was too easy. Meade would do nothing until Lee moved, and then he would attempt to counter it.

"Lee is not going anywhere for a while," Thorne said. He waved his arm and almost spilled some of his good German beer. A local brewer was making a fortune selling to the army. "He is going to sit in Pennsylvania and eat good German and Dutch food while his beloved Virginia recovers from the ravages of war."

"But he can't stay there forever," said Willis. His voice was slurred. The men had been drinking for several hours in this, their first chance to unwind after the retreat and the necessity of setting up an encampment. They all had new uniforms and fresh mounts for whoever needed them, along with decent food and regular opportunities to bathe. They also had new weapons—Spencer breech-loading carbines in place of the old 1855 pattern musket-rifles. The Spencer carbines were loaded by shoving a tube with seven bullets in it in the stock. The weapon could be fired much more rapidly than a standard Union rifle. Even better, the shooter did not have to stand up and expose himself in order to reload.

Thorne had been told about a gun that could shoot over a hundred rounds a minute, but he didn't believe that. How would you get the ammunition into the thing at that rate, just to start?

Thorne was not done strategizing. "Lee could head towards Wilmington or Philadelphia, or even north towards Harrisburg. My guess, though, is that he will attack Washington. No other place makes sense. Washington is where Lincoln and the federal government are, along with all the generals and politicians who've gotten us into this mess. If he can chase the government out of the nation's capital, the entire United States would look stupid and inept."

"I didn't think that our ineptitude was such a secret," said Willis, who then belched. Thorne was concerned that his friend might pass out and fall over into the fire. It wouldn't be the first time that had happened to a soldier.

Thorne stood and stretched. He'd been pacing his drinks so he wasn't as drunk as the others. "I think we should end this evening's discussions. We can pick it up again tomorrow. In the meantime, get some sleep and try not to show the men your hangovers tomorrow."

Willis tried to stand up, but instead dropped to one knee. Thorne was about to grab for him when one of the other officers, a newly arrived captain, took over and guided him into the darkness and towards his tent.

Thorne took several deep breaths. He felt like smoking a cigar, but decided that going to his bunk and getting some shuteye would be a better choice. He was exhausted. Getting the rump session of the regiment into some kind of order and overseeing their training had drained him. His decision to see Colonel Baird had been pushed into the background. Maybe he would get a chance this weekend, unless, of course, Bobby Lee came a-calling.

If it wasn't for the fact that he was part of one army that wanted to kill another army, the camp could almost be pleasant. The smell of burning wood from a thousand campfires was familiar and comforting. The sky was bright with a million stars that the preachers said proved the existence of God. Thorne had no answer for that. Once upon a time he'd believed in a generous and loving God, but that was before Gettysburg. Now he was certain that God did not live in Pennsylvania, at least not in this summer of 1863.

He was through with war but war was not through with him. He was twenty-six and had a law degree. He should have been home writing wills and contracts, but no—here he was, training men to kill other men. He also should have been married to a woman he couldn't quite visualize and have a couple of kids who were likewise vague figments of his imagination. He wanted to have a normal life before his dark-brown hair turned gray and his trim one hundred and sixty-pound frame turned to flab.

There had been a girl back home, and it was assumed by both sets of parents that they would marry. There had been some fond and even intensely passionate moments with Judith until she decided that she didn't want a man who was going to leave her alone for months, even years, to become a soldier. He didn't blame her.

A month after he'd joined the army he got word that she'd married a minister's son. He'd been angry for a couple of days until it dawned on him that he didn't actually miss her one damned bit. He did wonder if they prayed before having sex. He recalled Judith calling out for God when they were alone and mainly naked and she reached flood tide.

He smiled at the thought and let it hide the memories of war. He decided he would see the colonel this weekend. Definitely.

Once more the crackle and flash of gunfire came from the half-dozen closely circled supply wagons. "Idiots," shouted Colonel Corey Wade of Wade's Tennessee Volunteer Cavalry. He turned to Sergeant Jonah Blandon. He didn't like Blandon, a violent roughneck at best, but he was the man closest to hand.

"Those bluejackets are outnumbered at least ten to one, and they still fight. Goddamn fools." Blandon grinned wickedly. "Maybe they'd rather die fighting than starve in prison." He spat a shot of tobacco into the brush. "I would. Or maybe . . . maybe they think reinforcements are coming."

Of course, thought Wade. Maybe one of their men had ridden for help. They'd caught and killed one Union soldier trying to do exactly that, but what if there had been two?

He reached into his jacket pocket and fingered the watch his mother had given him. It had seemed so easy. A dozen Union supply wagons were proceeding lazily down the high road, guarded by little more than a squad of soldiers, when his three hundred men had swept from hiding in the forest and run them down. It was astonishing that the northerners had been able to circle the wagons and present a defense. Counting the wagon drivers, they couldn't have had more than a score of men and several of those now lay prone on the ground.

Captain Alex Mayfield slipped quietly to his side. The Yanks had a couple of decent shooters—three of Wade's men were dead and two others wounded, and for what? The Yanks were going to lose. It was just a question of when and what the final score would be.

But the thought of Union reinforcements chilled him. They were well behind Union lines, which was why this supply train had been behaving so stupidly. His three hundred troopers, though more than enough to take a supply train, were a piddling number if the Yanks got aroused and came after them. The Yankee cavalry wasn't all that good, but there were a lot of them.

One option was to withdraw, but his sense of honor would never accept that. "The men in place, Captain?"

"Ready and waiting, Colonel," said Mayfield.

"Then do it," said Wade. "We've got to get this nonsense over with."

Mayfield nodded and blew several piercing blasts on a whistle. Seconds later, a host of dismounted Confederate soldiers erupted from the grass where they'd managed to crawl to within a few yards of the wagons. Withering covering fire from their comrades protected them as they charged.

The Union troops continued to fire, dropping a couple more of Wade's troopers, until a gray wave poured over the wagons and into the perimeter. There were shouts and screams and then silence.

Wade was angry but satisfied. His men knew what to do. They would take anything useful and ruin the rest. Fire was not an option, as the columns of smoke would draw Union patrols even quicker than the sounds of musket fire.

He spotted Blandon leading three bluebellies into a stand of trees. A sense of misgiving seized Wade. He was turning to ride in that direction when he heard three pistol shots. He spurred his horse toward the trees. "Blandon, you son of a bitch, what did you do now?"

He found the sergeant standing over the three dead Union soldiers. "They was trying to escape, Colonel."

Wade was livid. The three men had all been shot in the back of the head. "The hell they were. You just shot them down in cold blood. What the hell is the matter with you?"

"After what they done to my home and my family, I don't much care. You want to bust me back to the ranks again, that's just fine. Or if you want to discharge me, even better. Maybe I can sign on with Quantrill or somebody like that, somebody knows about war."

Other soldiers had moved discreetly out of hearing. They were afraid of the colonel but terrified of Blandon. It was rumored that the short, stocky man had killed more than a score of men, and not always in battle. It was also said that he'd raped a number of women, although most of those were runaway slaves, so that didn't count.

Blandon eyed his commander a moment longer and turned to walk away. There was a touch of a swagger in his stride. Wade opened his mouth to call him back, but thought better of it. He really couldn't think of what to say.

The men of Wade's cavalry had loaded up one wagon with coffee and other luxuries and were destroying bags of flour by slitting them and dumping them out onto the ground. Some of the more imaginative were urinating on the flour to make sure no effort would be made to salvage it. Blandon had disappeared. He'd gone back to his squad knowing that the colonel wouldn't do anything.

Wade was a brave man, but not a strong one. This kind of thing made him wonder just who was in charge of the Volunteers, him or Blandon, and just who would the men obey if it came down to a pitched battle.

★ CHAPTER 4 ★

Abraham Lincoln, a good horseman, could have ridden back to the White House, but he knew that his long legs made him look foolish, as they dangled almost to the ground. Besides, he was getting old. Thus, and at his wife's insistence, he rode in a carriage to the Soldiers' Home a few miles from the President's House. He was fifty-four years old but felt much older. The war had aged him dramatically. He liked going to the Soldiers' Home because it allowed him to get away from the political stress of Washington. At the White House, there were always people lined up to see him. He'd been told by his secretaries and others that he could always shoo them away, but he had no heart for that. They had elected him and he would hear them out, no matter how exhausting it was and no matter how foolish their requests.

But going to the cottage in the summer months provided a degree of comfort in the suffocating heat. He was not the first president to so utilize the building. His predecessor, James Buchanan, had made it his summer residence. It was also where Lincoln had drafted the Emancipation Proclamation, an action he had hoped would bring an end to the war. It hadn't.

While the slaves in the South were still slaves, any who made it to Union lines were free, at least in theory. The North now had many more thousands of mouths to feed and that brought resentment. The fact that Negroes could form their own volunteer units and serve and die for the United States had toned down some of the angry rhetoric, but not all of it.

He entered the cottage by a back door in case someone was watching. General Meade had been summoned and was waiting, doubtlessly angry. Lincoln smiled at the thought. General Meade was always angry.

They sat at a plain kitchen table. This was the first time they'd spoken since the disaster after Gettysburg. It distressed Lincoln to see Meade looking like a beaten man and not his usual combative self. That was not good.

Meade glanced up at him and then lowered his eyes. "Are you going to dismiss me?" His tone seemed to indicate that such a course of action would be most welcome.

Lincoln shook his head. "No, General. I told my Cabinet, and I will tell you: I take responsibility for what happened. I should not have forced you and your army to chase Lee after suffering such appalling casualties. I should have realized that Lee would not let himself be captured."

Meade was puzzled. "Then do you wish me to resign to save you the trouble of removing me from command?"

"What would you do if Lee attacked you?"

Meade bristled, showing a spark of his old ferocious self. "Throw him back and defeat him, sir."

"But what would you do if, after rebuilding the army, you were ordered to find him and bring him to battle? Could you do that and defeat General Lee? No, not just defeat him, could you do find and *destroy* General Lee?"

General Meade hesitated before answering. "Mr. President, I think we have all become aware that it is possible to defeat an enemy by forcing him from the field of battle or by inflicting more casualties on him than he has inflicted on us, but the destruction of an enemy army might not be possible, at least not without incredible strokes of luck and fortune. Armies are too large to be annihilated and even the victor, like my army was for a few glorious days, would suffer enormous casualties in any battle or campaign."

"I have seen the reports, General, and I concur. Perhaps as many as twenty-five thousand Union soldiers were killed or wounded during the three days of fighting at Gettysburg and another fifteen thousand or so in the fighting north of the Potomac. At least most of those casualties suffered near Hagerstown were captured and not killed."

Meade winced. A full twelve thousand Union soldiers had either surrendered or been captured. "Will you arrange to have them exchanged?"

Lincoln nodded solemnly. "We will have to do something. I cannot abide the thought of all those thousands of young men being cooped up in those horrors that the Confederacy refers to as prisons. Of course," he added sadly, "our own prison camps are wretched places as well. Yes, we will have to do something."

"And what, sir, shall I do about the contrabands?" Meade was using the common term for the many thousands of slaves who'd escaped and were now camped close to the Union army. "There have been reports of slavecatchers trying to round them up like cattle and ship them back down to their southern owners."

"Former owners," Lincoln insisted. "The Emancipation Proclamation has freed them and nothing will change that fact. And we will not tolerate slavecatchers. The mere thought of it is distasteful. You will do what you can to protect the contrabands. I have not quite given up on my idea to send them back to Africa where they can join the Liberians, or perhaps even create a new nation of free blacks."

Lincoln's grand idea had run afoul of reality. The overwhelming majority of blacks in both the north and south were generations removed from Africa, had no true knowledge of the continent, and absolutely did not want to leave the sometimes dubious safety of the United States for the terrors and perils of Africa.

Meade continued. "Then I shall continue to ensure that the army grows stronger and able to defend itself. But I shall not venture out against General Lee until and if ordered to do so by you."

"That's probably the wisest course," said Lincoln. But, he thought, it would be highly unlikely that George Gordon Meade would be the one leading an attack against Lee. He knew a man who could, but not just now. He and the rest of the country would have to be patient. Patience was a virtue, the President thought, but he didn't feel terribly virtuous, at the moment. He wanted the damn war over.

With her father well on his way to recovery, Cassandra Baird and her mother, along with Mariah, rode several miles out to a field where several hundred Negroes were camped. Tents were well constructed and laid out in lines. It looked military and was run by the largest

Negro she had ever seen. His name was Hadrian and he was well over six feet tall and must have weighed over two hundred and fifty pounds. He was as black as night and there was a jagged scar across his left cheek. He had a rope belt tied around his waist and a Bowie knife stuck in it. He eyed them coldly.

"Are you fine ladies here for a good reason or are you just going to stare at us like monkeys in a zoo?"

Rachel flinched at the man's impertinence. She introduced herself and her daughter. "We have come here to offer you some assistance in learning to live and prosper as free men and women. It is our goal to set up schools so that your people can learn to read and write. Perhaps you'd like to join a class?"

Hadrian glared. "What makes you think I'm illiterate? I can read and write as well as the next man."

Cassandra blushed. "Sorry, we just assumed."

"Don't ever assume, miss," he said gently. "My father was a blacksmith for some rich folk down in Virginia. He learned his letters by watching his white master read instructions and such. Then he would teach me and I caught on fast. He shouldn't have taught me nothing. I got caught reading a book and the white folk gave me a good beating. Beat my father too. He couldn't stand that. He run away, tried to get to the north. He didn't make it."

"But you did."

Those stern eyes looked her over. "I suppose."

"So, will you support us with our school?"

Hadrian thought it over. "Why not? Wouldn't hurt to get something inside their wooly heads." He eyed her once again, and Cassandra blinked despite herself. "Just don't be too obvious about it, eh? White folk around here are as bad as the Rebs. Just like down South, they don't like colored people being smarter than them."

"Well, that's their problem," said Cassandra. "We would like to start out with a group of about twenty or so. We will have enough teaching materials for that many. If this goes well, we will ask benefactors to donate to the cause."

"Benefactors." Hadrian smiled to himself. It was just as fierce as his regular expression. "How long will it take to teach someone to read, at least enough to get by?"

Cassandra could only smile. "That depends on the person. You say you caught on quickly, but, really, how long did it take? Weeks? Months? And by the way, you are right that many of the people around here don't like what Negroes like you are doing. Should it come to it, just how will you protect us and your people? Do you have guns?"

"You should know that white people frown on colored people having guns. It makes them very nervous, even though we are up here in the north."

He said that so solemnly that Cassandra was certain he was lying. "If there is trouble, I will assume that your men all have knives like that one in your belt. Is there a military detachment near enough to here if things should go bad?"

"A small one, missy. But really, we're pretty much on our own and besides, there's dozens of camps just like this one. Hell, maybe there's hundreds of them. We will take care of ourselves and as long as you are in this camp, we'll take care of you."

Cassandra forced herself to smile. Yes, she would be safe in Hadrian's camp, but what about when she was not in his camp?

". . . the flanking attempt was stymied by Union troops holding the high ground of the elevation known as the Little Round Top . . ."

Jefferson Davis sat with his eyes half-closed, resting his head on one hand as he listened to General Chesnut read the most recent report on General Lee and the Army of Northern Virginia.

It was, of course, nothing new to him. He'd read the originals as they had come in. But it was a true pleasure to hear it read aloud, dealing as it did not only with a victory but perhaps *the* victory—the battle that won the South its independence at last.

". . . at that point, Pickett's division collapsed, and Longstreet's charge was turned back with extremely heavy casualties . . ."

Davis frowned as he recalled hearing that news. For a time, it seemed that all had been lost. Another Sharpsburg, if not worse, with Lee and his army forced once again to skulk back home across the Potomac.

". . . Meade chose to strike, evidently without properly marshalling his forces . . ."

But then Lee had turned it around completely, with one of the master-strokes that the Confederacy had come to expect from him. A swift riposte against Meade's scattered forces that routed them as completely as had occurred at Manassas and Chancellorsville, in the process demonstrating absolutely and finally, to anyone who cared to debate the matter, that the true spark of martial genius lay within Lee and not the poor dead Thomas Jackson.

". . . for the large part not even attempting to regroup until they had been driven well beyond Hagerstown. Fatalities among the Union forces are estimated at over 2,500, wounded at nearly twice that number, with no less than 12,000 prisoners taken. Confederate casualties were minimal. Under these circumstances, and considering the magnitude of the defeat, it is unlikely that General Meade and the Army of the Potomac will be fit for further operations for the balance of the summer."

"Excellent."

That was Memminger, secretary of the treasury. Davis opened his eyes to glance among his Cabinet. James Seddon, War, was beaming as if he was personally responsible. Mallory applauded with two fingers, as well he might, considering the record of the Navy in this conflict. Reagan and Bragg both smiled benignly. Judah Benjamin, as was his custom, kept his counsel at the far end of the table. Only Alexander Stephens, his Vice-President, was not present. He was back in Georgia, which was where he belonged as far as Jefferson Davis was concerned.

General Chesnut nodded to them and reached for a second sheaf of papers. "I have here the report on Vicksburg . . ."

Davis sat up. "That won't be necessary, General."

The men before him chuckled. Davis looked sharply around the table, but there was no real malice to it, as far as he could see. Still, what was the point in dwelling on setbacks? True, the loss of Vicksburg would render communications with Texas difficult, but what did that matter? Everyone knew that the war would be decided in the Virginia theater. The result would be determined here and nowhere else.

Besides—imagine if they had lost Vicksburg and Gettysburg in the same week. He was not sure how he would have taken that. Best not to dwell on it more than necessary.

"Robert E. Lee, the Alexander of our day," Seddon said.

"Yes, and a man of Virginia as well."

Davis retained his smile as best he could. He could clearly recall the comments about "Granny Lee" and "General Sandbags," some of them from the lips of the men sitting here before him, and not so long ago either. Davis had not doubted him at the time, and he did not doubt him today. Few who had met the man ever did. Sometimes it seemed to Davis that these years would feature in the histories to come as the Age of Lee, with all else appearing only as footnotes. But that would be all right. There were worse fates than becoming a footnote to the saga of Robert E. Lee.

"I wish he was here this moment," Mallory said, "that I might shake his hand."

That gained him a number of nods and grunts of agreement. Memminger turned to Davis. "When will Lee be returning, Mr. President?"

For a moment, Davis pretended he hadn't heard. Memminger repeated, "Mr. President?'

"What was that, Mr. Secretary? 'When,' did you ask?" Davis shot a glance at Judah Benjamin. "Not for some time."

"I beg your pardon?"

"He's not remaining in Pennsylvania, is he?"

"That would be foolish."

Davis leaned over the table. "'Foolish,' Mr. Mallory? Is that your choice of words? And who, may I ask, is the fool here? Myself, or General Lee?"

Mallory had the grace to look abashed. Davis considered tossing in a few words about the Navy's inability to field a single ironclad against the Federal blockade, but thought better of it.

General Chesnut licked his lips. "I think a more suitable term would be 'militarily inadvisable,' sir. Pennsylvania is the enemy's heartland. Our troops there are effectively surrounded, and beyond the assistance of any other forces. If we were to lose the Army of Northern Virginia, why . . . we would lose everything."

"I am inclined to agree," Siddons said. "I was under the impression that this operation was on the order of a raid." Several of the others nodded.

"Militarily inadvisable, General?" Davis put a slight but noticeable emphasis on the first word. "On the face of it, perhaps. The Army of Northern Virginia is in the midst of enemy territory, surrounded by foemen, with not a single secure supply line. That is your argument . . . General. Secretary Siddons."

He sat back, taking in the whole table. "In other words, Lee and his army are in the same position as Winfield Scott in the late Mexican war. You will recall, after Scott began his march on Mexico City, the entire world proclaimed his inevitable doom. No less than the Duke of Wellington exclaimed that 'Scott is lost.'"

He waited a long moment. "And what occurred then? General? Mr. Secretary?"

As he had expected, there was no answer. "He prevailed. He drove the Mexicans before him like rabbits, and took their capital with greater dispatch than Cortez did centuries before him. And I ask you, if the likes of Winfield Scott can bring off such an effort, who could doubt General Lee?"

No answer was forthcoming now, either. It never failed. No matter how trivial the matter, or how inexperienced and ignorant they might be, they had to bicker about it. What did they know of military affairs? Which one of them had commanded a regiment in battle? Which one of them had served as secretary of war for Franklin Pierce, the last capable President of the United States? There were times when he truly wished he had the dictatorial powers the Yankee papers accused him of exercising.

He recalled Scott himself, dismissing his request to arm his regiment with rifles. But as a congressman, Davis had the ear of the great James K. Polk. He got his guns despite Scott, and the Mississippi Rifles became renowned as one of finest regiments in the entire army—largely due to those very rifles. He'd shown Scott to be the fool he actually was. If Scott hadn't been fighting against Mexicans, Wellington might well have been proven right. Davis had been in no way surprised when the Federals had dropped the old fool only months after this war commenced . . .

"But Mr. President . . . at least Scott had a goal." It was as if Siddons had been reading his mind. "He was out to conquer the city and bring the war to an end. What can Lee accomplish in Pennsylvania?"

"What can he accomplish? What kind of a question is that, sir? General Lee can accomplish anything he sets his mind to. A day's march puts him at Harrisburg, the state capital. Two days puts him at Philadelphia. Three days to the west lies Pittsburgh. He also threatens Baltimore and Washington, along with the lines of communication between Washington and New York, and the middle west and the

New England states. Nor need he move anywhere. Simply by remaining where he is, he drains Yankee goods and supplies, as well as making Lincoln and his junto look like mountebanks before the entire world.

"What can he do? Better to ask what he cannot do. What could he do in Virginia? Let his army live off the Yankees while acting as a threat in being behind their lines. We can be certain that as long as he remains, there will be no Federal effort against Richmond." With the last two words he rapped harshly on the tabletop. There were nods of agreement, some reluctant. At the far end of the table, Benjamin sat with a half-smile on his face, but then he generally did.

"Wars are not won by military means alone," Davis continued. "There are other aspects as well, political and diplomatic . . ." He caught a slight gesture from Benjamin. He'd best cut it short. If this crowd became aware that negotiations with the British had been resumed after the death of the crown prince, it would soon be all around Richmond and in short order in the hands of Abraham Lincoln himself. "So we had best maintain our faith in General Lee."

"I never meant to suggest otherwise," Mallory said.

"I didn't imply that you did, sir." Davis decided this meeting had gone on long enough. "Now that we have settled this matter, perhaps some refreshment is called for." He gestured to James, his valet, who nodded and turned to the door.

Benjamin began conversing with Seddon and Memminger. Davis busied himself with some papers before him. He could sense Mallory's and Chesnut's eyes resting on him. Could they be considering one question that had not arisen—what did Robert E. Lee himself think of remaining in Pennsylvania?

At last, the coffee cart clattered through the doorway. Davis got to his feet, glad he was not going to be put in the position of answering that question.

For reasons he didn't understand, Thorne had been ordered to take his men on patrol near a place where a Union supply column had been ambushed. A captain from General Montgomery Meigs' Quartermaster Corps awaited him at the place where there the action had taken place. The remains of a number of wagons littered the field even though they'd been stripped of much of their wood and anything else that could be useful. Crows and other birds pecked in the dirt looking for foodstuffs that had turned into garbage.

Most compelling was a line of fresh graves. The raw earth mounds were mute testimony to the one-sided fight.

Thorne had brought two platoons of his mounted infantry, about forty men. The captain gestured, and a puzzled Thorne rode forward. A moment later, Brigadier General Meigs himself emerged from the shadows. A very surprised Thorne saluted sharply. The stern-looking Meigs was considered by many to be a genius for the manner in which he had organized the Quartermaster Corps' sometimes thankless work. Now soldiers were fed, even though they often didn't like what they had to eat, and they had decent uniforms, boots, shoes, and, most important, weapons and ammunition.

"Welcome to the scene of the slaughter," said Meigs. "I assume you know what transpired here."

"I do, sir. Twenty men guarding a wagon train full of supplies were overrun and killed."

"Are you aware that three of them were murdered?"

"I've heard rumors."

"The rumors are true, Major. If you count the graves, there are only nineteen and not twenty. One man, one very lucky man, survived the fight by pretending to be dead. Apparently he was so covered with a comrade's blood as well as his own that no one thought to check if he was alive. He said that three men survived and were shot in the back of the head by a Rebel sergeant. He believes the name was 'Blandon.' When our troops realized that the supply wagons were very late, they sent out a patrol and found the bodies and the badly wounded survivor. The officer in charge of the patrol confirmed that three men appeared to have been executed, shot in the back of the head."

Thorne's curiosity was piqued. But what did all this have to do with him and his men?

"Major, at some point in time there will be another titanic battle between Lee's army and the Army of the Potomac commanded by whatever unfortunate soul is nominated by President Lincoln. Until that time, there will be scores of skirmishes, perhaps even hundreds of them. This is just one example. We are seeing to it that Lee is aware of the murders. Killing in battle is accepted, but massacring prisoners is not. The wounded man was close enough to hear the sergeant who did the killing arguing about it with the commander of the Confederate unit, something called Wade's Tennessee Volunteers. If nothing else, they are a long way from home."

"Yes sir," Thorne said. "May I ask just what this has to do with me and my men?"

"Major, there will be many more wagon trains like this one. I want them to go through to their destinations. I am assigning a number of smaller regiments like yours to function as escorts. As circumstances warrant, I may attach other units to your regiment. But don't get your hopes up about another promotion. It isn't going to happen."

"I'm fine with what I have, sir."

The two men had wandered away from the main body and were now out in the middle of a small field where no one could hear them. "General Meigs, the idea of using good troops as guards is necessary, but I like to think they can be better utilized."

"And how is that, Major?"

"I would like to set traps for the Rebels. It is one thing to have a number of guards who can deter an attack, but another to be able to ambush the attackers. If an attack is simply deterred, the rebels can strike again at another time and place of their choosing and perhaps even succeed. If we defeat, or even destroy them, they won't do it again."

Meigs smiled tightly. "If you're asking for permission to be creative, it's granted."

Thorne was dismissed. He saluted and rode off with his men. Meigs watched them disappear. He had been told that the Indiana men had suffered enough at Gettysburg and should be given a chance to complete the war in relative safety. Too bad nobody thought to tell the aggressive young major, Meigs thought. Ambushing the ambushers seemed like a marvelous idea.

He turned to his aide. "Captain, let's get the hell out of here and back to Washington, the seat of all lunacy."

★ CHAPTER 5 ★

Cassandra Baird's first day at her school for ex-slaves was less than a flaming success. First, almost a hundred men and women wanted to learn, and most were adults, which was far too many for her to work with. Somehow, she'd naively thought that her students would be children and that there would only be a dozen or so. Second, the would-be students' eagerness to learn was almost overwhelming. Her feelings of inadequacy mounted as the day progressed. She decided to tell them straight out that she'd never done anything like this before and that she would be learning to teach just as they were learning to learn.

It seemed to work. The men nodded solemnly while the handful of adult women smiled. Mariah was a big help. A light-skinned black, she told them that she had learned to read and that anyone could. She further told them that she'd escaped from a plantation in North Carolina owned by a cruel man and had made it into Indiana just after the war began.

Her story was somewhat similar to Hadrian's except that Mariah hadn't had to kill anyone to get away. At least, Cassandra thought with a start, she didn't *think* her servant had killed anyone en route to freedom.

Cassandra also noticed that Mariah and Hadrian were stealing glances at each other. She would not tease the young woman. If she did, Mariah would retort and ask how long she was going to be in mourning for her lost Richard. Mariah had never cared much for Richard. For one thing, he'd been such a thin and frail-looking young man. While Cassie didn't think he was after the family money, Mariah wasn't so sure. It didn't help that Rachel thought he was sweet while her father could barely stand the man.

Their opinions had softened somewhat when Richard had been killed and both were wondering when she would come out of her self-inflicted period of mourning and use what feminine charms she had. Her father thought she was lovely, but he was her father, after all.

Some of the students picked up on the need to memorize the letters and their sounds very quickly. Others were puzzled by the fact that the scribbles actually meant something. This was, she thought, something that must confront teachers everywhere. Still others were surprised to realize that they could already read after a fashion. They knew what the name of their owners' farm or plantation looked like and could read signs telling them where they were if the place was familiar.

She was about to call it an uneventful day when she heard a shout and then Hadrian yelling for people to "circle."

Within seconds, she was in the middle of a group of Negro woman and children who were being protected by a cordon of their men. She was not surprised to see that several of them had pistols. Those who didn't had axes and knives.

There were several other groups of contrabands in sight and they were all taking up circular defensive positions. "What is it?" Cassie asked, her voice rising in alarm.

"Slavers," Mariah said angrily. Her face was contorted into a snarl. "They are not going to take me. I was a slave once and it's not gonna happen again. I will not be any white man's fuck toy."

Cassie recoiled in surprise. She'd heard the word, of course, just not in such a cold anger and definitely not from a woman.

Several dozen horsemen were visible in the near distance, cantering as if they didn't have a care in the world. They stopped and viewed the groups arrayed against them. Their very silence was sinister. She had heard of packs of wolves inspecting herds of cattle and sheep, looking for weak ones to separate and kill. These riders were predators.

"How do you know they're slavers?"

"We just know," Hadrian answered. She saw that he had a Colt revolver in his belt—an Army horse pistol, like her father's. "We got some mighty brave scouts watching this here gang. Them sons of bitches would like nothing better than to ride through here and take anyone with a dark skin down south. They don't give a damn about nobody being free, legal or not. Mister Lincoln's Emancipation Proclamation's just a scrap of paper to them."

This is incredible, she thought. They were only a few short miles from Washington and these poor Negroes were in danger of being enslaved . . . re-enslaved, she corrected herself. She had no concerns for her own safety. She was clearly a white woman, but she was worried about Mariah. Even though she was light-skinned no one would mistake her for white. It sounded as if she would choose to die rather than be enslaved again. Mariah had told her only a little about her life as a slave, except to intimate that it was sometimes brutal and that she'd had to do things against her will and which she found repugnant. Now it occurred to her that Mariah likely had been forced to have sex with her master, or other men. She shuddered. What kind of world was she living in? And how innocent and naïve was she?

Another invisible signal was given and the frightened band relaxed. A clearly agitated and angry Hadrian approached. "I think there's been enough teaching for today. Let these folks think on it 'til tomorrow. That is, if you ain't been scared off."

Cassandra glared at him. "I have not been scared off and will not be scared off. Nor do I care if you swear all the time. I have heard many such words before. Perhaps I will learn some new ones."

Hadrian blinked, then laughed and strolled off. He detailed a handful of strong young men with guns to watch their carriage as they rode off to the safety of home. Tomorrow they would teach anew.

Colonel Corey Wade had seen General Longstreet before, but only at a distance. Even then, he struck Wade as being an imposing figure. Up close and across a dirty wooden table, the general was even more so. Burly and taller than average, Longstreet had an intimidating glare and it was now totally focused on Colonel Corey Wade.

"Colonel, just exactly when did you find out that your sergeant had killed three Union prisoners in cold blood?"

"Shortly after he did it, sir. Actually, within minutes. I was present at the fighting but unable to prevent the shootings from happening."

And what did you do about it?"

"Sir, Sergeant Blandon is a very valuable man. He is my chief scout. He is the one who found the wagon train in the first place. I ordered him to control himself. I was at least partly convinced that he had killed in the passion of the moment."

"Passion of the moment. Does that condone murder?"

Wade began to get angry. "With respect, sir, the last I checked we're at war with the North and the men who were killed were enemy soldiers."

"They were soldiers who had surrendered, Colonel."

"They surrendered after killing three of my men and wounding five more. I felt that Sergeant Blandon had simply gotten carried away in the heat of battle."

"Bullshit, Colonel. The killings occurred a good ten minutes after the Union wagons had been overrun. Your man Blandon did it for the hell of it and you are trying to excuse his actions and your inaction. Where the hell is Blandon now?"

Wade felt his face turning red. "I don't know, sir. He and a dozen of his usual companions left this morning. They told one of my lieutenants that they were going to go do some independent scouting, which is what they do quite frequently."

"Did he know that you'd been ordered to report to me?"

"Sir, everybody did."

"Then he would have guessed the purpose of our meeting and he probably also guessed that I was going to order you to arrest him. I have a freshly printed Union greenback that says you'll never see him again. I think he's gone off to be an outlaw."

Wade was feeling less threatened by Longstreet. Blandon was his only target. "I can't argue with that, sir."

Longstreet eyed him for a moment, stroking his bread. "Colonel, you don't have to love the Yankees, but they remain, in a real sense, our countrymen. I will not have them murdered in cold blood. Not only did you and everyone in your unit know about the killings and not inform your superiors, but I had to hear it from a French liaison officer who showed up under flag of truce. If you should happen to lay eyes on this son of a bitch Blandon, you will either arrest him or shoot him dead. Is that understood?"

Wade stood even straighter and saluted. He was being dismissed and would live to tell about it. As he rode back to where his Volunteers were camped, he thought it very likely that Blandon would indeed try to get in contact with him. And what would he do then, he wondered? Why, Corey Wade would do whatever was best for himself and his Volunteers.

He began to get angry. Just who the hell was Longstreet to scold him? Everyone knew that it was Longstreet's inertia that had caused the attacks against the Union army at Gettysburg to go off late, thus condemning them to failure.

The hell with James Longstreet, Wade decided. Robert E. Lee might have forgiven the son of a bitch, but Corey Wade had not.

Abraham Lincoln was bemused at the audacity of the man standing before him. First, Lincoln sitting was just about as tall as George Brinton McClellan standing. He hadn't been referred to as the Little Napoleon for nothing. Second, McClellan's contempt for Lincoln was well known. On one occasion he'd actually snubbed his commander in chief, leaving the President cooling his heels in the living room of the general's residence while the Little Napoleon took a nap upstairs. He'd even been among those who referred to Lincoln as a gorilla. So why had he asked for the "honor" of a private audience with the President?

The President was determined to be polite, if a little cynical. "To say I'm surprised that you wished to see me would be an understatement. But here we are and I am curious. Do you have a plan to . . . save the nation?" He gestured towards a chair but McClellan continued to stand.

"Yes sir, I do."

"It is my understanding that you intend to run against me next year as the Democratic candidate."

"If that is what the people wish, I will serve. But I see no need to wait more than a year to resolve the nation's problem."

"I'm all ears, General." Lincoln had earlier decided he would not antagonize the conceited little man by ignoring his past military rank. After all, he was well educated and experienced. Halleck had told Lincoln there was no better staff officer. He might actually have something useful to contribute.

"As I see it, Mr. Lincoln, General Lee is safely ensconced in Pennsylvania and no move has been made to dislodge him. It is common knowledge that you have little confidence in General Meade and even less in the others in my old command, the Army of the Potomac."

Lincoln nodded. "I also vaguely recall that you also held the position of Commanding General of all the Union armies, a position now held by General Halleck. I also recall removing you from both assignments."

To his credit, McClellan showed no reaction. "And I recall stating that my removal would not accomplish victory for the Union. I believe I stand vindicated, sir."

"That's why you won't sit down."

"What?"

"Nothing, General," he'd forgotten that the man had little sense of humor. "What do you specifically propose?"

McClellan shoved his hand into his jacket in that infuriating way of his. In military uniform the pose was bad enough, but in a civilian suit it was ridiculous. "It's very simple. Restore me to my command. If you do not wish me to be in command of all the armies, then just that of the Army of the Potomac will suffice. I guarantee you that General Lee will not conquer either Washington or Baltimore."

"Will you drive him from Pennsylvania and back down to Virginia? Will you destroy his army in the process, or will you simply push it and him back south? And if so, how will that bring an end to this war, sir?"

"Sir, like you, I am appalled by the amount of blood that has been spilled and is still being spilled. I would think that by now you would realize that the Confederacy cannot be defeated in the manner you desire. Therefore, the only alternative is a negotiated peace that will bring the killing to an end. What is happening now is not war; it is mass murder."

Lincoln suppressed a bitter smile. Appalled. The man who had overseen the butchery of Antietam was "appalled." "General, I will readily admit that you did a superb job of organizing and training the army. Yet, when it was time to go forth and do battle, you flinched. You had the absurd belief that you were greatly outnumbered when, in truth, you always greatly outnumbered the rebels. I still wonder why?"

"There are good reasons, sir. First, I still believe we were the lesser force numerically. I stand by what Mr. Pinkerton's men reported and the method by which he carried out his calculations. Second, I was in the position of possibly losing the war in a few hours, and, third, the losses would have been horrific. One of the terrible truths of this Civil War is that all of the dead and wounded are Americans. Sir, we must negotiate an end to this tragedy, even if it means letting the South go its own way."

Lincoln got to his feet, towering over the diminutive former general. "But if we negotiate, the only thing the South will want is its independence and the right to own slaves. If the former occurs, then the United States will cease to exist and if the latter occurs, we will have condemned an entire race of human beings to lives of cruel and involuntary servitude. It would mean that the Supreme Court's Dred Scott decision would still be in effect and that the Emancipation Proclamation would be worthless."

McClellan was not impressed. "And there are those who believe that the Lord wants the Negro to be subservient to the white man. It comes from the bible, from Genesis, where Ham, the son of Noah and his descendants, are doomed to be slaves. I submit, sir, that this is just what is happening now. Following the recent debacle, does anyone really think the South can be conquered?

"I do," Lincoln said firmly. "Now I suggest you leave and make plans for your presidency should this nation be so unfortunate as to have you elected to this high office."

McClellan's face turned red. He wheeled and exited the room. One of Lincoln's secretaries, John Hay, entered to find a clearly distressed Lincoln. "You may do two things, Mr. Hay. First, you will remind me never to be alone with that absurd and conceited creature again and, second, pull the drapes. I feel a headache coming on and must rest."

Josiah Baird winced as he tried on his new crutches. They rubbed his armpit and he wished he had an artificial leg and a cane to steady himself with. He'd already tried a couple of wooden legs, and found them wanting. With all the money he had, he thought angrily, he ought to be able to find someone who could whittle a good one for him.

Again, he stood up and steadied himself. "Do you want me to help you?" Rachel asked.

"When I want help, I'll ask for it."

"I'm glad to see your temper is back to normal. Is this the thanks I get for bringing you back from the brink of celibacy last night?"

Josiah smiled quickly at the memory. "I am, as always, in debt to you. What happened was truly a miracle. I just want to be able to walk like I wasn't a cripple."

"But you're not a cripple, dear. You're a rich and powerful man who has a physical challenge that he will overcome. And since you are now a civilian, what will you do?"

He slipped some additional padding on the arm rest and managed to lurch around their room. They were no longer in the hospital. He had rented a large home several miles northwest of the District—he'd have preferred being closer to town, but that was a dream—and installed himself in a first-floor bedroom. He'd added staff, to include a young doctor and an old female nurse. It was far better than the hospital where, despite the fact that it was restricted to senior officers, was filled with noisy people giving treatments and wounded soldiers moaning and sometimes crying out in their pain and confusion. Once he thought he himself had cried out.

He hoped to God he hadn't. He would not show weakness. If he did, his business rivals would pounce on him like jackals.

"I am going to talk to some of our people in Congress and try to call in some favors. I believe they owe me a few. Then I'm going to talk to Mr. Allan Pinkerton about an assignment. I feel he can do a better job locating one particular individual than he did estimating the size of the Confederate Army."

"Does this have anything to do with our daughter?"

"It might just. I've picked up on a couple of rumors that need to be either verified or discounted. I'm also less than thrilled that she's teaching those Negroes how to read. I have nothing against colored people being literate. I just object to her being out of the range of the army or the police. I want her protected."

She smiled warmly and kissed him on the cheek. "Wonderful, dear husband, but don't exhaust yourself. I want you at least as fresh and spry as you were last night. And I want you as lusty and crude as you were when we first got married back when we were poor."

He grinned hugely and patted her on her bottom. "I am your humble and devoted servant. It will be as you wish."

The easiest way to protect the supply trains was to increase the number of guards, and this Thorne set out to do. Even better, now that his men had Spencer repeating rifles instead of muzzle-loaders, their firepower was increased by a factor of at least seven, perhaps even more when the psychological impact of rifles that seemed to fire forever was entered into the equation.

The number of men he commanded was a drop in the bucket when compared to the vast Union Army, while the number of supply trains seemed to be unending.

Railroads crisscrossed the land, but could not go everywhere, and even they were targets for raiders. Nor could the army be everywhere, either. There were enormous gaps between major units, which meant patrols and scouts were out looking both for those units and for changes in their locations and dispositions. Meade's army was being reinforced, and intelligence said that Lee's was as well, which might put their combined numbers close to a total of two hundred thousand men, an incredible number.

These numbers meant that Herculean efforts had to be expended to keep them supplied and, since the Confederates were always short on everything, plundering Union supplies was one way of keeping their men fed.

Despite the fact that the Army of Northern Virginia had moved into Pennsylvania, a rich farming area, they were already threatening to eat their way through that wealthy commonwealth. Anyone with half a brain understood that the status quo could not last forever. Something would have to give, and give soon.

Thorne had a reinforced platoon of thirty men on horseback guarding a wagon train of some forty covered wagons. In ten of them were four additional soldiers each. With the exception of the teamsters, who just wanted to deliver their loads and get home safely, they were hoping the Rebels would try an ambush.

Even though it was a relatively small wagon train, it snaked along for several hundred yards. Thorne placed himself in the middle and had Captain Archie Willis riding at the front.

As usual, it was a hot and sticky day and sweat soaked their heavy uniforms. Each man had been ordered to bring two canteens, with additional water on one of the wagons.

Thorne pulled out his pocket watch. It was only three in the afternoon. If his estimates were correct, they would not reach a Union camp until much later this evening. He did not want to spend the night in potentially hostile territory. What he really wanted was to get to his quarters and take a bath. He'd found a corrugated iron tub that would fit his lean body if he twisted himself just right.

A rider came from the front of the column and announced that a creek with clean water lay just ahead. With a grin the rider added that Captain Willis suggested that they all go and soak their heads in it.

The men and the horses needed a break and if it meant a further delay, then so be it. "Tell the captain that I agree and that he should be the first to go soak himself."

An hour later, the men had splashed water on themselves, refilled their canteens, and made sure that their horses had quenched their thirst. They'd been told by red-faced sergeants to piss well downstream. Thorne wondered what the people downstream would think of that.

They were just about to re-form the column when they heard the now familiar screech of the Rebel yell as scores of horsemen burst from where they'd been hiding in deep brush. The men of the Sixth formed up quickly and presented a bristling front to the hard-charging horsemen.

"Fire!" Thorne yelled and Spencer rifles opened up, and then without pause fired again. A continuous storm of bullets struck the attacking men and horses, their surprise and confusion clearly visible as the fusillade dropped them into ghastly piles of twisted and screaming flesh. One man waved an arm, evidently trying to rally the others. A shot blew him clear out of his saddle. Thorne lost sight of him amid the dust stirred up by the horse's hooves.

There was a brief pause as the men reloaded and replaced seven-shot tubes in the stocks of their rifles. The Spencers didn't have the range of the traditional muzzle-loaders, but today that was irrelevant. The Confederates halted and began sporadically returning fire. Now the screams came from the men in blue. But there were far fewer Union casualties, as they were either behind the wagons or lying prone. The attackers began to pull back, dragging some of their wounded with them. One man grabbed the stirrup of a horse and pulled himself up behind the rider. Thorne wondered if it could be the man he'd seen shot down, and found himself hoping that it was.

When they were far enough off, Thorne organized a skirmish line and advanced to the point where the dead Rebels lay thickest. He counted fourteen bodies and another five too badly wounded to move. There were a number of dead and wounded horses as well. These were disposed of quickly. He leaned over one man who was conscious. "What unit are you in?"

The man grimaced. "Fuck you, Yankee." There was a wound in his stomach and he was bleeding badly. It would doubtless prove fatal.

"You know you're going to die, don't you? Now do you want to die in agony or would you like some laudanum to make your passing easier?"

The man's eyes widened. "You ain't gonna take me to a doctor?"

"Sorry, but there aren't any doctors within ten miles of here and besides, you've been gut shot. Your insides are already spilling poison throughout your body and it's going to kill you just as certain as it will be dark in a few hours."

The Rebel shook as a wave of pain washed over him. "Ask me anything. Just get me something to kill this godawful pain."

Thorne assigned Willis to interrogate the man. Those other wounded who were conscious were already talking. The Rebels were in rags, which made no sense.

Lee had not only been reinforced, but his own supply lines were bringing him fresh equipment, to include uniforms. He concluded that these were bushwhackers or outlaws, irregular forces that sometimes supported one side or the other and sometimes just looted like vandals.

Fourteen outlaws had been killed with one more sure to join them. The four who might survive would last long enough to hang. His men had suffered only three wounded and only one was serious. It was a good day's work. Maybe tomorrow he could ride in to Washington and see how Colonel Baird was doing.

Blandon's riders were strung out single file. Since they were a part of neither army, they kept a close watch for any patrols. If they found something that the Confederates could use and that they didn't want, they'd turn it in to what had been their army. They conceded that was highly unlikely. Blandon and the others had become outlaws.

Pennsylvania was filled with large and prosperous farms and a goodly portion of the farmers were of German descent. There were many Quaker communities and Blandon found it amusing that people would not defend themselves.

Blandon signaled a halt and the men bunched up more closely. There were a total of fifteen of them and they were all well-armed deserters from the Army of Northern Virginia. If caught, they would be hanged. Looking down from the small hill on which they stood, they could see a prosperous-looking farm compound about a half mile away. People could be seen moving about and some had noticed the riders on the hill.

Blandon grinned. "Let's ride down and see what they have that they might want to share with good Christian men like us."

When they were a couple of hundred yards away, one of the farmers fired a shotgun into the air. Blandon guffawed. "Well, I guess they ain't Quakers."

They rode up, but more slowly. There were seven men and all were armed. Blandon counted five adult women and wondered if younger women and children might be hiding in one of the buildings. A couple of the women also had rifles.

"Damn," said Skinner, one of Blandon's companions, "this could be a tough nut to crack."

"Agreed. We could whip them but we would lose some good boys and then the rest might bolt." Blandon took a piece of cloth that could pass for white and tied it around the barrel of his rifle. "I'll go first and alone. I don't think they'll shoot me."

He was right. The farmers let him ride right up to them, although they kept their weapons covering him. Blandon thought that one of the women with a rifle was right handsome and didn't know shit about handling it. Her hands were shaking too badly. If she'd been alone, he could have taken it right off her. Then she would have had the pleasure of being fucked by a real Confederate cavalryman.

He put down his rifle and stood tall in the saddle. "My name is Jonah Blandon and I am an officer in the Confederate Army of Northern Virginia. I have been sent by General Lee to purchase supplies for his army. We will pay in money or give receipts, whichever you like best. We want horses, cattle, pigs, and even chickens. I see that your fields are bare, so we can send some wagons for whatever you might have in your barns. How's that sound?"

An older man of about fifty and with a long graying beard stepped forward. "I'd say we might be interested but for the fact that the Union soldiers were here and already bought everything we had. I would also tell you that we are Union people, don't like slavery, and wouldn't want either Confederate money or your receipts."

"Are you Quakers?"

"No, but we largely agree with them. We are peaceful people, too."

Blandon forced a smile. "Well then, I guess there's no reason for me to stick around here. We'll be off. You don't happen to know of any other farms like yours that might have provisions to sell?"

The bearded man spat brown on the ground. It was chewing tobacco and it had been a while since Blandon had had the luxury. "A lot of the farmers around here have packed up and left. We were just discussing that very thing and, since you Rebels are now so close, we likely will depart."

Blandon smiled again. "That might be wise. There are a lot of ruffians riding about. We are Christian men and mean you no harm, but there is a nasty war taking place and people sometimes do cruel things." He tapped the brim of his hat in salute. "I wish you a safe journey."

Back over the hill and out of sight, he told his men that they'd wait until well after dark. "If those people sold their belongings to General Meade, then he paid them in cash, which is a helluva lot better to cart around than pigs and cows. Besides, when we take the place we can have some real fun."

They made a normal and very obvious camp several miles down the road from the farm. His men cooked food, ate, and went to sleep. They were very tired so there was no need to pretend. About three in the morning, Blandon went around and woke them.

"No horses," he said to each one of them. "We don't want them hearing a thing. I wouldn't be surprised if they have a guard out keeping track of us. Make your rolls look like someone's sleeping and slip quietly into the woods. Two of us will be the pretend guards at our camp and will keep the fires burning just a little."

"I don't feature walking that far to no farm," said Skinner.

"You'll get over it." Blandon smiled. "Just think of them pretty white thighs awaiting on you."

"Some of us won't go for that neither."

"What?"

"That's right. Those women are Christian and white. Doing the colored may be one thing, but not white women. So, you don't want to lose these boys, you don't let it happen. I seen how you was slobbering at that brown-haired woman. Just let it go this time, Sarge. Let it go. We may not be part of the Confederate Army no more, but that don't mean we can't act like good, Christian soldiers."

Good Christian soldiers, thought Blandon. *Good Christian soldiers who loot farms and rob travelers.* "Awright, Skinner."

They crept away from the camp and walked parallel to the trail that led to the farm. One of his men was a good hunter and quickly spotted the boy that the farmers thought they'd hidden. They snuck up behind him and subdued him with scarcely a sound. They then tied him up securely.

"I hope the little bastard's not due to be relieved for a while," Skinner said.

"Then we'd best move right along. I very much misdoubt that there's a second guard. There aren't enough of them for that kind of setup."

He was right. They made it unseen to the main house and a bunkhouse behind the main building. They gathered by the doors and were about to burst in when a dog began to bark. It was followed by a second and a third. Inside the houses, people began yelling.

"Now," Blandon screamed and shouldered his way through the door. A man in a nightgown was just inside. Blandon shot him in the chest. The gunfire and flashes deafened and blinded him for an instant. More of his men pushed by him, screaming and howling. After a few more shots, it was over. Two farmers were dead and one of Blandon's men had been stabbed in the thigh.

Their prisoners were tied up and dragged outside where dawn was beginning to show. They looked up at him, both angry and terrified. Blandon smiled down at them, with special attention at the woman who had been holding the rifle. Her nightgown had been ripped across the shoulder and she was holding a small child. He wanted her so badly he could taste it.

"Now," Blandon said, "here's what's going to happen. You told us you sold your stuff to the Union boys and that means you got cash for it. We'll take that cash, thank you, and be on our way."

"We don't have it any more," the bearded man said. "That was days ago. We sent it on to Philadelphia. No way we were going to leave cash lying around."

Shit, Blandon thought. That sounded all too plausible. But then, maybe it didn't. "I don't quite believe you. You might have sent some of it on, but not all of it. Give it up and nothing much will happen. Don't and we'll beat the shit out of you men and burn this place down."

"You said you were Christians," the bearded man said.

"I lied," Blandon said and his men laughed.

"Where's my son?" one woman shrieked. "He was supposed to be watching out."

"He's resting comfortable. If you want to see him again, give up that money."

The bearded leader reluctantly agreed. He was untied and came back with a valise full of cash. It was still too dark to count but it looked like a good haul.

"Thank you for your cooperation. We'll leave you in a few minutes, but first we must make sure you are well tied up so you can't give a warning."

It was all too easy. After making sure the farmers were all trussed up, they were dragged off to the barn. While his men tore the house apart looking for treasures, Blandon stared at the woman, who kept averting her head. Why the hell had he made that promise to Skinner? He would have to get a few more men who thought like he did. Then he could get rid of the pansies.

Blandon went outside and lit up a small cigar. It had been a very good night.

Major Steven Thorne and the former colonel, Josiah Baird, shook hands formally and then embraced firmly and warmly. "It's good to see you, sir," Thorne said with a degree of emotion that surprised him. He and the colonel had never been close. He was unsure if Baird wanted to be called colonel or mister. "I'm sorry I couldn't get to see you sooner, but things have been quite busy."

"I can only imagine. I wish I could still be there in command, but a one-legged colonel is generally quite useless in the army. They said I could stay on in some administrative capacity, but I respectfully declined. I had enough of war and the army, although I will insist on people calling me 'colonel.' I rather like it."

Well, that's cleared up, Thorne thought. They were on the porch of the home Baird and his family were renting. Tea had just been served. Thorne didn't much like tea. He preferred coffee, but he sipped politely anyhow. Mrs. Baird had joined them and fussed over him. Their daughter, Cassandra, was friendly but still dressed as he recalled her the one time they had met—all in black for mourning. For whom, he wondered? None of the other Bairds were similarly dressed, so just who had died?

The colonel showed him how well he could navigate on crutches and said he was looking forward to getting an artificial leg that was being specially made for him. "Then I will either walk normally or with a cane. I will not be a damned cripple."

"I don't think you'd ever be a cripple, sir," Thorne said, which brought smiles from both women. He decided that Cassandra was almost pretty when she smiled. She should do it more often.

The colonel wanted to know all about the regiment and its new duties. He didn't ask about the casualties from Gettysburg. He'd seen the lists and had even visited some of the wounded in the hospitals. He just said it was so godawful depressing.

"At least you're away from the front lines," Rachel said and the colonel flushed. Thorne wondered if Colonel Baird had used his influence to get the regiment away from II Corps. He decided he didn't care. If it helped keep him and the others alive, it was a wonderful idea.

They talked, ate, and talked some more. Tea became wine and even the ladies joined in. Thorne began to wonder why the colonel had intimidated him so much. Of course his no longer being in the army had a great deal to do with it.

"Steven, what will you do when this bloody war is over?"

"Don't you mean if it is ever over, sir? Thanks to Meade, it may never end. Ah, I don't think I should have said that. He was in over his head and I may be in the same situation commanding the regiment, no matter how small it currently is."

The colonel and Thorne were both a little unsteady when they finally walked to the door. Baird said he would like to see his regiment and Steven said he was cordially invited and that it would always be the colonel's regiment. He also wished he hadn't had that last glass of wine.

Rachel Baird kissed him on the cheek and Cassandra even smiled. It had been a good night. He carefully mounted his horse, hoping he wouldn't stumble.

"A deserter, eh?"

The man Richard Dean was speaking to was dressed in the epitome of fashion—an embroidered waistcoat, a light-colored jacket, a cravat pinned at his throat. He was toying with his ebony walking stick. There was the beginning of a mustache visible on his upper lip.

"Nothing to be ashamed of," he went on. "Who wants to die in the army of the Great Ape of Pennsylvania Avenue?"

"That's how I look at it," Dean said eagerly. He himself had grown a rather scraggly beard over the past few weeks to disguise himself from the provost marshal's men. It also added a few years to his apparent age, something he was grateful for. His small build often made people take him for an underage youth.

Dean had been working as a stagehand since he'd separated himself from the army, moving between several theaters in Washington. On a couple of occasions, he'd performed on stage as a boy in his early teens. He hadn't spoken, since he was in his mid-twenties and his voice was far too deep to permit that. Still, he'd enjoyed his few moments in the limelight.

This day he was painting props backstage at Ford's Theater. It was hot and unpleasant work, but it paid. That he'd become entranced by what went on in the world of theater was obvious and not the slightest bit unusual. Star-struck young men and women showed up all the time. Normally, they came and stayed for a while and then went on with their lives. Some went home a little better educated about the world and others just disappeared. A few stuck.

Any one of them would give their right arm for the opportunity facing Dean right now.

"Abe Lincoln would be prime evidence that mankind had interbred with gorillas."

Dean allowed himself a chuckle.

"That is, if we didn't already have the niggers."

Dean chuckled once again. The man gave his stick a twirl. "You like that one?" He regarded Dean a moment before going on. "So you've been in battle?"

"Awful hard to avoid it the way things have been going."

"That's true. Ever kill anybody?"

"Yes I have."

The eyes regarding Dean narrowed. "You're telling me you killed a member of the Confederate forces?"

Dean felt his face redden. "Well, no . . . I actually never killed anybody."

The man smiled. "I didn't think so. Killing leaves a mark on a man. But you know your firearms."

"Yes I do. Explosives as well."

"Explosives?" He raised the stick to rub his chin.

Two men appeared from the stage entrance. They were clean-shaven, dressed in business suits and, despite being young and large, were not military officers. For a moment Dean thought they might be businessmen trying to sell something to Mr. John T. Ford, the founder and owner of the theater that had only recently reopened following a fire. He wished them well if that was the case. Mr. Ford was not free with his money.

"That's him," the taller man said. Dean had scarcely time enough to stiffen before they lay strong arms on him. He tried to break free but it was use.

"What the devil is going on here?" They had shoved the actor aside as they closed in on Dean. He stood facing them with stick upraised.

"Who are you?" the bigger of the two demanded.

"My name is Booth, and I perform at this theater."

The bigger man nodded at the other, who said. "Sorry, Mr. Booth. We didn't recognize you. This one here," he gave Dean a shake. "Is a deserter from the Army of the Potomac."

"A deserter?" Booth lowered his stick. "You don't say?"

Dean flinched as the bigger man clapped a pair of manacles on his wrists. "Mr. Booth . . ."

"This is nothing that concerns you, sir. We are from the Metropolitan Police. Now please step aside."

"I meant no harm," Booth said, and backed up quickly. Dean was dismayed. He'd idolized John Wilkes Booth, and had thought he was as brave as the parts he played. Now he knew it was all a sham. Booth had been acting, was always acting.

"Let's go." The two men ushered Dean toward the rear entrance. He looked over his shoulder. Booth was gazing after him with no expression at all on his face.

Dean shook his head. His position was hopeless. Out in the alley, the two men steered him toward the street. He heard a voice behind him and turned to see Booth heading in the opposite direction, calling out to someone.

Reaching the street, they came to a halt. "Where is the carriage?"

"He said he was turning around . . ."

"Ah, there it is." The big man gave him a shove and they started down past the theater façade. He was dragged to the closed carriage and thrust inside. The two men sat on either side of him as a third man drove the horses at a good rate of speed. It began to occur to him that the men weren't police officers at all.

"Cassandra, are you awake and dressed?" her father hollered up the stairs. "Come down to the kitchen. There's something you absolutely must see."

Cassie did as she was told and, curious, quickly made her way to the kitchen. To her surprise, the room was crowded. Two large men were holding a third and smaller man by his arms while her father sat smiling benignly.

"Turn him around," the colonel ordered and the men complied.

Cassie gasped and her legs felt weak. "Richard? My God, Richard, you're alive!"

Then it dawned on her. "Richard, how can this be? Everyone said you were dead . . . and yet here you are. Why didn't you tell anyone you'd survived the battle?"

Richard shrugged off the hands of the two men and addressed her father. "Colonel . . . if I may beg the privilege of conferring with your daughter alone?"

Colonel Baird snorted and gestured toward the dining room. The two large men glanced uneasily at each other but said nothing.

Cassie led the way into the dining room. She turned to Richard. He stood there smirking at her. "Well?"

Richard shrugged. "You see, my dear, I didn't survive the battle, so to speak, because I was never in it. Only fools go charging up hills to their deaths. I gave a man a twenty-dollar gold piece to take my place while I took his as a messenger. In the chaos afterward, I simply slipped away and began to live a new life."

"Richard, that's awful."

"On the contrary, dear Cassie. It's commonplace. Almost accepted procedure."

Her head was clearing from the shock of seeing the man she'd been mourning standing in front of her. "But . . . what if the other man had been killed?"

"He *was* killed."

"Richard!"

"Ah, Cassie, he was merely an Irishman. You wouldn't wish me dead in the place of some papist immigrant, would you? You've never witnessed their popish rituals. Horrible stuff."

She stared wordlessly at him. Sensing movement behind her, she half turned to see the duller-looking of the big men eying them from the pantry doorway. He touched his hat and retreated.

". . . and in any case, I have discovered where my real talents lie, and what path awaits me."

"What do you mean?"

He took a step away, eyes turned upward as if fixed on some far horizon. "I always told you I thought the war was wrong, that the Great Ape was wrong, and that freeing the colored was wrong. Or weren't you listening to me?"

"But then you went and enlisted, Richard."

Richard laughed. "So I made a mistake. At least I didn't compound the error by remaining where I wasn't meant to be. After only a couple of weeks, I saw the bloody results of what someone said was a small skirmish and decided I wanted nothing to do with risking my life for something I didn't believe in. I joined up to impress you in hopes that you'd marry a brave warrior. But Cassie, that is not what I truly am."

Cassie crossed her arms. "What are you exactly, Richard?"

He cast an arm into the air. "I have learned that I have a knack for the theatrical arts. That I can touch the souls of onlookers, and change their way of thinking, without them even being aware of it. Therein lies my opportunity to make a real contribution.

"You cannot know, dear girl, how corrupt is our commonwealth, how terrible the lies which we endure, and how difficult it is to put across the truth." He shook a fist in the air. "But I have discovered a way. The newspapers are all Republican, owned by abolitionists and lackeys of the Great Ape. To confront people with the truth, we must utilize another means.

"The theater will be that means. I envision a travelling program, making its way from town to town, both informing and entertaining the people at once. We will present a series of tableaus that will reveal the true nature of this war, the enormity of the Ape's crimes, the actual status of the colored. Ahh, you have not spent any time among the niggers, Cassie. I am here to tell you, they are but small children, little more than beasts of the field. They need a strong white Anglo-Saxon hand to—"

"I see," Cassie said. "And who, may I ask, is the Great Ape?"

"Why, that would be none other than Abe Linkhorn, soi disant president of this sorry republic."

She gazed at him in silence. Rubbing his hands together, he drew nearer. "So you see, Cassie, I need you to ask your father to dismiss those two detectives so that we can sit down and discuss how much he wants to invest in my effort."

"Invest."

He nodded. *And to think*, she thought to herself, *that I was willing to get married to* this.

Gathering up her skirts, she returned to the kitchen. Her father was saying, ". . . believed he was dead on the Fredericksburg battlefield. That's why my daughter is dressed in black."

"Well, she'll be able to treat herself to more colorful finery now, Colonel."

Colonel Baird looked up. "Ahh, Cassandra, are you finished?"

"Well and truly, Father."

"Very well, then. Gentlemen, take him away."

The two men got up. "What will you do with him, Detective?"

"Well, miss," the smaller man said. The other moved toward the dining room. "We will take him to Fort Monroe, and once there—"

From the dining room came the sound of a window sash opening. "Goddammit . . ." the dull-looking man shouted as he dashed from the kitchen.

"Excuse me," the other detective said.

Cassie turned to her father. "Oh dear . . ."

★ ★ ★

Dean didn't stop running until he was a hundred yards from the house. He paused to catch his breath with one hand on a tree trunk. Hearing shouts behind him, he pushed on.

He'd gotten no more than another twenty yards when he heard a crackling in the brush and stumbled to a halt. A man on horseback emerged from the trees to his right.

"Dean?"

He let out a breath. The face was familiar, even though he didn't know the name. The man was thin-faced, high-cheekboned, and glaring-eyed, an abolitionist's nightmare of the typical Rebel. The voice matched the face.

"Name's Jessup. Booth sent me."

Dean nodded wordlessly. Jessup swung the horse around. "Come along now."

They'd nearly reached the road when they heard the clop of horse's hooves up ahead. Jessup pulled his horse to a halt and stretched to look over its neck. Nodding to himself, he reached into his jacket and pulled out a large-caliber Colt pistol. He took aim and fired one shot. There was a shriek of animal agony followed by confused shouting.

Cocking the pistol, Jessup fired another round, then paused with the barrel held high. Dean heard the sound of footsteps receding through brush.

"They gonna need another horse or two," Jessup assured him. He spat to one side. "Pinkertons. I hate 'em. Come along."

He said no more until they returned to the road another half-mile on. "Let's get some speed on."

"Give me a hand up," Dean told him.

"You ain't sitting up here with me. You grab that strap on the saddle and you run."

Jessup rode forward about ten yards then stopped and glared back at Dean. He caught up and grabbed the strap. A moment later they were clattering along at a slow trot toward Washington.

★ CHAPTER 6 ★

All his life, Captain Steven Thorne had been taught that it was immoral—sinful—to keep a fellow human being in bondage. In his mind, it was both a blasphemy against the Creator and an insult to humanity. He didn't understand the rationale that asserted that people who were not white were not quite human, and could thus be bought and sold like cattle, and forced to work for the benefit of others. It was a foul and base excuse. All men were made in the image of God Almighty, and all men deserved the same treatment from their fellow creatures.

On the other hand, he had his doubts that the problems surrounding race and slavery could be solved peacefully. The war was evidence aplenty of that. It was a conundrum, one that he hoped that wiser heads than his own would be able to solve.

Even though Indiana was a Union state, there were many in it who sympathized with the Confederacy and there were some who'd slipped off to the South to join either the Army of Tennessee or the Army of Northern Virginia. There would be some interesting reunions and recriminations when the war ended. If it ended, he corrected himself for the hundredth time. He was almost resigned to spending the rest of his life in a uniform.

He'd applauded the Emancipation Proclamation, even wishing that it had included the slaves of the Border States. The lawyer in him understood the legal impossibility of freeing those poor souls at this time. The Supreme Court had pretty much decided that issue with the Dred Scott decision. A slave was still a man's property. Lincoln's Proclamation declared a southern man's property forfeit, thus freeing the slaves within the Confederacy. The rationale was that freeing the slaves in the rebelling states hurt the South's war effort just as much as burning her crops or defeating her armies did.

Again, the lawyer in him wondered what would happen to the freed slaves when the war did end with Union victory. Would they still be considered property and returned to their former owners? *Not bloody likely*, he thought as he considered the many thousands of contrabands camped around Washington.

He had no idea where the freed blacks should go. They might go back down south and work for pay instead of being slaves. Like most people, even hard-core abolitionists, he had no desire to work with Negroes or live near them. The freeing of millions of colored was already causing chaos as contraband camps sprang up.

Where would the freed slaves go? Well, *this* group would not be going back south in chains. Word had come that a group of slavers had gathered up nearly a hundred contrabands from nearby camps and were herding them like cattle south towards the Potomac and safety— so to speak—in Virginia.

Fortunately, the slaves could not move very quickly, which gave Thorne the opportunity to set up an ambush. A few miles behind the slavers, Archie Willis had one company of soldiers while Thorne commanded the rest of the regiment. Willis' men would drive the slavers on to Thorne's position. There were only a couple of dozen slavers, and using the regiment to take them might have been compared to using a sledgehammer to hit an ant, but it was a splendid opportunity to maneuver his men and get them used to each other.

Scouts had told him that the slavers suspected that they were being trailed and had picked up the pace. That was rough for those in chains. Thorne sent a scout back to Willis telling him to close in on the slavers but to avoid contact.

"Here they come," said Sergeant Maury. A number of men and women were spilling out of the stand of woods to their front and entering a farmer's field. The crops had been harvested, so they stood out clearly.

"Mount," he ordered. This day the Sixth Indiana Mounted Infantry would function more as cavalry than infantry. He signaled and sixty horsemen breasted the hill behind which they'd been hiding and cantered towards the slavers and their captives.

Thorne fought the urge to order a charge. His men were good horsemen, but not as good as true cavalry. He didn't want any injuries.

Some of the slavers turned and opened fire while their prisoners threw themselves on the ground. A horse screamed and collapsed, shot in the leg. The rider fell face forward, hit the ground, and lay still. "Shit," said Thorne. He aimed his pistol at a man with a rifle, fired and missed. The man threw down his rifle and ran.

Scattered gunfire came from the rest of the slavers. Another soldier fell and then the horsemen were among them. Thorne was just about to shoot a slaver only a few feet in front of him when the man dropped his rifle and held up his hands. A couple of slavers were down and the others were giving up. The former slaves looked about in stunned disbelief. A couple of them started punching and kicking a slaver. Thorne broke it up, one of the Negroes telling him through gritted teeth that the man had beaten and whipped them repeatedly on the road south. The slaver was bloody but would live. Thorne had no pity for him and was tempted to let his former captives work him over some more.

Thorne checked over his men. He had one dead. The man who'd fallen face down had broken his neck and died instantly. Another trooper had been shot in the flesh of the arm and would likely recover if infection didn't set in. Several others had bruises from falling off their horses, thereby proving that they were mounted infantry and not cavalry. Jeb Stuart would have nothing to fear from the Sixth Indiana. That said, it had been a good day. His men had fought together and fought well.

Perhaps he should stop by the colonel's residence and have another excellent dinner. The colonel would surely like to know just how well his old regiment was doing, wouldn't he?

The men of Wade's Tennessee Volunteers were facing an uncomfortable truth. The Commonwealth of Pennsylvania was no longer the land of plenty, the fabled Cornucopia spilling its largesse on the soil. The longer the Confederate army remained in position, the harder it became to keep it fed. Not only had the farms within an easy ride of Lee's camps been stripped of both cattle and crops, but so too had properties farther away. In many cases, crops had been burned so that the army could not get at them, and this was the case at the farm they'd just ridden through.

The usual pillars of smoke had attracted them to the scene and the Volunteers had arrived only a little after the Union patrols had left. There'd been some thought of chasing the Union detachment but the threat of an ambush ruled that out.

The family that had lived there was just leaving as the cavalry rode up. They were not harmed. Colonel Wade would not permit that—he was no Blandon. Instead, he had taken their horses and two oxen and given them receipts in the name of Jefferson Davis. The extended family would now have to walk, with all their possessions left by the side of the road for anyone to pick through.

There was pure hatred in the eyes of the Pennsylvanians as they realized the extent of their disaster. Their buildings would be burned as well as their fields. That was war.

"You are barbarians," said the oldest woman in the group. She doubtless felt that her age made it safe to say such things, and she was right. "How dare you invade our homes and steal our possessions?"

"I believe we bought them," Wade said calmly, although he wanted to punch all of them. There were even two Negroes in their group and they looked terrified.

Since Pennsylvania did not have slaves, these were likely free men. He would leave them alone as well. If they were caught by slavecatchers, well, it would be too bad. He hoped they didn't run afoul of Blandon.

"And as to our being invaders," Wade continued, "try telling that to the people of Virginia and Tennessee where your Union armies have marched and ravaged in a manner far more barbaric then anything you have seen today. You northerners are the cause of this war. You are the ones who will not let the people of the South go their own way. You want peace? You want to be able to farm without armies trampling over your fields? Well then, why don't you just stop invading our land and we'll leave yours alone as well."

Wade realized he'd made no impression on them. Their feelings were too deeply entrenched. Well, so too were his.

"No, my friends, we are not Yankees. We do not act as locusts to our fellow men. I have never damaged civilian property without good reason, though I'm almost ready to do it in your case. Now get the hell out of my sight. Let Honest Abe Lincoln feed and shelter you. Maybe you'll wind up in a tent city with all of those contrabands as your next-door neighbors. How'll you like them apples?"

He angrily wheeled his horse away from the farmers, only slightly aware that those men of his who'd been close by were applauding him. Damn, he realized, I finally did something right.

Robert E. Lee lay on his cot and tried to rest. His staff had urged him to simply take over one of the rich houses in the area north of York, but he was uncomfortable doing that. When operating in the South, folks had been honored to offer their homes to him, but in the north he was an invader. He would not steal from them even though his back cried out for a comfortable mattress for a night or two. One of the causes of the American Revolution was the quartering of British soldiers in American homes. He would not force himself on the people of the north and he wouldn't permit his officers and men to do so. In an irony, some of the houses dated from the Revolution—his father's war.

Of course, this meant that his staff had to sleep in tents as well. That made him smile. Almost all of them were much younger than he and in their physical primes while he, although only fifty-six, felt much older. He'd mused on the fact that he was only a couple of years older than Abraham Lincoln and wondered if the Union president was as exhausted as he. Probably, he decided.

Coffee was brought to him, along with bread and butter. He ate heartily, unlike other mornings when he had little or no appetite for food, just as he had no appetite for war. He was beginning to think that his decision to stay in Pennsylvania had been one enormous mistake. The Union Army was showing no inclination of moving against him.

The Army of Northern Virginia was growing stronger. He now had a division commanded by William Hardee, one of the better generals in the Confederacy. He, along with General Leonidas Polk, had requested permission to be transferred from the command of Braxton Bragg to anyplace else. He had ordered Hardee north, but decided that the bishop would do just as well where he was.

These men, along with the replacements trickling up from the south, were putting an enormous strain on the abilities of his quartermasters to feed the army. He would have to do something to alleviate that problem even if it meant sending large raiding parties far afield, even if it meant crossing the Susquehanna at Harrisburg and requisitioning supplies from the people in that part of Pennsylvania. He did not wish to cause harm to those people, but when he compared it to the devastation that had taken place in his beloved Virginia, he thought it just. *War is a hellish venture*, he thought.

General Lee finished his bread and put aside his now cold coffee. He called to an aide. "Please give my compliments to General Longstreet and tell him I wish to see him this afternoon. Tell him I would enjoy his presence at a quiet dinner."

The next several days spent teaching the contrabands went much better. Cassie was showing more confidence as an instructor and the Negroes' respect for her grew as it became obvious that she wasn't going to cut and run just because the task was difficult. She had also begun wearing dresses that were colored and not black and some of them wondered at the sudden change from mourning but were too discreet to ask.

When it came time for lunch, Cassie and Mariah would usually eat with the students. Today, Mariah had chosen to eat elsewhere. Hadrian was nowhere to be seen either, which made Cassie smile. Not that she much cared whatever Mariah did, except for not wanting her to be hurt. Her servant was a free woman and could do as she pleased.

Many of the students were showing real progress. It would be a long road for most of them, but she was confident that they would make it. Security in Hadrian's camp had improved as well. The massive Negro had gotten his hands on a number of rifles that looked suspiciously like what the Union Army used. She thought she saw the hand of her sometimes devious father in this. For once, she had no problem with his meddling in her affairs.

Mariah was only a couple of minutes late from her lunch. Cassie sweetly told her that her blouse wasn't buttoned correctly and that her hair was mussed. The women in the class had noticed as well and there were quiet giggles. Mariah straightened herself, apparently unconcerned. "Are you going to tell them about tomorrow?"

"Ah yes, tomorrow," Cassie said and turned to the group. "There will be no school tomorrow. I have some family obligations to attend to."

One of the women smiled gently. "We envy you. Not everyone here has a family. Our white owners saw to that. I had three husbands and two children and they were all sold away from me."

How could anyone not have a family, Cassie wondered? How could anyone separate those families that did exist? "You'll have your own family someday," she said hopefully.

She had often wondered just how any human being could sell or own another human being. She understood that the courts said that a Negro was property, which meant that anyone of color could be bought just like the fabric she'd bought to make new dresses from. The law would have to change. Maybe Mr. Lincoln could bring that about. First, he would have to defeat the Confederates, thousands of whom were gathering not all that far from where she was trying to teach former slaves how to read.

And as to tomorrow, her father had accepted an invitation from Major Thorne to visit the regiment and have an early dinner. She was looking forward to it. Since finding out that Richard Dean had betrayed her, she had stifled her anger and was determined to live her life.

Perhaps, she thought impishly, *she would even flirt*. Perhaps she wasn't quite ready to be an old maid.

The dinner went well. The regiment's former colonel was delighted almost to tears to see his old companions. He offered a toast to all of those who weren't there and they all mourned the fact that there were so many empty places.

The dinner was not normal military fare. Thorne had hired a man from another regiment who had been a chef in his previous life and he roasted a goose along with half a cow. Wines were served and a kind of ice cream made by nearby Quakers was the dessert.

Thorne was pleasantly surprised to see that Cassandra was no longer in mourning. He considered asking the reason and decided in favor of discretion. He had to admit that she looked far more attractive and there was color in her cheeks that hinted at the use of some form of cosmetics. He was no expert on the topic, but he'd seen his sister apply colors and recalled mocking her. Cassandra was an engaging conversationalist and Thorne quickly realized that her mother was pushing them in the same direction. He wasn't particularly thrilled at the thought of being romantically connected with his former colonel's daughter, but decided there were worse fates. He could at least be polite.

On the other hand, Cassandra was fairly attractive now that she was taking care of herself. The fact that she was teaching a school for Negroes showed she was both intelligent and determined. He gathered that neither her father nor her mother liked the idea of her working in a camp surrounded by hundreds of colored people and decided he didn't either. He made a point to find out where the camp was and see what he could do to provide additional protection. It couldn't be too far away.

After dinner, entertainment was provided by a group of the regiment's soldiers who'd formed a chorus. They sang a number of patriotic songs and sang them quite loudly and enthusiastically. Captain Archie Willis also sang and Thorne was surprised that his companion had a really pleasant voice. Mariah and Cassie then sang duets, primarily spirituals from Mariah's youth and what they'd heard in the contraband camp. A few Stephen Foster songs completed their repertoire. Thorne was certain that Mariah's was the stronger voice.

The day ended as pleasantly as it had begun. The colonel again got emotional on taking leave of his regiment. He was invited back, of course, but who knew when the war would start up again and cause a further and tragic reduction in their ranks? Thorne did get Cassie aside and suggest that they have dinner or lunch—with an appropriate chaperone, of course.

Cassie had responded by laughing at him. "Major, I am twenty-three and I no longer have any need for a chaperone or a nanny. In case you haven't noticed, I've had an epiphany and am going to live my life to the fullest. And, if you're curious, I just found out that I was mourning someone who wasn't dead—and who didn't deserve an instant of my life in any case. On the other hand, I am not foolish and we will be discreet."

Thorne thought it was a wonderful idea and they made tentative arrangements for a picnic the Sunday after next. That is, if the war didn't intervene.

★ ★ ★

The town of Bensonville, Pennsylvania, looked too small to have a bank, but there it was. An ugly red brick block that tried to exude security, telling customers that their money was secure within. Several score buildings and dwellings surrounded it.

Of course it was largely abandoned, thought Jonah Blandon. Bensonville was in the area between the two armies and many of the homes around the bank and the stores had been left empty. Their occupants and owners had prudently opted for the safety of Washington or Baltimore, or had crossed the Susquehanna and gone deeper into Pennsylvania.

Blandon and his men had found very slim pickings of late. Farmers' crops had either been harvested or burned, and the farmers moved away. Blandon decided that what his band needed wasn't some farmer's damn crops, it was money.

By giving out the word that they were going to attack the bank, a score of new recruits had joined him.

Just before dawn was the best time. It was when people were either asleep or so groggy they might as well be. Taking a page from other raiders like Quantrill, his men stormed through the town, hollering and shooting in the air, herding the civilians ahead of them like so many geese. Within a few minutes, they'd rounded up more than thirty men, women, and children to use as hostages. Happily for him, one of the women angrily identified herself as the wife of the bank manager. She then pointed out a short, plump, and balding man as her husband, Marvin Hill, who looked as if he wanted to strangle her.

"Mr. Hill," Blandon said with a smile, "you will now please open the vault. We have a need to make a very rather withdrawal for the good of the Confederate States of America."

"I will not," Hill huffed. "In a very few minutes, the army will be here and you will wind up hanging if you are still here."

"And which army might that be, Mr. Hill? You are closest to Confederate lines and we are southerners, and God bless Robert E. Lee. On the other hand, if you're waiting for Lincoln's boys, you'll have one long wait ahead of you. At any rate, we will be out of here in a very few minutes and, one way or the other, we will have the contents of that vault. Now open up and don't make us do something that would bring your wife misery."

Hill stuck his chin out proudly. "I will not."

Blandon punched him hard in the stomach and, when he bent over, hit him in the kidney. Hill fell, clawing the ground in agony. "Open the goddamn vault, Yankee," Blandon snarled.

"No," Hill gasped and Blandon felt a degree of admiration.

Blandon gestured and an old man was dragged from the crowd of hostages. Blandon put his revolver against the man's skull and cocked it. "Open it."

"You wouldn't," said Hill, his face going pale.

Blandon fired once. The bullet blew the hostage's head apart. Blood and brains splattered the ground. The remaining hostages groaned or shrieked.

Blandon laughed. "His death is on you, Mr. Hill. Now open the fucking vault or God help me, I'll shoot every last one. And when I've killed them all, including your bigmouth wife, I'll shoot you in the gut just so you take a right long time to die."

Hill's face collapsed. He began sobbing. He staggered into the bank with Blandon at his heels and worked the combination to the vault door that was almost six feet tall. There were several small canvas bags of cash. It was nowhere near what Blandon had hoped, but it would have to do.

Blandon mounted and pointed his pistol at the manager. "Let the word go forth, Mr. Hill. When I give an order, I expect it to be obeyed instantly." He aimed and fired once into Hill's knee. He shrieked and doubled over while his wife wailed. Blandon signaled and he and his men rode off.

Richard Dean was spirited away to Baltimore, a city where southern sympathies ran deep. Booth saw to it that his hair was dyed and he was fitted with a pair of glasses that featured just plain glass. He was given a cot in a room in a small warehouse near the waterfront and told to stay there until he was informed otherwise. He was given enough bread and water to last a while.

Two days later, he was bored to tears and debating going out on his own. He studied the surrounding area through a window and saw nothing blatantly dangerous. There were some men lounging around and he wondered if they were to guard him or if they were just locals.

He had checked the door and found to his dismay that it was

locked. He was a prisoner. He had escaped one form of captivity for another.

The next day, just when he was beginning to wonder about his food, the door opened and Booth walked in. "You tried to leave, didn't you?"

Richard bristled. "I wasn't aware that I couldn't. I didn't know that I was your prisoner. Besides, the bread you left me is getting stale and the bucket I have to use stinks to high heaven."

"If you're going to be ungrateful, I'll send you back to those Pinkerton men, or maybe I'll just drop you off at Fortress Monroe with a note pinned to your shirt. My men and I put ourselves in great danger to rescue you. I think we deserve more than you acting like a spoiled brat. I was hoping we could use you for a very important task."

Richard was both chastened and intrigued. He apologized profusely and swore that he would be a good boy. Booth laughed. "Don't worry, I wouldn't have turned you over to the Yankee scum, and I don't blame you for being upset at what's been happening. Now, would you like to hear about our plans?"

"Of course."

"What's the worst thing that could befall the Union other than Washington sliding into the ocean?

"Why, something bad happening to Lincoln, of course."

"'Of course' is right, and we, my friends and I, are having intense discussions as to what that might be. There are those who wish to kill him and that is very possible since he is not very well guarded. If necessary, I would do it myself."

"I would be honored to assist you, sir."

Booth laughed, "As would a lot of people, which is why we are safe here in Baltimore. This is a southern city. Maryland is a border state and many, perhaps most of her people would like to see Maryland as part of the Confederacy. Lincoln's troops have so far prevented that, but that may change when Lee defeats the next fool Lincoln sends to command his army."

"So why hasn't Lincoln been killed?"

"Because there is at least one other idea very much worth pursuing, and that is the kidnapping of the abolitionist bastard. That has considerably more appeal than simply killing him. Lincoln dead becomes a martyr, a rallying point for the north, while an Abe Lincoln in Libby Prison in Richmond becomes an object of scorn. There is also the fact that a dead Lincoln would be succeeded by his Vice President, Hannibal Hamlin, who is as staunch an abolitionist as they come. No, the idea of kidnapping him is becoming more and more attractive. If he is alive but incapacitated, then who will be President? Why, who knows? Might it be Hamlin, or Stanton, or God knows who. At any rate confusion would have been sown at a critical time."

Richard smiled. "Would you be the one to take him?"

"I would certainly hope so."

"As would I, Mr. Booth. And I would like to assist you in any way possible. And you further have my assurances that I won't do anything stupid like writing to my mother."

★ CHAPTER 7 ★

Early on, Edwin Stanton and Abraham Lincoln had been bitter rivals. Stanton had thought himself superior to any other candidate for the presidency, and it had been only with great difficulty that he had swallowed his pride and accepted the office of secretary of war. Thus, it came as a surprise to him that he had gradually but genuinely come to respect the tall, gangly frontiersman who had been elected President. Stanton now believed that Lincoln had the will, the resolve, and the intellect to carry the war to its ultimate conclusion—victory over the South.

Like so many others, he had bemoaned the fact that there seemed to be no one with enough military talent to successfully confront Robert E. Lee. Stanton had no particular fear of other Rebel generals, especially now that Stonewall Jackson was dead, accidentally killed by his own men at Chancellorsville. Yes, the South had Longstreet, a very good general, and Hardee, a man who had written books on infantry tactics that were being used by both sides, but there was no one of stature who would intimidate Union generals like Lee did. Why had Lee's almost mystical presence on the battlefield turned so many Union generals into soft clay? The closest to have tasted victory was Meade, but even his success had been flawed. There were those who said that Meade had been in a nervous frenzy throughout the battle at Gettysburg and that the true victor had been Major General Winfield Scott Hancock, who held the line during the fateful second day of fighting.

Under other circumstances, Hancock would be a logical choice to replace Meade, but he'd been badly wounded in the fighting. He would recover, but it would take time.

So who did that leave? Stanton was a burly man who was used to having his way, and it was frustrating to be unable to solve a problem for his President and his country. Therefore, he would take a trip and see a man.

Travelling across the country was an ordeal, especially if it was to be done in secret and without interference from the Confederates. Stanton boarded the *USS Mohican*, a steam sloop, at the mouth of the Potomac. He promptly took over the captain's cabin and the ship sailed for New Orleans at a steady ten knots per hour. The better part of a week later the *Mohican* anchored off Fort Jackson at the mouth of the Mississippi. He did not disembark. That night, a large slope-sided City-class ironclad, the *Carondelet*, brought a short and rumpled man on board the *Mohican*. Stanton came to his feet as the man entered the captain's cabin.

Stanton had been prepared to be disappointed and initially, he was. Ulysses Grant was short and slight and dressed in a well-worn uniform without insignia. For a moment, Stanton thought that perhaps someone was playing a joke on him and that the real Ulysses Grant would somehow emerge and say "surprise."

But no, Stanton had seen enough photos and drawings of the man to know that this was no imposter. Grant's eyes betrayed him. They were of a man who was in total control and who did not need the trappings of power that so many high-ranking officers in the Union Army considered their due. Stanton had come to the unwelcome conclusion that a surfeit of vanity was a prerequisite for high command and Lincoln had laughingly concurred. McClellan, the Little Napoleon, was only one example—if one of the more extreme.

"He fights," had been the comment by Lincoln when Halleck had wanted to fire Grant based on rumors of his drinking.

The two men shook hands firmly. As host, Stanton waved Grant to a chair. "May I get you a drink, General?"

"Are you testing me, Mr. Stanton?" Grant said with a smile. "Regardless, no thank you, but go ahead if you wish."

Stanton flushed. He didn't like being on the defensive. "Perhaps some cold water would be appropriate," he said and Grant concurred.

"But please don't light one of your famous cigars. The air circulation in this floating prison is bad enough. Now, sir, do you understand why I am here?"

"I do. But first, let me tell you that I had an interesting and lengthy letter from retired General Winfield Scott. I was astonished when I received it because I thought he had no recognition of me when I served with him during the Mexican War. Either I was wrong or he was being exceedingly polite. He said that I would soon be offered command of the Army of the Potomac and that I should decline the honor."

Stanton was shocked. "But, sir, there is . . ." He bit off the words.

"No one else?" Grant smiled. "I hope this doesn't sound too conceited, Mr. Stanton, but I agree. However, I would insist on preconditions before taking the position. General Scott, whose early and initially reviled strategies are being vindicated, told me what one part of the problem is. It is General Halleck, a man who despises me and who is incompetent in high command. If I were to report to him, he would be looking over my shoulder every hour of every day, questioning my decisions and even reversing them. I would be willing to report directly to Mr. Lincoln out of respect for him and his office, but I would not permit even him to change my strategies."

"General Grant, are you saying that you already have a plan for defeating Lee?"

"I have a rough draft, yes, and I am confident that it will succeed."

"Will you tell me what it is?"

"No sir, I will not. The simple fact that General Scott found out about your errand and was able to contact me is proof that there are no secrets in Washington City. To tell you the truth, sir, I will not even tell the President the plan until it is too late for him to do anything about it. Since it is highly unlikely that he will agree to this, I will respectfully decline the command of the Army of the Potomac under the current circumstances."

Stanton took a swallow of his chilled water and wished there was some bourbon in it. He waited for him to go on, but Grant said nothing further. He sat back and invited General Grant to dinner.

It was not a sumptuous feast, little better than what could be scraped up by the ship's cook. But there was no complaint from Grant. They spoke desultorily as they ate. Stanton inquired about Rosecrans' chances against Joseph Johnston in any advance from Chattanooga. Grant was noncommittal. Only when they spoke of General Sherman did he show any sense of liveliness. "When you require something of General Sherman," Grant said. "It will be done, and it will be done as you wished it, if not better."

Afterward they went up on deck to allow Grant to smoke. "So what are your plans now, Mr. Secretary?"

"I was considering a brief stop at New Orleans. I've never visited that city."

Grant nodded. "Well worth the trip. Nothing like it anywhere else in the Union." He took the cigar from his mouth and examined the glowing tip. "Within living memory, New Orleans was a polyglot city, home to the French and Spanish as well as Americans. The streets are divided by walkways. These represented neutral ground. You see, different neighborhoods were held by different nationalities. The walkways were where they met when they wished to do business. If they took a step into the territory of another nation, they were fair game."

"Somewhat representative of our current situation."

Grant took a puff of his cigar. "Yes it is."

The night was quiet, nothing more than the sounds of a river and the surrounding swampland. The only lights were those of the *Carondelet*, riding low on the water.

"That ship was originally built for the Army, and transferred to Navy control last year."

Grant raised his eyebrows. "I didn't know that."

The order had crossed Stanton's desk and the time and somehow stuck in his mind. "I know very little else. I am the secretary of war. I have little to do with the Navy."

"With respects, sir, perhaps you should learn a little more. The *Carondelet* is one of a number of City class ironclads. The ship is short, squat, ugly, brutish, and very dangerous." Grant smiled engagingly. "Some will say I fit that description and they may well be right. Of greater importance is the fact that she and her sister ships draw only about six feet of water and her load can be lightened so that she would draw even less. One Navy engineer bragged that he could sail her in a puddle."

Stanton was intrigued. "And that capability interests you?"

"Yes it does. We couldn't have taken Vicksburg, or advanced down the Mississippi valley at all, without ships of this type. Right now, though, it's just a thought."

He knocked the ash off the end of his cigar and then butted it out. The two men shook hands. Stanton watched as the general climbed over the side and was rowed back to the ironclad.

The secretary of war was again surprised at how strong Grant's grip was. He would inform the President of Grant's response and Mr. Lincoln would be upset, even angry. But Stanton understood Grant's reluctance to work under the thumb of Halleck, or even Abraham Lincoln. Yes, Grant would decline and Lincoln would have to abide by that decision.

But Stanton wondered if the time might come soon when the President would accept the small but intense man's conditions. McClellan was a short man, too, but Grant inspired confidence, even a degree of fear, while McClellan did not. Still, there were large numbers of soldiers who remembered how the "Little Napoleon" had trained them and cared for them. Stanton could not ignore the fact that a presidential election would take place next year, 1864. Who would those soldiers support? Would it be the man who promised them continued war or the man who pledged peace but at a terrible price? Lincoln had to achieve at least one major victory before the election if he and the Union were to be victorious. And what the devil did Grant plan to do with an ironclad with a shallow draft?

When Otto Bauer emigrated from Bavaria to the United States in 1858, he thought he would work on a farm or even in a store. Not for one minute did he think he would become a soldier. But history had caught up with him, and he'd found that he made a good one. In large part, he knew, it was because of his skills with a rifle. In Bavaria, he'd been a hunter. Most of his catches he'd taken legally, but there were other kills that could have gotten him flogged or even hanged by the representatives of the dictatorial king of Bavaria, Maximilian II. After one close brush with the authorities, he'd taken his savings and shipped off to New York. He'd finally moved to Pennsylvania where he got a job in a machine shop, mainly repairing rifles and shotguns. He also joined the state militia to show that he wanted to be a good citizen. His new neighbors had welcomed him warmly.

Another reason he'd left Bavaria was the fear that it was going to be swallowed up by Prussia. Along with many Bavarians, Otto was a Catholic, and Prussia was Protestant. When he found that Protestants were dominant in the U.S., he'd been dismayed. But he'd quickly learned that most people didn't much care about anybody's religion and that freedom of religion was a real thing. He'd never thought much about freeing blacks, but this new thing called the "Confederacy" threatened the nation he now called home. True, he'd never even seen a black person until he arrived in New York. But slavery—that was a terrible thing, an offense against both God and man. He fully supported ending it. Still, he couldn't see how the problems of dark-skinned people affected him. He wanted stability and a chance to prosper. He was thirty and time was running out on his ambitions. He had a job, an income, and a couple of the eligible women in the area had been very friendly towards him.

But now, he had more important things on his mind. The Rebel army was south and west of his position along the Susquehanna River near Harrisburg, the state capital. The militia was commanded by a Major Granville Haller, who reported to a general named Darius Couch.

Otto's problems with the English language had largely disappeared. He still spoke with a heavy accent that some found amusing, but he understood what was written and what was said and most people could understand him just fine.

Otto had been named a temporary corporal commanding a dozen militiamen. Many were immigrants like himself. Their job was to cover a ford across the river and west of Harrisburg that would permit an army to cross the Susquehanna. Just how a handful of poorly trained part-time soldiers would hold off the rebel army was not his concern.

Otto understood the lay of the land and positioned his men well. Even the major had complimented them on their skills. They had dug trenches in the soft soil and would give their best if and when the Rebels came. Then, they all joked, they would run like the devil was after them, and he likely would be. Before that happened, Bauer hoped he would be able to use his skills as a rifleman to shoot at least one of the damned Confederates. He'd seen a few of them. Their patrols had come to the river, but not close enough to take a shot. He'd seen motion and movement and believed that at least one Rebel was in the bushes examining their position. Otto swallowed. He wondered what would come of that fact. He thought about firing into the bushes but discarded the idea. He might not hit anything. That would be a waste of a good bullet. Otto hated wasting rounds.

Sergeant Jonah Blandon looked through his telescope at the laughable Union position. Shallow trenches did not make a fortification. He counted a dozen men with no one else close by. Jeb Stuart would be pleased with the information.

Blandon patted the shirt pocket by his heart. In it was a letter from Stuart absolving Blandon of all his sins and welcoming him and his men back into the good graces of the Army of Northern Virginia. He had promised to be a good little boy and help Stuart again be the army's eyes and ears.

Blandon had done so in part because pickings had become very scarce indeed. He had no firm idea why the generals wanted information about this and other river crossings but guessing was obvious. The army was either going to cross the Susquehanna or pretend to cross it. Either way they needed solid intelligence and he could now provide it.

Armed with Stuart's letter, he had presented himself to Colonel Wade, who had initially been none too pleased to see the prodigal returned. But Blandon's apparently sincere act of contrition had won the colonel over. Blandon tried not to laugh. The colonel was such an innocent little shit. One of these days, Blandon was going to help himself to that nice watch Wade was so fond of.

Blandon froze. There was activity on the Union side. A group of horsemen rode over a low hill, dismounted, and examined the trifling Union position. It was obvious that they were officers. They said something to the large man in charge, a corporal or a junior sergeant. Whatever questions were asked were answered to the officer's satisfaction. They mounted, exchanged salutes with the corporal and rode off.

Blandon penned a brief note to be taken up the chain of command. He and his small group would stay put until told to move elsewhere. He could not imagine the Army of Northern Virginia crossing at this miserable point, but he could visualize Wade's Volunteers storming ashore and raising hell in the rear of the Union positions. He liked that thought. The confusion would give him a chance to do some real looting. With a little bit of luck, he might find some plump Pennsylvania farm wife to do his bidding, willingly or not. He smirked at the thought. It had been so long since he'd had a woman.

"Steven, I am more than pleased to see you again, but I am also a little embarrassed. I have come to the conclusion that my parents are pushing us together and I'm not terribly comfortable with that fact."

Thorne smiled and let the swing sway very gently. He and Cassie were seated side by side on the swing on the front porch of the Bairds' rented home. Since it was broad daylight and there was a discreet distance between them, there would be little hint of scandal. Even so, he could sense the perfume she was wearing and almost felt her thigh against his. He wondered what she'd do if he reached over and put his hand on her knee. He did not think she would scream, but he believed she would move it away and scold him. But how long would it be before she removed it?

As always, he was full. Too many more dinners cooked by Rachel Baird and he would have to have his uniforms sent to a tailor. "Well I don't mind it at all," he said with sincerity. Cassie Baird was totally out of her shell and he'd found her to be a most engaging woman. Not a traditional beauty, whatever that was, but a vivacious and intelligent lady who intrigued him.

"This can't last forever, can it, Steven?"

"What can't?"

"This prolonged period of peace. We can't have two huge enemy armies staring at each other from a few miles away. Sooner or later something's got to give and there'll be another titanic battle like Gettysburg. Thousands will die and thousands more will be wounded."

He decided to take a chance. He sneaked his hand over and covered hers. She smiled and did not move it. "Of course you're right, Cassie. This has to end somehow, some way. Some shocking finale to this war."

"Are you saying that one more battle and the war will end?"

"Perhaps. Even the Hundred Years War came to an end. I don't remember how or why. Maybe people just got sick and tired of fighting. But I'm afraid of an Armageddon, an all-consuming battle that will leave next to nothing for the survivors."

"And who would win that battle, Steven?"

"That's easy, Cassie. Right now, Robert E. Lee would trample the Army of the Potomac. Our leaders are fearful of him and those that aren't fearful are incompetent."

"And you could get hurt, or even killed. I worry for you."

"Unfortunately, yes. And just as you would worry for me, I'm afraid for you working with those Negroes. They will attract danger and vengeful people if the Union Army retreats and leaves you and your friends stranded."

"Enough of this sad talk," she said and stood, determined and unsmiling. "Come inside with me."

She took him by the hand and led him to a small storage room off the kitchen and closed the door behind them. The room was empty and dark. Once inside they embraced and kissed. He thought he could feel her heart pounding. He knew his was.

"We can only stay here for a minute," she said gasping.

"Then find another place for us," he whispered and tried to hold her even tighter.

"Let me loose. I can't breathe."

"Sorry."

"Don't be," she said and his eyes had adjusted enough that he could make out her smile. She took his hand and put it over her breast. "Now try to think of me when you go to sleep tonight in your rude army bunk."

He gently squeezed her breast, and she gasped. He regretted those insane rules of fashion that dictated that she had to wear so many layers of clothing. "If I do that, I won't be able to get much sleep."

She smiled and buried her head in his shoulder. She did not remove his hand.

Hadrian could read the portents as well as anyone. The days of his group being safe on the fringes of the Union-occupied area were numbered. New arrivals were still trickling in. There weren't many of them and they all reported the same thing: the Confederates were getting bolder.

Toby, a young man in his teens, had been particularly observant. "Everywhere you look there's Confederate cavalry. They was watching the roads and every trail they could. But they couldn't be everywhere, so we snuck through. I saw and heard black people getting stopped and caught. They were even stopping and roughing up white people. The Rebs are up to no good and that means bad things for us."

Hadrian agreed. He didn't like it one damn bit. The Rebels were about to cause trouble. That meant they would have to move closer to Washington and his group would not be alone. Thousands of now free slaves would be doing the same thing.

"Toby, did you by any chance see Union soldiers trying to get through to the Rebel army?"

"Not really, but I really wasn't in any position to find out very much. Come to think of it, though, I did see one patrol spot a Rebel group about the same size and skedaddle back where they come from."

Hadrian stood. "Get yourself some food and find a place to lie down. If you need a blanket, ask for a man named Charles. He'll find you something to keep you warm."

As Toby walked away, Hadrian strolled casually over to where the white woman was teaching a bunch of Negroes how to read. She was down to about twenty now and was disappointed. Well, she was doing her best and learning to read wasn't the easiest thing in the world. It had taken him a long time to figure out that all those squiggles and marks actually meant something. Sometimes students would get discouraged and stay away for a couple of days and then come back. When that happened the white woman welcomed them warmly. She seemed to understand that sometimes a body just needed to step back, take a deep breath and pick up the pieces. He had the feeling that she had done something like that in her life.

As usual, Cassandra Baird was working alongside her servant, Mariah. Cassandra was a lovely woman in her own right, just too damn skinny for Hadrian to seriously consider. That is, if any black man could seriously consider involving himself with a white woman. Now Mariah was a different story. Yes, she had a lot of white blood running through her, but she was still a black and a woman who was both handsome and robust. They'd pleasured each other a couple of times and had enjoyed it immensely. Too bad her teaching duties kept her so occupied. It was very difficult to find the time and place to be with her in private.

Mariah saw him walking up to the group and smiled knowingly. He returned the smile and winked. He gestured that he wanted to talk to Cassandra. Mariah took over the class and Cassandra walked up to him.

"Hadrian, I keep forgetting how large you are. I believe you would scare a grizzly bear."

Hadrian laughed. He had only recently found out what a grizzly bear was. He had read it in a book about strange and wonderful animals. He'd been stunned to find out about elephants and whales and lions and tigers. There was so much to learn. He was happy he knew how to read.

"Miss Cassandra, I've been hearing some disturbing news about the Rebels. People are telling me that they are waking up, and that is no good. We are going to plan on moving closer to the Union Army, where it might just be a little bit safer."

"I think that would be wise. Let me know when you plan on going and Mariah and I will come with you."

Hadrian shook his head. "I don't think so. We will set up camp some new place and I'll send one of my boys to tell you where we're at.

"I have something else to ask you. Apparently, you have been seeing a Union cavalry officer."

Cassandra rolled her eyes. "Is nothing private in this world?"

"Nothing much, Miss Cassandra. I'm asking because you might want to tell him what we've been observing and see if he thinks it's important."

"I will ask Steven, I mean Major Thorne, what he thinks and I'll get back to you."

"Good enough, Miss Cassie."

Later that evening, Cassandra and Steven were again sitting on the swing. This time one of her damn cats had snuggled between them and was purring loudly. Cassandra wasn't certain whether she'd adopted the stray or the stray had adopted her. No matter, it was firmly ensconced as a ten-pound chaperone.

"Steven, do you think Hadrian's right?"

"Yes. We've picked up many indications that they are up to something. They are aggressively using their cavalry to screen their movements. I'm afraid our days of peace and quiet may soon be over. And yes, I would suggest that Hadrian and any others he knows move closer to Washington City. I can't guarantee their safety, but logic says they'll be better off closer to the city's defenses.

"Oh God," she sighed. "This talk of the war returning is so

depressing. Of course, we all knew it couldn't last. Lee or Meade would have to do something and the bleeding would start all over again. Why can't we all just live in peace?"

"That's what McClellan and others like him want to do. But that would also mean an independent Confederacy and sending people like Hadrian back to bondage."

"That cannot be permitted to happen," she said sternly and Thorne almost laughed. "Therefore, we must fight and damn the consequences. But enough of this depressing talk. Tonight, you will go back to your army and tomorrow I'm sure you will tell your generals just what Hadrian has discovered. In the meantime, I wish this evening to end on a happier note."

"What do you propose?" he asked with a smile. He hoped he knew what she was going to suggest.

She pulled him to his feet and took him by the hand. "Yes. You're absolutely right. There is so much more to inventory in that darn storeroom. It's amazing how people let things go, isn't it?"

The large brick warehouse on Baltimore's waterfront was burning brightly. Richard Dean and his companions whooped and hollered. The supplies it contained, intended for the Union Army, were now being reduced to ashes. Lincoln and his damned blue-coated dragoons would have to shop elsewhere for their goods.

Something in the building exploded, sending embers high into the night. It was almost like Fourth of July fireworks, only better. Finally, Dean felt like he was doing something for the Cause. Some of the embers floated over the shipping packed tightly in the harbor and crewmen began scurrying about their decks to make sure their ships didn't catch fire. Other embers landed on buildings and a couple of fires started. For an instant, Richard hoped they didn't belong to southern sympathizers, but then realized he didn't care.

The stated reason for the rioting was the hated Draft Act. It would require men who opposed the Union to be forcibly enlisted into the Union Army. Nor was it universally applied. Rich men could hire poor men to be their substitutes. The irony that this was essentially what Richard had done in paying someone else to take his place was not lost on him. Still, he and the man he'd paid had volunteered. But the draft, that was tantamount to enslaving white men and that infuriated many in Baltimore and other large cities. The worst riots had taken place in New York, with rioters killed or wounded and a number of Negroes lynched. Negroes would have been lynched this night too, but they'd been very prudent and had stayed out of sight.

"They're coming," someone yelled. Either Union soldiers or the Baltimore police would soon arrive to break up the crowd, so that the fire crews could try to contain the raging blaze. Putting it out would be an impossibility. The warehouse was too far gone. It would have to burn itself out.

As he thought that, the rear wall of the warehouse collapsed and a thunderhead of embers soared upward. Once again, ashes and embers were swirled about by the wind.

This first wave of responders consisted of a few dozen Baltimore police. Some of them hallooed the pro-secession mob that now numbered several hundred men and a handful of women. The pro-Lincoln members of the police quickly disappeared while the others took off their uniform tunics and joined the mob.

Back when the southern states first seceded, it was presumed that Maryland would join the Confederacy. Maryland was one of the four Border States along with Delaware, Kentucky, and Missouri. These were states in which a large portion of the population supported the South.

There had been bloody and deadly riots when the newly elected Abraham Lincoln been forced to slink his way through Baltimore on his way to Washington. Despite the fact that Union General Ben Butler now had large numbers of soldiers in the area, equally large numbers of secessionists announced themselves openly and vocally.

The Maryland legislature had not been permitted to meet or vote on secession. Richard had been told that Governor Thomas Hicks had supported what southern sympathizers thought was a series of illegal acts ensuring that Maryland stayed loyal to the Union.

Richard noticed another group approaching, a large one. As it emerged from the smoke he saw that it was a battalion-sized detachment of army regulars, soldiers that had fought in the streets before. Slowly but steadily, they marched forward with bayonets pointed directly at the mob, which began to back away. Rocks and bricks arced toward the troops and a few of them went down. That infuriated the bluecoats. Richard quickly realized that the situation was getting out of control with the danger increasing every minute. He could not afford to be taken prisoner—it was all too likely that he'd be recognized.

Someone grabbed his arm. "Richard. Come with me."

It was a young woman who scarcely reached his shoulder. She was dark-haired, plump, and very concerned. "Richard, I said come with me."

"Who are you?"

"Does it matter? My name is Mary, and Mr. Booth sent me to watch over you. He was afraid you'd get yourself into a terrible mess and he was right. He also said you were a fool, and he was right about that as well."

Well, I can't say she's wrong, he thought. *Not completely, anyway.* "Slow down. Those troops will think you're running"

"Who the devil cares? Everybody's running," she snapped. "And besides, we don't have time for a conversation. Bend over," she ordered and he complied. A second later, something wet and cold had been dumped on his head. "It's a red coloring that only looks like blood. Lean over and grab your empty head and let me lead you away. Everyone will think you've been wounded."

He did as he was told. He grabbed his skull and groaned loudly as Mary guided him away from the fray. They'd just turned down a side street when a volley of rifle fire stunned them. They paused and looked back. Dozens of the people he'd just been among lay on the street in bloody piles. Some were moving but very many lay still as their lives flowed into the gutter. *Damn*, he thought, *that could have been me.*

"What did you say?" he said. Mary was continuing to guide and steer him. Now the remnants of the mob were running for their lives. The soldiers advanced slowly and in formation. There was still a danger of getting caught.

"Mary, whoever you are, I see no further purpose in pretending that I'm hurt. I suggest we simply run like the devil and I hope you have someplace to take me."

She did. Instead of taking him back to his quarters, they went to yet another warehouse. She informed him that they would wait out the night, and in the morning she would see if the police or provost marshal's people were at his old place. Richard couldn't help himself. He went to a window and looked out. The glow that had been the warehouse was larger and brighter now. It was clear that adjacent buildings were burning as well. He laughed. It had been a good night.

"Richard, you will sleep on this pile of whatever it is, while I will sleep over there. You will not make a move towards me. If you do, I will hurt you badly, and I don't care what Mr. Booth will think."

She lifted up her skirt to show him a bit of leg and a large knife strapped to it.

"You are quite safe, Mary. But do you have a last name?"

"My last name is Nardelli and I am a refugee from what will someday be Italy. Now go to sleep."

Thorne got his own confirmation that the Rebels were on the move when he took the regiment out on patrol. Thanks to additional men, the Sixth Indiana now numbered just over two hundred. Along with additional horses, they presented an imposing sight as they rode towards the distant Confederate lines.

Thorne knew better. Two hundred men wasn't even a drop in the bucket. If he ran into a sizeable enemy force his duty was to run and report the contact. "Nobody likes cowards but they often live longer," Captain Archie Willis had said, and nobody had disagreed.

Scouts were out in advance of the column, and several pairs of flankers were on station. The rolling hills and the lush foliage that covered them could hide a force that could overwhelm them.

"Halt," he ordered. One of the scouts was galloping towards him, frantically waving his arm.

"Rebels to our front, sir, in about brigade strength," he gasped, wide-eyed with what he'd seen. "They're coming slowly, but they *are* coming."

Thorne rode on in grim silence to the top of a hill, where he could see about two miles to his front. "Rebels, all right," he muttered. A long line of horsemen was coming down the road. Behind the horsemen he thought he could see infantry. A quick look through his telescope confirmed it.

"And a lot more than we can handle," Willis said.

"Concur. Let's get out of here."

The regiment wheeled and cantered quickly towards the Union lines. They had only gone a few hundred yards when Rebel yells came from their left and several hundred enemy cavalry burst from the woods, yelling and screaming.

"Here they come," cried Willis.

Their canter became a gallop, but the Rebels gained on them all the same. It was clear to Thorne that they would be caught before they could reach friendly lines. "Into the woods and dismount," he ordered. "And hold your fire."

The Sixth did as ordered, leaving their horses in the thickets and finding spots for themselves behind trees. They waited for the charging Confederates to get within range. Discipline and training held. When the Confederates were within two hundred yards, Thorne ordered his men to fire.

The Spencers barked once, then once more, and then repeatedly. The Confederate horsemen were staggered as if by an invisible blow. Men and horses went down in piles. The Rebels wavered and pulled back. Some raised their pistols and carbines and fired at their unseen enemies in the woods as they continued to withdraw.

"I think we pissed them off," said Willis.

"Inclined to agree, Archie. We'd best mount up again and ride like hell before they get hold of their big brothers and come back."

Willis pulled at his sleeve. "Steve . . . Major . . . just when the hell did you get shot?"

Thorne looked down to see the blood staining his uniform trousers. The wound started hurting at the same moment, as if it had to be noticed first. He instinctively laid his hand against it, drawing away a palm full of blood.

He looked up in surprise. Willis shook his head. "Come along now, Major."

★ CHAPTER 8 ★

Thorne was barely conscious when he got back to the regiment. He was eased from the saddle and laid down on his cot. A medic came and quickly confirmed the obvious—he had been shot in the left thigh. He was given some laudanum and while he was asleep, Willis sent a messenger to Colonel Baird. An ambulance arrived at Thorne's tent the next morning and transported him back to the Bairds' home.

He did not awake until dusk of the next day. The first person he saw was Rachel Baird, who was looking down on him in a motherly manner.

"Mrs. Baird," he managed to whisper. "I am surprised to see you."

"You are in one of several spare bedrooms we have in this large mausoleum. Do you recall getting shot?"

"No," he answered truthfully. The sight of blood running down his leg had come as a complete shock.

"It doesn't matter. What does matter is that you are here with us and we have the colonel's personal doctor taking care of you. He will give you a little more morphine, but not too much. It might become a habit. He said that the bullet went through your thigh and out, leaving a clean hole. There should be no infection, and he swore that he used clean instruments to probe the hole. If he hadn't, one of us would have killed him. The bullet wedged itself into your saddle and we've kept it in case you want it as a souvenir."

"I'll have to think about that."

"You will stay here and rest and eat until you've gained enough strength to return to duty. I've been told that a diet heavy on beef will help replace lost blood. You will be eating a lot of steak, I'm afraid."

"May I ask where Cassie is?"

"She's waiting downstairs. We've been taking turns watching over you. It's just as well I was here and not her, because you might notice that we had to cut your uniform away and be embarrassed."

"I see," said Steve.

"Yes. You're wearing one of my husband's nightshirts, one of his longer ones. And no, Cassie did not take part in the cutting off of your uniform. Mariah and I took part in those festivities. You are fairly muscular but you could still stand to put on a little more weight."

Steve grinned weakly. "A few more meals like those you serve and I'll have to start losing, not gaining."

The bedroom door opened and a tearful Cassie barged in and threw herself across his chest. "Careful," Rachel said. "Stay off his left leg." With that piece of sage advice, she departed and closed the door—but not tightly.

"Don't scare me like that," Cassie told him. "Do you have any idea what you looked like when they brought you here, all torn and bloody and pale? Of course not, but you looked awful. I thought you were going to die."

"Only the good die young, Cassie. God's not ready for me."

"Don't joke," she said and kissed him hungrily. He returned the favor with just as much passion, even more.

"Cassie," he said when they finally broke apart and he lay back, exhausted. "Are you at all concerned about your reputation?"

"At the moment, no. Why?"

"Because all I'm wearing is your father's nightshirt and I'm a good deal taller than he is."

She grinned wickedly. "Then I should duck in beside you," which she promptly did and cuddled along the length of his body. "You may be undressed but it would take you an hour to get me in the same situation. Presuming, that is, that your wounded leg would permit it. As we speak, your uniform is being cleaned and mended, so don't worry about anybody's loss of their precious virtue. My father is visiting some politicians, and both my mother and Mariah are well aware that I am here, and doubtless have some idea what we're doing."

"And they don't object?"

Cassie laughed. "Mariah is my friend as well as my servant, and she has her own male friend in the contraband camp, and I only recently found out what fun and games my parents played at before they were married."

He pretended shock. "Are you telling me they had a storeroom as well?"

She giggled and guided his hand inside her bodice and onto her breast. Other than the now despised Richard, she had never let any man touch her like she was letting Steve. And she never thought it would feel so good. Too bad they would have to stop in a few minutes.

"Cassie," shouted Rachel. "I'm coming up with Steven's uniform."

"Yes, Mother," she said. She turned to tell Steve that his virtue was also safe, but realized that the young major was sound asleep.

Abraham Lincoln was the sixteenth president of the United States. He was the commander in chief of the army and the navy. His army contained close to a million men and his navy consisted of more than a thousand ships, although most of them were small. He was one of the most powerful men in the world. So why did he feel so helpless?

He gazed about the room at his council of war. Secretary of War Stanton was there, glowering as usual. Commanding General Henry Halleck looked both owlish and puzzled, while George Gordon Meade, commander of the Army of the Potomac, would not look Lincoln in the eye. Only the Quartermaster General, Montgomery Meigs, appeared confident. Secretary of State Edwin Seward completed the group. Lincoln thought Seward doubtless had more bad news to share. He couldn't wait to hear it.

Lincoln, of course, chaired and spoke first. "Gentlemen, let us be blunt and brief so we can all get back to our respective duties. First and foremost, what the devil is General Lee up to?"

Stanton responded. "I think it's obvious, sir. He is launching the long-awaited attack on Washington. I believe this will be an all-out attempt to take the city and bring us to the negotiating table."

Lincoln nodded. "General Halleck, do you concur?"

"I do, sir. And if you ask me, you should be making preparations to evacuate the government from Washington to whatever place you designate. Already, people are beginning to leave and, just as hordes of refugees are trying to take shelter behind our defenses."

"Thank you," said Lincoln. "General Meade, if Lee comes, can you defeat him as you did at Gettysburg?"

"I can and will," Meade said stoutly. But Lincoln had caught the momentary hesitation and flicker of doubt in his eyes before he answered. Yes, he might stop Lee, but would he drive him away or would there be another stalemate? The answer was easy—he would not be able to do either.

Lincoln stood and towered over the group. "General Meigs, your thoughts, please."

Brigadier General Meigs was the lowest-ranking man in the room, but he was not intimidated. "Lee will not attack our defenses. I rather wish he would. If he were to be that foolish, his army would ruin itself by being impaled on the fortifications that circle the city."

"That's ridiculous," said Halleck scornfully. "Why wouldn't he attack and if he isn't going to, just what on earth is he up to?"

Meigs responded. "Gentlemen, kindly recall that I am responsible for seeing to it that the massive Union Army is properly supplied in all ways. It is an enormous and sometimes thankless undertaking. However, it is the same with the Army of Northern Virginia, which, by many estimates, is now close to a hundred thousand strong. These men must be fed and clothed and, as at Gettysburg, Lee's men are running out of food. The Army of the Potomac requires at least five hundred tons of supplies each day, and the same must hold true for Lee."

Lincoln smiled. Meigs' thinking paralleled his own. He thought highly of Meigs. For one thing, the general was the only army officer who took the Ager gun seriously. The "coffee-mill gun," as some called it, was a rotary weapon that could fire well over a hundred rounds a minute. Lincoln had been quite impressed by it on seeing it demonstrated. He had tried to get General Ripley interested in the gun, but neither he nor any of his staff in the Ordnance Corps could be bothered with it, any more than they could repeating rifles. "I agree with General Meigs. Lee will not launch a major attack against our rings of interlocking forts that have made us possibly the most fortified city in the world. He would destroy his army even if he were able to punch his way in. No, gentlemen, this is nothing more than a massive and impressive feint, which, of course, we cannot ignore. We must honor the threat to Washington, but the hammer will not fall here unless we do something inordinately foolish, like sending the Army of the Potomac out to duel with Lee. Tell me, General Meigs, what would you be doing if you were Lee?"

Meigs gazed off into distance, as if in contemplation of the mystery of Leehood. "Sir, confident that we will not move aggressively against him, I would send a major component of the army out on a massive foraging expedition to bring much-needed supplies to the army."

"How much of a component do you think Lee has sent away?" asked the President.

"A quarter, perhaps a third. And I would have it commanded by someone reliable, like Hardee or Longstreet," answered Meigs. He was almost radiantly happy to be listened to and be the center of attention.

"I find all this hard to believe. It absolutely flies against logic," said Halleck, and Meade nodded. Stanton and Seward merely looked thoughtful.

Lincoln again turned to Meade. "General Meade. I believe that General Meigs is right and that Lee's army is severely weakened. Will you, therefore, take the Army of the Potomac out and attack him?"

Meade paled. "If I am so ordered, I will do so to the utmost of my ability, sir."

Halleck's eyes bugged out even more than usual. "I would be honored to take command."

And neither one of you will succeed, thought Lincoln. *Neither of you is anywhere near the equal of Robert E. Lee, even if his army was severely reduced.* "Thank you for volunteering, but that won't be necessary. The Army of the Potomac will hold back and protect Washington on the off-chance that General Meigs and I are wrong."

There was an audible sigh of relief around the table. Only Stanton and Meigs looked unhappy, while Seward looked puzzled. "Secretary Seward, do you have anything to add?"

"Only that the French are back to being French again. Their invasion of Mexico, in defiance of our Monroe Doctrine, is not going very well for them. I have heard rumors that they will massively reinforce their army in Mexico if we are unable to corral Lee. If we are defeated, there will be pressure on their government to recognize the Confederacy, which would cause all kinds of problems for us."

Lincoln looked out the window. There was a long line of people waiting outside the White House to see him and the line inside was just as long. "And to think, gentlemen, when I awoke this morning, the only thing I thought I had to worry about was my wife's latest shopping spree. Yesterday, dear Mary bought God only knows how many pairs of gloves, and God only knows why. Thank God I am not poor and can afford her profligacies."

There were smiles and polite chuckles. Mary Todd Lincoln's shopping adventures were well known. "We will adjourn," said Lincoln. "We will watch and wait."

When the room was emptied, the President again looked out the window. He was in despair. He had a magnificent army and no one to lead it. Was it time to reconsider Grant's terms? He would have to think on it. He needed rest. He felt a headache coming on and there were all those people who wanted to see him.

Otto Bauer waded the last few feet and clambered up the mud bank of the Union side of the Susquehanna. A couple of his men laughingly handed him towels. "Did you find Lee?" one of them asked.

"No, but I found that my boot will fit right up your arsch."

The men all laughed some more and Otto laughed along with them. They were good men. Better, they were comrades. "I will report nothing to the major because there is nothing to report. I saw signs that people had been around and watching us and they likely were Confederates, but I saw no army."

"How far did you go?" asked one of the older men.

"About three miles. I managed to get on a hill and climb a good-sized tree where I could see a whole lot further, but, again, there was nothing. Therefore, I will not report. The major is a good man although a little too full of himself. I will not add to his burden."

Coffee was brewing and there were beans and some fresh bread. The beans even had some chunks of pork floating around in it. The meal was good and he was exhausted. He informed his squad that he was going to take a nap.

It was dawn of the next day when he woke up. When he realized that his men had let him sleep that long he swore. They were unrepentant. "You were tired. We need you alert so we let you rest. You snore like a hog, by the way."

Otto shook his head and went down to the Susquehanna to relieve himself. He looked across and into the woods about a mile away and froze. There was motion in the woods and he thought he could see some color. Whatever it was it definitely wasn't part of the Union Army. And was somebody watching him? And might that somebody have a rifle aimed right at his thick skull? Why hadn't he anticipated that the Rebels might move at least some units at night? Damn it to hell!

As nonchalantly as he could, he finished peeing and buttoned up. He casually walked up to his men, who had sensed his concern and had stopped laughing. They awaited his orders.

"There are a handful of us and maybe hundreds of the enemy closing in on this spot. We will quietly gather our goods and get over the top of the hill. Then we will stop and see what is actually coming. Henry, you will be prepared to run as fast as you can to any officer to report what I will tell you. Is that understood?"

Henry was fourteen years old and understood that Otto was sending him away because of his youth. Henry decided he didn't mind at all. "Yes, Otto, I mean Corporal."

They gathered their gear and made it to the top of the hill without incident. The woods that hid monsters were well out of range of rifle, but not of cannon. Several cannon barked and sent shells towards them. The soldiers scattered as round shot hit and sent gobs of earth flying. They made it over the crest of the hill, where Otto counted noses. One man was missing, Henry.

Otto slid over the crest, trying to make himself either invisible or a small target. It didn't take long to find Henry, or at least what was left of him. The shell must have struck him cleanly, a one in a million shot that had torn him to red shreds. Otto wanted to weep. Henry was just a little boy. He should have been home with his mother.

But he quickly realized he had bigger problems than grieving for one young soldier. Large numbers of cavalry were coming down the trail and rows of infantry were forming up. More cannon fired. The shells went over the hill and there was no place to hide. Nor would he and his squad make any attempt to stop the entire Confederate Army from crossing the river at this point. They would retreat and try to make contact with the major. He would know what to do.

★ ★ ★

Wade's Tennessee Volunteers were not the first cavalry detachment to cross the Susquehanna River. A couple of Virginia regiments commanded by Jeb Stuart had taken that honor. The men yelled and waved their hats as they crossed into a fresh part of Pennsylvania. The state capital, Harrisburg, was within easy reach. Was that their target? They didn't know, but they were looking forward to punishing the Yankees one more time.

They fanned out and created a safe perimeter that permitted a long line of Confederate infantry to cross in safety. When it was their turn, Wade's cavalry felt exultation. Like mischievous kids, they whooped and hollered and splashed each other. Wade joined in the merriment until he saw the human remains on the hill.

"Jesus," he said. "It looks like this poor son of a bitch tried to catch a cannon ball with his chest."

"At least he went quickly," said Captain Mayfield. "It beats the hell out of yelling and screaming in a hospital for days, maybe even weeks."

"You're right. Let's get some men to bury him or at least cover him with enough dirt so that we don't have to look at the poor boy. I know there's not much left to look at, but I would surmise that he's only about twelve or so. If the Yanks are drafting them that young we've got this war all but won."

Mayfield laughed and averted his eyes from the grisly sight. They'd all seen violent death, but this one struck them hard. "Naw, this lad wasn't drafted. I'll bet you a one-dollar Union greenback that he's somebody's little boy who had run off to see the elephant."

"And I won't bet against that," said Wade. "Now if only we knew what we are going to do and where, we'd all be a lot happier."

"Well, Corey, here comes Jeb Stuart and I'll bet you that Longstreet is close on his heels. I will bet you another dollar that we are going to take part in the biggest, baddest raid in the history of the Confederacy."

Otto was too far away to hear what the two men had to say and he couldn't read lips. They were just barely in range and any shots from him would bring and instant and angry reaction that could easily prove fatal. It was a shame that Henry Watson was dead, but that's what war was all about. He'd tried to tell that to the boy and had failed. His mother had insisted that Henry go with him, thinking that he'd be safer with the man who had been courting her. Now, he thought sadly, Martha Watson would likely not want to have anything to do with him, and he couldn't blame her.

He was incredulous when he saw a trio of rebels dig a shallow grave and pour Henry into it. It was a sign of respect he hadn't anticipated. Maybe there was hope for man on this globe after all.

There was a knock on the door and his valet James announced his visitor. Davis got to his feet and brushed his coat. He glanced at the door behind which his secretary of state awaited.

The British envoy entered to room, still carrying his walking stick in one gloved hand.

Davis stopped forward. "Mr. Wallingford."

Slipping his walking stick under his arm, Wallingford eased off a kidskin glove and took Davis' extended hand. "Mr. President."

Davis gestured him to a seat. The meeting was taking place at his home rather than his presidential offices. It was not "official" by any means. The British could not be seen in discussions with the Confederacy at this point, at least. For similar reasons there was no presentation of credentials. Charles Wallingford, as far as Davis knew, was merely a businessman with interests in British North America that brought him across the Atlantic on a regular basis. Whatever other status he held Davis knew nothing, and didn't need to know.

Wallingford appeared younger than he would have thought. Trim white trousers, a tight waistcoat, an impeccably tailored jacket, a riot of light-brown curls brushed back from the forehead. Add the gloves and stick and the first word that came to Davis' mind was "fop."

"How did you find your journey to Richmond, sir?"

"Not as difficult as I'd feared. Your opponents are not maintaining an effective interdiction by any means."

"They have other worries to occupy their minds."

The envoy smiled. "Indeed they do, sir." He bent forward in the chair. "I must admit that General Lee's performance has been most impressive. Though some of our officers believe his current position in Pennsylvania is untenable."

"Many thought the same of Winfield Scott's advance into Mexico."

Wallingford nodded. "So they did, sir. The Iron Duke among them."

"But to give you a clearer picture . . ." Davis handed him the report. Wallingford accepted it and sat back to leaf through it.

After a moment he looked up. "Lee seems to have Meade checkmated."

"So it appears. After Gettysburg, our hearts were in our throats. But Lee's riposte totally negated any victory Washington might have claimed. What other commander since Wellington could have accomplished such a feat?"

"None to my knowledge." Wallingford shifted in his chair. "This adds some point to the matter under consideration . . ."

"Indeed it does, sir. That being the case, I would like to include my secretary of state as we proceed."

Wallingford raised both hands in concurrence. Davis got to his feet and went to the door at the rear of the room. He opened it to find Judah Benjamin waiting in the hall.

Davis made the introductions. Benjamin greeted Wallingford with his broad face wreathed in a smile. Davis was pleased to see that the Englishman took Benjamin's hand with no hesitation—they had been warned of the common British antipathy toward Jews. But then, the notable British politician Disraeli was also a son of Israel.

Benjamin went over the situation in detail. Wallingford listened, asking only a few questions. "The North has more resources, more industry, and more men," Benjamin concluded. "But they have not been able to marshal them effectively. The reason is lack of leadership, from Lincoln on down. Mr. Lincoln has been reduced to empty gestures, such as his recent 'proclamation.' He seems to think that instigating a servile revolt will make up for ineptness on the battlefield. He has spent this war looking for a general. We do not believe he will find one."

Wallingford pursed his lips. "And what of Vicksburg, sir?"

"A setback. We will not deny it. But the cockpit of this war is in the northeast. The decision will be made there and nowhere else."

"It is a pity that General Lee is not here to speak his piece," Davis added. "I believe you would be suitably impressed."

"General Lee is an impressive figure."

"Not to forget his army," Benjamin said. "The Army of Northern Virginia is one of the finest military forces ever assembled on this continent."

"I am inclined to agree." Wallingford smiled. "A confession, gentlemen: I visited the army on my way here from Canada."

Davis reared back in surprise. "Sir?"

"You did?"

Wallingford nodded. There was more to this young man than Davis had assumed.

"Yes. I went amongst them. Both armies, in fact. I found it much as you say."

Getting to his feet, Wallingford stepped toward the window. A few childish cries could be heard from outside. He contemplated the scene beyond the window in silence for a moment. "There is a moral aspect to war that is often overlooked. Buonaparte once put it that in war the moral to the physical is as three to one. So it is no uncommon fact found throughout history for the weaker, least capable force to prevail over a much larger enemy, as David did over Goliath. 'The race does not always go to the swift.' This appears to be the case with the Confederacy.

"I found the army of General Lee to be confident, vigorous, and expectant of victory, an unusual case for an army that placed itself at the table of its enemies.

"The army of Mr. Lincoln, on the other hand, is ill-led, at loose ends, and suspended between indifference and despair."

"As is the Union as a whole," Davis added. "Evidenced by the New York riots."

"Excellent point. It would require a remarkable leader to reverse this situation, and as Mr. Benjamin alluded, no such leader is apparent."

Davis got to his feet. He hesitated to speak, fearing a trembling in his voice. This was a climactic moment. It was what they had hoped for, planned for, since this horrid struggle had begun. With Britain backing the Confederacy, this war would be over. The new nation would be independent, the peace guaranteed by a Royal Navy flotilla in the southern reaches of Chesapeake Bay. "I am pleased to hear these words, Mr. Wallingford."

Wallingford shrugged. "Any objective observer would draw the same conclusion. When I have returned to London, I will present my findings as we have discussed them here."

As he reached the window, Davis fought an impulse to grip the man's hand in thanks. "I can ask for no more than that."

Wallingford smiled and glanced once again out the window. In the distance a group of children were playing under the eyes of an older woman.

"My son Joseph and his little friends," Davis said.

"Do I note an African child among them?"

"Yes—that is James, my son's companion. 'Limber Jim' they call him."

"Companion?" Wallingford turned toward Davis, his face expressionless. "And yet a slave."

It was not a question. Davis drew himself to his full height. "No sir. We do not think of him as such."

"You do not." This close, Davis could see that Wallingford was older than he had first taken him to be. "And what, sir, does James think?"

Davis felt his face flush with anger. He cast a glance at Benjamin, who looked on with a fixed smile. "Perhaps, Mr. Wallingford, you are unfamiliar with our Peculiar Institution . . ."

"Oh, but I am, sir. Quite familiar. I have encountered it previously elsewhere, among the Tatars of the steppes and the sheiks of Arabia."

He gazed at Davis for a long moment and at last smiled. "But as I say, I am but an instrument. I will report objectively, as a loyal subject of the crown." He stepped away from the window. "And the mill-owners of the Midlands miss their southern cotton."

Benjamin spoke first. "Uhh . . . how will you proceed, Mr. Wallingford?

The Englishman had retrieved his cane and was donning his gloves. "I will recross the lines into Washington, take a train to New York, by sea to Halifax and on to London. You should have your answer by the time the snows return."

Davis found his voice. "I wish you a pleasant voyage, Mr. Wallingford."

"Good day to you, gentlemen." He gave them each a short bow. "I will see myself out."

Davis gazed after him before turning to Secretary Benjamin. "Is that is how it will be for us, Judah? A pariah among the nations?"

Benjamin smiled sadly, and Davis belatedly thought of the suffering of his own people across the ages. "We can live with it."

★ CHAPTER 9 ★

Charles Rutherford introduced himself as being from the Provost Marshal's Office in Washington and showed credentials to prove it. His visit had been expected. A very thin man in his forties, he looked as if he'd once been deathly ill and had barely recovered. He was courteous and gracious enough but was also very reserved.

Josiah Baird shifted his weight and tried to make himself more comfortable. This latest artificial leg was brand new and, so far, appeared to be working nicely. "Mr. Rutherford, you say you represent the army but you show no indication of rank. May I ask why?"

"My military rank is somewhere between corporal and major general. It is sometimes quite useful to keep it hidden. If I told you, a colonel, that I was a captain, you might just try to bully me. If it was the other way around, you might be intimidated and be disinclined to talk openly. Sometimes a little dramatic license is a good idea."

"I see," said the colonel, who clearly remained dubious. They were in the ornate parlor of his rented house. Along with Colonel Baird and Rutherford, Rachel and Cassandra sat demurely and frankly puzzled.

Colonel Baird smiled without warmth. Like most soldiers he didn't like the provost marshal's office. They were police and they were snoops. There was the feeling that the provost men were always trying to trip up good people. "Well then, if you will not divulge your rank, will you kindly tell us why you wanted to speak with us?"

"Of course. The reason is a young man named Richard Dean."

Cassie gasped and Rachel said, "Oh my God. What has that foolish, stupid little boy gone and done now?"

"He's not a little boy, Mother," Cassie snapped. "He's a traitor and maybe a murderer."

"No, he's not. His childhood ended some time ago," said the colonel. "At the very least he's a lying snake who finagled his way into our home and embarrassed us dreadfully."

This time Rutherford did smile genuinely. "Well, well, I see we are all of one opinion regarding the dear lad. But tell me, Miss Cassandra, why do you call him a murderer?"

"Because he hired somebody to take his place in the army and that young man was killed. Don't you consider that murder?"

"You and I might, but the law wouldn't. But don't worry. Desertion alone is a hanging offense. But that isn't why we want him."

Colonel Baird frowned. "Then what is the reason?"

"Until a very short while ago, we didn't even know Richard Dean existed. Then you had him kidnapped and brought here as a deserter. That got our attention somewhat, but not too much, because there have been a number of desertions. What really pricked up our ears was his rescue by persons unknown, which told us that Richard Dean might be in one of the many plots percolating and circulating around Washington and Baltimore, just to name a couple of places where unrest is common. Now we want Richard Dean so he can tell us who rescued him and who any of his coconspirators might be."

"You must have your suspicions," said Rachel.

"Indeed, Madam, and therein lies the problem. The President and the Congress have suspended certain constitutional rights for the duration of the war so that we might make arrests to save the nation from those who would destroy it. Some are obvious, like former Congressman Clement Vallandigham, who is making a nuisance of himself in Canada. He and the other Copperheads are of great concern to us and are being watched. But we are equally concerned about the new players, and Dean is one of them. We must find him and get him to tell us who rescued him and why."

"And how will you do that?" Cassie asked softly.

"We will interrogate him."

She pressed him. "Does that mean you will torture him?"

"I suppose that depends on your definition of torture, Miss Baird.

He will be kept in isolation at Fortress Monroe where he will be cold, lonely, and hungry. Will he be flogged? No. Will someone get carried away and beat him? Possibly. The men in the provost marshal's office hate the Rebels."

Rachel was puzzled. "And besides, Cassie, I thought you hated him."

Now it was Cassie's turn to look puzzled. "I do. I hate him with every fiber of my being. That said, I feel sorry for the pathetic, lost creature he has become and now I wonder what, if anything, I had to do with it."

"Damn it, Cassie," her father said. "You had nothing at all to do with it. He came in here with the intention of gaining a foothold in hopes of looting our family. It's not your fault things didn't work out for him. He was and is a crook and now he's a traitor. Whatever he did, he did of his own free will. You are blameless."

"For what it's worth, I agree," Rutherford said.

Cassie took a couple of deep breaths. "Thank you."

Rachel smiled at the group. "Would anyone like some tea?" She glanced between the two men. "Or would a shot of whisky be more appropriate?"

Steven Thorne had promoted himself from bedridden to semi-active duty and was not present when Rutherford made his visit to the Bairds' home. He walked with a limp and rode in a carriage instead of on horseback. He'd been told of the meeting with the provost marshal's office and decided he didn't want to be present. Like most soldiers, the provost made him very nervous even though he had nothing to hide.

The private serving as his driver was trying to avoid bumps, which was impossible, as none of the roads in the area were paved. If Thorne's wound continued to heal, he'd give serious thought to finding the gentlest, slowest horse in the world and riding it. Being driven about in a carriage was almost embarrassing.

He found the regiment coming back from patrol. They were dusty and tired, but still greeted him with grins and waved hats. "Captain Willis, have you found Robert Lee? President Lincoln stopped by and wants to know."

Willis saluted for the benefit of the soldiers riding by. "When I find the old fox, Abe will be the next to know. Seriously, all we ran into were distant cavalry screens. Since our orders were not to bring on a battle, we just stared at them and let them be. What lay behind them, I do not know. Who knows, there may be absolutely nothing out there when you consider what is happening around Harrisburg."

"I believe we may be experiencing what some German or other referred to as the 'Fog of War.' Bobby Lee does not want us to know what he is up to, so he blocks us from seeing him with a cavalry screen that is effectively impenetrable. Even our observation balloons can see only so much farther. In the meantime, the old fox sends troops up to Harrisburg and across the Susquehanna. Once on the other side, they cause chaos and confusion and apparently you and I know about as much as Abraham Lincoln does."

Willis took out a small cigar and lit it. "None of which speaks well of our army. Lee could be dining in the White House while we chase our tails around the Pennsylvania countryside. From what you've heard, it's true that the Rebels have taken Harrisburg, is it not?"

"It is. The only question is why and I haven't heard from Lincoln either. It may be as simple as his needing food or as complex as doing something to get France and England in the war on the side of the South."

"Maybe Lee is just toying with us," Willis wondered.

"I don't like being anybody's toy," said Thorne. *Except Cassandra's,* he thought with a smile. He would return to their home this evening and find out what the provost marshal's man was after. He would sleep over in the guest room he now thought of as his, and hope that Cassie would come to him during the night. She hadn't yet, but one could always hope. He shook his head in wonderment. How could he not have seen how lovely she was when he first met her? Of course, she had still been in mourning for that cretin she thought she'd driven to his death. Damn, that had been silliness.

As the last of his small regiment passed by, the long line of refugees began anew. It was sickening to see so many hundreds, perhaps thousands of American citizens being driven away from their homes in fear of an enemy army. Apparently only one civilian had been killed at Gettysburg, but that number could rise to the hundreds as a result of the next battle.

Colonel Corey Wade had never been a cattle driver, had never even seen a herd of cattle driven anywhere. He'd owned a farm that had cows and he knew they gave milk and were delicious to eat when cut into steaks and roasted rare over an open fire. To actually drive a herd of the creatures someplace had never crossed his mind.

But now the men of his Tennessee Volunteers were responsible for getting several hundred of them across the Susquehanna and safely behind Confederate lines. Along with his herd, there were numerous others like it crossing the solid bridge at Harrisburg. It had been damaged, but not seriously, and repairs had been quickly made. The cattle, being smart, did not like the unstable swaying motion of the pontoon bridges the army had thrown up.

The pontoon bridges were for the literally thousands of wagons loaded with supplies that General Longstreet had gotten hold of one way or another. Everyone in Longstreet's part of the Army of Northern Virginia understood the basic agreement. After a few sharp skirmishes that had resulted in the withdrawal of Union General Crouch's Department of the Susquehanna Army, Pennsylvania's governor Andrew Gregg Curtin had agreed to the basic contract. In return for all the food and cattle that could be gathered, Longstreet would not set fire to Pennsylvania. The civilians were paid with Confederate IOUs which everyone acknowledged were worthless. This meant that the Confederate Army was stealing and the resentment was fierce.

However, there would be no looting or plundering of personal property. The people of Pennsylvania would endure this setback and rise again. Longstreet's men would endure hatred that would last for generations.

Captain Alex Mayfield rode up and saluted casually. "That's about it, Colonel. The bridge is nearly ankle deep in cow shit and it's really slippery. You fall and you could drown in cow crap."

"Then God help the ones who will follow us." Another herd was approaching and there was doubtless another and another behind it.

Other drovers were taking charge of the herd as it crossed. They would drive it down to the rest of Lee's army, where the cattle would either be slaughtered immediately or kept grazing for future needs. The resupply of the Army of Northern Virginia was running like a well-oiled machine. Corey could only guess, but it looked like the army was well set for several months at least and it only cost a couple of dozen killed or wounded and a few million royally pissed-off Pennsylvanians. And the Pennsylvanians could all go to hell and stay there as far as he was concerned. They had voted for war by electing Abraham Lincoln and his abolitionist brethren. There was a price for such folly.

For Sergeant Blandon, the foray across the river had brought mixed results. Since becoming part of the military again, he'd been kept on a fairly tight leash. His crimes had been forgiven but the good Colonel Wade had not forgotten.

Thus, it was with a good deal of surprise that he found himself and five others out on patrol and well away from prying eyes. Better, the men with him were all of like mind. They saw no problem enriching themselves by taking the wealth of the Yankee civilians in the area. And, lord, was there wealth! Down south, only rich folk had houses like the one they were in, but here they were all over the place. Well, maybe they weren't quite as large or ornate as the plantation houses he recalled, but they were close enough.

Along with identifying cattle and other foodstuffs that had not been turned in, they felt it was their obligation to relieve the Yankees of small items such as jewelry and cash that they thought they'd hidden so well.

It was almost laughably easy to find spots in the yards that had recently been dug up or parts of walls where the plaster was fresh or a picture hanging where no orderly minded woman would ever hang a picture. Finding trap doors under rugs was just as easy.

They were in the process of prying open a strongbox they'd found in the floor of a large house, when Blandon heard a scream. A middle-aged woman was standing in the doorway and staring at them. Behind her were a couple of older men.

"You thieving, lying bastards," one of the men said. "You people agreed you wouldn't take personal property."

Blandon laughed. "First of all, I didn't sign any agreement and second, it looks to me like all this shit was abandoned and we got first choice on anything that's abandoned."

"I'm going to have you arrested," the second man said and turned to leave.

"The hell you are," said one of Blandon's men. A shot was fired, almost deafening them in the crowded kitchen. The man crumpled and fell, his chest bloody. The second man reached under his jacket and was shot by Blandon. The woman looked at the carnage and began to scream as she pulled a Derringer from her purse. Blandon fired again and hit her in the forehead, killing her instantly.

"Now what?" asked Skinner.

Blandon was as shocked as anyone by the sudden turn of events. This was supposed to have been a simple burglary of an empty house. At least nobody seemed to have heard the shots. The house was in an isolated area, which was why they had chosen it. "We got three dead people to hide."

Blandon shrugged. "We'll drag them down to the basement and leave them. And we don't burn the place. That'll attract too much attention. Just hide the bodies in the basement and then we up and go on our way. It'll be a long, long time before anybody misses them."

It was time to get back to the main body and pretend he was interested in the war. He'd managed to gather more than five hundred dollars in greenbacks and gold along with some small pieces of jewelry that, sadly, would bring him only a fraction of their worth when they were fenced to some unscrupulous Jew. He idly wondered if it would be better to melt the things down.

★ CHAPTER 10 ★

The nightmare was pretty much always the same. Sometimes the cast of characters was subtly different, but the results were always terrifyingly similar.

On the first day of Gettysburg, the regiment had fought alongside Brigadier General John Buford's regular cavalry. Fighting dismounted, they had held off vastly larger Confederate forces until reinforcements from Major General John Reynolds' I Corps arrived to stabilize the position and permit them to withdraw. Thorne knew nothing of the grand strategy. He was merely the second in command of a small, almost amateur, regiment of mounted infantry. His vision of the battle was that of hundreds of armed and angry men howling, shooting, and trying to kill him. Some of them he recognized as faces from his youth, which, even in his dream state, made no sense whatsoever. And why were they so tall and fearsome? Thorne had never considered himself a coward, so why did he have an overwhelming urge to flee that was only held back by the fact that his feet were leaden and wouldn't move as the monsters closed in on him?

Then the dream shifted.

Prior to that engagement, the regiment had only fought in minor skirmishes. They'd suffered a handful of casualties and only a few of those had been killed. It had been shocking, but it had not been a slaughter. When I Corps had arrived to relieve Buford and the Sixth Indiana, the regiment had been withdrawn through the town of Gettysburg and had taken up position on Cemetery Ridge.

The nightmare seemed to skip over the second day's fighting. They'd lost a large number of men and were pulled back to be reorganized. They'd hoped their part in the battle was over. In the dream, his men were lying down and joking while he tried to yell and warn them that something terrible was about to happen. They paid no attention.

But then came the third day and the horror of Pickett's Charge. It had begun with a cannonade that had made the earth tremble. He and the others had hugged the dirt and prayed for the onslaught to end. Around them, men and horses were torn to shreds. The horses were worst. When wounded, they screamed louder than a score of men could have and their cries were crazed and panicked . . . and why not? The poor beasts had no idea why men were trying to kill them or why it hurt so much. Normally, they'd have been put down as humanely as possible, but there was little humanity at Gettysburg. This part of the dream was pure terrible memory.

The third day's images were the worst. When the cannonade mercifully ended, Steve had moved to where he could see the field from the ridge. The sight of thousands of men marching toward them in good order across the field was something he would never forget. But then the Union cannon began to chew them up, leaving clumps of dead and wounded to litter what had once been some farmer's land, a place where crops would someday grow peacefully.

The Rebels came closer and he could see that the point of the attack was aimed almost directly at where he stood. Closer they approached, growing larger with each step. Dusty shapes became people and then people with faces. Some of them were grim and some were yelling that high-pitched scream called the Rebel yell. They fell as bullets and canister whipped through their now chaotic ranks, but still they came. Bodies piled up and they still came on.

"This way," a disembodied voice hollered and the regiment ran towards the back of the Union line. They were plugged in just behind the Pennsylvanians. Steve saw a man with his wide-brimmed hat on the point of his sword and thought that was silly. The hat would be ruined. The man waved his sword a few times and then disappeared.

The Rebels climbed over the low stone fence and piled into the Union soldiers. Now it was a brawl. Grown men were stabbing each other with bayonets and clubbing each other to the ground with rifle butts. They struck each other with fists and tore at each other with their teeth and Steve stood watching it all unfold, each strike, each wound, each gout of blood as clear as the morning.

He found himself on his hands and knees, trying desperately to crawl away, but hands kept grabbing at him and pulling him back. He tried to stand, but his wounded leg wouldn't let him. His wounded leg . . . but this was Gettysburg . . . He started awake, with real hands touching him.

"It's all right, Steve." He recognized Cassie's voice and he reached out to her. She took his head and held it against her bosom and rocked him as if he was a small child. He shuddered and wished that were true.

"Are you better now?" she asked softly.

"Yes, much better. In fact, I'd just as soon you never let me go."

"That works both ways, you know," she said kissed him on the forehead. "Does this happen very often?"

"Too often, and a lot of the men get it too. When it happens, their friends wake them up and they shake it off. New guys don't understand yet, but they will. Usually, I just wake up in my cot and will myself back to reality. Being held by you is a lot better."

"I'll bet it is."

He sat up with a jolt. He'd just realized she was wearing nothing more than her nightgown. "You shouldn't be here. Your parents will be furious."

"You worry too much. My father was out with friends and is sound asleep and my mother's waiting outside. We both heard you and she felt it would be so much better if I was the one to come in."

Steve laughed, "Definitely the better idea."

She poured some water from a pitcher into a basin and dipped a cloth into it. She used it to wipe his head and neck.

"There, doesn't that feel better?"

"Much, much better. How much time do we have before your mother gets suspicious?"

"Not too much at all, I'm afraid, and you'd better stop what you're doing before she comes barging in."

She had been sitting on the edge of the bed and the nightgown had ridden up above her knees. Like most men, he had rarely seen a woman's legs and he found hers to be both fascinating and lovely.

"You are so beautiful," he said as his fingers traced a path from her ankle to her outer thigh.

"You are very bold," she said as she both gasped and laughed. She reluctantly removed his hand and straightened her gown. "You don't want to get thrown out of here, do you?"

"Not for anything."

"And I wouldn't want that to happen either. I am now going to tell my mother that the patient will live. She will fuss over you, just not like I did, and we will both try to go back to sleep."

And she would have to ask her mother about the bulge at the base of Steven's stomach. She thought she understood how men and women worked, but, like so many demure ladies of her station, her education in that area was far from adequate. Of course, none of her friends knew anything they would talk about either. But being caressed by Steve had been extraordinarily pleasant.

Hadrian's people had pulled into a tight perimeter. Those who had guns showed them, while others held axes, pitchforks, and anything else that could be used as a weapon. One old man had gotten his hands on a sword. Even the women had hatchets and knives of all types. In the middle of the defenses were the children and the elderly along with others who were helpless. Torches lit up the night and made the scene garish.

Faced with this bristling threat, the mob of several hundred white men and women had pulled back. Much of their courage had come from a bottle and the effects of the alcohol were starting to wear off. Regardless, it was evident that black people were not wanted in this part of Maryland. The group had moved south toward the formidable defenses that ringed Washington without incident. The military garrison saw that they weren't Confederates and let them pass without incident.

During the nighttime they could see the glow of the city in the distance and it gave them hope. Abraham Lincoln could not be that far away.

Even though the city was filled with soldiers, that didn't stop roaming mobs from assaulting small groups of Negroes. Whenever Hadrian's people had to move, they did so in large and well-disciplined groups. So far, this had kept them safe. This Saturday night, a number of white citizens of Maryland had gotten liquored up and were hunting for human prey.

One brave soul worked up the courage to come close and throw a rock. Others followed. "Damn it," Hadrian raged as a rock struck home, causing a woman to scream in pain. He hoped it wasn't Mariah, who had casually "stopped by" that afternoon to visit.

He organized a flying squad of men, but chose none with guns. The last thing he wanted to do was have a black man shoot a white man. Then the mobs would be out in full fury and the police would arrest everyone associated with them. The guns Hadrian's people had were for intimidation and last-ditch defense.

With a shout, he and the dozen others charged the loosely grouped attackers, who appeared surprised at seeing the worm turn. It was over in seconds. A few heads cracked and the rioters ran off shouting curses. A couple of them were dragging their wounded.

"Well done, Emperor Hadrian," said Mariah as she slipped her hand in his.

Hadrian grinned and accepted the praise as his due. One of the advantages of being able to read was that he had picked up a fair knowledge of history. He thought that Hadrian was one of the great Roman emperors. And if his name and actions impressed the delightful Mariah, all the better.

A troop of cavalry arrived. They looked exhausted. Doubtless they'd been chasing reports of similar fights all night. A young lieutenant looked down on them and glared. "What's been going on here?"

Hadrian answered, "Just some boys making some noise, sir. Ain't nothing to be worried about."

The lieutenant took the comment as an insult, "I don't recall saying I was worried about anything, boy."

"Didn't mean it that way, sir. We're peaceful," he said, hoping that all the guns were tucked away.

"Where y'all from?" the lieutenant asked, mollified by the apology.

"Just about everywhere, sir. We've travelled a long way to be free."

The lieutenant actually laughed. "Well don't let me stop you if you want to keep on moving."

The troopers rode away. Mariah took Hadrian's arm and steered him back to the tent he called home. "I don't think it would be too smart for me to try to make it back home tonight. You don't happen to know where an innocent young woman of color might stay the night, do you?"

Otto Bauer spat in the general direction of the departing Confederate soldiers. He thought about standing up and urinating in their direction, but passed on the idea. Some southerner without a sense of humor might take a shot at him with one of their cannon. Several batteries were arrayed on the other side of the Susquehanna, pointed in his general direction. He thought he was out of range, but that kind of thinking had gotten young Henry Watson blown to pieces by a cannonball.

Longstreet's rear guard was about to cross the ford. They were laughing and joking. He assumed they could see him as well as he could see them. Their orders remained the same. The governor said they should hold their fire and the general had concurred. Rumors had it that General Couch was incensed, but rumors meant nothing. You couldn't call what they were doing "retreating" as much as simply sauntering out of the way of any possibility of action. The Union had been defeated in more ways than one. What little fighting there had been had resulted in an effective surrender. The Confederates could do whatever they wished with the property of the people of Pennsylvania.

At least he had made peace with Henry's mother. Martha Watson had made the short trip and he was able to use a telescope and show her where her son had been buried. She talked about digging him up and reburying him in a churchyard and Otto had silently hoped they'd find enough to exhume and rebury.

Martha had surprised him by fully understanding the situation. "I know what happened and that you were sending him back to be safe. Life is cruel and unfair, Otto. I had him go with you because both of us respected and admired you and nothing has changed. I felt he had a better chance of surviving the war with you, but God had a different plan."

Otto could only nod mutely. He ached at the thought of what she might say next.

"And I will not be present when he is dug up. I am not strong enough to handle that. I lost my husband and now I have lost my son and now I must start over again."

Otto recalled that her husband's death had not been considered any great loss. He and Martha had gotten married when he was thirty-five and she fourteen. He'd been a drunk and a bully and he'd liked to beat her. Martha today was pale and haggard, but she was still lovely. Her late husband had gotten drunk one night and ridden his horse so hard that it had stumbled and he'd been thrown and broken his worthless neck. Toby had been but a little boy and the two of them had been helped by Martha's relatives.

Nor had young Henry been a saint. He'd been showing disturbing tendencies that he might be very much like his father. He'd hadn't yet struck his mother, but Otto heard that he'd come close. He'd also been involved in petty thefts and some beatings of fellow young boys. He'd needed a strong hand and Otto was disappointed that he hadn't been able to provide it.

"Otto," she said. "Most men wouldn't have done what you did. I respect that. I . . . would like you to come back." She raised her head and looked at him frankly. "I want you to come back."

"Well, Mrs. Watson . . ."

"Martha," she said.

They took each other's hands and squeezed. Otto smiled, unable to find any words. Was it marriage that beckoned him here? A family, children? Perhaps so, but first he had a task to perform.

Otto crossed the river alone and upstream from the ford. His horse had little trouble swimming the deep water and nobody appeared to pay him any attention. It was a cloudy night with but a sliver of a moon to betray him.

Once across, he didn't have to look hard to find the Rebel camp. The lights from hundreds of campfires created a glow that couldn't be missed. It was perfect for a hunter, a stalker.

As he drew closer, he didn't have any particular target in mind. He just wanted to strike out at the invaders who had caused so much harm to his adopted nation.

Nor was he out to commit suicide. He would fire once and escape quickly amid the chaos and confusion.

The Confederates had guards and patrols out, but they were not paying much attention and were easy to evade. They were victorious and there was no Union army in the area. They laughed and joked among themselves, sparing no notice for the man moving slowly through the trees. He had put a brown shawl over his blue uniform, hoping it would help him pass for a Rebel if he had to.

This night he didn't have his army issue Model 1861 Springfield percussion rifle-musket. It was too big and cumbersome for his purpose and not all that accurate at long distance. Instead, he had a Whitworth rifle that he'd paid for out of his own funds, buying it from a dealer in Pittsburgh. It even had a telescopic sight, as if he needed one. The British-made rifle had a tendency to foul after only a handful of shots, but that was fine by him. One shot and he'd be gone.

Otto swore as he looked over the area. There were too many targets. Several clusters of men appeared to be officers, but there were so many it implied that no single one was very important.

Cheers erupted as another group rode into view. One rider waved his hat and the cheers rose again, much louder this time. The hat had a plume or feather on it. Otto nodded to himself. The choice had been made for him. He had set up a stable firing platform out of rocks. He took careful aim, caressed the trigger, and squeezed gently.

He fired and absorbed the recoil. He didn't stop to see if he'd made a hit. That was not in doubt. Instead he got up and made his way quietly and carefully into the dark woods. Behind him, chaos had erupted, with men shouting and running in every direction. That actually helped him by covering any noise he might make. He found his horse, mounted it, and rode towards the river. Again, he splashed across without incident.

After a short ride, he reached the farmhouse where Martha was staying with friends. She greeted him wearing a robe over her nightshirt. When he told her what he had done and whom he thought he had shot, she smiled. "It's not as good as Jefferson Davis or Robert E. Lee, but it will more than do. I want you to promise one thing. You will promise that you will never again stalk and kill someone. It's bad enough that people are killed in battle, but not the way you just did. You may have helped the Union cause, but you put yourself in great danger and for no good reason. You will not do that again. Is that understood?"

"Yes, ma'am," he said solemnly. Inside he was rejoicing. She truly cared for him.

"Good. But Otto . . . I am honored. Don't doubt that." She took him to her room and closed the door. "By the way, I don't care what anyone thinks."

She snuffed out the candle and took off her robe. She slowly lay down on the bed. "Get undressed, Otto, we don't have all night. Well maybe," she smiled warmly, "we do."

Robert E. Lee warmly grasped the hand of his most reliable general, James Longstreet, Old Pete. "The prodigal has returned and I could not be more pleased."

Longstreet returned the handshake firmly. His emotion was so great he almost reached out to hug the older man. "We succeeded, but we paid a great price, perhaps too great a price."

Lee shook his head. "People die in battle. It's a tragedy, but killing is the nature of war. Killing in wartime is just so easy. Jeb Stuart will be missed, but, after all is said and done, he is only one man."

"But to be killed in the middle of the night by a sniper, a lone wolf, is hard to fathom. Stuart had his faults, but he was an inspiring leader and he didn't die easily. The bullet went through his shoulder and into his chest. He bled to death but never lost consciousness. He was as shocked as a man can be. He told me to tell his wife how much he loved her. He thought he was safe among his comrades, but there isn't any safe place in wartime."

"Which is why this war cannot drag on forever," Lee said. "We will run out of people."

"The men are taking it as if we had lost another Stonewall Jackson. The circumstances aren't quite the same, but they are close enough. Jackson being killed by his own men and now Stuart being shot by a sniper at long range—that's weighing heavily on the troops. For whatever it's worth, we found the killer's trail, but it ended at the river. We presume the shooter rode across to safety."

Lee did not comment. When he'd gotten word of Stuart's death, he'd been shaken to the point of withdrawing to his tent for privacy. Jeb Stuart had been the South's dashing cavalier. Even when he failed, as he had when he left Lee to go on a long ride around the Union lines at Gettysburg, he did so with flair. Lee had chastised him and that appeared to crush Stuart for a brief while, but he recovered and soon found himself back in Lee's good graces.

"Wade Hampton will do well as Stuart's replacement," Lee finally said. "But I do wonder just how many losses of key men can this army endure. I've said it before and I'll say it again, you and Hardee and the others must stay out of harm's way to the extent that it is possible. I fear that the North is beginning to develop some first-rate generals."

Lee smiled wryly. "Fortunately for us, they seem to be avoiding the Army of the Potomac. Grant, Sherman, and Thomas are out west and I pray that they stay there."

Longstreet wiped his brow and sat down on a folding camp chair. He was exhausted. "Did you ever meet Grant?"

"I've been told that I have, but I have no recollection of it. He performed well as a junior officer in the Mexican War and I may have congratulated him or mentioned him in reports, but I simply do not recall the man. If we do not bring this war to a favorable conclusion, I'm afraid that I will be meeting him on the field of battle."

Longstreet grinned. "Not a bad fellow. But sir, you are by far the better general."

"Quite right. I am the better general. But he has the resources and appears to understand how to use them. He seems to be that type of dog that bites and never lets go. The Confederacy cannot afford to fight battles of attrition against a tenacious and fearless hound. And unlike other Union generals, he appears to learn quickly from his mistakes."

Lee stood and Longstreet did as well. "When Grant does come east, I hope I can beat him decisively before he gains the experience of ccommand in this theater, that lack of which will be his only shortcoming. In the meantime, you have brought us enough supplies to last us for months and perhaps prod President Lincoln into doing something foolish. His election to a second term is no foregone conclusion. A single sharp defeat and someone more malleable, like McClellan, could be in the White House and perhaps an honorable peace could be negotiated."

Longstreet yawned and was too tired to hide it. "I do not understand why they just don't leave us alone. We want peace as much as they do. I just cannot fathom that slavery is all that important to them. Given time, it will die a natural death. But they don't want to give us time."

"In all fairness to the abolitionists, once you agree that slavery is a moral wrong, then extending it until it dies a natural death is like sending an innocent man to prison."

"I understand the point, General. I've read a great deal about the issue. If the North wins, I do fear for the South if all the slaves are turned loose."

"As do I, General Longstreet, but let us withdraw from this discussion and get some well-earned sleep."

"I hate beards," said Cassandra as she wielded the straight razor over Steven's cheek.

"Do you have any idea what you're doing?" he croaked.

"On a number of occasions I had to shave my father and he has survived quite nicely. The scars are barely noticeable. His losing his leg was not the result of my barbering skills."

They were in the kitchen and both Rachel and Mariah were watching. It was true enough many women shaved their men, though it was a new experience for Thorne.

"All it takes," she said, "is hot water, hot towels, and a steady hand. I will try hard not to sneeze. But if I do, Mariah has a number of cloths that can be used as bandages or even a tourniquet."

The decision to shave off his beard had not been taken lightly. Most men these days had beards and some of them were grown and styled in almost fantastic ways. It made sense in its own terms— shaving regularly on campaign was a peacetime procedure that troops could easily do without. Cassie, however, had let it be known that she didn't care for them, and besides, Steve's beard was neither full nor dramatically combed. It anything, it was scraggly and made him look younger than he wished to appear. Thus, and by popular demand, it would have to go.

She lathered him up and began to shave him in smooth, gentle strokes. In a surprisingly short period of time, he was clean shaven with skin that was as smooth as a baby's. He looked in the mirror and laughingly handed her a brand new thin dime. "I'll be back in a couple of weeks for an encore."

Brandies were passed around. Mariah discreetly departed. Even though she was Cassie's friend, she was still an employee and it would not be seemly for her to be drinking alcohol with them on anything but a special occasion, like Christmas.

As happened frequently, Cassie's father was out playing cards and smoking cigars with political friends. His latest new leg seemed to be working out well. Either that or he was ignoring the pain.

Lee had withdrawn and any threat to the District of Columbia had abated. Soldiers from both sides had settled in to a routine that included scouting and probing. Shots were fired and supply wagons ambushed and burned, but no great battles appeared on the horizon.

Cassie and Steve had left the kitchen and were seated on a couch in the parlor. "Lee made a great fool out of Abraham Lincoln and his generals, didn't he?" Cassie asked.

"Sometimes I wish you didn't read so much and weren't so knowledgeable, but yes. And a lot of people, some of them congressmen, are furious. They are rightfully wondering just when the war will be brought to a conclusion. The longer it drags on, the more likely it is that there will be a negotiated peace that anyone who wants to free the slaves won't like."

"And that would be a terrible shame," said Rachel as she entered with tea and cookies. Steve would drink the tea to be polite, but he loved the cookies Rachel made.

He made a note to ask Cassie if she knew how to make them. If yes, then it was reason enough to ask her to marry him.

"Will you be staying with us tonight?" Cassie asked sweetly. She clearly did not want him to leave.

Steve sighed and took another cookie. "Sadly, duty calls. I must return to the regiment. I think they're beginning to suspect that I would rather be here with you than camping out in the mud with them."

★ CHAPTER 11 ★

"... and that, gentlemen, is the state of this republic in this, the year of our Lord, eighteen-hundred and sixty-three."

Booth was working himself up to a fine fettle. Sid and Nate, two of his Washington crew, sat watching him wide-eyed, Sid with what seemed to be considerable puzzlement. For his part, Dean was stifling an impulse to reply. It was clear enough to him that Booth didn't care to have people interrupting his soliloquies.

Booth took another gulp of his drink. "The republic. A republic of Irishmen, Silesians, Bavarians, the gutter sweepings of Europe. And now they want to throw in the colored on top of it. What next? Sicilians? Jews? Perhaps a nice sprinkling of Chinamen? The Great Ape and his henchman are turning this country into the world's sewer."

Dean took a surreptitious glance around the tavern. Several drinkers were staring directly at them, while others had that doing-their-best-to-ignore air.

"And what is standing against that, gentlemen? I ask you. What force stands alone against abolitionism, servile war, and race-mixing?" He slammed a fist on the tabletop. "The South. It was the South that founded this country, and the South that will save it. Aristocratic, English, and white, the way God Almighty intended. Let the Celtic riffraff and the Sons of Ham start their own country. This is ours!"

He raised his glass. "Gentlemen—to the South! May she long be—"

"Treason!"

An old man had stepped away from the bar and stood glaring at Booth. "You'll not speak in favor of sedition before me, you insolent pup."

He glanced around him. "Will no man join me in defending our Republic?" No one else in the bar leapt to their feet.

The barman stepped out, a billy club dangling from one hand. "We want no trouble here," he said to Booth. "If the bluebellies appear, you'll be the one to answer for it."

"We were just leaving." Gulping the rest of his drink, Booth got to his feet. "Drink up, boys."

As he walked past the old man, he cracked his elbow with his walking stick. Grabbing his arm, the old man shot a curse at him. He turned just in time for Dean to shove him against the bar. Nobody said another word as they walked out into the street.

Outside, Booth straightened his cravat. "Well, Richard—would you say I got carried away?"

Uncertain of how to answer, Dean simply laughed. The other two echoed him a moment later.

Booth started down the street. "So, Richard," he said, his tone still conversational. "Could you kill a man?"

Booth's question rattled Richard Dean. "I suppose that I could, in battle. I have it on good authority that many soldiers don't even fire their rifles and, if they do, they don't bother to aim . . ."

"Yes, yes, That's not quite what I mean. I want to know if you could sneak up on a man and . . ." He struck Richard lightly with his stick. Sid and Nate started laughing. ". . . stab him in the ribs or reach across and slice his throat . . . 'Who would have thought the old man to have so much blood in him?' Would you be capable of that?"

Dean paled. They were walking along Baltimore's crowded waterfront. There were no riots planned for today. Richard had minimally disguised himself with a workman's jacket and cap. No one seemed to care. Booth was dressed, as always, to the peak of fashion, if not beyond. He seemed to own fifty hats, and at least that many walking sticks. He didn't care either.

"I haven't given it much thought, Mr. Booth, but I suppose I could if I had to and if it would help our cause."

"Good answer. Now, could you shoot someone in the back, or, for that matter, in the chest or the face at point-blank range?"

Sid made a shooting noise. Dean gave it a moment's consideration. "I believe it would be preferable to stabbing, and yes, I think I could do it."

"You *think* or you *know*?"

Richard managed to laugh. "I don't think we'll really know until it actually happens. I saw a number of men proclaim their bravery before a battle and then run when the shooting started."

"Does that include your own actions?"

"Indeed it does, although I didn't desert out of cowardice. I left because of the futility of it all. I think I'm as brave as the next man, although I do wonder just how brave the next man is." He found himself glancing involuntarily at the two boys. Nate made a face at him.

Booth laughed. A passing fishwife gave him a glance.

"Mr. Booth, may I assume that you have some thoughts in this regard and this discussion is not philosophical?"

"You may indeed. However, there is nothing more to divulge at this time." He paused at a shop window to straighten up his hat. "Come along, gents. Time for some soft-shelled crabs."

This particular section of the B&O Railroad line ran from Baltimore to Philadelphia, among other destinations, and the company liked to brag that it was the first railroad line in the United States, a contention open to considerable argument. What was certain, however, was that Union railroads were vastly superior to those found in the Confederacy. The reasons for this were strictly commercial. Southern lines were short-haul lines built to enable planters to bring cotton and other crops to markets where they could be sold. In the north, tracks went from large ports and commercial centers to other centers. In the south, there was nothing to compete with New York, Chicago, Baltimore, or any of a dozen other economic centers.

Southern lines were often of a narrower gauge than those in the north and, at this point in the war, had been savaged by the fighting, whereas the northern lines had been largely insulated from the violence and devastation. Nor did the South have the resources to repair those lines that Union soldiers had gleefully torn up.

All of this ran though Colonel Corey Wade's mind as he and his men waited patiently for the train that ran with almost clockwork precision from Washington City to Baltimore. They were well behind Union lines and scouts were keeping a sharp eye out for anything that smacked of danger. Once again, they were comforted by the fact that even the large Union Army could not be everywhere. Wade's scouts had carefully analyzed Union patrol patterns. They had determined that no bluebellies would be anywhere near their location or the site of their planned ambush.

The train would be a small one. Unless some changes were made and an additional car or two was attached, the train would consist of a locomotive, tender, two freight cars, and a caboose. Their goal was to make off with the contents of the second freight car. Along with many bags of mail, this consisted of several million dollars in paper money, greenbacks, newly printed by the Treasury in Washington and needed for circulation in New York and elsewhere.

While the Army of Northern Virginia had more than enough food and other supplies, thanks to the Harrisburg raid, it was short on the cash needed to buy weapons and ammunition. Even those merchants who believed in the Confederacy's cause weren't so foolish as to accept Confederate paper money. They wanted gold or Union paper money. It was ironic that the North had only recently introduced paper money as a means of paying for their mounting bills, which far outstripped the value of any specie they might get their hands on.

A distant whistle interrupted his thoughts. Captain Mayfield cocked his head. "Do I hear a train coming, Colonel?"

"Your command of the obvious is refreshing," Wade said with a smile that hid his real emotions. They were about to go into action and, while they should be able to overwhelm any defenses the train might have, nothing in combat was guaranteed. You never knew when a lucky bullet or a stray shot had your name on it. Hadn't the sudden and shocking death of Jeb Stuart proved that? One bullet out of the night. In Wade's opinion—and he was far from alone in this—the killing of Stuart had been an act of murder, not war.

A mile away, signal flags were waving. "Damn," said Wade. Two additional cars had been added to the train. His signalers said they were passenger cars and he wondered if they were loaded with Union soldiers. If so, it would complicate matters, but a passenger car could only hold thirty or so soldiers. He would still hold an overwhelming numerical superiority.

Another whistle and now it was much closer. As ordered, his men deployed to either side of the track. Charges had already been set and now the fuse was lit. The train just came into view when the gunpowder detonated, dislodging a rail.

The engineer saw the explosion and hit the brakes, which squealed hideously, before the engine stopped a hundred yards short of the broken line.

Wade yelled and waved his hat. His small force of volunteers closed in on the now-immobile engine, with several of them firing in the air. His orders had been simple: clean and quick, with no massacre or unnecessary killing. Anxious faces looked out from the passenger car windows and he was relieved to see that almost all were all civilians. There was one freight car and it was closed. He rode up to the door and pounded on it with the handle of his pistol.

"Open up and you won't be harmed."

"Damn you Rebels," came the muffled reply.

Wade had expected the bravado. "If you don't open up, we'll blow the car and you to pieces."

The engineer arrived and he pounded on the door as well. "Jesse, don't be a fool. They blew the tracks, and they can blow you to kingdom come as well and for no good reason. Open the damn door."

A moment later, the door opened and a half a dozen uniformed and unarmed guards climbed down and put up their hands. In the meantime, the civilians had been taken from the passenger cars and were lined up along the tracks. Their emotions ranged from anger to fear. A few children stared at the Confederates in disbelief and excitement.

Wade was curious. Four unarmed Union soldiers stared at him. "Where are you boys going?"

"We're going home," said one, a corporal. "We were wounded at Gettysburg and we've been released from duty. Now I suppose home will be a Confederate prison camp."

Wade pretended to think for a moment. He didn't want the responsibility of prisoners, especially wounded ones. "And home is where you're going to go. You've fought your war and I have no desire to interrupt your journey." He turned to the civilians. "And as to the rest of you, you will not be assaulted, molested, or robbed. We are not like the monsters who killed General Stuart. We simply want the contents of those sacks that my men are hoisting on their horses. Another train will doubtless be along in a while and the line will be repaired by tomorrow."

And doubtless it would. The Union Army was damnably efficient at building and maintaining its railways. He feared that the South would never catch up. Union workers were just too damned efficient and there were just too damned many of them.

The warehouse contained stores for the Union Army. As such it was one of scores of similar buildings along the crowded and dirty Baltimore waterfront. The building was guarded, but neither Richard Dean nor his two companions were impressed by the two old drunks who carried clubs and walked around the large building with the speed of arthritic turtles.

If his watch was anywhere near accurate, it was about three in the morning. They slipped quietly up to the rear door and unlocked it with a key that had been provided by a disgruntled employee.

Like in other warehouses they had seen, supplies were piled to the ceiling. "Where are the guards?" Dean asked. They had to be silenced before the warehouse could be destroyed. If either of them ran outside hallooing and shouting, they might have to call it all off, and Booth would not like that.

This chill night, he was assisted by Sid and Nate. If this was what the Confederacy was going to use in key operations, Richard wasn't impressed. They did not split up to search for the guards. They believed they would be found in the rear of the building where there was a coffee pot and some couches, and they were right.

As they tried to sneak close, Nate managed to stumble and send some packages tumbling. "What the hell was that?" A suddenly alarmed guard jerked awake. "Who goes there?"

The time for subtlety was over. "Now," Dean yelled, and the three men charged. The guards had their clubs and each, to Dean's shock, had a large blade, much the like the type called a "Bowie knife" in their belts.

"Copperheads!" shouted one guard as he lunged towards Richard, who parried easily and rammed his own knife into the man's gut. He thrust upward and turned, just like Sid had told him. To his astonishment, it worked. The man staggered backwards and let out a guttural scream. Richard pulled out the knife and turned to the second guard, who stared at him in disbelief before dropping his own knife and running for an exit, grunting in fear as he went.

Richard swore and took off after the man who'd begun gasping after only a few strides. Richard caught him and wrapped one arm around the guard's neck while slicing at his throat with the other. Enormous fountains of blood poured out as the guard staggered and died.

"Jesus." Nate stared at him wide eyed. "I didn't think you had it in you. And, Lord, are you ever a mess."

Richard's clothing was covered with congealing blood. He couldn't go outside like this. The guards' quarters provided him with a solution in the form of a long and weathered frock coat. He slipped it on and the three of them began setting explosives and laying out fuses. Containers of oil were set alongside the explosives. It took about an hour to get everything ready. Richard pulled out his watch. Everything was supposed to explode at four-thirty and it was five to four. Other fire bombs were scheduled to detonate throughout the city at the same time to maximize confusion and prevent any useful response from the police or the fire companies.

The three men waited for a few minutes and tried to calm themselves. They also tried to ignore the stink coming from Richard's ill-fitting coat. "Now," he said and struck a match. The explosions would be a few minutes early, but who would care. Primary and secondary fuses were lit and they ran out the rear door and into an alley. Nobody was there.

They forced themselves to walk slowly, casually, just three friends who'd had a little too much to drink. They walked along a beach and Richard waded in. The water was icy cold and made him gasp, which the other two thought was funny. Dean could care less. Louts would be louts. As for him . . . he had proven to John Wilkes Booth that he could kill efficiently and coldly. Now he was confident he would be an asset to the Confederacy and Booth. He smiled widely in the darkness.

There was a rumble behind him. In the distance, explosions began to rock the warehouse and dock areas of Baltimore. Sid began dancing around on the sand like a loon. Dean waded back to shore. He thought the fireworks were lovely.

Confronting one general was bad enough, but now there were two angry brigadiers to deal with in the offices of the War Department. At least, Thorne thought, he wasn't alone. Along with Montgomery Meigs, the Quartermaster General, was Brigadier Herman Haupt. General Haupt's specialty was railroads, and he was considered a genius at building them and maintaining them. Thorne was accompanied by a select group of other field-grade officers who'd been tasked with keeping the supply lines open. If evidence of the last few days was accurate, all had failed miserably.

"Another train was destroyed yesterday," said Meigs. "This time it was by a raggedy group from Tennessee led by a Colonel Wade. To give the devil his due, no civilians were robbed or molested. He even let a handful of convalescing soldiers go on their way. All of that says that Wade is a gentleman, but he made off with two and a half million dollars in Mr. Lincoln's greenbacks which will be put to use supplying our enemies. Something has to be done about this. The newspapers are having a wonderful time at our expense. Colonel Wade's attack was not the only one and some of the others have been fairly bloody confrontations. Obviously, we want these stopped. The President is most anxious that they cease.

"The only successful efforts were those in which soldiers were hidden on trains and gave the Rebels more than they could handle. Unfortunately, raiders like this Wade's are larger than any number of soldiers we could hide on a train."

"On the other hand," said Thorne, "do the Rebs really want to suffer the heavy casualties that would be required for them to take a well-defended train?"

"And what if that train was armored?" suggested another officer.

"And how did the bastards find out about the money that was on the train in the first place?"

Meigs replied stiffly. "The provost marshal is working on that obvious problem. Someone in the Baltimore and Ohio or in the Treasury has to be informing them. Scores of trains take that route every day and it cannot be a coincidence that they attacked this particular one."

"Or some of the others they've robbed," said Haupt. "Some attacks may be random targets of opportunity, but I don't think this one was. They had information. A Mr. Rutherford from the Provost Marshal's office will be in charge of the investigation. He believes, and I agree

with him, that the traitor will turn out to be someone in the Treasury—
or perhaps another department—who supports the South."

Annette Cosgrove was a nothing, a cypher. She was middle-aged,
lonely, and hated her job and Abraham Lincoln. To her, the Great
Emancipator was the Great Destroyer. She loved only two things in
this life: the South and John Wilkes Booth.

She had been born in what was now West Virginia in a small town
near Wheeling. She hated the fact that her home country had deserted
the South and joined the Union. There should have been battles and
bloodshed. West Virginia should have remained part of the grand state
of Virginia. She despised Jefferson Davis for not fighting more
strenuously to keep West Virginia in the Confederacy. She was more
lenient towards Robert E. Lee, whose conduct in the brief campaign
against the Union had been less than stellar. Now he was the only man
who could save the Confederacy.

So Annette did what she could. Her job at the Treasury Department
at 1500 Pennsylvania Avenue was to record planned shipments of
money and send out the necessary communications. The building, still
under construction, had been designed to emulate a Roman place of
worship. It was huge, and many columns rose to impress visitors.

Annette was far from stupid. It had taken her more than a year to
make legitimate contacts with the Confederate government in
Richmond. Even then, there was a distinct lack of interest from
Richmond. She concluded that the South had no way of utilizing the
information. But now, with the South's army on the doorstep of
Washington, there suddenly *was* interest.

Her contact was a man named Jessup. She didn't like or trust
Jessup—he was tall and thin and he looked mean. But he was the man
designated by the Confederacy—and he worked with John Wilkes
Booth. When she had heard that, she knew that destiny had touched
her. She would be helping both the South and her idol, whom she had
seen on stage on over one hundred occasions, at the same time.

Jessup's eyes had widened when she told him of the money
shipment and added that she could give him many more. Her job as
a clerk was to make schedules, not decisions. Days later, when she
read the newspapers that told about the multimillion-dollar train
robbery, she knew she'd made the right decision. It was also quite

pleasant to see her superiors running around like the proverbial headless chickens.

Since money shipments had to be set up in advance, there was plenty of time for her to provide information and for the Rebel army to react. Each Friday, she would have her lunch at a particular modest restaurant and, if she had anything of note, she would ostentatiously put the information in a particular wastebasket. She always made sure that Jessup was present for the drop and loitering across the street. A day later, slipped beneath the door of her room, she would find a note of thanks, just a word or two, never more than that, but signed by John Wilkes Booth. Her life was now not quite as dull as it had been. She was doing something for her country, the Confederate States of America. And for Booth.

Lord Richard Lyons, the first Viscount Lyons, was shown in to the President's office. He was accompanied by Secretary of State William H. Seward. Neither man looked pleased. While Great Britain supported the North, it was a strained relationship. Early on in the war, the Union and Great Britain had almost gone to war as the result of a regrettable incident called the Trent Affair. A Union warship had stopped a British ship on the high seas and taken off diplomats accredited by the Confederacy. No matter that the Union did not recognize the Confederacy or its diplomats, Great Britain had been outraged by the seizure of its ship and war seemed inevitable. But cooler heads had prevailed. The men were released to go on to London where they continued to pester Queen Victoria's ministers, but to no avail.

There would be other problems, in particular the fact that a number of Confederates had taken refuge in Canada, where American law couldn't touch them.

There was also the nagging rumor that Lord Lyons considered Americans to be little more than barbarians. He and many in his class would have happily sided with the more aristocratic Confederacy had it not been for the Confederacy's stubborn and, in Lyons' opinion, insane insistence on retaining slavery. Southern plantation owners were gentlemen in the manner that northern factory owners and merchants could never be. But Great Britain had abolished slavery in the early years of the nineteenth century and it would have been anathema to support a nation that kept humans in bondage.

Lyons accepted his tea, sipped, and spoke. "Mr. President, my country and my queen are sorely conflicted. Weeks ago, when your General Meade was victorious at Gettysburg at the same time that Vicksburg was falling to Union forces, it looked as if the war was all but over. But now the situation has changed and not in your favor or ours. Simply put, sir, the war is dragging down our economy. Labor is getting restless. There have been strikes and even some rioting. The economy is down and unemployment is high, in large part because of the shortage of cotton. Right now, my party does not believe there is any likelihood that the British government will recognize the Confederacy and just turn a blind eye towards the issue of slavery. But another reversal like the last one, or a lack of progress in the war, could result in Parliament changing its mind. Her majesty would not like it, but she is, after all, a constitutional monarch who reigns but does not rule."

Lincoln seethed but did not let it show. How dare this snob lecture him on the situation confronting him? This was the United States, not a nation dominated by a medieval aristocracy.

Lyons continued, apparently oblivious to Lincoln's growing discomfort. "And the situation with France could only get worse. Napoleon III has gotten himself into something of a mess in Mexico. His puppet ruler, the emperor Maximilian and his wife, the empress Carlotta, are barely hanging on. The brave Mexicans don't want any foreign power governing them. They are back fighting savagely."

Lyons continued. "Maximilian is convinced that your government is providing covert aid to the indigenous Mexicans."

Lincoln smiled tightly. "We have a little item we call the Monroe Doctrine, your Lordship. You will note the French waited until we were embroiled in the current conflict before making their move in Mexico. While we cannot as yet confront them directly, we will use whatever means we can to make their Mexican sojourn uncomfortable."

"Monroe Doctrine," Lyons said in a dismissive tone. "Mr. President, many in France, as well as a number in Great Britain, feel that Mexico is not ready for nationhood. They believe it is true of all the Latin American countries. Just look at all the wars and upheavals that have occurred since they forced Spain to leave Mexico."

Lyons had a point, but Lincoln would not concede it. "While we have not been able to enforce the Monroe Doctrine because of the greater war we are fighting against the Confederacy, I'm sure both

Great Britain and the French realize that once this war is over we will assist the Mexicans in driving the French out of Mexico."

"Unless, of course," said Lyons, "France is firmly ensconced in Mexico and is allied with Great Britain. In that case, the Monroe Doctrine would be nothing more than an interesting bit of philosophy that somebody thought to write down."

Having made their points, they diverted the conversation to less bothersome topics. Seward took the opportunity to ask Lyons a question concerning a matter that he had been pursuing.

"What's that? Russian Alaska?"

"Yes, sir. What is Britain's interest in that region?"

Seward had a bee in his bonnet about the czar's North American territories. As Lincoln understood it, the Comte de Tocqueville's study *Democracy in America* (Unread as yet by Lincoln—there were many worthy volumes awaiting him. When this was all over, he'd have to make up a list.) had predicted that the great national rivalry of the epoch to come would be between the United States and Imperial Russia. Seward had developed a firm belief that Alaska must be acquired to gain an advantage.

"Sir, I assure you that Great Britain has no interest whatsoever in a barren icefield."

Seward sat back, looking far more content.

A British nobleman annoyed by the work of a French count concerning Russian territory while in Washington D.C. *There*, thought Lincoln, *was the makings of a first-rate yarn*.

". . . please believe me, sir," Lyons said as the meeting drew to a close. "when I say that I want nothing more than for the Union to prevail. But this cannot deteriorate into another Thirty Years War. There must be progress and it must occur soon. Bluntness may not be diplomatic, but I must bluntly implore you to solve your command problems. There is no reason for the Union to lose this war. You have all the tools and resources. You lack only the man to lead you to victory."

It took several scrubbings for the blood to come off Richard Dean's skin, leaving him raw and feeling as if he'd been lightly burned. The clothes he'd been wearing had been burned as trash. Nobody noticed. Burning trash was just one way of getting rid of it and one more fire in a city that was suffering through dozens of them.

Mary Nardelli handed him a clean shirt and helped him pull it over his head. Despite the fact that he'd been standing naked in his own room, there had been nothing sexual about the situation.

"Did you enjoy it?" she asked.

"Enjoy what?"

"Killing those two men, Richard. Did it give you pleasure to stab them and watch them die as their blood poured all over the floor?"

"Lord, that is lurid. Have you been indulging in those terrible books that sell for a penny?"

"You forget, sir, that I am Italian," she smiled.

"Well, let me assure you that I did not enjoy it. First, I was afraid for my life and, second, those were human beings whose life I snuffed out."

"Would you do it again?"

"If I had to, of course. But there is nothing that says I would have to like it."

"That's reassuring, Richard. You're a nice but confused man and I would not like to see you turn into a monster."

"Or an Italian." He laughed. She was several years younger than he and not terribly attractive. He thought she liked him and he liked her but could not see himself taking her to bed. Unless, of course, he was totally desperate. This had not yet been the case. There were enough whores along the Baltimore waterfront to satisfy an army.

"Mary, how did you meet Booth?"

She giggled impishly. "Are you implying that I'm not his type? Well you're right, I'm not. He prefers them much prettier than plain little me. I met him because I chased him. At first he was annoyed when I kept showing up, but then he thought it was funny. I let him seduce me and that pleased him. If you're curious, we did it once and there was no second time. And he wasn't really all that good in bed."

Richard roared with laughter. So the fabulously famous John Wilkes Booth wasn't a great lover. How wonderful. Mary really was a sweet thing. Perhaps he should go to bed with her and find out if he was better than John Wilkes Booth. And he had lied to little Mary Nardelli. He had enjoyed the hell out of butchering those two men and would love doing it again.

Both Confederate troops and Rebel sympathizers were angry, and this included the criminals who passed themselves off as soldiers. The cause of their anger was what they described as the murder of the beloved Jeb Stuart. Direct communication with the Confederates didn't happen, but it didn't have to. Marauders had decided to become their own versions of Jeb Stuart's cavalry, forgetting the fact that neither Stuart nor his troops intentionally committed atrocities. They were soldiers, not bandits.

Cassie and Mariah had overstayed at the latest place that Hadrian called home and it had turned dark as they drove their carriage back into the city. At least they were close to the Union lines. The fortifications surrounding Washington City were massive and all encompassing. It was a shame that contraband camps were forced to locate outside the safety of the defenses. She suspected that racial animosity was at the root of it. The average northern soldier could not abide Negroes and wanted them back south where they could be free alongside their white neighbors. That the whites would kill the blacks, or at least try to, was of no concern.

It was a dangerous world, and now they were two women foolishly alone in the dark. They had been offered an escort, but had declined. Hadrian hadn't been there, otherwise he would have insisted. This close to the defenses, the two women had decided that they did not need an escort.

But other people did.

They heard shots and the screams. They came from several hundred yards down the narrow dirt road.

"Should we turn around?" asked Mariah.

"And go where?" snapped Cassie. She was driving and held the reins tightly.

They could hear the thunder of horses' hooves coming down the road from the other direction. They would be trapped if they didn't do something quickly.

"There," said Mariah as she pointed to a path that probably led to some farmer's house.

Cassie turned the carriage quickly and headed down the road. After a hundred yards or so, she halted.

"Why are we stopping?" asked Mariah.

"If we keep moving we make noise and motion can be seen. I want us to become invisible."

They hopped off the carriage and held the horses' heads down to prevent them from whinnying. Seconds later, a number of horsemen cantered past the cowering women. As hoped, they weren't noticed. The horsemen appeared to have rifles and, a moment later there was a fresh eruption of gunfire.

"We stay right here," said Cassie. "We wait for the dawn or for the arrival of the army."

A scream pierced the air and they shuddered. More screams followed. "Those are women," Mariah said, "and we can guess what's happening to them."

Cassie squeezed her eyes together until tears came. The cries became sobs and then silence. They simply did know what to do. That people would be looking for them was a given and their route back to Washington was a constant. They decided that they would simply wait. They were cold, thirsty, and hungry, but no one had noticed them.

Just after dawn, Cassie walked down the trail towards the road. Even though it was far more difficult and doubtless was ruining her dress, she stayed off the path and in the brush. When she reached the road she stopped, looked and waited. She wasn't alone for long. Mariah came to her side. Her clothes were tattered and covered with leaves and twigs. Despite her concerns, Cassie managed to smile.

"You look awful. May I assume I do as well?"

"Indeed. And nobody's come down this road? That's surprising."

"Not for long," Cassie said. Her ears had picked up the sound of horses approaching. They ducked back into the brush and well into the shadow. Moments later, several troops of Union cavalry trotted past them.

They yelled and screamed and the column halted. They explained their situation and their commander detailed a troop to stay with them and escort them to the Bairds' house. The troopers helped get their carriage onto the road.

"I'm not too sure you ladies want to be seeing what's up here," the officer said. "We got word that it was a real nasty raid."

"We heard much of it," Cassie said. She was mildly amused that the young Yankee had referred to Mariah as a lady. She was, of course, but she was also a colored woman.

They didn't have to travel far to arrive at the scene of the carnage. Bodies had been laid out in a neat row and covered by blankets. They were all fully clothed except for three who were women. She could tell because their bare feet stuck out from the blankets. Articles of women's clothing were strewn about.

"You don't have to look at this," Mariah whispered.

"Yes I do," Cassie said firmly. "If this is what war is about, then everyone should see."

A quarter-hour later they were back home. There were hugs, cries, and recriminations, and Cassie admitted that she'd been very foolish, that she'd endangered both herself and Mariah. She should never have left that late and should have insisted on an armed escort, although she wondered just what use an escort would have been. Those other travelers had been more numerous and armed, and what good had it done them?

An hour later, they were clean and in fresh clothing. Mariah was in the kitchen, where a friend of Hadrian's was waiting, and Cassie had joined the others in the parlor. Steve had also arrived.

Josiah Baird's hand shook as he took another healthy swallow of Kentucky bourbon, his favorite. "If you ever do anything like that again, you'll send me to my grave."

"I understand," she said, sincerely contrite. "But what I don't understand is what makes the Confederates behave in such a barbaric manner."

Thorne answered. "Don't count on those raiders being Confederates. As close as they were to Union lines, my bet is that they were Union deserters out to prey on the helpless. And just to be truthful, it isn't only the Confederates who are becoming outlaws. If you're down South and close to a place with a Union garrison, you'll see Union patrols seizing crops and cattle and from there it's a small step to outright banditry. No, Cassie, there are no saints in either army. When there are no police or soldiers to maintain order, then people become like wild animals. Not everyone, of course, but enough to create terrible situations like that of today."

Cassie's hands shook. She'd had a couple of glasses of sherry and was feeling it. The events of the night and the day were overwhelming her. She needed sleep. She wondered if her parents would let her nap with Steven beside her. Not likely, she decided. "I have learned a terrible lesson this day and I will not forget it. I will also try to learn from it."

★ CHAPTER 12 ★

Otto had become a celebrity of sorts after the shooting of Jeb Stuart. Everyone wanted to shake his hand and the story got embellished with each telling, although not by him. He told it straight, and now people thought he was playing too humble. Now the range of the shot had been extended to more than a mile and the night had been pitch black. All the new versions didn't have, Otto thought whimsically, was him having his rifle hanging upside down while shooting between his legs.

On a more positive note, he and Martha had gotten married the next day. With his newfound celebrity, there was no problem finding a pliant Lutheran minister. After that he'd been given time for a brief honeymoon. Otto and Martha had made love almost every minute of every day. They were trying to make up for all those days lost in the past. He'd also gotten promoted and had another stripe sewn to his sleeve.

Too soon, it was over and he returned to duty, where he found a note saying that General Couch wanted to see him as soon as he returned. And yes, he should bring his rifle.

He managed to find a clean uniform and reported. Couch returned his salute and shook his hand. "Damn fine shooting, young man. Is it true that the distance was over a thousand yards, in the dark?"

"Nein, mein Herr . . ." Otto said, in his nervousness slipping into his mother tongue. "Uhh . . . no sir. No more than four hundred yards."

"Yet you still managed to slip away?"

"The Rebels were thrown into utter confusion, sir."

"Nicely done. I sent a dispatch to Washington advising them of your feat. They could use the good news."

Otto smiled, though actually he was less than pleased. The fewer Rebels learned his name, the happier he would be.

General Couch was a small man and looked frail. Rumors had him being very ill on a number of occasions. So how did that square with his being such a fighter?

"Your action against Stuart has caused a lot of people to think, and that includes me. I have guards, it is true. I would hope a sufficient number of them. However, their task is to form a defensive circle around me and protect me from any close-in dangers. On the other hand, your successful attack on Stuart showed the futility of all that." The general eyed him a moment. "What I need is a hunter, someone who can operate at a decent distance, stalk trouble, and snuff it out. Someone familiar with such action, who knows how to carry it out, and is aware of what to look for. Do you find the description intriguing?"

"Yes, sir."

"Good, now let me see that rifle, Sergeant." Otto took it out of the leather case and handed it over. The general took it in his hands and admired it. "How the devil did you get the money to buy this rifle? . . . and if you did anything illegal, I don't want to hear a word."

Otto grinned. "Nothing illegal, I assure you, sir. When it became obvious that I was going into the army, I simply worked harder, saved, and some of my new friends here in this country gave me the rest of the money. If I was going to fight, I wanted the best weapon money can buy. I already had a reputation as a shooter, so it struck me as wise to get the best rifle I could. I have a specially modified 1860 Colt as a handgun."

Couch chuckled. "Sounds like you don't want to fight fair, son."

Otto shook his head. "Nothing's fair about war, sir."

Couch passed the Whitworth to several other senior officers. Catching Otto's expression, he laughed. "Nobody's going to steal it, Sergeant."

"Sorry, sir."

"Don't be. Now what do you think of yourself and maybe a couple of others being my long-range security detail? It might just keep you out of the next big battle that everyone knows is coming down the road. And I know it would make your young bride happy."

Did everyone know about his personal life, he wondered? "General, I'd be proud to serve under you."

"Excellent. My aide will have your orders cut posthaste and you'll begin your new job as my guardian angel just about right now."

"Thorne, would you like to take this train out for a while?"

General Meigs was clearly proud, and why not? The train was a marvel. It consisted of a pair of locomotives, a coal tender, three flatbed cars, and a caboose. The flatcars were edged with sandbags, covered with tarps, to a height of a man's chest. The train rested on a spur that led to the New Jersey Avenue Station of the Baltimore and Ohio Railroad. As this was an extremely busy station, the train itself was, in effect, hiding in plain sight.

"If you order me to, sir, I'll take it to hell and back. As long as I have a choice, however, I think I'll stick to my horse and bring up the chase."

"Do you think it'll work, son?" Meigs asked grimly.

"It might. Depends on how badly they want that money. We know that they already spent the greenbacks from the first robbery, so an attack wouldn't surprise me."

Meigs smiled. After all, this semi-armored train had been his idea. The sandbagged flatcars held a platoon of infantry each and firing holes had been worked into the bags. If nothing else, there was complete agreement that the Confederate attackers were in for a nasty shock. Still, the Confederate force that had attacked the earlier train would be large enough to overwhelm the men behind the sandbags. That was where Thorne came in. The men on the train were infantry, while his men would be mounted. The engineer would be ordered to maintain a slow enough speed to attract the Rebels, yet not be so fast as to let them slip away from the men on horseback.

They would be cutting it very close. The flatcars could be overwhelmed in a matter of minutes. The soldiers could be massacred and yet more money seized to assist the Confederate cause.

"Welcome to the White House, the President's House, or whatever you want to call the disgusting place." Booth leaned over and whispered conspiratorially. "I prefer to call it the Gorilla's Den. But not too loudly. There are those who might take umbrage. But we'll have the last laugh, young Dean. Don't you worry yourself about *that*."

Booth had simply dropped by Dean's apartment in Baltimore and said let's go to Washington. With a little bit of makeup and a few tufts of fake hair, Richard was transformed into someone who worked on the docks or in a factory. Booth had done the same for himself and they laughed as they left the apartment.

"Where are we going?" Richard asked.

"To the White House to see the king," Booth laughed.

A few hours later found them in the capital of their enemy, the United States of America. Booth rested one foot on the stone retaining wall and stared at the building. "This place is nothing," said Booth. "You should see the true palaces of Europe. You could put the White House in a closet and still have room left over. A circus cage for a trained ape, that's what this is."

He eyed Dean. "You want to see him?"

"Well . . . why not?"

"Then go right ahead." He pointed toward the line stretching out the front of the place. "It's the People's House. You can walk right in. Maybe you'll run into him shambling down the hallways. I've heard he does that since he's lost so many battles."

"But . . . you mean alone?"

Booth nodded. "Old Abe is a theater hound. Likes the bright lights and the pretty ladies. He might well recognize me." He smiled. "Not you, though."

Dean made his way toward the long line, looking back over his shoulder at Booth more than once.

"Long wait," said the well-dressed young man just ahead of him.

"Why don't they give up?" asked Richard.

"Would you give up if you had the chance to talk to a man who could change your life?"

After a surprisingly short time he was inside the building, facing a staircase leading to the second floor. A large red-faced man was pushing his way down. "Sumbitch ain't giving away anything today, boys."

"Giving away what?" asked Dean.

"Jobs, sonny. Everybody's done it before him. It's called Lar-Chess, boy. He makes me a postmaster or a county sheriff, then I gets a lot of money and he gets my undying gratitude and support."

The red-faced man departed. Dean hunched his shoulders. He was half-convinced somebody was about to lay hands on him from behind and drag him off. He had a sudden nightmare vision of Colonel Baird limping down those stairs, shouting and waving his stick as he caught sight of him.

Stepping from the line, he began moving toward the open doorway. But Booth was waiting. He'd know that Dean hadn't been inside long enough to see Lincoln. He'd ask him what Lincoln had said, and what would he tell him? Booth would know he was lying. What would he say then?

Dean turned back to the stairway. He stood rubbing his arm for a long moment. Then he started toward the stairs.

A few of the petitioners shouted at him, telling him to wait his turn. But most just stared at him quizzically as he made his way up the stairs. At last he pushed his way past the man waiting at the top and walked out onto the landing. And there he was, right through the open door.

Lincoln was sitting behind a desk, resting his head on one hand as he spoke to the man seated opposite him. His voice was so low that Dean could not make out the words. Lincoln's eyes looked sad and he was very thin. The man got up and Lincoln smiled and shook his hand. When the man turned, he looked slightly disappointed by not really unhappy. It was if he'd gotten something more interesting than just a job.

Dean studied Lincoln as the man at the head of the line went in. He didn't look like an ape. He didn't look like a devil. He didn't look anything at all like what Dean had expected—though he couldn't quite say what he'd actually expected in the first place. Something out of a political cartoon? Something like Booth's word-pictures? It was suddenly all very vague and hard to recover in the face of this patient, smiling man.

A thought struck Dean at that moment: suppose he was to go in there right now and announce to Lincoln: "I am here to warn about a grave, impending danger. There is a plot afoot aimed at yourself, sir, a dastardly scheme to lay hands on you and deliver you to—"

"What are you doing, fella?"

All visions of a grateful president and an admiring nation vanished from Dean's mind as he turned to see a grim, square-faced man advancing on him. He was wearing a dark frock coat and a derby hat. He looked a like a police detective. "I said, what are you doing?"

The waiting job-seekers snickered behind him. "I . . . I just wanted to see the President."

"Well, you've seen him. Let's go." He grabbed Dean by the arm and pushed him toward the stairs.

"What's this, Crook?"

The last petitioner was just leaving the room. Behind him appeared Lincoln. He was stretching his legs before him as if he'd been sitting for a little too long.

"He was trying to jump the line, sir."

"Oh no . . ." Dean said. "I wasn't . . . I didn't . . . I'm not asking for anything. I was in town visiting and I just wanted you to know how much we all appreciate everything you've done. For the country. And everybody."

Lincoln blinked in surprise. "Sweet Lord . . . Here's someone who doesn't want the sun, moon, and evening stars to play with." He smiled down at Dean, then reached out and shook his hand. Dean was surprised by the strength of his grip.

Dean smiled openly as he was led away. "Well, you cheered him up, sonny. That's something, anyway. Now be off with you."

The men waiting in line smirked as he descended the stairs. Dean paid them no mind. At the bottom he stopped to look back up the stairs once again, then left the building to find Booth.

Precisely on time, the train rolled slowly down the tracks. The locomotives and caboose had been freshly painted black and seemed to shine. At six in the morning only a handful of passersby were present in the station. Most took a single incurious look and moved on. One prosperous-looking gentleman asked what the sandbags were supposed to protect and a soldier said it was to keep what they were shipping dry in case it rained. What were they shipping, the man asked? Rice, was the reply. Satisfied, the man walked off.

"Who decided on the name?" Thorne asked.

Meigs grinned. "I did. I thought the 'Spirit of Columbia' painted in red on the side of the lead locomotive was uplifting. It's also where I was born."

"Wonderful choice, sir," said Thorne, and both men laughed.

"There's supposed to be six million freshly printed dollars in the boxcar," added Meigs. "I guess I can tell you that no real money is being shipped. It's all counterfeit."

"Sir, I think it's time I joined the rest of my regiment."

"It is indeed, son. And good luck if you do confront the bastards."

Thorne saluted and the two men shook hands. The regiment was waiting about two miles away and with luck, away from prying eyes. One hundred and twenty mounted infantry would clamber aboard and fill in the sandbagged squares, while the rest of the Sixth Indiana would be mounted and would attempt to keep up with the train.

That should not be too difficult. Thorne had absolute faith in Archie Willis to keep the speed down.

Soldiers were swarming over the flatcars searching for comfortable spots. A tarp was being spread to both hide the men and provide a level of shade. The men had been told to bring extra canteens and water, along with food from a mess hall that had been opened up just for them. If there was no Confederate attack, the men would have a lovely picnic.

Finally, the train was loaded. Someone yelled "all aboard" and it began to crawl forward. An enormous cloud of black smoke mushroomed from the smokestack and settled on the soldiers on one car who swore and yelled, to the delight of the men on the others.

"I hope this works," said Meigs. "We can't continue chasing will-o'-the-wisps. We need to get on top of this thing and end it."

There was nothing to say, so Thorne prudently said nothing.

Provost Marshal agent Charles Rutherford waved happily as he spotted his new friend, Josiah Baird, at the back of the restaurant. The seating was strategic for both of them. As a police officer, Rutherford always wanted to be seated so he could catch the comings and goings of the clientele. Prior to the war, his powers of observation had enabled him to identify and arrest lawbreakers as their meals were being served. The criminals had always been astonished. Some had complained that being collared before eating was somehow unfair and that they should at least be allowed to finish their meal. They were assured that their meals would not go to waste.

Baird chose his seat for much the same reason, but without any particular target in mind. He simply wanted to observe who arrived with whom and who left with whom. His business rivals were always choosing sides, either for him or against him, and it behooved him to stay alert. He was the predator and had no urge to be reduced to being prey.

The two men shook hands and Rutherford took his seat. He saw the waiter and signaled him over. When the man left with their order, it was time to talk. "First of all, Charles, how is life in your new world?"

"Once upon a time my world was peaceful and serene. All I had to do was chase and catch criminals within the military and it wasn't very difficult since most of them were foolish sods. But not now. It is a hurtful world, both physically and emotionally. This war could end tomorrow and the hatreds would last forever. It's been said that a civil war is the worst possible conflict. It splits families apart and destroys friendships. I'm sure you've heard that several of Mary Todd Lincoln's relatives are active Confederates, who have chosen to ostracize her. This has put a great stress on the President's marriage."

Baird thought it well past time to change the subject. "And how goes your search for the leak? Who is informing the Rebels about the money shipments?"

Rutherford shook his head. "There are only a handful of higher-up people who are privy to that information, and they, sir, have been investigated time and again. We've even set traps, but caught nothing."

Baird relit his cigar. "Then perhaps, sir, you are looking in the wrong places. Don't clerks and others have that information? Aren't they the ones who actually make the schedules and pass them upwards for approval?"

Rutherford clamped down on his unlit cigar. "Could well be. But that's the thing. Do you have any idea how many clerks there are in the War Department alone? Washington is crawling with them. The number could run into the hundreds."

"Well then, my friend, you'd best get started."

The wig-wag signals told anyone who could see them that the train was on its way. Wade's hundred-plus cavalry were primed and ready. Somewhat uselessly, a Union balloon could be seen as a black dot floating in the distance. He wondered what the men in the balloon could see. He shook his head. It was time to return to reality.

They were three miles from the site of the first attack by Wade's

Volunteers. In Wade's opinion, this was a much better position. His well-hidden troops could stay that way until the last minute.

The train was approaching at about twenty miles an hour when he gave the signal to light the fuses. The track blew with a satisfying roar with the train about a half a mile away. Perfect, Wade thought. But what the hell were all those sandbag barricades? Heads popped up and he could see men with rifles. The realization went through him like a shock: he'd been ambushed.

Wade tried to recall his troops, but they were wild to finish the attack and walked right into concentrated Union rifle fire. Dozens of his men and horses fell in sickening heaps. An aide grabbed his arm and pointed him towards the north where at least a hundred Union cavalry were approaching as fast as they could gallop.

"We'd better run," he said to Mayfield. A bugler sounded the call and the Tennessee Volunteers commenced pulling back. Several of his men had shells filled with gunpowder. These they lit and hurled at the flatcars packed with blue-coated figures. One exploded inside the wall of sandbags, sending several Union soldiers into the air. Another Volunteer chucked his package underneath a flatcar and the explosion broke the car in half.

Union reinforcements were close now, very close. Wade's remaining men smashed into the flank of the Union troops, scattering them. Wade and his men whooped and yelled as they retreated.

As Wade rode off, he checked on as many men as he could. They may have been driven off, but they weren't defeated. On the other hand, he would bet all the money in Washington that there never had been any cash in that armored freight car.

They'd been euchred and diddled again. Somebody had told the Yanks of their plans, just as the Yankees had found out about their own.

It had just cost too much to cut up some Federals. He would have to do much better. More likely, however, they would have to find new targets.

It was a delightful day. Outside, fall was in its glory as the leaves started to change from vibrant green to yellow. Thorne had just been congratulated by Meigs and had his hand shaken by a thoroughly pleased Henry Halleck. Even better, a radiantly smiling Cassandra

Baird stood beside him and held onto his arm so tightly that she might have been afraid it would fall off. The railroad menace was not over— far from it. But now they had a tactic that, even if it didn't work all the time, would keep the southerners off balance and alert to enemy forces that might not even exist. The Army of Northern Virginia had just had its lunch stolen. It felt good. Morale was sky high and the Sixth Indiana had begun receiving reinforcements and he'd been promised the time to train them. Of course, that depended on the whims of Robert E. Lee.

Later that afternoon, Thorne issued himself a three-day pass and headed directly for the District of Columbia. He detoured through Washington to drop off some reports that would probably not be as detailed as the War Department would like before heading for the Bairds'.

Inside the city's defenses swirled a mass of humanity, much of it in uniform. Washington's roads were unpaved and rains had reduced them to mud that was further churned up by passing soldiers. Mud, plus horse dung, plus the feet of tens of thousands of soldiers, had turned the roads into deep quagmires. Nor were the city's parks any better or cleaner. The Mall between the capitol and the Potomac River was a stinking horror. Trash and garbage flowed freely and every dawn showed the bodies of men and animals floating in the city's creeks. The lawn itself was covered by soldiers or refugees. It seemed that every available place to pitch a tent was taken. He wondered just how many more people could fit into Washington before the city exploded. He was thankful that he was only passing through.

He left the city behind and rode northwest through much cleaner and more pleasant county. All the same, he arrived at the Bairds' house dirty and angry. He slipped Lem, their stable boy and all-round hand, some coins to clean his tired horse and give it a good rubdown. The poor dumb thing deserved so much better.

In order to keep the carpets clean, he entered through the kitchen. Cassandra spotted him immediately and smiled warmly. "You stink," she said happily. "Fortunately, I had a suspicion you'd come in smelling like a piggy so I've got some bath water heating and a clean uniform is being ironed while we speak."

"You are a pearl beyond price, or whatever the Bible said."

"I certainly am and, no, I am not going to wash your back or any other part of your anatomy you'd desire me to clean."

The water was only lukewarm, but the soap was strong and took care of the filth that was caked on the lower part of his body. After a number of scrubbings and rinses he decided enough was enough. He dressed in a uniform that he'd prudently decided to keep at the Bairds' residence. Dinner was nothing special, just cold meat, fresh bread, and butter. But Cassie was present, which made it a banquet fit for a king.

"Steven, as you've said so many times, this cannot go on forever. I too was in the city and I have no idea where all these people go at night. Perhaps they hide in caves or under rocks. I just don't know."

"I do and I almost wish you wouldn't ask."

"Tell me," she insisted.

"Cassie, the army has controls and General Meigs' organization to ensure that the soldiers are fed and dry. However, the civilians go anywhere and everywhere to get food and shelter. They eat whatever they find no matter how bad it might smell or taste. And the plight of the children is gut-wrenching."

"What can be done for them?"

"Ending the war would solve a lot of problems."

"I know that there are charitable groups trying to help them, but they are so few. Why doesn't President Lincoln do something, and don't tell me it's because the war takes priority."

"Then I will remain silent." He yawned. "And I think I should get some sleep before I say something I might regret. These are terrible times, Cassie. Just think—here we are enjoying ourselves while a deadly and determined enemy is only a few miles to the north and west."

She agreed that they should say no more. They kissed and went no farther. This was neither the time nor the place. They smiled and went their separate ways to their separate rooms.

Across the lawn and the dirt road, neither had noticed a lone horseman pull up and take out a small, cheap telescope and aim it at the house. Richard Dean knew that Cassandra Baird, the bitch who had nearly gotten him hanged, was only about a hundred yards away from him. Oh, how he longed to take vengeance on her and the rest of her family! While he was somewhat satisfied to be working for John Wilkes Booth, he was beginning to think that Booth was a little mad.

Of course, Booth probably thought the same of him, now that he'd become a killer.

Dean was longer the tidy, educated gentleman that Cassandra Baird had once known. He was an agent of her country's enemy, hardened and brutal. A predator who had tasted blood, who had taken lives and would soon take more. He yearned to make that revelation to her. She would sneer at her first sight of him, those prissy little lips quirking with distaste. But then her expression would change—fear overtaking self-assurance, her mouth quivering, her eyes growing wide as he seized her, pounded her with his fists, tore her clothes off, and possessed her. She would whimper and cry and beg and call for her father, that old cripple. For that matter, he ought to start out by giving the old man a good beating, right in front of her. That would show the Bairds who Richard Dean was.

That day would come. Until then, he would maintain a high degree of self-control. He would also remain invisible to her. Booth would have been angry if he'd known that Richard had gotten so close to the Bairds. Not that he cared what Booth thought. He walked slowly and carefully to where he'd tethered his horse. He admitted that it had been a mistake to come so close to where Cassandra and the others were living, but the anticipation of his vengeance felt so good. He would be back.

Hadrian's latest place of refuge was, like the others, as close to the Union lines as he could make it. All the same, he wasn't a fool. He had no idea whether or not the bluecoats would defend and protect his colored charges. The Copperheads were becoming bolder and cannier. Just the night before, over the country line, a group of about fifty had attacked an equal number of contrabands, killed several and carried off a dozen others, all female.

Hadrian knew the South all too well. Many southern whites were live and let live, but others were simply vile, like the Romans of the preacher's Bible, lynching and beating when opportunities presented themselves. He was now considering moving his flock far to the north, someplace like Minnesota, or even farther, once he got a clear picture of how large the country was and what was where. He'd heard it got bitter cold up there come winter. That was good. That might discourage the southern whites from following them, but as for the northern whites . . . He shook his head.

They'd all heard rumors that Uncle Abraham wanted to send them all back to Africa, the supposed land of their origins. Trouble was, nobody knew anything about this place called Africa. Some of the older folk recalled it as the land from which they'd been captured by their own kind, people with skin as dark as their own, and then sold into slavery. Who the hell would *want* to go back to such a place? It was also a place with giant horned animals that liked to trample people and enormous wild cats the size of horses that stalked and ate people as well. Hadrian thought he could do without that.

Hadrian accepted that there was likely a high degree of exaggeration in those tales, but didn't want to be the first person to find out the truth. Then there was the question of who ruled Africa. They did not want to be sent back to those who'd sold them into slavery in the first place. And what language did the Africans speak? Hadrian laughed to himself when he thought of the difficulty some of his charges had with English.

"What's so funny?" asked Mariah as she stirred beside him. Unlike most other nights, she'd decided to spend the night with him. Cassie hadn't accompanied her to the camp this day, which made it easier for the two of them. Mariah felt responsible for Cassie, since she was such a naïve young woman. True, she had come a long way and was no longer in her self-inflicted emotional prison, but she still had a long way to go. Mariah despised Richard Dean for putting her there, but she was puzzled by someone who would allow herself to be deluded by a man who was such a snake. She'd tried to warn Cassie, but had been rebuffed. At least this Major Thorne seemed to be a decent sort and not one to go after her money.

"Go back to sleep," she ordered him firmly but gently. A few seconds later and his deep breathing showed that he'd complied.

"Once more, Mary. Just why does your pope think he needs an army?"

Mary Nardelli laughed, half out of good humor and half out of frustration. Richard Dean seemed to be totally unwilling to comprehend the complexities of life in nineteenth-century Italy.

"He doesn't, and that is at least part of the point. The pope is supposed to be appointed by God and God should not need an army. Yet he does because he owns lands called the Papal States which must be governed and government requires an army. Pius IX may be a good and holy man, but he is a prisoner of his own aristocratic world. He must be shaken free of it even if that means war for the Papal States against the rest of the freedom-loving world."

Dean yawned. "And just how does that affect you and me?"

"It affects us because the conflict has brought people like me across the Atlantic to fight for freedom. You want freedom from the dictators of the north and I am here to help you."

He grinned at her sincerity. She wanted so much to help him. "You support the South even though the South supports slavery?"

"Slavery will go away in its own good time. But what is even more wrong is the tyranny of the north. It simply amazes me that more people in Baltimore and Washington don't see that and haven't risen up."

Now Dean did laugh. "Perhaps it has something to do with thousands of General Butler's Union soldiers with their boots on their throats. It is awkward at best to think clearly from that position. All we want is the freedom to determine our own future and that of our property. Any attempt to take away our slaves would be nothing but stealing."

Mary nodded happily. "Have you met any of the others that Mr. Booth has recruited?"

"Some, and I have to admit I'm not terribly impressed. First, Booth's idea that the two groups, Baltimore and Washington, should be kept separate, seems to be falling apart. I thought it was a good idea. Second, at least a couple of the Washington recruits seem to be very slow mentally. I cannot help but wonder just how they will stand up when we go into action."

"I agree, Richard, but I can only hope that Mr. Booth and the others that back him have a good idea what to do."

"Mary, what others are you talking about?"

"Richard, surely you must realize that Mr. Booth could not have thought of this and planned it all by himself. He just isn't all that smart. He must have backers and they must be powerful people in either the Confederate government or some other nation, like Great Britain or France."

The idea of powerful nations supporting the Confederacy pleased him. For a moment he allowed himself to think that he was at the forefront of a mighty endeavor, instead of being a confused deserter from the Union Army. Yes, with another nation's backing their plans might actually come to fruition. Perhaps he would live through this ordeal and survive to become a great hero. Perhaps too, he would see the day when Cassandra Baird would grovel at his feet. He would like that very much.

Annette Cosgrove had been crying a lot lately. What had begun as a game had devolved into a morass of violence and death. How could she have been so blind, so foolish? The north and the south were at war, and war was synonymous with death. She had exulted when the first raid on a train carrying cash had resulted in humiliation for the north and with no serious casualties. For some reason she had thought that would be the way of it. The Federal government would be robbed of its ill-gotten gains and her beloved South would be strengthened.

But of course, she should have realized that the feral north would lash out and punish those who dared defy it. Blood had been spilled, poor southern boys were dead, and it was all on her hands. Worse, there had to be those who suspected her of what they would call "treason." She had no doubts that what she was doing was right, so how could it be treason and she a traitor? Still, if the investigators who swarmed her office at the Treasury could connect her to the attacks and subsequent deaths, she would hang. The thought of slowly choking and strangling terrified her.

So distraught had she become that she had taken the liberty of writing a letter to Booth seeking his guidance. She had not used the drop—she didn't trust Jessup, for one thing—but instead had sent it directly to his dwelling place, which she had discovered by following Jessup there one day after he had left the drop. As an introduction, she had mentioned how many times she had seen him perform, hoping that would soften his heart toward her. Then she had gone into her anxieties and fears concerning the raids and their results. A simple word from Booth would calm her fears, of that she was sure.

But she had heard nothing. It had been over a week, and there had been no reply at all.

The stress had affected her emotionally and she was now prone to outbursts of crying. Once had nearly fainted while at work. She'd passed it off by explaining that a dear young cousin had been killed near Chattanooga and that she'd only recently gotten the word. It had worked and she'd even gotten sympathy from her coworkers.

"How are you today, Miss Cosgrove?"

At the sound of the voice, she nearly jumped out of her skin. It was Mr. Rutherford from the Provost Marshal's office, and a deadlier enemy did not exist.

"You startled me, sir. You shouldn't do that to an old lady."

"I do not see any old ladies," he said graciously, "Just charming mature ones."

She recovered sufficiently to smile and even forced a simper. Rutherford was the most dangerous of the men investigating the source of the leaks. As usual, he was accompanied by a pair of young, tough-looking enlisted soldiers. She assumed they would jump into action if Rutherford simply pointed in her direction and said "arrest her." They were his attack dogs.

Rutherford nodded and moved on. She wished she had called in sick as she had so many times before. But that was a card she could not play too often. Too many times sick and she might be dismissed. The job didn't pay very much, but it was her sole source of income. Without it she would be destitute and on the streets. She was trapped. She had relatives down south near Charleston, but they might as well be on the moon for all the good they could do for her.

Across the noisy and crowded room full of overworked and underpaid clerks, she spotted Rutherford speaking to her supervisor. He turned his head, and it seemed to Annette that he was staring directly at her. Lowering her head, she pretended to be busy with her work.

★ CHAPTER 13 ★

The Sixth Indiana had a large area to patrol and they took their job seriously. Thorne thought that it was too much territory to handle, but his complaints fell on deaf ears. Along with watching out for the unlikely forward move by Lee, there was the constant possibility of saboteurs entering Union lines. With lines now stable, the Army of the Potomac had accumulated vast quantities of supplies. All were considered targets.

"Just who thought they saw something, Captain?" asked Thorne.

"Several of the boys," said Willis. "Granted the damned rain has washed away most of the footprints, but they were pretty certain that they led from the road into the storage depot."

"Dismount," ordered Thorne, "and let's spread out and see what we can find."

The men had done this before, many times before. Any sense of excitement had long since disappeared. Whatever human trace somebody had thought they had seen would likely be nothing more than somebody taking a shortcut or a drunk looking for a place to pee. It wasn't even a break in the monotony of camp life.

Thorne and Willis tried to set a good example. Their pistols were drawn and ready. "Dear God, there is so much of this," Willis said as they walked through small mountains of wooden crates.

"Don't forget it's not all ours. We're sharing this cornucopia with the division and, who knows, maybe the corps."

"And all of it'll burn, even though it's been raining," said Willis. "Let us not forget that Rebel saboteurs have become very adroit at setting fires. I hear rumors that half of Baltimore has been torched, along with a good deal of Washington. Washington they can burn, but I rather like some parts of Baltimore."

They were moving as quietly as two companies of dismounted infantry could, which meant they were making a considerable amount of noise. The crash, when it came, startled them and everyone froze. It was as if a whole pile of boxes had collapsed.

"I don't think that was a squirrel," Willis said. Now the men moved forward more purposefully, weapons at the ready.

They reached the point where they thought they'd heard the noise. "Surrender and come out," yelled Thorne.

"Come and get us, you goddamned Yanks."

Us, thought Steve. There was more than one man or at least he said there was. They smelled something burning. "Those are fuses," a soldier yelled. "He's gonna blow us all up."

With that, the men began to withdraw. In an instant, almost everyone was running. Thorne cursed. There was no ammunition or gunpowder stored here, was there? Nobody in the Quartermaster service could be that stupid, could they?

Just as the men were getting under control, something exploded, followed by loud popping. *Damn it to hell*, he thought. Some jackass had indeed stored black powder with the supplies, and it was blasting God alone knew what all over the place. Small fires were developing and he could see where they would quickly form into larger fires, rain or no rain.

The area alarm had been sounded and hundreds of men were running up and forming bucket brigades to put out the fires, all the while ducking as the powder exploded. Fortunately, the exploding missiles flew at low velocity. Still, nobody wanted to be hit by a piece of flying wood or metal.

Several hundred men with shovels slowly brought the fires under control. It helped that the rain increased, drowning the smaller fires. Steve ordered a nose count of the regiment. With everyone all mixed up, it took a while to ascertain that no one had been killed, though three men had been injured or burned badly enough to require medical care.

"We're going to need more guards," Willis said. Steve concurred. They were already stretched thin and this would not help. His shadow of a regiment had just too much responsibility.

"We're comin' out." Someone called from within the smoke. "We surrender." Three men, their clothes smoking, emerged from the flames and the ashes. Two of them were coughing and retching uncontrollably. The third looked warily between Thorne and his men. His facial hair had been badly singed, his face covered with ash. He looked like a burned rat.

The Rebel hopped backward as a trooper swung a shovel at him.

"That's enough," Thorne shouted.

"In the name of God, get us some water. We got trapped when the fire got too big. We thought we was gonna die."

"I say shove 'em back in," said Willis.

The first bucket was splashed directly on the men. Only then did the Union soldiers allow the Rebels to drink. They swallowed the water in huge gulps, though one seemed to cough most of it back up.

Thorne shook his head. "I don't know if you men are the bravest I know or the dumbest. What the hell were you thinking of, setting off explosions like that?"

The Rebel laughed as best he could. "Hell, we didn't know some fool put ammunition in there. We was just thinking of all the hurt we'd be putting on you Yankees by destroying all your supplies."

"You think this is all we got?" asked an incredulous Willis.

"Well, hell yes," said the first man. He smiled broadly, that typical jackass Rebel smirk made all the more infuriating by the gray ash surrounding it. "You may have some other piles of shit here and there, but this has got to be the truly major one. We've really set your asses back a long time."

Thorne did not reply. If the Rebels thought that this was a "major" depot, did it indicate that the enemy was running low on supplies again? Maybe the great raid across central Pennsylvania hadn't been such a flaming success after all. The damage to this storage depot had been significant, but it was nothing that wouldn't be replaced before this time tomorrow.

If this was what a group of Rebels thought was a large stockpile, what did the Confederates actually have as reserves?

★ ★ ★

Otto Bauer took his job of protecting Major General Darius Couch very seriously. Of course there were guards around the headquarters, but they were tasked with protecting the whole operation and not just the general.

The duty was a hell of a lot better than being an ordinary soldier. He didn't have to worry about inspections or even keeping regular hours. And with the weather turning bad, he didn't have to slog through the mud.

Couch was a physically small man in his early forties, which should have put him in his prime. Instead, he was nervous and insecure and complained of a number of physical ailments. Otto overheard a number of soldiers wondering if the command was too much for him. Perhaps that was why he kept seeing danger in the shadows. But if the man wanted additional protection, then Otto and his friends would provide it. The simple fact of his presence seemed to calm the general.

Bauer spent his time looking for *die Besonderheit*—"anomalies" was the English word. He'd set a series of patrols in the area surrounding the camp, particularly the high, forested ridge to the east, which was the easiest avenue of approach. Otto, along with the two enlisted men assigned to him, both experienced hunters, swept the area at irregular intervals, looking for anything out of the ordinary.

He had found exactly that this afternoon. Clear signs that someone had visited the ridge, their tracks and the disturbed ground showing that their attention had been directed at the camp below.

He scratched at his mustaches as he walked just beneath the crest of the ridge. He was considering shaving them off. Molly had mentioned that her late husband had been clean-shaven, and Otto had detected a hint that she preferred it that way. Otto had first grown them back home, largely because so few men were wearing them. He'd gotten a lot of teasing, with people calling him the "Little Chancellor" or "Young Bismarck." Much as he'd detested being associated with that bloody-handed old butcher, he'd kept the mustaches out of simple defiance.

But over here it was different. When he'd first arrived, ten years ago, whiskers of any sort had been uncommon. But as soon as the war started, you saw them all over, some of them quite fantastic, such as those of General Burnside. Otto sometimes wondered if perhaps they might not do better leaping on horses and attacking the Rebels by themselves . . .

He paused and dropped into a squat. Otto gave a lot of credit to instinct. Thus, when he felt a draft on the back of his neck and the hairs seemed to come alive, he paid attention. Something had alerted him just now—he couldn't say what, a sound, a shadow, a change in the background buzz of the forest. He checked his '55 musket—his rifle was little heavy for this kind of duty—and the Colt on his belt. He cocked his head at a sound, a low voice *there*, ahead and to his right.

He got up and approached the patch of brush. Someone was behind it, of that he was sure. Carefully chosen to hide them from above? That would be his guess.

He found the thinnest part of the brush and, after a pause to listen, burst through with his musket barrel high. On the other side were two men in Union blue. They shot to their feet as Otto appeared. They had been studying the camp, clearly visible through the trees.

"Hey there, Sergeant," the smaller man said. His partner stood without speaking.

Otto nodded without answering.

"We're up here looking for a chicken got loose."

"A chicken? Ahh . . . chicken dinner's nice on a cool day. A fine stew, maybe."

The small man smiled and nodded. The other stuck his thumbs in his belt. "Where ya'll from, anyway? Germany, sounds like."

The other man's accent had been unremarkable, but this *Lümmel's* was clear enough. "And where are you from, Alabama?"

The man cursed and reached into his jacket. Otto drew his pistol and shot him in the knee. He fell howling, gripping his leg, his blood spraying out over the pine needles. The smaller man raised a hand, but Otto cocked his pistol and switched his aim between the two of them.

He heard shouts from the camp below. Men had begun running toward the ridge. Above him Otto heard the sound of running feet. A voice shouted, "Sergeant Bauer?"

"Here, Kernan," he called out.

The wounded man snarled up at him. "You done kilt Jeb Stuart, you sumbitch." The first man opened his mouth to speak but evidently thought better of it.

"Just like a goddamn sneak," the second man went on.

"*Ja?* And who's skulking around this hillside?"

Kernan burst through the brush and came to a halt, staring wide-eyed at the two Rebels.

"Here's our *spionen*," Otto told him.

"What?"

"Spies," Otto said. The first man lowered his eyes at the word. Otto told Kernan to search the two. He came up with two pistols and several knives.

By that time the men from the camp had reached them. They stood looking breathless between Otto and the Rebels. Otto gave them a brief explanation. "All right, let's bring 'em in," a lieutenant said.

"This one's wounded."

"He can walk."

"No, no, no—get him a stretcher."

The lieutenant bit his lip, but evidently thinking of Otto's relationship with the general, finally nodded.

"Go on," Otto gestured toward two enlisted men. "*Mit einem affenzahn.*"

He sat on a fallen branch, not looking at the two Rebels. They were spies, there was no question about that. They had seen their last sunrise. They would likely be hanged before dark. It was a pity—the smaller one looked like a decent fellow.

At last the stretcher came, and the two of them were led off the ridge. The lieutenant asked him if he wanted to come along, but Otto refused. General Couch would certainly have much to say, but he didn't need to hear it from him just now.

He watched as they descended the slope. Those two hadn't been after Darius Couch. Oh, maybe they had, but as an alternate target. No, they had been after one Otto Bauer, expert marksman, late of the Kingdom of Bavaria. They'd been looking for a German with a rifle, that was clear enough.

"What we do now?" Kernan, a fine woodsman, but nobody's idea of a scholar, wanted to know.

"We go back on patrol." He took in Kernan's expression. "You don't think they're the only Rebels in Pennsylvania, do you?"

Kernan considered it. "I suppose."

"Let's go." Otto shouldered the musket and started up the slope. He was fingering his mustaches when it occurred to him—he might not be able to help his accent, but there was certainly one thing he could change.

Those mustaches were going to go.

Abraham Lincoln stood waving a copy of the previous day's New York *Times*. Slightly older copies of the Detroit *Free Press* and the Chicago *Times* were scattered on the table. Their editorials all said the same thing. The White House, the government, and the army were all slacking. Robert E. Lee was making an international ass out of the American Republic. The Confederates had to be expelled from their stronghold in Pennsylvania posthaste.

"Stanton, this article has the gall to say that Washington City is withering and dying because it is in a state of siege. And there are other newspapers saying essentially the same thing. The implication is that people are starving or eating rats in order to survive. Worse is the publicity they are giving to those generals of ours who have tried and failed in the past. Do they actually think that McClellan would do any better today than he did earlier? Now the insufferable man wants to be President and not a victor in the battlefield."

Stanton laughed. "And what about the editorial that calls on you to give the command to Burnside for a second attempt at total disaster? Dear God, it is as if they never heard of Fredericksburg and the catastrophe of Marye's Heights. At least Burnside was an honest man. He said he wasn't qualified to command the Army of the Potomac and then went out and proved it."

Lincoln allowed himself a smile. "God save us from honest men."

"All of which brings us back to George Gordon Meade. He is and will remain commanding general until you make a change, sir, and it doesn't sound like you're ready to do that."

Lincoln looked out a window, keeping himself in the shadows in case a madman with a rifle was lurking about. As always, there was a large crowd around the White House and in the parks surrounding it. A good-sized group was forming to march. They had been present for the last several nights and they bore signs urging the President to launch the Army of the Potomac at the forces of Robert E. Lee. They didn't seem to care who commanded. They just wanted action, and Lincoln sympathized with them.

He stepped back from the window. He regretted not going to his second residence at the Soldiers' Home, where there would be a little more peace and quiet. Mary was already there, and she was feeling melancholy as she kept recalling the deaths of two of their children, Willy and Eddie. Now even Robert had come down with a fever.

"Edwin, I will direct General Meade to take the Army of the Potomac on the offensive. He will fight General Lee and let the chips fall where they may. If he can be the general he was during the first days of Gettysburg, we will be able to drive Lee from Pennsylvania. If not . . . then I will have a momentous decision to make regarding General Grant."

Stanton departed, leaving Lincoln alone with his thoughts. Once again he was launching the Union Army into a series of bloody battles. Visions of the thousands of dead and wounded that would result nearly overwhelmed him. He felt he could picture every last one of them—and they all had poor Willie's face. That was what made it so hard to bear; the fact that he knew exactly what they felt, those bereft parents in those homesteads all across the northern United States. And yes, the South, too.

He sat down on a couch, stretched out his long legs, and rubbed his forehead, trying to alleviate the anguish. Knowing as he did, feeling what he felt, made things very hard. But really, he wouldn't have it any other way.

"The war is our Sword of Damocles," Josiah Baird announced a trifle pompously. He'd had a couple of brandies and was on the edge of being tipsy. Steven thought it interesting that a man who was politically active could not do a better job of holding his liquor.

"It hangs over our head and threatens to destroy us and soon it will not matter whether the north or south wins. The damage to the United States will have been too severe to be repaired in our lifetime or a hundred lifetimes. We may come back to having one government, but there will be two nations enduring under it."

"And what's the solution?" asked his wife.

"Rachel, my dearest, there is but one answer. The war must end. Sadly, there seems to be no real interest in bringing it to a conclusion, even if that means additional fighting. The real curse is that good men must die in order for there to be a real peace."

Cassandra was shocked. "Father, are you saying that not enough blood has been shed already?"

Her father bowed mockingly and poured himself a little more brandy. "More than enough blood has been spent. The problem is getting people to realize it, and maintaining the status quo regarding General Lee and his omnipresent army in Pennsylvania is a case in point. Lee has to be expelled and, unless he decides to visit his family in Richmond, the only way to get rid of him will be through battle. Even if we should send him back to Virginia, we will only have reestablished the battle lines as they were before the Gettysburg campaign."

Thorne yawned. It had been a long day and he was feeling warm standing by the fireplace. He glanced across the parlor to where Cassandra sat, surprise still evident on her face.

"War is a terrible thing," Josiah said, "and a civil war is the most terrible of all. It would be one thing if we were fighting off an invasion of the Huns or some other barbaric entity, but no, we're killing off our cousins and brothers. Just about everyone I know has friends or relatives in the Confederacy and that includes us. I hope that doesn't upset you, Major Thorne."

Thorne laughed. "I have cousins in Charleston and New Orleans. Of course, I haven't seen or heard from them in years. I hope they're safe and well and out of the war."

"And I also don't think we're living in a state of siege," added Josiah.

"I wouldn't be too certain about that," Steven said. "Our movements are severely constrained by the presence of Lee to the west and north. Granted, Washington is not surrounded, but there are many who feel the city is in such danger that it should be evacuated. I believe, however, that these are the same people who ran like rabbits after the first battle of Bull Run. Lincoln was made of sterner stuff then and I don't see him changing now."

Cassandra was intrigued. "And what do the rumors say this time, Steven?"

"They say that President Lincoln has decided that the Army of the Potomac is as strong as it's ever going to be and that it should go on the attack. There are no secrets in this town and, even though it is only a rumor, it has the ring of truth. There's only one way General Lee can be driven back south and that's through battle."

A few moments later, Cassandra and Steven went out onto the porch. She had wrapped a shawl around her shoulders as protection from the cool evening air and let him put his arm around her. It was just about time for him to return to his regiment.

"The idea of another bloodbath battle is horrifying," she said. "Unfortunately, I cannot think of another way of ending this either. But it does have to end. This cannot be the opening days of another Hundred Years War. This has to end and if that means another battle, so be it. I just want you to try and stay out of it. You've seen enough action and you've been wounded." She turned and hugged him. "And I don't want to lose you."

Steven just held her. There was nothing he could add. Her fears were his as well. Would this war ever end? God only knew.

Richard Dean was tempted to get a placard of his own and march around the White House proclaiming his dislike of the war along with his contempt for Abraham Lincoln. But he decided against it when he saw how many police and provost marshal's men were watching the marchers. It seemed that the lawmen almost outnumbered them. So instead, he stepped back and let the fools parade by. Many of them were old men and women and he laughed silently at their sincerity. Did they really think anyone in the federal government would listen to them or give a damn what they thought? They were living a dream.

At least he, Booth, and the others had a plan. They were leaning toward assassination. Kidnapping Lincoln was just too complex and dangerous. Following an assassination, on the other hand, the killers could simply split up and flee or hide, while kidnappers had the task of controlling and hiding their victim. And then, of course, they would have to negotiate with the federals for the man's release, all of which could be quite perilous.

But what did the conspirators have to offer? When negotiations were over and a captive Lincoln was released, he would simply go back to his old tricks and doubtless renege on any agreement that had been made. He would claim that it had been made under duress which, of course, would be absolutely correct. He would have had a pistol at his head all the time.

The deciding factor against kidnapping was that they would have to be in contact with the government, which put them all at risk of getting caught and then hanged. No, it would be far better to kill the man, cause chaos in the government, and then flee to safety. The Confederacy was only a day's ride away.

The only unresolved question was just who would fire the gun. Booth was adamant that he be the one, but Richard thought it would boil down to which one of them had the opportunity.

He was so wrapped up in his thoughts that he almost bumped into a city policeman. "Excuse me," he muttered and the officer glared at him.

"Be more careful, young man." Dean solemnly assured him that he would. He turned and hurried away from the White House grounds, toward the rooming house where he shared a room with two other men, both government clerks. To them he was a nobody, a faceless clerk like themselves. Other than a handful of people, nobody had ever heard of Richard Dean. That was going to change.

Major General George Gordon Meade was uncertain, a feeling he'd been having frequently of late. The close-run victory at Gettysburg and the subsequent crushing defeat at Hagerstown had sucked much of the vigor from him. He had a history of being bad tempered and irascible and this day he was in a truly foul mood.

The summons to the White House had come as a complete surprise. He'd been all but ignored by Lincoln and Stanton since the debacle north of the Potomac, and expected the situation to continue until the president found a suitable replacement for him. That Lincoln was having a hard time with that was common knowledge. Meade was proud enough to know that he was at least as good as any of his contemporaries with the possible exception of the relatively unknown but inexperienced Ulysses Grant. He was confident that Grant would not replace him, at least not for a while. A crisis was brewing at Chattanooga that would require his handling. In the meantime, Meade would head the army and keep it ready to repulse any attempt by the Army of Northern Virginia to capture the nation's capital.

On receipt of the orders, he'd gone directly to see Lincoln and Stanton, huddled together as usual in the White House.

Meade fought to contain his temper. "Mr. President, your orders are astonishing. We are within weeks of the end of the year's campaigning season. Now you wish me to use the army to attack Lee? May I ask what has caused this shift?"

Lincoln was grim. "Reality, General, reality has changed my mind. The pressure to do something, anything, has simply become too much. The people want something done about Lee and they want it done as soon as possible. The army—your army—must march forth and attack General Lee wherever he might be found. And that raises a point—do you know precisely where Lee is?"

Meade bristled. "Of course we do and they know exactly where we are as well. Our patrols have been probing each other since Lee decided to camp. Their cavalry screen is very good, but not impenetrable, and besides, it is difficult to hide an army of that size."

Stanton grunted. "It won't matter what we know. As soon as he hears that you're on the move, he'll come out of his hole and attack. When he does that, can you whip him?"

Meade started to sweat. "If he attacks me, I will beat him, just like I did for the first three days at Gettysburg. But I will be honest. If I have to attack him, the advantage will be his. His army is much more maneuverable than mine. I have so many men now that I am afraid the Army of the Potomac will be quite cumbersome."

"Are you saying you now have too many men?" asked Stanton, aghast at the possibility that the Army of the Potomac was too large to control.

Meade's face turned red. "Of course not," he responded angrily. "A general can never have too many men. I'm merely pointing out that a smaller, more agile Confederate army will be able to maneuver more easily than mine."

Lincoln was not sympathetic. "General, you have more than a hundred thousand men to Lee's seventy or eighty thousand or so, or do you believe the reports that he outnumbers you?"

The President was referring to the fact that Allan Pinkerton, the owner and founder of the detective agency that bore his name, had again come out with estimates of Confederate manpower that appeared to wildly exaggerate Rebel numbers. This was consistent with the advice he'd given McClellan during the Peninsula Campaign of 1862. Pinkerton had fed McClellan with projected numbers that had the large Union Army greatly outnumbered, which fed the Little Napoleon's fears of defeat.

"Sir, we all know that Pinkerton's numbers are rubbish. I merely submit that any campaign against Lee will be a bloody one."

"Then so be it," said the President. "If at the end of the day, we have a few men standing and they have none, we will have won and we can begin to forge a peace."

Meade was calming himself as he saw the extent of Lincoln's wishes. "But sir, a peace built on so much blood? Is that even possible?"

Lincoln stood and gestured for the others to remain seated. "Unless the South sees reason and negotiates a true peace that involves the Confederate states returning to the Union and abolishing slavery, it will be a case of pay the blood price today or pay it tomorrow. May I suggest, General, that you return to your command and determine just when you will be able to bring General Lee to battle?"

Meade departed. He retrieved his horse from a groom and, along with a few staffers, rode down Pennsylvania Avenue. Some people recognized him and a couple of soldiers saluted, but most did not. He was just another grumpy-looking man on a horse.

Meade was deep in thought. He would be leading the largest army ever brought forth in the United States and he had serious doubts as to his ability to handle it properly. He would never admit it, but the events surrounding Gettysburg had shattered him. Even the so-called victory after the first three days was not without controversy. There were those who said that the battle had been won by others, such as Hancock, who was still mending from his wounds.

He spurred his horse faster. He needed to purge himself of his doubts.

Cassie got up quickly as she saw the dozen or so horsemen approaching. Around her the students picked up their things and retreated toward the trees. A glance showed the children running to their mothers. The men had slipped out of sight, but they were no doubt very close.

Mariah approached her, her hands clenched tightly. She remembered how Mariah had been sexually used by white men and how she had sworn to die before she would let it happen again. She quelled an impulse to take her by the hand.

Cassie stepped forward to meet the riders. They came to a halt about ten yards away.

The lead rider was a stocky man in his thirties in a frock coat and a top hat. He glanced around him, looking down his nose as if confronted with something of gross unpleasantness. At last he took notice of Cassie. "And what do we have here, young lady?"

"I beg your pardon, sir?"

He frowned at her. The rider to his right, an unshaven man with more than a touch of the village lout to his appearance, let out a snigger.

"Would you care to introduce yourself?"

"My name is Dover. I am a councilman from the town of Cabin John."

Cabin John was a river town to the south of here. Cassie had never been there and knew little about it. "Good afternoon, Mr. Dover. My name is Cassandra Baird and my father is, or was, colonel commanding the Sixth Indiana Mounted Infantry."

Dover looked from side to side. "Doesn't look like a mounted infantry unit to me."

That got a bigger response from the rest of his crowd than it strictly deserved. Cassie waited out the laughter. "That is because it is no such thing, Councilman. It is in fact a very rough school. We have been authorized to teach these emancipated Negroes how to read and write."

"Who authorized this school for niggers—or is this something you're doing on your own?"

Cassandra flinched at the venom in his voice. "Captain, this is the brainchild of President Lincoln. He is contemplating starting a government program that would help freed slaves become productive members of society when the war is over."

"The Apeman himself," one of the riders said. Cassie felt her lips go thin.

"Productive," another one muttered. "From the numbers of pickaninnies hereabouts, I can believe that."

Dover wasn't laughing. "Why were not local authorities consulted in this matter?"

"The President failed to consult the village council of John's Cabin, sir? I shall make a point of mentioning that." She heard a sharp intake of breath from Mariah.

Dover's face darkened. "We do not approve of this education of the Negro. Darkies will become productive members of society when pigs learn to fly. They are little more than brutes who require direction and oversight from white people. Your so-called school is making them think they are as good as whites and that is both wrong and dangerous." He glanced about him to assure himself that his men were all listening. "That is not my opinion, miss. Those are the words of Scripture."

"Scripture, sir?" Cassie took a couple of steps forward. "Would you care to recite chapter and verse? No? Because I recall another passage, from the Gospels. Matthew, I believe, in which Jesus Christ bade his disciples to preach to all nations. *All* nations, sir. Not only the white people of Maryland."

"You leave Jesus Christ out of this."

"I didn't bring up the Bible, Mr. Dover."

Dover gritted his teeth. "You listen here, you young hussy. You may think your authorization allows you to run this nigger school among decent white people, but you are mistaken. I warn you, the next time I catch you trying to teach Negroes something they shouldn't learn, I will go very hard on you."

"Sir, are you threatening me with violence?"

"I wouldn't think of it, ma'am. You're white." He gave her a nasty grin. "Or at least you appear so to me."

With that, Dover and his small group rode away. Mariah, who remained prudently silent, came forward.

"Did that man frighten you?" Cassie asked.

"Yes. Yes, he did. You shouldn't have spoken to him that way."

"Oh . . ." Cassie took her by the arm and led her back to where the others were gathering. "Don't pay him any mind. He's all talk."

A glance told her Mariah was not so certain.

★ CHAPTER 14 ★

Blandon didn't hold with paper money. Give him a good, solid coin of gold or silver, one that rang right loud when you slapped it on the counter. Paper money was most often issued by scores of pissant little banks throughout the country that frequently failed, leaving holders of their money up the creek. But he had to admit that old Abe's experiment with paper money had its points. He had several thousand dollars in paper tucked in his money belt right now. Greenbacks, widely accepted and backed by a strong government. The fact that he was fighting that government meant nothing to Blandon. Rumor had it that it was even gaining acceptance down South, although he doubted that. Good old Jeff Davis would never stand for it.

Once again, he was staying clear of his own people. Incredibly, the bodies of the three Yankees he'd murdered and thrown down that basement had been discovered and there was quite a ruckus. They should have rotted away in that basement for months and before anybody bothered to look. He had not been accused of anything or even been associated with the massacre, but he was worried that the others who'd been with him might break down under pressure and implicate him.

The good Colonel Wade had likely heard about these murders, but hadn't connected them to Blandon. To the colonel, war was an affair between soldiers, and civilians just didn't come into it, which struck Blandon as humorous. Why was everybody so upset over three dead civilians when tens of thousands of soldiers lay rotting in shallow graves? It didn't make sense. Yes, those civilians might have been 'innocent,' whatever that meant, but what about all those soldiers? He guessed the concerns arose because this war was what some people referred to as a "civilized war", another thought that made him laugh. Civilized war? What the hell was that?

So Blandon stayed out of the way and out of sight. The colonel would wonder why he'd disappeared, but he'd cross that bridge at some later time. He was a loner by nature, so this kind of life suited him. He had built himself a den in the nearby woods and was comfortable. He also had a piece of paper with Colonel Wade's forged signature on it authorizing him to work independently as a scout.

It was getting toward fall now and the Pennsylvania weather was surprisingly chill and moist. He would need a more permanent place to hide before long. Either that or he would go back to Wade and take his chances. But to go back safely he would have to bring something of value, and that did not mean the money strapped to his waist. Wade was the kind of honorable bastard who didn't take bribes.

He heard a noise and froze. A horse whinnied, fairly close. He slid deeper into the bushes and waited. A short while later a lone rider appeared. It was a Union soldier and he appeared to be lost. The Confederate lines were just too close for him to have come this way intentionally. He judged the rider to be in his late teens and the confused expression on his face confirmed the fact that he was lost. It would be only a little while before a Confederate patrol picked him up. Blandon smiled as he saw the leather pouch draped over the rider's saddle. The foolish boy was a courier and what was in those pouches could easily be valuable.

He moved stealthily but quickly towards the rider, approaching him from the rear. He didn't want to spook him and send him riding off. Likewise, Blandon didn't want to shoot him. Even in the woods, the sound could easily carry to ears that didn't need to know about him.

The soldier had actually taken out a small compass and was trying to fathom its meaning when Blandon pounced. He grabbed the rider and dragged him off the horse and onto the ground. For a second, the soldier didn't resist, but then realized he was in deadly peril. He began to thrash wildly, kicking and punching. Blandon was the more experienced fighter and got his hands around the boy's throat. He began to squeeze with all his strength. The soldier was strong and became even more desperate, using his hands as claws that almost gouged out one of Blandon's eyes. Blandon was in agony, but forced himself to continue the pressure. He had a knife, but he would have to stop strangling the courier to get it. Finally, the soldier's body sagged and there was the smell of urine and shit as he fouled himself in his death throes.

Blandon lurched back from the body and fell down. Blood was running down his cheek and he was covered with scratches and bruises. *I'm getting old,* he thought, as his breath came in gasps. Once upon a time he would have killed that boy in only a couple of seconds, not the eternity it seemed to take this day. And he wouldn't have gotten hurt. Already, his eye was swelling. It would close soon and his vision would be seriously impaired until the swelling went down. *Shit,* he thought, *what a mess.* What the boy was carrying had damn well better be important.

He staggered to his feet. Where the hell were the horse and the saddlebags? He smiled through a badly swollen lip when he saw that the horse was a few steps away and grazing contentedly.

He took the saddlebags and opened them. As he'd hoped, there were many messages, all neatly bundled for delivery. His eyes widened as he read them. They were virtually identical and all directed to commanders telling them to get their men ready for a major offensive operation that would commence in a week or two. This would all become common knowledge in a few days, since no one could keep secrets in the District of Columbia, but right now it was priceless information. He would take the saddlebag and the messages back to the colonel and come out of this a big hero.

Blandon ignored his pain and mounted the horse. He did so awkwardly, since he'd managed to hurt his knee in the fight. Damn, he really was getting old.

Thorne had heard the news from brigade. Immediately, he began getting his men even more prepared than they were already. He would purge them of the bad habits that they'd accumulated after living in what amounted to a garrison. The enemy was close and the army was finally going after it.

Thorne had never been the type of commanding officer to let the men lose their fighting edge for any extended period of time. He had them marching and maneuvering until he was confident that many of them hated his guts. *Well, so be it*, he thought.

Other officers disagreed with him. "Let the boys have some fun, blow off steam. They'll be ready for a fight when the time comes."

Thorne was confident that the Sixth Indiana was as ready as any regiment in the Army of the Potomac, but there was still room for improvement. There always was.

Both General Meigs and Josiah Baird visited, professing pleasure at the shape the regiment was in. Baird had laughed. "If you can control my daughter the way you do these troops, you might have an interesting life ahead of you."

Steve had turned red with embarrassment. There had not yet been any mention of marriage between him and Cassandra. Even their earlier and intense passion had cooled. Of course, the major reason for that was the lack of any opportunity. They were too old to go sneaking into the storeroom off the kitchen although they did use it for some furtive kissing and caressing if no other place was available.

Cassie did not mention her encounter with Dover to her father. If he ever learned of it, he would halt her visits to Hadrian and his people. She would not have been able to bear that. But she had gone over it with Hadrian, who had simply frowned and nodded to himself, as if he'd expected as much, then went off to speak in low tones with the rest of the men.

Shortly thereafter, Cassie had noticed a cluster of horsemen eyeing the camp from about a half mile away.

She quickly borrowed Hadrian's telescope and focused on the horseman in the middle. It was Dover and he appeared to be examining their camp through his own telescope.

"Can we go to the soldiers and have them chased away?" Mariah asked plaintively.

"Not likely," Cassie told her. "You see, there's nothing actually illegal about it. Dover is an official and he's keeping an eye on something in his area. He could simply argue that it's his responsibility."

Mariah made a disgusted sound and moved away. Cassie decided that the two of them would make no attempt to go home this night. Instead, they would bunk on the ground and be thankful that the weather, while chill, wasn't all that miserable. Or maybe she and Mariah could squeeze into somebody's tent. Mariah would be in Hadrian's while she would have to find one of her own.

She would, of course, send a messenger to inform her father. Perhaps her father could arrange for something terrible to happen to one Councilman Ronald Dover.

She would have to depend of her own wits, Mariah's, and of course, Hadrian's. She smiled. It seemed like a fair fight. While she was contemplating this, the horsemen wheeled and departed. Dover waved his hat at her, verifying that they'd been staring at each other. It infuriated her, but what could she do?

The highest rank in the Union Army was that of major general. There had been no lieutenant generals since George Washington held the rank. Now, Winfield Scott was a brevet lieutenant general, but he was the only one.

The result of this stinginess with rank was a logjam of two-star generals trying to figure out who was senior and, thus, who was in charge. Sometimes presidential orders enabled men to leapfrog over generals who were old and doddering. It was also a dangerous policy since it meant that a political general, like Major General John Alexander McClernand, was senior to the aggressive and skilled William Tecumseh Sherman. So far, Lincoln had managed to keep the political generals, so titled because of their political clout and ability to bring support to the war and, oh yes—the 1864 presidential elections. What truly galled other generals was the fact that McClernand was running for the presidency, and was not terribly interested in commanding an army. Nor was he particularly skilled. It was widely conceded that the political generals would have their heads handed to them in a battle with any one of a number of capable Confederates. Giving them an independent command of any size would be equivalent to murder.

Thus, Major Generals Henry Halleck and George Meade were both equal and unequal. Halleck was the commanding general of the armies while Meade commanded the Army of the Potomac. Generally, they tolerated each other well, but this was not one of those days. Halleck wanted to know everything and Meade was neither able nor willing to accommodate him. In Meade's opinion, Halleck was a goggle-eyed staff officer who had failed at command and was jealous of anyone who might do better. A case in point was Halleck's intense dislike of Ulysses Grant. Once Halleck's subordinate, it now looked as if Grant would be put in command if he, Meade, faltered. Thus, Meade had good reason to dislike both Halleck and Grant.

"General, I will not give you the details of my plans for the simple reason that they are not fully formulated yet."

Halleck had had a fine reputation as a thinker and a military theorist. One of his nicknames was "Old Brains," which had been a compliment until it was noted that his army moved extremely slowly, even stopping to dig field fortifications each night. Finally, Halleck had been replaced and returned to Washington with the nominal title of commanding general. There, he did what he did best in organizing the army.

Meade cared nothing about all that. He just wanted Halleck out of his hair. Rumor had it that both Reynolds and Grant had turned down command of the Army of the Potomac for the simple reason that they would have to spend so much time dealing with Halleck and his preoccupations.

"General Halleck, you tell me you represent the wishes of the President. However, I see nothing in the way of proof to support this contention. I am beginning to believe that you want nothing more than to be given credit for this campaign which, I am certain, will go a long way towards ending this awful war."

"Meade, I pray that you are correct in that it will end the war. However, I must admit that I have my doubts. You have seven infantry corps and one of cavalry and they all report directly to you. That is far too much responsibility for one man. Lee has apparently split his army into two grand corps, Hardee's and Longstreet's. Might I suggest that you do so as well? If might prevent a debacle like that which occurred when Lee was retreating."

Meade bristled and his face turned red, "Kindly recall, sir, that both you and the President wanted me to do exactly what I did, and that was to chase Mr. Lee and destroy him." Meade ran his hand through his mussed red hair. "How in God's name was I to even suspect that a badly beaten Lee would turn around and become a tiger? I was the commander in the field and I bear responsibility for the defeat. Keep in mind, however, that I was following direct orders that made no sense. Part of the reason for that defeat was because I lost control of the army. That will never happen again. This time they will all report directly to me and I will keep my finger on the pulse of the army. It will be difficult but it will work."

Halleck's expression told Meade all he needed to know. Halleck disagreed vehemently but was not going to say a thing that would offend the hair-trigger Meade. Well and good. Halleck might be "Old Brains," but he, George Gordon Meade, was a fighter. He would pin Lee into a position of his own choosing, grab onto him like a bulldog and never let go. In a brawl at close range, a fighter would always prevail. *Now,* he thought ruefully, *all I have to do is find Lee.*

The men of the Sixth Indiana cantered out of their encampment in a long column of twos. They were in high spirits. They were actually going to try to do something, rather than ride patrols around their camp with their thumbs up their asses. The column included several wagons that carried additional supplies and that could be used to transport wounded.

The regiment owned two very small six-pound cannon, but these had been left at their camp. Most of the officers considered them to be nothing more than loud toys. Thorne wasn't that comfortable with denigrating them or leaving them behind. With their barrels stuffed with pieces of glass and metal, they could do some terrible damage to human flesh. Well, it was too late now.

The regiment was at the head of the column heading down this particular dirt road that seemed merely to connect four or five farms. He wondered if they were all related. Archie Willis thought it was a clear case of incest.

As always, Thorne had scouts and outriders keeping an eye open. Thus it was no surprise when one of the scouts came galloping down the road towards him. "Damn it, soldier, you kill that horse and you pay for it."

"Sir, the horse is in fine shape. She just got a little lathered up because of the heat and the fact that so many people in this world seem to hate us."

"I sure as hell hope you're right. Now what's got you all hot and bothered?"

"Sir, there's a hill up ahead and this excuse for a road goes right over it with trees on each side. Looks like a perfect spot for an ambush, if you ask me."

The scout had done excellent work in the past, so there was no reason to doubt his assessment. Thorne spurred his horse and, along with the scout and half a dozen men, rode to the crest of a hill that fronted the enemy position. The potential enemy position stood higher than the hill they were on. Of enemy soldiers, however, they could see not a one.

Willis rode up. "What's your pleasure, Major?"

Thorne continued to stare through his telescope. It told him nothing. "Well, if I was either Pleasonton or Custer I'd simply mount up and have the regiment ride though yonder trees. But I'm not either of those men and I have too much respect for the lives of our troops to even consider it."

"That's why we all love you, Major."

"Go to hell, Willis. No, instead send one company around each side of the woods and attempt to penetrate from the rear." He looked over Willis' shoulder. "Damn it, here comes Pleasonton. Get the men started real fast before that man gets here and tries to change everything."

Willis rode off quickly and within minutes had two companies of mounted infantry performing an attempt to envelop the hill which, he realized, was smaller and lower than he had first thought.

"Thorne, what the hell is going on here?" snarled Pleasonton. "Are your men going to dance around that shitty little hill or are you going to drive any Rebs off it?"

"Sir, I thought I'd figure out how many there were before maybe getting my men shot."

"I'll tell you how many Rebs are up there, Thorne. Not a one, and you're holding up the entire column and with it, my reputation. Don't ever pull a trick like that again."

"Understood, General." Thorne also understood that Pleasonton did not get along with anybody and desperately wanted to get promoted to the rank of major general. As the annoying regular cavalry officer prepared to ride off, Thorne noticed two things. First, the men around them were looking elsewhere and ignoring Pleasonton. Second, he noted with dismay that the two companies he'd sent were entirely into the woods.

Pleasonton noticed it as well. "See, Major, there's not a damned thing to worry about. No Rebels here, there, or anywhere else for that matter."

No sooner had Pleasonton spoken than the woods erupted in gunfire, in seconds covering the hill with smoke. Thorne responded quickly, before Pleasonton could say a word. "Willis, get the rest of the regiment up there and tell them to hack their way through to our men." He wheeled and saluted his commander. "By your leave sir, I'm going to join the fight."

The cavalry general grinned wolfishly. "Not without me you aren't."

The remainder of the regiment fell in behind them and they galloped up the hill. "Thorne, where the devil is the rest of your regiment? They told me it was a small one, but this is ridiculous."

"Most of the missing are either healing in a hospital or lying dead on Cemetery Ridge, sir." The general went silent and Thorne was afraid he'd pushed the bad-tempered cavalry leader too far.

Finally, Pleasanton spoke. "We lost too many good men. There are a lot of prima donnas in this army. I know I have the reputation of a shit, but I don't want to waste lives."

Thorne had heard otherwise about him, so he kept silent.

The actual site of the skirmish was nothing much. A number of trees and bushes had been scarred or broken down and there were a good dozen dead and wounded lying about. Captive Rebels clumped together sullenly while the Yankees were unabashedly relieved that they'd survived another encounter with death.

"What now, Thorne?"

"That's easy, sir. We'll ask our wounded Union men and anyone else who has an opinion as to what happened. The captured Rebels will be questioned about anything they might know and then they'll be forwarded to any one of a dozen prison camps where they will starve for the duration of the war. I don't envy them." Prisoner of war camps on both sides were a disgrace and the death rates among inmates was extremely high.

"It sounds like you don't approve, Thorne."

"I'm fine with killing people in combat, but to neglect them, leave them to starve and rot, is just plain barbaric."

"I'll agree with that, Thorne, but don't let anyone hear you. There are still a lot of people who think we're too soft on those we do put in prison. Now, I am going to do you a helluva favor. I am going to write up a report about this little skirmish and I am going to praise you to the skies. I will mention that I am doing it because you deserve it, which you do, and because it showed intelligent initiative."

Thorne was flabbergasted. Pleasonton was very slow giving out praise to anyone. Was something going on here?

Pleasonton answered it for him. "No, I am not getting soft in the head. I know I am controversial and make enemies without breaking a sweat. I still want a handful of people who will give me a fair judgment. You're an honest man and you're even a lawyer, which means you won't go far in your chosen profession."

Musket fire in the distance told them the fighting had spread. Again it was punctuated by the banging of small cannon.

A tall, lean colonel from Pleasonton's command rode up. He was accompanied by another man in grubby civilian clothes. Salutes were exchanged. The civilian did not salute.

The colonel spoke. "We found them, sir, a whole bunch of them are digging a great big long trench in on a hill to our right front. There may be at least twenty-five thousand of them, General."

Pleasonton nodded and urged his horse slowly forward. "Spread out. Don't make a target for some cracker with a twelve-pounder."

The party did as instructed. Before reaching the crest of the hill, they dismounted and continued on foot to make themselves even smaller targets.

And there was the Rebel army, at least a goodly portion of it. They were directly confronted by at least a brigade, and all that separated them was a fairly steep ravine. As usual with Lee's men, they were digging in. The King of Spades was living up to his reputation for entrenching.

Pleasonton was no coward, but he kept himself well hidden. Thorne and the others did the same. They were almost within rifle range.

"Colonel, that's a lot of Rebels there, but it ain't twenty-five thousand men. Where the hell are the rest of them?"

"Stacked up behind them, sir. What we're looking at is the point of the spear."

The general nodded, "And a point that can't stick us. Whoever is leading them has managed to put himself out on a limb. Look, they're starting to pack up and find a way around the ravine."

Despite himself, Thorne grinned. Some officer was going to get sent to bed without his dinner for leading so many men astray. In a way, it was good to know that even the Army of Northern Virginia was capable of making a dumb mistake.

A cannon fired and a shell screamed overhead before burying itself in the soft ground. Pleasonton laughed. "Damned if I don't think they've spotted us and offered a personal invitation to hell."

Lieutenant General Robert E. Lee had received the messages and reports and was more than pleased. "Thank God. Finally, grumpy old Meade is going come out and play with his army. Only thing is, we are the ones who are going to be playing with it."

The others gathered around the large fire that tried to keep away the fall's chill. "You don't think he's trying to trick us, do you, sir?" Longstreet said drily.

"Why of course he is, General. However, by his losing and our finding those orders, his secret is out and we will have stolen a couple of day's march on him. Meade is no fool. I've already said he will make no mistakes, and his losing those orders does not qualify any more than the misplacing of my orders before Sharpsburg. No, he will fight well. However, he will fight quite slowly because he has a huge army that he has decided not to divide into more flexible groups. It will be ponderous and vulnerable to attack, in much the same way as the Spanish Armada."

Longstreet looked mildly surprised. "I thought you had determined not to attack Meade, that he was too strong, just as he was at Gettysburg."

Lee flushed. It was clear that he did not like remembering that battle. "Of course we will attack him. We must. This time, however, we will attack where he is weak, not strong, and he cannot be strong everywhere. Further, there will be no frontal assaults. We will attempt to turn his flanks at every opportunity and leave him thoroughly confused. General Meade is a very highly strung man who may have been given more responsibility than he can handle. We must play on his insecurities until he and the Army of the Potomac collapse. When that occurs, we pick up the pieces of what was once his army and march into Washington."

General Hardee nodded sagely. "And when the Union is totally humiliated, we will again have our ambassadors present their credentials to the governments in Paris and London, perhaps even Madrid and Berlin. The Confederacy will be recognized and peace negotiations can commence almost immediately."

Lee broke out into confident laughter, something his staff hadn't heard that much lately.

Warned by the sounds of the approaching horses, the guard stiffened to attention and snapped off a smart salute. When the President and his party had passed, he relaxed and thought of home and his family. It was late and dark and he did wonder what the great people were up to. He wondered what the President and the others were planning and if it involved him. Like most soldiers, he had a healthy respect for combat and wished to avoid it if at all possible. No false bravado for him. No sir. If it became necessary to lay down his life, he was ready to do so, but he was not planning on volunteering.

He peered into the darkness, down the direction Lincoln had come. There was nothing out of the ordinary. He took a deep breath and willed himself to relax. He had another hour until he was relieved. He prayed that it would pass peacefully. His prayers might be answered this night, but not too many more times, as the army was stirring itself.

Inside the Executive Mansion, Lincoln attempted to warm himself by standing with his rear end close to the fire. "Don't fall in," said Stanton in a rare display of humor.

"Not enough of me to burn for very long," Lincoln responded. He wrapped a shawl around his shoulders and sat in his rocking chair. On a table beside the chair rested a stack of telegrams.

"General Halleck, just how many of these telegrams can be deemed important?

"Perhaps one in ten, while the remainder are important only in the minds of their creators."

"Yet I have to read them all."

Halleck shook his head. "We've been over this before, sir, and the truth is that you don't have to respond personally to more than one in a hundred. In Nicolai and Hay you have fine secretaries and they are more than capable of separating the wheat from the chaff and responding on your behalf."

"But then I would risk losing touch with the people, and that includes men in the army who constantly complain about their lot." And sometimes with great justification, he did not add. Corruption and incompetence had been rooted out by simply reading the mail.

"On the other hand," said Stanton, "you could work yourself into an early death and a freshly dug grave. The nation would be leaderless. If you are not here to guide us, who will? Vice President Hamlin is a good Republican but so harsh and strict in his abolitionist beliefs that a lasting peace would be impossible under his regime. No sir, you must preserve yourself and your health. Your nation needs you."

Lincoln rubbed his eyes. Everything that had been said was so very right, but also so very wrong.

The downpour had been sudden and drenching. One moment it had been a fairly pleasant fall afternoon, the next, gusts of wind and rain had soaked Cassie and torn her frilly umbrella to shreds. She swore and threw the useless thing onto a trash pile while Mariah giggled.

With great dignity, the two women walked the remaining blocks to their home. "We need hot water," Cassie shouted as she entered through the kitchen. There was no way she was going to shed gallons of rainwater on the parlor rugs.

Cassie let herself drip dry as best she could on the kitchen floor, and then dashed upstairs by the rear stairs. Two servant girls, friendly, lazy and Irish, were preparing her bath with more haste than she'd seen in them for quite some time.

While they filled the tub with warm water, she laid out some fresh clothing and stripped off her dress and much of her underclothing, which she left in a sodden pile on the floor.

"Enough," she said and ordered the two women to leave. Once they were gone, she stripped down to her shift and climbed into the water. It was hot and would stay so for a while. When it cooled, the two girls would add buckets of hot to keep her comfortable.

There was a tap on the door followed by her mother's voice. "May I come in?"

"Of course," Cassie said. She had expected her mother to come calling. It was well past time to have a talk and was one reason she'd kept her shift on. She felt she was a little too old for her mother to see her naked. Besides, she didn't need a full bath anyhow. She'd had one only a couple of days prior.

"Is it time for another talk, Mother?"

"Perhaps. I would like to know your intentions regarding Major Thorne."

Cassie smiled wickedly. "My intentions are totally dishonorable. I plan on using all of my feminine wiles to seduce him and make him my slave. We will marry and I will have him chained to my bed for the rest of his life. And I will punish him if he does not please me."

Rachel smiled. "Well, thank God you're not being impractical."

"My intentions are honorable and, so far, his are as well. We've had some pleasant moments when we could be alone, but your daughter's virtue is intact. Unwanted perhaps, but intact."

"Cassandra! Please . . ." Rachel shook her head, then stepped out and returned with two snifters of brandy. "I felt the same way before your father and I got married. Which reminds me, in your wanderings, did you pick up any news about the army?"

"Not even good rumors, Mother. And I assume that our father is at the telegraph office in Washington along with scores of other people trying to pick up crumbs of news. Just think of it—two giant armies could be out there clawing each other to shreds and causing thousands of deaths while we sit here and do nothing. Enough." She stood and grabbed a blanket which she wrapped around herself.

"Give me a few moments to get dressed and let's go see what we can find out ourselves."

Rachel rose. "And I will see if Mariah is ready and wishes to join us."

★ CHAPTER 15 ★

The ground north and west of Washington was as cold and wet as the ground in any other direction. It had finally stopped raining, but the water still lay in large dirty puddles. If the troops were lucky, maybe they could get a fire going and have a hot meal.

Archie Willis handed Thorne a cup of lukewarm coffee. "Beggars can't be choosers, honorable Major."

"At least we can console ourselves with the fact that Bobby Lee and his minions are as cold and miserable as we are. I've been looking for a reasonably dry plot of mud to sleep on tonight but haven't found anything yet. This means, of course, sleeping in the mud." He shuddered at the thought. "May I assume that guards are properly positioned and ready if the Rebels decide to raid?"

Willis grimaced and threw away the rest of his coffee. "That was truly shitty coffee. Tell me, Steve, what did we learn today?"

Thorne paused before answering. The regiment had spent all day looking for Lee and determining that an army of a hundred thousand men could actually disappear into the mist. Lee was out there someplace and if there was any rhyme or reason to their patrols, they were to find him, pin him down, and then attack him. They had patrolled slowly and cautiously to avoid an ambush. They were not to start a battle, merely find the enemy and, so far, they had failed. *Of course*, he thought ruefully, *the Army of the Potomac was used to failure.*

Nor did he or anyone else he knew have an abiding faith in General

Meade. Meade had been lucky, was the consensus. Lee had acted out of character at Gettysburg and it had nearly cost him his army. Only the desperate counterattack on what was commonly being referred to as the Day After had saved him, and no one was counting on Lee making the same kind of mistake again.

"Well Archie, first, we learned that the Confederates are just as likely to get lost as we are. I wonder how badly Lee chewed out whoever led what could have been a full corps to that ravine."

"I understand that Lee is too much of a gentleman to do any real chewing."

"Then we learned that the Rebel cavalry under Wade Hampton is as good as it was under Jeb Stuart. They did a very effective job of keeping us away from their main army. We really don't know where they are, and that worries me."

"Me too, Steve. It's almost night time and they could come charging out of the darkness and cut us up pretty badly before we got organized."

Steve wished he had a dry cigar, but couldn't find one. "I guess we should all be thankful that neither army likes to fight it out at night. There's nothing but chaos and confusion at night with soldiers shooting and killing men right and left, including their own. Personally, I can think of no worse fate than to be shot by one's own side."

"Like what happened to Stonewall Jackson?"

"Yep. From what I've heard, Stonewall and some of his staff had been scouting outside his own lines and maybe got lost. At any rate, it doesn't matter. His own men killed him and now we have Wade Hampton to contend with."

A few miles away, Meade was thoroughly confused and frustrated. He was receiving information in such quantities that he could not process it all. Yet it all left unanswered the primary question—Where the hell was Robert E. Lee?

The Army of the Potomac was advancing on a broad front. Meade was almost daring Lee to attack. His army would be a bludgeon that would advance to and through the rebel army. His flanks would be well protected. There would be no surprise assault, as had happened at Chancellorsville when the late Stonewall Jackson had launched a devastating flanking attack against "Fighting" Joe Hooker. Meade almost smiled. Fighting Joe had practically collapsed from the shock of that attack and the subsequent bloody defeat. No, the Army of the Potomac would not be surprised this time, and if that meant moving more slowly than either Halleck or Lincoln wanted, well that was just too damned bad. Not only was he not going to be flanked, but the army would not run blindly into Lee as had happened just north of the Potomac. If Lincoln had let him pursue Lee in his own manner, the country wouldn't be in the mess it was.

"I see you haven't found the old fox." It was Halleck. He had arrived an hour or so earlier and had been just "looking around."

"I think that is painfully obvious, General Halleck. Even though I have a hundred thousand men looking for a creature that must stretch five miles from one end to the other, the area to search is so vast it precludes a quick conclusion."

"Yet we must find him and bring him to bay. The army cannot simply march around and use up supplies until it has to retreat in ignominy back to its previous positions."

"Don't you think I know that?" Meade snapped. "And I also realize that I have to keep my army between Washington and where I think the rebels might be to prevent an attack on the capital. Losing Washington, if only for a short while, would be catastrophic."

"For once we agree," Halleck said softly. "And despite Lincoln's protestations to the contrary, I believe he would be quite happy to have Lee south of the Potomac instead of us wasting lives and supplies in an attempt to destroy him. I cannot believe that he truly wishes an Armageddon where tens of thousands would be killed and wounded. To corner Lee and force him to fight a desperate battle and subsequent bloodbath would be more than the nation could handle."

"So what are you suggesting?"

"Only that we do our duty. We have our orders and we must obey them. I am certain that your scouts will be out looking for the elusive Lee at first light if not sooner."

"A number of them are out as we speak," Meade said. "Of course, the rebels are seeking us out as well. However, they will doubtless find us before we find them. It's a sad fact that Hampton's cavalry is superior to Pleasonton's."

Halleck glared at Meade, making his eyes pop out even further. The effect made him look ridiculous. "But when you find Lee, I trust it will be a battle, not a slaughter. You will not allow him to launch another counterattack, and will not push him so hard that he becomes desperate."

Meade grimaced. "I've learned my lesson, General. But what if he defeats me? That could easily result in my being fired and replaced by Grant."

"General Meade, you cannot permit that to happen. I remain firmly convinced that putting that drunken incompetent Grant in charge would result in disaster. I will do everything in my power to prevent Grant from taking command."

Then who had been in command at Vicksburg, Meade wanted to ask? Instead, he kept his counsel as Halleck and his entourage departed. Meade had another reason for wanting Lee found as soon as possible. His own vast army was stretched out over a number of miles and he was beginning to wonder if he shouldn't have divided it into two or three smaller groups that would still report to him. Yet he was afraid of losing touch with his various corps. That had almost happened at Gettysburg when Dan Sickles, another political general, had moved his III Corps too far in front of the rest of the army. As a result, III Corps had been savagely mauled and Sickles grievously wounded, losing his leg. Though some thought Sickles was a hero, his actions had actually endangered the Union Army and nearly cost the Union the battle.

The truth—which he was reluctant to admit—was that Meade had lost control of one of his corps. He could not let that happen again.

Perhaps he should have copied what he understood of Lee's changes. He had to admit that he really had no idea what was going on with his own soldiers at the other, farther, end of the Army of the Potomac, several miles away.

His stomach had been upset all day long and now it was like a fist had grabbed his gut and wouldn't let go. Maybe his critics were right. Maybe he really wasn't up to this important a command. But if he couldn't do it, then who could? Grant? But Grant wasn't ready and maybe never would be. Meade was determined to do his best. But would it be enough?

A shrieking in the night was followed by the sounds of many guns firing. Thorne threw himself off his cot and on to the wet dirt floor of the tent. As bullets whistled outside, he reached up and grabbed his trousers. A moment later, he was dressed and armed. The firing had not abated. If anything, it was even closer and the shrieking rebel yell was enough to stand up the hairs on the back of his neck. He ducked down and slipped through the opening of the tent and into chaos.

Dozens of soldiers, dressed and half dressed, were trying to form a skirmish line and shoot back at an invisible foe. Rifle fire was coming from several directions. Was this a major attack or just a raid, Thorne wondered?

A soldier cried out and crumpled beside him. "Put out the fires," Thorne yelled. "They can see us but we can't see them."

A few looked puzzled, but most caught on and began kicking dirt into the fire pits. Soon, only the flashes from the rifles provided any illumination. The surprised Union soldiers steadied and began to aim at the flashes. Cries of pain told them they were scoring hits.

Thorne sensed that the Confederates were pulling back and ordered his few score men forward. The Rebels abandoned the woods with a few parting shots and some obscene taunts. But the skirmish was over. Thorne wondered just what had been accomplished apart from causing a number of casualties.

In the distance, the sounds of fighting could be heard in all directions. Gradually, even these died out and a strange silence took over. Fires were lit again and patrols began to prowl. This time they would be more alert.

Willis had a bandage wrapped around his left arm above the elbow. "Didn't we decide that nobody liked to fight at night, that it smacked of desperation and that it ran the risk of shooting one's own men?"

"Quite obviously we were misinformed. Either that or Lee is more of a gambler than we expected. But what did he accomplish besides letting us know that he's around and very, very close?"

"Which means that we're going to look for him tomorrow and find the entire Confederate army. All I know is that I would not like to be in Meade's shoes."

Thorne laughed. "But we *are* in his shoes. Whatever he decides we'll wind up doing. And however many of us get killed or wounded, I doubt it will bother him much. Generals have to be cold, unfeeling bastards, otherwise there'd be nobody who'd want to lead us in battle. What kind of a war would that leave us with?"

"Maybe a pleasant one," Willis said. "Maybe there'd be no wars at all if nobody wanted to play at being a general."

The wind shifted, blowing smoke over them. Thorne wondered if he would ever be able to smell a campfire or a fireplace without first thinking of a battlefield. This time at least, there was no scent of burning flesh.

Richard Dean was in Baltimore when word of Meade's move and the subsequent fighting reached him. The first thing he did was to get himself a bottle of rum. The rum was cheap, since he was again short of funds, but it was good enough to toast the destruction of the enemies of the Confederacy. He did so quietly and discreetly in his room. Baltimore might be sympathetic towards the South, but northern troops still patrolled it and took great delight in smashing the heads of people who voiced support for Jefferson Davis's new nation.

Dean had spent much of the evening with Sid and Nate. They were not bright, but even they could see the problems inherent in kidnapping Abraham Lincoln. Even though they agreed with him, Richard knew they could easily be swayed by Booth into doing whatever he wanted. Once again, Richard wondered about the success of the plot if that pair were responsible for important tasks. It was very discouraging. Why couldn't a man of Booth's skill and stature attract more qualified conspirators?

Dean took a deep swallow of the rum and nearly gagged. It was truly wretched stuff. He was sitting cross-legged on his bed and had removed his outer shirt and shoes. He was tired and almost didn't notice when the door opened and little Mary Nardelli rushed in.

"It's happening, Richard. It's true; it's all true."

"Mary, what the hell are you talking about?"

"Lincoln's army has finally woken up and has moved out. They're going to bring Lee to battle, and you know what that means."

Richard was fully awake. "Yes, you silly goose, it means chaos and confusion for our enemies. It means that there may actually be a chance for us to do something final about that goddamned gorilla, Abraham Linkhorn. I think it's highly likely that the Union army will be badly defeated. Robert E. Lee is without a doubt the greatest war leader of our times—perhaps all time. I could almost feel sorry for the Union general and I assume it's still Meade."

Mary sat down on the bed beside him. Not that long ago she would have been shocked at the very idea of her being alone in a room with a man. Now, much had changed. She was no longer the shy virgin who'd fled the Papal Armies in Rome. Her first love had been the great John Wilkes Booth who, it turned out, wasn't so great in bed. Her second, and so far last, was Richard Dean. He'd been reluctant at first— perhaps because she was overweight and not very pretty—but he'd succumbed, just like he would this night. It didn't hurt that Richard Dean was a much better lover than Booth.

"Richard, tomorrow we should go to Washington."

He pulled her to him and began to undress her. *Good*, she thought. "Because that's where Lincoln is and if we're going to move against him we shouldn't be a city away."

He laughed. "As always, little Mary, you make sense. Tomorrow I will disguise myself and we will take a train to Washington City. We will find Mr. Booth and see what he has up his sleeve. And whatever he wants to do, kidnap or kill, then I will go along with it."

"Us," she corrected him. "I have to get away as well."

They were both naked now. He handed her the bottle of rum. "Drink quickly. I'm way ahead of you." She took a long swallow. It was bad but it was still better than the swill her father used to make back in Italy.

The day after the fighting had ended at Gettysburg, Thorne, Willis, and a couple of others had ridden down from Cemetery Hill and across the valley to the abandoned Confederate positions on Seminary Ridge. They followed the route taken by Pickett's men on the disastrous third day. The field had not been cleaned up. Bodies and fragments of bodies littered the field, stinking beneath the July sun. At least the wounded had all been taken away. *Or*, he thought sadly, *they'd died while waiting for succor*. Just as terrible were the other pieces of debris, articles of clothing and equipment thrown away while their owners tried to escape the hell that had been unleashed on them.

"Remind me why we're riding out here," said Willis.

"I want an idea of what they went through before they hit our lines." He turned and looked up the gentle slope leading to the Union positions. A human wave had dashed itself against the rocks that were the Union defenses. The rocks had won. The Sixth Indiana had been positioned a few yards behind the fence that had been the target of the Confederate human wave. They had stood in shock as half-crazed soldiers clambered over the fence to go hand-to-hand against the waiting Union soldiers. They'd gone at it with fists and teeth, they'd kicked and clawed and used knives until the Union's weight of numbers prevailed. When it was over, thousands of rebels lay dead or wounded while thousands more retreated in disarray.

Thorne leaned down and picked up a canteen. It was clearly marked "CSA" and had a bullet hole in it. For a moment he wondered if the owner had survived, then realized he didn't much care. He threw the canteen away.

"It was pure murder to send men out in the open to attack that Ridge," Willis said. "Why didn't Pickett or Longstreet protest?"

Thorne shaded his eyes from the sun. Back on Cemetery Hill he could see people walking around, near the area where his men had been fighting and where Colonel Baird had lost his leg. Yes, it was insane. Thank God no Union general would even think of sending his men out to be slaughtered like that.

But he had been wrong. He shook his head, clearing it of all thoughts of Gettysburg and focusing it on the similar hill the Union II Corps was now assaulting. It was a gentle slope like Cemetery Hill and the distance from the start off point was a little more than a mile. From where he stood, he could see lines of blue dots advancing. First puffs and then clouds of smoke obscured events, but he could see blue uniforms crumpling and lying on the ground. Dozens of cannon had pounded the Rebel positions, as always to little or no effect. The attack was being shredded.

Several waves of Union soldiers followed the first, which was clearly getting mauled. But still they advanced. They appeared to be slowing. He hoped it was an illusion. To stop in the face of such fire was to die. They had to advance. Even the best defensive-minded soldiers wanted nothing to do with a hand-to-hand brawl or, worse, a fight with a man who was trying to run a foot of steel into your gut.

Thorne was mildly concerned by the great distance between the Sixth Indiana and Union forces to his left. He'd sent a messenger and had been brusquely informed that all was well and that he should be prepared to attack when the Rebel lines collapsed.

If they collapsed. The gunfire was intensifying and it did appear that the attackers had halted and were dueling with the dug-in Confederates. A bad move. Someone had to take charge and either send the Union troops on up the hill or pull them back.

It was growing clear that the planned assault by the Sixth wasn't going to occur. Their orders had been to ride though any breach in the Confederate lines and, along with expanding the breach, continue onward and raise holy hell in the enemy's rear.

Like all plans it seemed like a great idea, but reality was intruding. The attack wasn't being pressed and the Rebels were regaining their confidence. They had been shaken by the sight of the larger Union force, but no longer.

Suddenly, the Union soldiers shook off their torpor. With a shout they surged up the hill and over. "Well," said Willis, "I guess it's just about our time to make a grand entrance."

Thorne was about to agree when the Union force reappeared. They were retreating, and not in good order. Moments later, the Confederates came into view. The hill's defenders had been greatly reinforced and a horde came over the crest of the hill.

Thorne gave his orders. "We will open our lines and let our men pass through. Then we will close our lines and give the Rebels bloody hell. Now let's move!"

The men complied, and soon a large Union force had passed through to safety a few hundred yards away and to a chance to reorganize. Thorne was dismayed and angry to see that a number of his men had seized the opportunity to retreat as well. He grabbed a corporal. "Run down there and get those men of ours. Tell them to get their asses back up here or I'll see them hanged."

He ordered his men to dismount and horse-holders took themselves and three horses a short way away. He hated the idea of reducing his small force by even one, but it was necessary if his regiment was going to have any chance to retreat and join the main body.

The Confederates were within range. "Open fire!"

Close to two hundred Spencer repeating rifles blazed away, adding more smoke and noise and curtailing the Union soldiers' ability to aim. Still, the massed firepower staggered and then halted the Rebel advance. Thorne yelled at his men to get to their knees and to aim low, the way they'd been trained to do. Still, they would have to retreat. There were just too damn many Rebels to even consider holding on.

Someone tugged at his sleeve. "Colonel Barnwell says you did a great job and it's now time for everyone to pull back."

Thorne stole a look at the Rebels. They were not advancing and there were bodies piled everywhere. He closed his eyes against the sight as well as he could, then gave the order to withdraw. The men responded with alacrity. The Confederates did not follow—the Spencers had done their damage.

A scant handful of miles away, General Meade wondered pretty much the same thing. He attempted to concentrate on the large map spread before him, but that was useless. What troop dispositions were shown raised more questions than answers. He had launched major attacks against what scouts assured him were the Confederate far left and center left flanks. The attacks had failed and now II Corps and III Corps had been badly handled. They would not fight again tomorrow.

But he had his orders. The Army of the Potomac was to seek out and destroy the Army of Northern Virginia. He had the numbers and his men were well trained, well equipped, and well supplied. The only thing that might be lacking was leadership. Meade understood that he was part of that lack.

"Well?" It was that damned Halleck again. Meade fought the urge to grab him by the neck and choke him until his eyes really did pop out. Instead, he kept his composure.

Meade raised his hand to wipe his forehead. "The issue is still in doubt, General, and is likely to remain that way for some time. You may return to Washington and inform the President that we have taken heavy casualties and have inflicted much the same on the enemy."

"Are you saying you've won a Pyrrhic victory?" Halleck said, his voice almost a sneer. "Another victory that will ruin us—Like Gettysburg and all the rest?"

"You just don't grasp it, do you?" Meade said furiously. "That's what it's about, damn you. We can take the losses and Lee can't. Lincoln wants Lee destroyed and I fully intend to do the honors."

Halleck was about to respond, but suddenly looked alarmed. "General, are you all right? Your face is all red."

Meade shook his head. For the past several minutes, he'd been feeling first hot and then cold. He would sweat profusely, then begin shaking from a sudden chill, as he was right this minute. His head was aching horribly, and he was having a hard time gathering his thoughts. He was only dimly aware of Halleck taking his arm. "I think you should sit down for a while."

Yes, thought Meade. *Sit down. I need to sit down, but only for a little while.* There was so much to do, and so little time. Soldiers were dying, because he'd sent them out to die. But they were not dying for him. No—he could not think that. They were fighting for the Union, or to free the slaves, but they were not fighting for George Gordon Meade.

It was growing dark now. Not the dark of night—this darkness was deeper and more final. He knew this darkness. He had always known that it awaited him and that he would encounter it eventually. Just as he had always known that the only thing he could do was surrender to it.

They laid Meade on a cot and covered him with a blanket. His staff looked shocked at this sudden collapse. Some glared at Halleck for having caused it. Halleck grabbed a pad of paper and a pencil and began to write. "What I am doing," he announced, "is informing President Lincoln of this unfortunate turn of events. I will also inform him that there will be no further attacks this night unless he gives me a direct order to continue. In the meantime, we inform no one of General Meade's problem. It is Lincoln's to resolve."

The first ambulances from the battlefield arrived by mid-morning and it was quickly apparent their numbers were inadequate. The army had contracted for hundreds of the specially built vehicles, but they had been overwhelmed by demand and now anything that could be pulled by a horse or mule had been dragooned into service.

The wounded were staged at the mall. There they were separated according to the severity of the wounds. Those likely to die were given morphine and set aside and allowed to pass on in peace, while those who were likely to live were treated. The wounds were generally ghastly, and Cassie wondered just how some of them had survived as long as they had. A rifle fired a large bullet at high velocity and the effect of a bullet to the arm or a leg often resulted in the limb being torn off or the bone shredded and the limb rendered useless. Far too many wounded recovered but never returned to duty. All too many of the recovered were amputees or had mangled, useless arms and legs.

The women were tired and filthy, but would not give in to their physical complaints. If they could save but one life, their efforts would have been worth it.

They also felt that they had seen just about everything and were now able to joke among themselves about once leading sheltered lives.

The next ambulance was a case in point. Designed to carry four, it was clearly overloaded. The springs sagged and the two horses trying to pull it through the mud were exhausted. The driver looked as if he was about to collapse as well.

"Good lord," Rachel exclaimed. "How many are in there?"

The driver sagged against the ambulance and rubbed his face with his filthy forearms. "I dunno. Maybe a dozen. I wasn't counting. If there was room, we put them in."

"Why did you even think of stuffing so many men in this contraption?"

The driver took a deep breath and gained some strength. "Because there were so damned many of them and because the damned officers told me to, that's why."

Cassie and Mariah had begun pulling limp bodies out of the wagon and laying them on the ground. "These two men are dead."

"As God is my witness, they was all alive when we put them in," the driver said. "I was told to get them to an aid station as quickly as possible. We passed a couple on the way, but they told me they couldn't take any more wounded, that they was full up. I'm just glad I could unload here."

Rachel calmed down. It was clearly not the driver's fault. The ambulance had brought eleven souls back to the mall. Three were already dead and two others were not going to live more than a couple of hours. That left six who might make it, and four of them had badly mangled limbs that would have to be amputated.

Stretcher bearers came and took one young man away to the tent where amputations were being carried out. A stack of pale and naked limbs lay a few yards off to the side. Little more than a boy, the young man cried out for help. "Miss . . . Miss . . . Don't let them take my arm," he moaned. Cassie saw that his arm was hanging on by threads of flesh.

She was reassuring him as he broke into sobs and called out for his mother. Beside him, two others were unconscious and the remainder stoically awaited their fate. She would have sworn that a couple of them looked happy. Their war was over. If they could learn to function with missing or mangled limbs, they could lead productive lives.

Much like her father.

Cassie realized just how lucky he'd been. Her throat went tight and she felt her eyes grow moist. *Get control of yourself. These boys need you.*

A few feet away, the driver was leaning against the side of his wagon. "Driver, what's your name?"

"Fred."

"Well, Fred, you did marvelously. We're sorry we yelled at you, but this has all been so overwhelming."

"Been pretty much that way for me too. I've got a wife and two kids to worry about as well as these boys. Army's supposed to pay me but I'll bet you I won't see much of that money."

They took up a quick collection and gave several dollars to Fred. He swore that he would go back up to the battlefield and collect some more wounded as soon as his horses were strong enough. That was good enough for the women.

Cassie had one question. "Tell me, did you see anything of the Sixth Indiana Mounted Infantry?"

Fred immediately understood that they were looking for loved ones. "Sorry, ladies, but I didn't see hide nor hair of anything like the Sixth Indiana. Of course banners and stuff have been shot away or lost so I could have been standing right among them and didn't know it. Don't worry, ladies, there were a lot of men killed and wounded this night, but a whole lot more didn't even get scratched."

Yes, Cassie thought, *we must always hope for the best, while we prepare for the worst.*

★ CHAPTER 16 ★

Lincoln gazed down at the unconscious body of General Meade. "I thought someone said he was recovering?"

The doctor shrugged. He was exhausted, but not fazed by the fact that he was talking to the President. "A little while back he seemed to be coming out of it. His eyes opened and it looked like he was trying to talk. But then they simply closed again and he went back to sleep. It's called a coma."

"I know what it's called, Doctor," Lincoln said testily. "But does he recover or does he spend the rest of his life sleeping away any memories of yesterday's battle?"

"Sir, there are those who believe that's exactly what happens. Just as you and I feel refreshed after a good night's sleep, it may be that going into a coma is the way the mind repairs itself."

Lincoln nodded, "Sounds plausible. But aren't there times when the mind doesn't fix itself and the mind's owner is mad for the rest of his life?"

"There are indeed. Back home there is a man who fell into a coma after some fighting in the Mexican War twenty years ago. He just sits in his rocking chair and stares at nothing. His family feeds and clothes him and sometimes the neighborhood kids come by to see the crazy old man, but everyone has given up any hope for his recovery."

Lincoln thanked the doctor and dismissed him. He waved an

195

exhausted Halleck over. "You did fine work last night, General. I don't know if Lee was chasing Meade or not, likely not, but you got things under control and I'm convinced we would have handled him if he had tried to attack."

"Thank you, sir."

"The army's yours now, General Halleck. If you want it. You know that, don't you?"

Halleck sagged visibly. "Yes, sir. I realized that the moment General Meade collapsed. He won't be back, at least he won't be able to command the Army of the Potomac ever again. But . . ."

"But what?"

It took a moment for Halleck to collect himself. "Mr. President . . . I have seen things that before this war, I could not have imagined. I have seen good, strong men, men I admired, men who came up in my command, utterly broken. I have seen our army transformed into little more than a howling, craven mob. I have seen plans that could not have failed torn asunder and tossed to the four winds. And I have seen these things repeatedly."

Lincoln said nothing. He had seen all this too.

"I used to think I knew something about war, sir. But now . . . I doubt that I know anything at all."

"I see." Lincoln measured his words. "That would leave us with but one alternative."

"I know."

"Do you feel yourself capable of working with General Grant?"

Halleck drew himself up. "I will do my best. Grant is . . ." He thought better of going on. "What choice do we have?"

Lincoln allowed himself to relax. "Very well, then. We'll send for Grant."

"As soon as possible," Halleck whispered.

Colonel Corey Wade, CSA, pirouetted in his long coat and laughed, albeit a trifle nervously. He was alive and a lot of other people weren't. And if his coat was any indication, he should have been dead a half-dozen times over.

"See. That's one more, boys, and that makes nine bullet holes in this fine piece of material. I had it made special for me by the finest tailor in Nashville. Cost me a small fortune but it's been worth it since each bullet hole represents someone shooting at me and hitting the coat instead."

The other officers gathered around the roaring fire laughed and cheered. Colonel Wade was clearly a very lucky man, and everyone would rather be lucky than smart . . . or brave.

Wade and the others were only a little bit drunk, which was understandable. They had just finished chasing a part of Meade's army back to Maryland. They were proud and confident that they could handle anything the Union could throw at them even if they were a little bit worse for wear. It was just too damn bad that Jeb Stuart wasn't there to see it. Fortunately, Wade Hampton had proven to be up to the task. While he lacked the flair of Stuart, he was a fine general.

"Anybody care to guess when the North will get decent cavalry? I know they've improved but they are a long ways away from being as good as we are. Ain't I right, boys?"

The men of Wade's Tennessee Volunteers stood and cheered. "And we got Pleasonton, too, didn't we?"

"Damn near," said Wade. "We either killed his ass or wounded him pretty badly. The Yankees are going to have to find someone else to lead their cavalry and do it real soon."

"Colonel, what do you think of the rumor that Meade's done and got himself crazy?" asked Mayfield.

Wade stifled a belch. "Well, I think he had to have been a little bit crazy in the first place to even think of fighting Bobby Lee and us."

That brought on more cheers and a call for more of the homemade whisky they'd been drinking. Wade pulled a bottle from a saddlebag. "This has got to be the last one, boys. Tomorrow we've got to be ready in case the Yankees decide to see if we want to come out and play again."

A chorus of jeers greeted this pronouncement, but the men passed the bottle, finished it, and broke up to go to their blankets or, in the case of a lucky few, their tents and cots. Wade, of course, had his private tent. He wasn't surprised when there was a light tap on the piece of wood he used as a knocker.

"Come on in, Sergeant Blandon. Sit down and tell me what's on your evil mind. You haven't been robbing corpses again, have you?" As usual, he felt a mixture of irritation and affectionate contempt at the sight of that beefy, unshaven face. Blandon was quite the toast of the regiment since he'd ambushed that Union courier the other day. Granted, he should have returned to Wade immediately, instead of riding directly to Lee's headquarters, but as he'd said, he'd wanted to get those orders to Bobby Lee as soon as possible.

"No sir. Never have and never will. Only thing I've been doing is acting like a banker for the boys. They have no idea what a Lincoln greenback is worth so I've been buying and selling the things."

"For a profit, I presume."

"Absolutely, sir. But what I'm here for is to ask for another chance to do some good for the South. I'll admit I was damn lucky when I took down that courier with all those orders, and I think I can do better the next time." he glanced slyly at Wade. "What I want is a pass so I can go into Washington and snoop around. Who knows what I might dig up?"

It seemed that every other word out of Blandon's mouth was "courier." Wade wished he'd shut up about it. According to Blandon, he'd pretty much won the battle of Manchester all on his lonesome, even though he hadn't quite made it to the battlefield himself. James Longstreet had welcomed him like a long-lost son. He—along with General Lee's entire staff—been overwhelmed by the intelligence that Blandon had brought in. Wade wished he'd shut up about it.

"Do you have any idea how insane that sounds, Blandon? You would have to pretend to desert, then you would have to try to blend in with a northern army while you are speaking with a southern accent. And then what the hell do you think you would find that the army would find important? Some days I would like to see your ass hanging from a gallows tree, but I will not send someone out on a suicide mission. Your request is denied, and I just wonder if you didn't want me to deny it so you could tell everyone you tried but I wouldn't let you be a hero."

"Sir, I would never do any such thing and I'm almost insulted."

"And I *almost* care, Sergeant. Now get the hell out of here and let me get some sleep. And don't bother to salute. I'm too tired to lift my arm."

Hadrian was dismayed. When the mighty Union Army had sortied against the Rebels, he had pictured it in all its majesty. Regiment upon regiment; long lines of cannon; thousands of supply wagons. How, he wondered, could anyone, any other army, stand up to the might that he had seen, if only a small part, heading north toward Pennsylvania? The war was as good as over. He and his followers could begin to think of ways they could exist and maybe even thrive in a peaceful world.

But then the North had gotten itself whipped. Nobody said as much, but it was as plain as the nose on your face. The soldiers were returning in ambulances, not on their own two feet. As he'd done many times before, he got his people hidden and away from vengeful white deserters. He'd picked up enough comments to know that the soldiers lamented the fact that they really didn't have a leader, a commander, a warrior. He'd heard the soldiers bawling that this or that general didn't want to fight, which was something inconceivable to him.

As far Hadrian was concerned, when you were faced with something that had to be done, you went and did it. That was how it had been when he'd brought these people up north. He'd known it had to come the very first time he'd heard some whites carrying on about Mr. Lincoln's Proclamation. Then, a few weeks later, he'd heard the overseers talking about how Judge Fenton was planning to send his slaves down to his sister's plantation in Carolina, an area Hadrian had never seen and had no desire to, and well, that had made the decision for him.

That very night, he'd gotten them all up and moving. No plans, no long discussions—and no chance for any shifty nigger to turn them over to the whites for a reward, either. They had tied up the overseers and left them in their cabins. Some of the men wanted to work them over, but Hadrian put a stop to it—Freddie and Clem had not been bad as far as crackers went.

They had loaded up the wagons, taken the mules and horses, said a short prayer, and set out immediately. Slipping past Lynchburg by the old farm roads they knew well, keeping the Pole Star always ahead of them. By dawn they were thirty miles to the north, well out of the range of the local slave patrols.

By the end of the week they had reached the river, with no trouble at all beyond one skirmish with a group of what might have been Home Guard, or a patrol, or just random white trash who had been surprised to learn that the colored could shoot back. Losing two men had been enough for them.

That original sixty-odd had grown to over two hundred by then, all bondsmen who had heard of Lincoln's great Proclamation and were eager to set foot on free soil for the first time in their lives. Freeing two hundred slaves was a good job of work, one that pleased Hadrian as much as he ever got. He thought he had a thing or two he could tell those Union generals about how to get something done. Not that they'd ever pay attention to a colored man.

He had about decided to say his goodbyes to this section of America. All he wanted was to take his new tribe into an area where they would have enough food and water and safety. It didn't have to be ripe and fertile land, either. With hard work and good planning, he was confident that he could make even a barren-looking land prosper. And he wouldn't mind doing it with a young woman named Mariah. He smiled as he remembered the two of them with their legs wrapped around each other. She was one hell of a woman.

But first the damn Union soldiers had to defeat the southerners. Then he could take his people out west or even up north into a land called Canada where he'd heard that they were kindly towards black people, a lot more kindly than the Americans.

But what could he do to affect his own fate and that of the others? Sitting by and letting others fight and die for him was against his nature. He had to fight. There had to be something he could do, but what?

Charles Rutherford of the Provost Marshal's office had the uncomfortable feeling that someone was staring at him, and that the person was in the front window of the first-floor apartment that was his destination and target.

Even though it was a clammy and soggy day, it was good to be out on the streets looking for criminals and traitors instead of dealing with the mountain of paperwork that was piled on his desk. There hadn't been much action lately. Even the rumors had dried up and his usual informers had nothing to say. He bullied and threatened them, but to no avail. At least there was the opportunity to solve the crimes that had him standing in the rain and which had stuck in his craw for a long time.

Rutherford considered himself a good detective, so it annoyed him that he hadn't been able to solve the problem of who had leaked information about the two money trains. Granted, there hadn't been any further attacks, but they could always begin again. He was confident that he had scared away the perpetrators by his presence in the Treasury. But he knew they could always regain their courage and come back. Or try something else.

But then he had caught a lucky break. An informant had told him of a southern agent, name of Jessup. While Jessup himself had slipped away, either to Richmond or to the devil, he had left behind a number of interesting documents in his room. Among them was a pile of romantic notes addressed to "John" from "Annette C." It hadn't taken Rutherford long to put it all together, particularly after reading the final note, which detailed Annette C's doubts over the entire scheme.

Annette C. lived in the apartment he was facing. Her last name was Cosgrove and she was a low-level clerk. It was ironic, he thought. They had spent so much time looking for someone higher up when the villain was a lowly clerk with no authority of her own. She was so innocuous that he didn't even recall what she looked like. She was just the short of shadow person who could get away with murder because nobody noticed her.

He took a deep breath and walked across the street to the apartment door. He was just about to knock when a voice said, "Come in out of the rain, Mr. Rutherford. It's unlocked. I saw you standing there across the street."

Rutherford was pleased that his instincts had been correct. He pushed open the door and walked into a darkened room. An older woman he now dimly recognized was seated in an overstuffed chair directly in front of him. A shawl was draped over her lap.

A glance revealed no one else in the room. There were a lot of pictures on the walls, knickknacks and statuettes on every flat surface.

"Would you like some tea, Agent Rutherford?"

"No thank you."

"Then please have a seat. We have a lot to talk about."

Rutherford sat in another overstuffed chair that creaked when he lowered himself onto it. As his eyes adjusted to the darkness, he could see that she looked haggard. Her eyes were wild and her hair was unkempt.

He glanced again at the walls. All the pictures seemed to depict historical themes—men in togas, Renaissance getups of doublets and tights, and the like. His eyes widened as he realized that they appeared to all feature the same person—a handsome young man with dark curly hair who struck Rutherford as somehow familiar.

Reaching into his pocket, he pulled out he envelope containing the final note. Slipping the sheet out, he unfolded it and handed it to her. "Did you write that note?"

Cosgrove examined it for only a moment before letting it fall into her lap and gazing off into some remote distance.

"Why did you do it, Mrs. Cosgrove?"

"It's Miss Cosgrove, if you don't mind. I never married. You may call me Annette if you wish. And as to why I did it, that should be obvious. I tried to help my country, the Confederate States of America, free itself from the rapacious claws of Abraham Lincoln and his Republican Party. All men should be free and that includes the South. When I found out that I had such important information, I made contacts and you know all the rest, I'm sure. I failed at everything and now so many are dead. Do you know that I see the dead every night? I'm afraid to go to bed, perchance to dream, because those dreams will show me the dead who died at my hand."

"I'm not too sure I understand." A cheap statuette stood on a settee to his right. It looked like the same person as in all the drawings on the walls. It suddenly occurred to him who it was: a theater person, an actor. Damned if he could remember the name, though. Edwin? Julian?

"The first attempt at robbing the money train was partly successful. A few people might have been bruised, but nobody was killed. You must understand that I never meant to kill anybody. I guess I'm naïve. I thought it was a big game. He misled me, really. John did. He let me think of it that way."

John, he thought. *That must be the name.* But he was still drawing a blank on the rest.

". . . then there was a battle during the second attempt and how many died? Hundreds, and I see them every night. All those poor young boys. They stand by my bed like ghoulish characters from *A Christmas Carol* and they won't go away. They are all broken and bloody and they blame me."

A glance to his left showed even more pictures of the same man, of John. By God—there were dozens of them. Drawings, paintings . . . even a daguerreotype.

She's mad, he thought. *Utterly and completely mad.* She might be a traitor, but he had no desire to put her in jail. "Do you have friends or relatives in the South?"

"Of course," she sniffed.

He decided it would be useless to tell her that only a handful had perished. One would clearly be too many for her fragile mind. "Then why don't you pack up some things and come with me. I'll arrange for you to go through the lines and down to Richmond."

"I'm afraid it's too late," she said as she pulled back the shawl on her lap. She had a small pistol in her hand. It was cocked and pointed at him.

Rutherford held out his hands to show he was unarmed. He had his own weapon in a shoulder holster, but that would do him no good if she pulled the trigger of what he recognized was a Colt 1849 pocket revolver that fired a .31 caliber bullet. Although the caliber was small, it would be deadly from across a room.

"Where did you get that, Annette?" he asked, still trying to keep his voice steady.

"I'm an old woman living alone. I bought it for protection."

"Shooting me will accomplish nothing," he said in what he hoped was a calm and soothing voice.

"I can't go with you, sir. I can't betray John. Even after everything. He is stronger than I. John will see it through to the end."

"John Wilkes Booth," Rutherford said.

Annette Cosgrove stared at him for a moment, then raised the pistol and fired. Rutherford reached for his own gun, but the second round shattered his wrist. The third caught him as he was rising from the chair. He collapsed atop the threadbare rug.

Annette got up, took a step or two and gazed down at him. She let out a choked sound and ran her eyes across the pictures on the wall. She returned to the chair, straightened her dress, stuck the barrel under her chin and pulled the trigger. The bullet entered her throat and took out half her skull when it exited. The force threw her chair against the wall. She lay with her arms and legs splayed out.

Rutherford eyed the pictures. He could hear shouts and footsteps on the street outside. *John Wilkes Booth*, he thought as the darkness closed in. *He'd have to take a closer look at that . . .*

★ ★ ★

Abraham Lincoln was cold and shivering. He'd paid another visit to a nearby hospital and gotten ambushed by a sudden shower. Behind him, the fire in the fireplace was raging, but the heat didn't seem to penetrate his tired frame. He felt alone, even though Stanton was with him, watching and waiting for him to make up his mind. He wanted to talk with Mary. She would comfort him. Many in Washington didn't like her. Some of the more radical abolitionists didn't care for the fact that a number of her relatives were supporters of the Confederacy—not to mention slaveholders. They snubbed and insulted her, which hurt both her and her husband.

At times she drove him to distraction with her shopping sprees. Lincoln was not a poor man—far from it. He'd been a very successful lawyer before going into politics, and gave her a more than adequate allowance that she constantly exceeded, leaving him to pay the overdue bills. He suspected that she shopped so incessantly to compensate for the lack of friendship in Washington. He didn't blame her. Assuming he won reelection, he would begin to count down the days when he could leave and return to Illinois, or perhaps someplace else. Right now he would take anyplace that was warm and dry.

"Mr. Stanton, am I making a mistake with Grant?"

"I do not see where you have a choice. We've been over this many times, and he is just about the only general who hasn't been tainted with major defeats. And, as you once said, he fights. We do not have many generals who do. God knows what they expected out of a war."

"And who do you think he will bring with him?"

Stanton thought for just a moment. "Why, I would presume he would bring General Sherman with him, and perhaps others. Thomas, I understand, is highly thought of."

"The Virginian."

"That's right. One of the few southern officers to remain loyal."

"We could use a few more of those."

Lincoln tried to laugh but it became a cough. "My critics will have a field day. Grant, they will again accuse of drunkenness, Sherman, they will say, is insane based on some bad days early on in the war. Thomas is a southerner who cannot be trusted, and so forth."

"You paint a bleak picture, sir, but all it will take is one victory and all will be right with the world. Rumors that Grant will take command are everywhere. People are looking to him to be the savior of the Union."

"I certainly hope so. It appalls me that I am giving so much power and responsibility to a man I don't know and have never met. Good lord, he could walk in to the White House right now and nobody'd know who he was."

Stanton chuckled, this time with genuine humor. "Don't forget that I've not only met the man, but tried to negotiate with him. Anybody who doesn't know who he is and thinks they can overawe him will be in for a rude awakening. He's barely forty, which makes him one of our younger generals, but I count that as a plus. After all, he's several years older than McClellan, our erstwhile boy Napoleon."

"As usual, Mr. Stanton, you have calmed me. However, I wonder how he'll be received when he arrives."

"I hope somebody recognizes him. I've made arrangements for him to stay at the Willard. It's both prestigious and very close by."

"Excellent," said the President. "Now all we have to do is wait for him to make an entrance and solve all of our problems."

If only it were that easy, Lincoln thought-*If only, if only . . .*

Josiah Baird was beside himself with anger. He stomped so hard that his artificial leg came unstrapped and sent him sprawling into a settee. Despite themselves, Cassie and her mother both thought it was funny. After a few moments, Josiah did as well. But he became somber very quickly when he thought of all the casualties.

"I simply do not understand what anybody was thinking when they either ordered or permitted Meade to attack. Now, not only have we lost the battles, but we've lost Meade as well. The country, the Union, is in serious trouble. If Lee makes a move towards Washington, the whole army could collapse. I understand the morale is extremely low. Do you concur with that, Major Thorne?"

Thorne had just entered and helped himself to some brandy. "I have never seen morale as miserable as this. The army truly thought it would march out and smash the Rebels and then go home. Now nobody can see an end to the fighting, although how much actual fighting there might be under Halleck is questionable. Somebody else has to command and it will be either Hancock or Grant. Hancock, unfortunately, is still laid up by the wound he suffered on Cemetery

Ridge. There's a tale going around that he was struck in the leg by a piece of metal and he had to dig it out of his thigh with his bare hands."

Cassie shuddered, thinking of what she'd witnessed in Washington, "How awful."

"You'd be surprised at what you can do if you have to. Did I ever tell you that I had to tie my own tourniquet when I was wounded?"

"A number of times," said Rachel, "and I'm sure I'll hear it many times more in the future."

Steven grinned and winked at Cassie. She flushed and winked back. Too bad, he thought, that he could only stay for a very short while. It looked as if Cassie was in an adventurous mood this evening. Well, so was he. Unfortunately, he had a regiment to care for, even though it was getting smaller with each passing skirmish. If he didn't get some more reinforcements it'd be unable to function and might just be disbanded.

"So that means it must be Ulysses Grant unless Lincoln decides to resurrect somebody else, like Burnside or, God forbid, McClellan."

"I understand that Grant is quite crude and drinks too much," said Rachel.

"I like him already," said her husband. "Personally, I don't care what his personal habits are just so long as he can lead this army to victory. And I'm not alone in those feelings. How about your troops, Steven, what do they think?"

Thorne thought it was interesting that Josiah had not referred to the Sixth as "his" regiment which, of course, it had once been. Now it was Steven Thorne's regiment.

"They're all looking for a savior, someone who can lead them to victory and the Promised Land. They've all seen that Grant not only fights, but wins, which intrigues them." As well it ought—they'd seen little enough of it here in the east. "They know that more fighting will mean more casualties, but if that's the price that must be paid to end the war, then they will fight for Grant. Unless, of course, he does something stupid like Burnside did at Fredericksburg. Then they would turn on him like wild dogs."

Soon it was indeed time for him to go. Despite the cold mist that had replaced the rain, Steve and Cassie stood outside and embraced fervently. For the first time, they said that they loved each other. This declaration was followed by an even fiercer series of kisses and hugs.

"Are we going to get married?" he asked, "If so, I'd like the wedding to take place as soon as possible."

"So would I. Should we go back inside and tell my parents?"

"Yes, but only for a minute. I've still got this damned regiment to put to bed."

She smiled wickedly. "Well, when we get married, you can put me to bed all you want and I promise not to complain. You won't either."

The desk clerk at the Willard Hotel was an older man whose feet hurt. He was hungry because his relief was late. He was also bored and tired. He was also a snob, which was appropriate, since the hotel was the most exclusive and sought-after establishment in Washington.

The Willard was located only a short walk from the White House, and had been rebuilt and renovated a few years earlier. Everybody who was anybody wanted to see and be seen at the Willard. The important and the self-important rubbed elbows in a perpetually crowded bar and restaurant and often spilled over into the hallway or the area where the clerk had his domain.

This resulted in a clientele that the clerk sometimes thought were barbarians. He couldn't keep them all away, but he tried to see the worst offenders off from the clean and elegant rooms.

The clerk winced when he saw the short, grubby man with a young boy of about twelve approach. The man wore a slouch hat and had on an overlarge coat badly in need of cleaning. His beard was unkempt and he had an unlit cigar in his mouth. The clerk hated cigars. He first thought the man was in sales, an occupation which he considered crude, but the presence of the boy said otherwise. Perhaps the man was just tired and disheveled from a long journey. Well, that might prove to be too bad. The man was dragging a suitcase that was dirty and worn and must have weighed a ton. *A shame*, he thought. There were many other hotels in Washington that might be able to accommodate him. He decided to encourage the gentleman to seek one of them out.

"May I help you?" he said in a voice that said he was in charge.

"My son and I would like a room."

"I'm so sorry, but we're full. May I direct you to another hotel in the area?"

"Excuse me, but I forgot to mention that there is supposed to be a room being held for me."

Now the clerk was puzzled. Of course, he had several rooms vacant and a couple were indeed reserved for important people who were coming in later. He always held back. Everyone in the hotel business did. It was the prudent thing to do. Something began to register in his overtired mind. Oh dear, the man was beginning to look familiar. He'd seen that face in the newspapers . . .

"And what name would the reservation be under?"

"Grant, Ulysses Grant. And son."

The clerk's knees began to shake. This nondescript little man was going to save the Union? The face abruptly came into focus. Grant's eyes . . . they were as cold and icy as any he had ever seen. The clerk mentally juggled some rooms. Grant would have the best one available and if the senator from Maine who might or might not arrive tonight didn't like what was left, that would be a shame.

"Of course we have a room, General Grant, a very good one. Please accept my sincerest apologies for not recognizing you right away." He now noticed that Grant wore a uniform under the dirty coat. He turned to the bellhop lounging against a wall.

"Boy!" he said in an overloud voice that cut through the noise, "Kindly take the luggage of General Ulysses Grant to his room."

The crowd in the lobby froze. Then they surged forward chanting Grant's name. Some reached out timidly as if he was a religious relic. Grant ignored them as he stood chewing on his cigar.

"We can't see you," someone yelled and, after some urging, Grant stood on a chair. He looked astonished at the reception he'd been given. He waved and smiled almost shyly, then got down. "Please show me to my room," he told the bellhop.

A portly colonel stepped up and saluted. "General, I'll get some men and seal off the floor you're on so you can have some peace and quiet."

"Excellent."

"And with your permission, sir, I'll send a message to the White House telling them of your arrival."

Grant nodded. He just hoped he would get a little sleep before he was summoned.

★ CHAPTER 17 ★

Grant had arrived. The savior was here. Like the rest of the Army of the Potomac, the men of the Sixth Indiana were of two minds. Some were pleased, while others were angry and defiant. Another general meant more fighting and more of a chance of getting killed. End the damned war, they said. And besides, what had this Grant fellow done besides beat a bunch of roughnecks and crackers who weren't proper soldiers? They wanted McClellan back, not some new guy. They all knew that Meade was recovering someplace and would likely never return. A shame, but he hadn't won either and didn't have the army's confidence.

After long arguments and not a few fistfights, the majority agreed that Grant could not do worse than any of his predecessors; therefore he should be given a chance. If Grant failed, there might not be anybody else to take the reins of the Army of the Potomac and they could all go home.

But most felt that the war could not end without victory to honor the dead and maimed, and not without freeing the slaves, chorused more voices. To do otherwise would be criminal.

"Now we finally have the right man to win this damn war," said Josiah Baird as he again held court in his home. "At least I hope we do. Grant's a predator and he's brought others with him. Good Lord, I still can't believe he travelled here all alone except for his son. But if he does what he's done before, there will be action."

Cassie shook her head. She hadn't seen Steve in a couple of days and now wondered just when the next time would be. "That prospect doesn't thrill me at all, Father. I don't want to see Steven as one of those casualties I tried to help."

Josiah saw her distress and softened immediately. "I don't want that either, and I don't want it for anybody, and that includes the Confederates. Only thing is, I can't see a way around a lot of fighting."

Mariah entered the room, concern on her face. "There was a strange man looking at the house."

"Dear God," said Cassie, "please tell me it wasn't Richard Dean again."

"Oh good Lord, no," she said. "I would recognize that little snake anywhere. No, this was a stranger and, when I confronted him, he ran off. Although I suppose it could have been somebody sent by Dean. More likely it was just a wanderer or a vagrant, but I thought I should tell you."

Cassie did not find that thought comforting. She hadn't thought about Richard Dean and his treasonous beliefs in quite a while. But then, if it wasn't Dean, then who could it have been? Perhaps they were jumping at shadows. Maybe it was just a vagrant or a wanderer. Dean would not show himself in Washington again. If caught, he might be hanged, since he was now suspected of several acts of sabotage in Baltimore.

"Hey, Yank. I hear tell you got a new general." The voice came from maybe two hundred yards away, although it was hard to tell in the night.

"True enough, Johnny, and he's gonna kick your ass clear back to Richmond and then we can all go home."

"Well, Yank, I like the going home part but there's no way in hell that he's going to beat Bobby Lee.

"We'll see. Now let's get serious, Yank, you got any tobacco? And I mean the good stuff and not the dog turds you usually smoke."

"I might. How are you set for coffee?"

"I reckon we can spare some."

Thorne listened as the negotiations went on. A price was set and two men, one from each side, stepped cautiously out into the open.

Each carried a sack. They met and exchanged them, and after a few remarks retreated toward their lines. The soldiers did not check the contents. These trades were built on trust, and besides, they were too exposed to be comfortable spending time counting and weighing.

"Don't you think we should have stopped them?" asked Willis. "I mean, aren't there rules against this kind of bartering or trading with the enemy?"

"Of course there are, but we're running dangerously low on coffee."

"And that takes precedence."

"It absolutely does, unless, of course, you've given up drinking coffee."

The two men retrieved their horses and rode back to where the regiment was camped. All was quiet on the Confederate side, matched by silence from the obviously close-by Union forces. It was as if both sides had decided that there had been enough fighting for the time being. Of course, the North was wondering just how life would be different under General Ulysses Grant. When, everyone wondered, would he attack the South? Or would Lee take advantage of Grant's perceived inexperience and launch an assault on the Union lines? The consensus was that Lee would wait for Grant to move first and then lash out and destroy him just like he had done with so many other Union generals.

The two armies were encamped only a few miles from each other. It was as if, after having searched for so long, neither wanted to let go of the other. It looked to Steve that this would be a campaign without any surprises. He could not think of anything that Grant could do besides use his greater numbers to bludgeon the Confederate army. He also could not see Robert E. Lee letting that happen. In the back of everyone's mind was the fact that the two largest armies in the history of the Americas were poised to destroy each other.

He shuddered and it wasn't from the cold. He wondered what Cassie was doing and desperately wanted to be with her. The constant talk of war and dying was utterly depressing. He needed her smile, her laughter and her body crushed against his. He smiled at the thought. Now, that was something worth fighting for.

Standing next to Lincoln, Grant was absolutely diminutive, a fact that amused both of them. Lincoln felt that he had a wonderful view of the top of Grant's head while the general had an equally charming view of Lincoln's belt buckle.

Shortly after he arrived at the Willard, a detachment of soldiers had been sent to rescue Grant from a growing mob of well-wishers and the curious. The press was so great that there was a real fear that Grant might be crushed. Several had fainted and needed to be rescued.

A wedge of soldiers had whisked him to the White House, where the President hosted an informal dinner that included Stanton, Seward, Halleck, Meigs, and Grant's son Fred. Fred was eleven and totally unawed by being in the presence of so many important people.

A huge crowd outside chanted for Grant, who finally went to a window and waved almost shyly. That satisfied many of them and the crowd began to break up. As it was obvious that Grant was tired and young Fred exhausted, the others soon departed, leaving Grant and Lincoln alone while Fred slouched on a chair and dozed.

Grant smiled fondly at his oldest of his four children. "It's amazing how children can sleep anywhere. I sometimes envy them that skill."

"Indeed. I know you're as tired as young Fred, so I won't detain you.

"We need you well rested. However, indulge me. I do want to know if you have any plans for dealing with General Lee."

"Sir, I have a number of thoughts but nothing definite yet. I want to meet with my corps commanders first and determine what changes need to be made."

Lincoln nodded solemnly. He had agreed to let Grant get rid of some of the political generals who had proven lacking in the past. Lincoln himself would have to deal with the repercussions and hope that they didn't impact negatively on the upcoming elections. He would have to find a home for those politicos who didn't want to resign from the army, someplace safe where they could parade around as generals but not harm the war effort. He admitted to himself that it was something that he should have done a long time ago. He assumed that Grant would also avail himself of the opportunity to replace failures like Burnside and Hooker. Perhaps Benjamin Butler would be added to the list. Everywhere that man went, trouble seemed to follow. He had insulted the women of New Orleans shortly after that city had fallen to the Union forces by threatening to charge those who caused disturbances with being prostitutes.

But who would replace them and how long would it take? Perhaps Grant would be better off with the devils he already knew.

"And you are still planning on keeping secrets from me?"

Grant smiled engagingly. So far he and Lincoln were getting along famously and neither man wanted to jeopardize the growing relationship. "There are no secrets to keep as of yet. But when there are, I may just keep a few cards close to my vest. But when I finally play them, be assured that I will do everything in my power to make them a winning hand."

Cassie and Mariah sat side by side on the buckboard in companionable silence. The fall sun that had warmed them all afternoon was just beginning to set. Cassie was content. Her long day of working with some of her better students had gone well. She had come to realize that some of Hadrian's people would never master the skills necessary to read and write. The smart ones, however, were leaping ahead of the others. She had formed three groups: the haves, the maybes, and the never wills. Of course, she didn't mention any of this to her students, although she was fairly certain many of them had already figured it out. Working with the smarter ones gave her the most satisfaction, although she made certain she didn't cheat the others of their opportunities. And every now and then one of the dimmer lights would suddenly comprehend and she would laugh and say "Eureka."

She didn't see the horsemen approach. Suddenly the shapes were simply *there*, black against the still-golden sky. Cassie drew her breath in sharply as Mariah clutched her arm and let out a stifled scream.

The shape that was Dover reached for the brim of his hat and for a grotesque moment Cassie though he was going to greet them. "Grab that horse," he called out. One of the others rode forward and grabbed the horse's harness before Cassie gathered the presence of mind to give the reins a snap. The horse neighed nervously as it was brought to a halt.

"Bring them down," Dover commanded. "That godless jade in particular. Try to quote scripture to me, you strumpet."

"Lemme get a handful of this one here," one of them said, as he reached for Mariah. She shrieked and jerked away, colliding with Cassie. A man gripped Cassie's arm and began pulling her from the bench. She drew back, but then, aware that it would avail her little if at all, threw herself out of the buckboard. She slammed against him, half knocking him to the ground. Finding her feet, she started running, but the man holding the horse blocked her way. A second later the first man was clutching her by the shoulders.

Mariah was still struggling with the other two. Dover was hollering to no one particular. As Cassie was being was being dragged back to him, her horse let out a panicky shriek and started down the road, buckboard clattering behind it.

"Stop that wagon!"

The man on horseback stared after it and protested, "Well, I can't do two things at once, can I—"

"What are you talking about?"

"Well, she was runnin'—"

"Never mind that! Get that buckboard. Bring it back here."

The rider started down the road, muttering to himself.

"Bring them along," Dover told the others as he started off through the brush. They had only gone a few yards when Cassie smelled a harsh odor that made her heart skip a beat: somebody was boiling tar.

Moments later they arrived at a clearing where a good-sized pot was hung above a fire. Dover hitched his horse to a tree branch and turned. It was just light enough to see the expression on his face. "Well," he said. "Well now. As you see, missy, we have our own little school here. We're going to teach you a lesson. And I guarantee you, it will stick."

One of the others started cackling. Dover glanced around, pleased with himself. "That's right. An education. That's what we've got here."

One of the other men was standing before Mariah, cooing and running his fingers though her ringlets. The other laughed. "I like this," the first man said. Mariah shook her head to knock his hand away. Reaching out, he gripped the throat of her dress and tore it open, revealing her full breasts. "And I like this even better."

He was closing in with both hands when Mariah jerked forward and sank her teeth into his cheek. He let out a shriek and fell back. Cassie could see Mariah's face clearly, her eyes wide, her teeth gritted. It was an expression Cassie had never seen before. Thrusting herself against the man holding her she kicked out with both feet. The one in front of her let out a shriek and fell to his knees.

Dover waded in, shouting once again. Cassie wrenched against the arms holding her tight, but did nothing more than swing herself around slightly. Reaching Mariah, Dover struck her twice across the face. She sagged against the man holding her.

Cassie let herself drop backward. Unprepared, the man gripping her arms stumbled backward. He came up against something and let out a shrill cry. Cassie gritted her teeth as something terribly hot splattered on her foot. There was a blow to her head and she fell to her knees.

She looked to see Dover standing over the kettle, which lay half on its side, dripping tar. A large puddle lay on the ground beside it. He peered into the kettle mouth and nodded to himself. "There's enough."

One of the men was clutching his face and muttering to himself. He kicked at Mariah. "Dirty animal."

Cassie attempted to get to her feet, but the man holding her slammed her back onto the ground. "I'll fix you, you bitch. You ruined my good shoes."

She twisted her head toward him. She could see nothing of his face, but smelled his foul breath clearly enough. "Wait'll my father gets hold of you, you bandit."

"Yes, her father, the cripple—"

"Man enough for you, Dover. You're a coward. Look at you. Four men against two women."

"That's enough—"

"My father will see you flogged. You Copperhead. You dirty, stinking little Rebel."

There was a disturbance within the brush. They all turned to see the man sent off to chase the buckboard come into sight, leading his horse.

"Well?"

The man—more of a boy, really, barely out of his teens—raised a hand. "I couldn't catch it."

"What do you mean you couldn't catch it? Couldn't catch a buckboard pulled by a single horse . . . ?"

"There was people."

"What's that? People? What kind of people?

"People. Up ahead. On the road."

Dover gestured at Mariah. "Drag her over here, now . . ."

Still dazed, Mariah raised her head. "Cassie . . ."

"Don't you dare touch her! Leave her alone! You'd better start running now. All of you! My father—"

"Your father had best be ready to invade Virginia to find us. I've got people there."

"Virginia?" The boy said. "I don't wanna go to Virginia. I don't like it over there. They ain't friendly thereabouts."

"Oh, shut up . . . Drop her right there."

Mariah let out a moan as they let her fall into the puddle of tar amid the brush.

"Now, grab the handle . . ."

The moaning rose to a shriek as the hot tar poured over her. The man she had injured stood behind the others, kicking at her legs. Cassie let out a wordless shriek of rage.

"It's Miss Baird's turn now. Bring her over here."

Cassie jerked against the man's hands. He lost hold for a moment and let out a curse. One of the others raced eagerly to help him.

There was a hallooing from the direction of the road. Cassie let out a scream as loud as any sound that she had ever uttered.

The man reaching for her looked up, then turned and vanished into the brush. The pressure on her shoulders eased and she momentarily lost her balance. Pushing herself erect, she stumbled away from the fire. "Help . . ."

"Corporal, circle around there . . ."

"Smell that? That's tar . . ."

Cassie let out another shriek. She looked over her shoulder. All of them had vanished except for Dover, who stood staring after her as if undecided what to do. She heard footsteps approaching. Running to his horse, Dover grabbed the reins and vanished into the darkness.

A shape appeared to her left. "Miss? What's wrong here?"

She wordlessly waved in the direction Dover had gone. He went on, followed by two others.

Mariah was sobbing by the fire. Cassie went over to her. Her fingers encountered warm tar. She pulled them back, but there was no helping it. Putting her arms around Mariah, she drew her into her lap. Mariah's chin was quivering and she was making small noises like those of a child. Her eyes opened and gazed into Cassie's. "Did they . . . did they touch me?"

"No darling. They didn't."

"Miss . . ."

She looked up. A man in an officer's broad-brimmed hat was kneeling on one knee. "Who were they?"

"They were . . . Copperheads."

He nodded and called his men over to help.

Robert E. Lee contemplated his paladins, seated around the sturdy table of the farmhouse he was using as a headquarters. They were discussing the latest victory over the Federals with some pride, as was understandable. Mugs of coffee littered the table and at the far end of the room, the fireplace blazed.

Longstreet sat stolidly to Lee's left. Hardee, Hill, and Anderson sat at either side of the table. Beyond Hill was General Porter Alexander, looking far too young for his responsibilities. Across from them sat Jubal Early. He had yet to meet Lee's eyes. Ashamed over his tantrum at Gettysburg, perhaps? Lee dismissed the thought from his mind.

He considered the faces that were not present. John Bell Hood was recovering from his terrible injuries in Richmond. George Pickett had failed to appear. That pleased Lee more than he cared to admit. The thought of that nightmare moment at Seminary Ridge was never long absent from his mind. It had been worst moment of the war for him— worse than Malvern Hill, worse than Sharpsburg. He knew Pickett was not to blame, but the sight of that prissy face, those carefully ringletted curls, annoyed him no end. He couldn't help it. It was better the man stayed away.

The cavalier, Jeb Stuart, was dead, at the hands of a sneaking rifleman. Unable to overcome him on the field, his foes had sent an assassin.

The face he missed most was that of Thomas Jackson, his firm right hand. There had never been such a soldier. Jackson had been like one of Napoleon's marshals—unbreakable, utterly dependable, ruthless in his loyalty to the southern cause. If you told Jackson something must be done, you could consider it accomplished, no matter how desperate or unlikely.

He cast his eyes over the men before him. Good soldiers all, fine commanders many of them, with perhaps some reservations. But there was not a Jackson among them.

Emerging from his reverie, he cleared his throat. The men ceased speaking and gazed attentively at him. "We have learned the name of the new commander of our opponent's forces. General Ulysses Grant."

They murmured the name after him. Lee was certain they had heard it already. The rumor mill of the army was a marvel beyond understanding.

"Ulysses Grant," Lee repeated. "West Point 1843."

"Desdemona," Longstreet said under his breath.

Lee frowned at him. Several of the others bent closer to the table. Ambrose Hill touched his ear as if he hadn't heard correctly.

"During the Mexican campaign," Longstreet went on. "Some of the troops put on a performance of *Othello* while we were waiting in El Paso. Grant played Desdemona."

"Did he now!" Hill brayed. "Well, that's something I'm sorry I missed."

Longstreet nodded. Anderson was smiling, and even Hardee had an amused look on his face. "That's right. I didn't see it, mind you, but I did see Ulyss in costume, with his dainty gown and sweet blond curls . . ."

"Who is this here Desder Moaner?" Early demanded.

Hill waggled his head. "Shakespeare," he said. "from *Othello*."

"Oh, them plays." Early said. "I see. And this Desdermoaner is a female, I take it?"

"Gentlemen," Lee bent forward. "It was not Desdemona who took Vicksburg this past summer."

A chorus of "yes sirs," echoed around the table. Longstreet had the good grace to look abashed.

"So he served in Mexico," Hill said. "Were you acquainted with him, General Lee?"

"No, I was not. I don't believe I met him during the Mexican campaign. I don't recall so, in any case. But he had a fine reputation. Very innovative. In one encounter our troops were being held up by Mexican forces who commanded the streets. Instead of confronting them head on, Grant smashed his way through the adjoining houses and came out behind them." He nodded. "General Scott was very impressed."

Hill nodded. "I understand there are some character questions?"

Hardee grunted. "The man is a drunk."

There were a few murmurs of agreement. Longstreet made a face, difficult to interpret amid that mass of beard. Lee swung toward him. "General Longstreet—you knew him rather well."

"Yes sir. Ah, he had his bad days before the war . . ."

So Lee understood. Resigned from the army for obscure reasons, living hand to mouth in some farm town in Ohio. On the charity of family, according to some, selling firewood from a wagon, according to others.

"Grant is a very quiet, reserved man. But there is steel underneath and total determination. He may stumble against you in the beginning, but he will learn and he will not quit. He is also far more intelligent and learned than people give him credit for. They mistake silence for stupidity when, in reality, he is intently plotting the best course of action, and when he decides on that, he will pounce. And he will not give up."

Hardee frowned. "And the drinking?"

"I believe the drinking is exaggerated." Hardee looked unsatisfied. "Well, sir, to paraphrase something just said at this table, a drunk didn't take Vicksburg."

No—nor Fort Donelson, nor Shiloh Church, nor Cedar Ridge . . . Lee did not know quite know what to make of Grant's advance down the Mississippi. The strategy—if there had been a strategy—was opaque to him. It followed no pattern of warfare with which he was familiar. He suspected that he lacked the information to judge it clearly. Obscure, almost aimless meandering would be followed by swift, decisive strokes, as if the Union forces were being commanded by two distinct individuals. Entire armies disappeared and then suddenly burst forth into existence once again in the last place conceivable. Union forces often appeared to be doing their best to avoid contact rather than confronting their adversaries, before attacking targets that seemed to be of no real importance. There appeared to be no trace of rationality to any of it. And yet it had worked. Grant's advance down the valley had been nearly unstoppable after Pittsburgh Landing, one victory after another, with scarcely a single serious setback.

He explained this to his generals as clearly as could manage. ". . . Grant follows no pattern. He is of no school of strategy that we would recognize, not that of Jomini, or Clausewitz, or any other. He is an innovator, and that can be dangerous." Lee sat back. "Any comments?"

"I beg to disagree, General Lee." Hardee was staring fixedly at the fire. He turned to face Lee. "In my opinion, Grant is nothing but a butcher. I've spoken to soldiers who fought at Pittsburgh Landing. Many of us have. The man made no effort at maneuver or tactics. He simply continued funneling men onto the field as into a meat grinder. One unit after another, the livelong day. And his mad assistant there . . ."

"Sherman," Longstreet said.

"I thank you. Sherman did nothing to interfere." Hardee shook his head. "He is a butcher and nothing more. His actions seem irrational because they *are* irrational. And we know how to handle that type. We've done it before."

There was a rumble of agreement from around the table. Lee was pleased at Hardee's words, much as he might disagree. It was difficult to gain any kind of meaningful dissent from his lieutenants. All too often, his officers would take whatever he said as the final word. That was not a good situation for any commander—consider Napoleon and his marshals. Ney, MacDonald, Soult . . . had any of them advised against the Russian adventure? And would Bonaparte have listened if they had?

He looked at each of his generals in turn. They were confident. He could feel it. Plainly, this last victory had raised their spirits, made new men of them, the same as all the other victories before it. They believed that they were invincible, that they were forces of nature, like Alexander's Companions, like the Imperial Guard. They wanted to go on, to sweep Lincoln's armies aside, to take Philadelphia, Baltimore, or Washington, and give the hated Yankees a drubbing they would never forget.

It was catching. Despite himself, Lee felt it too. At this moment he half-believed he could lead them anywhere, against any enemy, and prevail no matter what the odds. After all, look at what they had accomplished already.

He knew better. Their time in Pennsylvania was limited. Soon they would have to decamp and return to Virginia. But not quite yet. He had received a message from Richmond yesterday. President Davis had asked him to hang on as long as he could. They were awaiting an answer from Great Britain. Another week, perhaps two . . .

With these men, Lee could give Davis his necessary weeks with ease. He felt the hard knot of anxiety within him fade away. At least

Lincoln had not done what had most concerned him—reappointed McClellan, the one northern general whom Lee viewed with trepidation. Those final moments at Sharpsburg, with his right being rolled up and the reinforcements from Harper's Ferry not yet arrived . . . Lee wondered if the Yankees had any idea how close it had been.

Grant might be a mystery, but Lee had no fear of mysteries.

"Very well, then." He turned to Jubal Early. "How is your army, sir?"

Early sat up straighter. "Well fed and ready to march, General Lee."

"I'm pleased to hear it. Gentlemen, we are not going to wait for General Grant." He bent over the table. "General Early, here is what I would like you to do . . ."

★ CHAPTER 18 ★

Cassie went to her room to check on Mariah. She had insisted that she be given her own bed, and her mother had concurred, though her father had made some noises about "her own quarters" being sufficient. Cassie had spent the night on a cot in the guest room.

The poor thing was fast asleep. She had been given another dose of laudanum this morning to ease her pain. Cassie bent close to see more clearly in the dim light. Nearly three days later, the blisters were still visible on her face. Cassie bit her lip and let out a sigh. Mariah made a small noise and wriggled underneath the blanket. Reaching out, Cassie stroked her forehead. The girl quietened. Cassie hoped she wasn't dreaming about those men. The doctor had said it would take several weeks for her to heal. He had been rather huffy about being called on to treat a Negress.

She closed the door carefully and paused in the hallway. She cast her gaze at her mother's room. Her mother too lay in a drugged sleep. Seeing Mariah in her brutalized condition had shaken her considerably, and the news that the Rebels were attacking Washington had pushed her into a state of near hysteria that only grew worse when she awoke this morning—if she'd slept at all. According to Mother, Jubal Early was going to smash his way into Washington, hang the President and the Congress, and then run wild across Maryland. None of her father's patient explanations concerning the defenses of Washington and the unlikelihood that Early's bandits were carrying much in way of supplies or ammunition had any effect. At last she had agreed to return to bed until the great Confederate invasion was finally turned back.

It had been quite a relief for Cassie. Ministering to hysterical females was a daughter's duty, but she had grown a little tired of the poor dear's overwrought theatrics.

She put on her bonnet, quickly tied the bow, and then pulled on her gloves. At the top of the stairs she paused, not looking forward to what was to come. She listened for a moment. She could not hear her father anywhere.

She descended the stairs. About halfway down, the bow came loose. She gritted her teeth to hold back a man's curse. She hated it when that happened. Holding the bonnet on her head as she reached the first floor, she swept into the kitchen.

As she'd suspected, all the food she had packed earlier remained on the kitchen table. "Bridget!"

The girl emerged from the larder. "Yes, missy?"

Cassie pointed at the table. "Why aren't those on the buckboard?"

The girl's eyes grew wide. "Well . . . the colonel said . . ."

"Forget what the colonel said. Call the boys and have them load it immediately. Right now."

"Cassie!"

Her father's voice boomed from the front hall. Cassie glanced once in that direction. The girl walked toward the back door, shaking her head miserably.

"I'm not angry with you," Cassie called after her.

"Cassandra!"

For a moment Cassie considered ducking out the back door, but instead she took a deep breath and headed toward the front of the house.

Her father was waiting in the hallway. He had neither stick nor cane but, feet spread wide, was trying to balance on his one good leg along with the new one, and not doing too impressive a job of it. He had his head thrown back and was glaring down his nose at her.

"Where do you think you're going?"

Cassie paused to tie the bow once again. "Father—don't play pretenses with me. You know full well where I'm going. We discussed it this morning."

"And I made my wishes clear at that time, did I not?"

"I believe that I did the same."

He made an effort to stamp his foot. For a moment it seemed that he was about to keel over, and Cassie had to hold herself back from running to help him.

"Young lady, you are not leaving this house."

"Sir, that is not your decision to make."

He pointed a finger at her. "As long as you are under this roof, you will do as I say."

"Then perhaps I shall not return at all."

Her father gave a sharp shake of his head. "Don't be ridiculous, Cassandra. Confederate troops on the march, Copperheads roaming the fields and highways . . ."

He gestured over his head. "Think of that girl upstairs. Do you want that to happen to you?"

All of Dover's crew had vanished except for the younger boy, who had been captured leading his horse aimlessly though the woods. "Those Copperhead Democrats have trotted off to Virginia with the rest of the trash. As for the Rebels . . . what did Captain Kemp say?" The captain had stopped by while leading a patrol yesterday to reassure them after the news of Early's attack had arrived. Confederate foragers were sticking close to Early's column, and were unlikely to bother them. Evidently, Early didn't have enough troops to provide cover for them.

"Nonetheless, you are going nowhere."

"I am going to Hadrian and his people, where I am needed. They must be fed, and reassured about the Rebels, and that is what I intend to do."

"You are not needed . . ."

"Everyone is needed . . . ." She said in a singsong voice. "Everyone must put his hands to the wheel. The nation calls in its hour of need, we all must do our part, carry our share of the burden . . . where did I hear those words, Father? From a patriotic Union Army colonel, or in a play, perhaps?"

"You are not going to endanger yourself over a gaggle of . . . rogue Negroes."

"Rogue Neg . . ." She yanked her skirts from the floor and advanced toward him. "What an awful thing to say! I suppose that's how you lost your leg, fighting to set free some rogue Negroes?"

He blinked down at her. She could see that the words had hurt him, and wished she could take them back, but it was too late to retreat now—for either of them.

"Young woman," he said in a low voice. "You will return to your room and wait to be called to supper. Or I will send for the boys and have you carried there by force and locked in."

"Will you now, Colonel?" A buggy whip lay upon the sideboard, something that Cassie's mother would surely not have allowed had she been awake. She strode over and picked it up. Swinging back to her father, she lifted it high and gave it a shake. "Then do so, sir. But I warn you, you will see them thoroughly thrashed before your very own eyes."

She gave the sideboard a sharp whack. It left a mark, something her mother would not be happy about either. Her father visibly started and stood blinking at her. He, who should have been the first in the world to have been aware of it, had finally arrived at the simple realization that he was facing Josiah Baird's daughter.

They stood gazing at each other for a long moment. Then Cassie negligently dropped the whip and swept past him. He made no move to stop her.

"Cassandra . . ." His voice was nearly a whisper.

She halted at the door and looked back. He stood there with his shoulders hunched, staring at her as if at some being he had never before seen and could not imagine actually existed.

She cut him off as he opened his mouth to speak. "Best not to wait supper for me."

He followed her out onto the porch. "Cassie . . ."

At the buckboard, Lemuel, a local farm boy hired to help with the chores, was loading the last of the boxes. She thanked him and stepped up onto the driver's seat.

"Uhh . . . Miss Baird . . . ."

"Yes, Lemuel?"

He gaped at her from a luxuriantly spotted face, then touched his hat. "Nothing, miss."

She looked back the house. Her father stood at top of the steps, leaning against the post as if it was the only thing keeping him from falling over. "Good day, Father. We will speak later."

Turning to the horse, she snapped the reins and started off.

★ ★ ★

Dean trudged down Pennsylvania Avenue eating candied fruit from a paper sack. He had spent the early afternoon at the battle line out past the 3rd Ward, eager to see his former colleagues in blue get a good mauling from Jubal Early's forces. He had been disappointed— all that was visible were a few rifle exchanges and a desultory cannonade or two. The Confederates seemed reluctant to come to grips with the Union troops behind the fortifications at Fort Stephens.

They had proven themselves already, that much couldn't be denied. Early had burst across the Pennsylvania border and crossed the width of Maryland to D.C. without a single move made to delay him. Not one Union soldier had raised a musket in defiance. The Union forces in Maryland had evidently skedaddled straight out of Early's way. That was the only logical explanation. Dean shook his head. It was pathetic. From his point of view, the Union army had shot its bolt. It was a good thing he'd got out when he had.

Some kind of rumpus was breaking out in front of the White House up the street. Dean hastened his step, stuffing fruit into his mouth. He paused across the street at Lafayette Park. A carriage was pulling up at the mansion steps, with a number of mounted troops at either side. And . . . lo and behold! Here came none other than the Great Ape himself, lumbering down the White House steps toward the carriage.

He was wearing his customary high stovepipe. Dean wondered how he'd get it inside the enclosed carriage. Maybe he'd have to squat down. Dean chuckled at the image.

Beside him walked another man, one of his Cabinet, evidently. Dean couldn't put a name to him. His knowledge of Lincoln's circle was perhaps not as deep as it should be.

Lincoln swept off his hat as he entered the carriage, the other man following him. Dean ran his eyes across the horsemen. He frowned to himself, chewing a little more slowly. Then it came to him: there were only a few cavalrymen in the escort. Six . . . no, seven. That was it. Usually, it was a squadron or more. Dean would bet that most of them were up at the front lines, reinforcing the city garrison.

He had been largely at loose ends since returning to Washington. Security was a lot tighter now than it had been—something about a spy ring in the Treasury Department. Booth had been keeping his head low. He discussed many plans, but put nothing, really, into effect. Dean could understand that, as restless as it made him after his exploits in Baltimore.

Booth kept putting off his plan to strike at Lincoln, surrounded as he always was by troops often numbering in the dozens. These days he spoke of it offhand, as if it was a daydream he'd like to see come to pass. Now the scheme was to kidnap one of the Cabinet, Seward or . . . Stanton, was it.

And yet here the Gorilla was, with only a handful of cavalry to protect him.

The horsemen were lining up ahead and behind the carriage. Their commander shouted a single word and the horsemen began trotting toward the avenue. The carriage jerked into motion. There were a few catcalls as it appeared on the avenue.

Dean looked around. A man in a checked suit and a derby was writing something in a notebook. A reporter? Discarding the empty sack, Dean wiped his hands on his trousers and walked over to him. "Where's the President headed?"

"Up to the battle line," the man said without looking up.

Dean's eyes followed the carriage as it passed, but he failed to take it in. Instead, he saw an image of something totally different: the magnificent raid that would bring the war to a close, the bold stroke by Booth and Dean that no one had considered possible, the smiling face of Jefferson Davis as the Confederate crowds cheered themselves hoarse, Booth's firm hand on his shoulder, his own grand but quiet heroism.

Turning away, he went off in search of Booth.

The sun was nearly touching the horizon as Lincoln unfolded his lanky frame from the carriage. He put on his stovepipe as he waited for Stanton to clamber out. General Heintzelman, the XXIInd Corps commander, was waiting along with several officers. Lincoln reflected that he couldn't recall seeing Heintzelman without his saber before.

Heintzelman saluted and then shook Lincoln's and Stanton's hands before introducing his staff. He seemed to be in a jollier mood than might be expected of a man at grips with an enemy army right at the edge of his country's capital city, but Lincoln supposed that meant good news.

"He's not getting any farther, Mr. President. He's smack up against our fortifications, and that's where he stops."

Lincoln could hear the crackling up ahead of them. A cannon boomed; a small-bore weapon, from the sound of it.

"He just doesn't have the manpower," Heintzelman went on.

"How many, would you say?" Stanton wanted to know.

"Four thousand or so, five thousand at most."

Lincoln nodded to himself. That had been the big question back at the White House. Estimates of Early's manpower had ranged from five to ten thousand. His lips quirked. If it had been McClellan, he'd have been claiming twenty or thirty thousand, with a dozen Pinkerton spy reports to prove it.

They were nearing the parapets of Fort Stephens and the battle line beyond. Some troops resting up ahead sprang to their feet as they approached. Lincoln waved while they saluted. A few of them cheered. That was heartening to hear. On the drive over, the catcalls and jeers had easily outnumbered anything else.

"I'd take off that stovepipe if I were you, Abe."

Heintzelman glared behind him. "No . . . quite right." Lincoln reached up and swept off the hat. "We don't want to make it easy for Johnny, now do we?"

They reached the fortifications, if that was the proper word. Hastily-dug trenches with mounds in front of them, piles of wood and brush, the occasional stone wall. More cheers rose from the men in the trenches. He waved the hat as he stepped down into the nearest trench.

Lincoln leaned against a rail bulwarking a mound of dirt and peered carefully over the top. It was the first time he'd ever truly laid eyes on a battlefield. There wasn't much to see, actually. The Rebels across from them were keeping their heads down as well.

A sudden burst of rifle fire broke out to his left, flashing brightly in the gathering darkness.

"It's been like this all day," Heintzelman was telling Stanton. "Random firing, and that's about it. There was brief demonstration early this morning, but I wouldn't even call it an attack."

"So this is just a raid," Lincoln said.

"Yes, sir. A welcoming party for General Grant."

So Grant had been right. He had dismissed the attack when they'd first gotten word of Early's approach yesterday. The Cabinet had clamored for him to detach some troops from the Army of the Potomac and send them here. He had adamantly refused, saying that was exactly what Lee wanted. The troops already in Washington could easily hold Early back. After a brief inspection of Heintzelman's lines, he had headed north for Pennsylvania, upsetting a number of the District's inhabitants, as well as the city's press. Lincoln had to admit that he admired Grant's cool.

"I just wish we had a bigger force out there now," Heintzelman said. "We could put a bit of a nutcracker on our old friend Jubal."

"What of General Wallace?" Stanton asked.

"Lew Wallace has a brigade. He's being reinforced steadily from Baltimore and Pennsylvania. That's all I know, Mr. Secretary."

"Do think Wallace can engage with Early?"

"Well, let me put it this way, Mr. President. If I were him, I would." Heintzelman gazed out over the battlefield. "Early must be aware of that too. Wallace has been picking off some of his foraging expeditions. Jubal must be getting a little nervous." He turned back to face them. "He'll be gone by this time tomorrow. Wouldn't surprise me to know that he'd started pulling back already."

Lincoln looked back out over the field. From somewhere to his right, a cannon roared. A shell arced out over the Rebel lines and exploded. The blast was followed almost immediately by a scream, clearly audible in the twilight. Lincoln bit his lip as the sound died out. Some poor boy was taking his final breaths. A home in Old Virginia, the Carolinas, or points south would soon be plunged into despair.

He made a gesture to put on his hat but checked himself. He turned to Heintzelman. "Well, General, thank you for the tour. And for holding back our Rebel guests as well, needless to say."

"Just wish we could do more, Mr. President."

"You've done plenty."

They walked silently back to the carriage. Lincoln felt obscurely disappointed. He was unsure of what he'd been looking for here, but whatever it was, he hadn't found it.

In a moment they had reached the carriage. Lincoln hoisted the stovepipe and gazed at Stanton. "Isn't that life, Edward? Just when it's time to put the hat back on, it's time to take it off again."

The general looked a little perplexed. Stanton smiled. "So it might seem, Mr. President."

"There he is, swinging his old hat. The Apeman in person."

Booth stroked his mustache as he watched Lincoln speaking to a man in uniform. There was a good-sized crowd milling around the road, being kept away from the line by a squad of pickets. "And there's Stanton, Mr. Roly-Poly."

"Stanton, that's right," Dean said. He started at the crackle of rifle fire from the front.

Booth turned to Sid. Nate, for his part, had been caught pilfering a shop and was relaxing in the district jail. Mary Nardelli was back in Baltimore, following a fit of temper from Booth. They could have used both of them tonight. "When that carriage starts moving, you run straight down to that corner to tell us."

Sid frowned slightly, as if putting effort into remembering the instructions, and nodded curtly. Booth turned to Dean. "Come along."

In a moment they had reached the spot where Jessup, glare-eyed as ever, stood leaning against a fencepost. He fell into step with them without a word. Jessup was wearing a long coat and holding his arms close to his sides.

Booth pointed ahead of them. "There, where the road narrows. That's where we'll take him."

"I don't see a lot of plannin' here, Booth," Jessup said.

"Which is the way it should be. We go by instinct, my man. There is a tide in the affairs of men, and it's flowing in our direction now at full flood. We will go where it takes us."

Jessup shrugged.

"Now, you take Hillyard . . . . Where is he, anyway?"

Jessup nodded toward a dark spot down the road in which a tall figure was barely visible.

"You get on either side of the road . . ."

"No, we ain't doin' that. We'd just shoot each other."

"All right. Set it up however you want." Booth looked over his shoulder. "But do it now."

He turned to Dean. "Okay now, Dick . . ."

"I did pretty good, didn't I?"

"You did fine." He pointed at a building with blazing lanterns hanging from the front porch. "Go to that shop there and buy a half-dozen packets of pepper. Quickly, now."

Dean did as he told. When he emerged, Sid had just arrived, out of breath. A few feet beyond them, Jessup was speaking to Hillyard, a man who could have been his twin. Dean handed the twisted paper packets to Booth.

"Halloo there, you young sports," Booth called out to a gang of layabouts sitting across the street from the store. "How would you like to each earn a whole silver dollar?"

Their interest piqued, the street Arabs got up and approached Booth. They were all in their teens, seemingly of every ethnic background imaginable. At least one was clearly a mulatto. Booth conferred with them for a moment. The boys cackled as they accepted the packets and coins. "Straight for their eyes," Booth said, as he stepped away.

He walked up to Dean. "Check your weapon."

Dean obediently lifted the Colt Navy pistol out of his coat pocket. He opened the cylinder and checked the balls by hand, then snapped it shut again. He slipped it under his arm where it wouldn't be seen.

Booth was gazing up the street. The first horses of Lincoln's escort were in sight, the carriage right behind them. Slipping off his kid gloves, Booth shoved them into his pocket. He turned back to Dean. His eyes were shining, his jaw working beneath the mustache. "Nervous, are we?" He put a hand on Dean's shoulder. "Don't be. This is a God-sent moment. We have a firm grip on the fulcrum of history, young Dick, and we will now move it as we will't."

He swung away and went on up the street, a well-dressed figure taking in the evening. If Lincoln's guard noticed him at all among the crowd, they gave no sign, any more than they did to Jessup and Hillyard standing together a few feet on, as if in deep conversation.

Dean looked nervously about him. What had happened to the street boys? Only two of them were visible. Where were the others? As he glanced around, a passerby, an older man, caught his eye. Dean dropped his head. The pistol under his arm felt as if it weighed a ton.

He snapped his head up at a sudden explosion of shouts and animal cries. In the street before him, the two lead horses were rearing backward while their riders fought to control them. The boys, having unloaded their packets of pepper into the horse's eyes, were now running off, throwing shouts of scorn over their shoulders.

Gunfire roared to Dean's left. Booth was firing a derringer at the cavalrymen to the rear of the carriage. Jessup pulled a sawed-off double-barrel from under his coat and opened up on the next horseman, while beyond him Hillyard blasted away with a pistol much like Dean's own.

Dean shifted his attention to the riders in front of him. Raising his pistol, he aimed at the closest bluejacket, but at that moment the panicked horse shook him off and he fell to the street. Dean shifted his aim to the second rider and pulled the trigger. He couldn't see if the bullet had hit, so he fired again. The man threw his arms up and dropped from the saddle.

Dean took aim at the carriage driver, but the man leapt off and ran for his life. A glance at the first rider showed him lying unmoving as the horse's hooves stomped his torso repeatedly.

Jessup was firing once again. Hillyard, crouched down, seemed to be in full-bore gunfight with the remaining guards. And Booth . . .

Booth was loping toward the carriage, his face intense as he reloaded the derringer. He grabbed the handle, but the door wouldn't open. As Dean watched, he kicked the door once, and then again, before once more gripping the handle. This time, the door swung wide. Leaping forward, Booth raised the derringer. The blast sounded like a cannon going off.

Lincoln and Stanton sat together in easy silence as they thought about what they had seen on the battle line. Stanton was turning toward him when the carriage jolted and a sudden uproar of shouts and the neighing of horses broke out on the street.

Stanton was clutching at his glasses. "What the devil . . ."

The stovepipe had fallen from Lincoln's lap. He was bending for it when the first shots rang out.

Stanton's eyes went wide. "Abraham . . . Mr. President . . ."

Several blows struck the carriage door. It suddenly burst wide and a pistol roared, the muzzle blast blinding in the twilight. Lincoln would have been hit if another jolt of the carriage hadn't thrown him back at that very moment.

A man clambered inside, his face shadowed. Lincoln could make out a mustache and nothing else.

With an inarticulate cry, Stanton lunged at him. The man clubbed Stanton several times with the pistol and then shoved him back into the seat. Grabbing for Lincoln, he raised the pistol.

Time seemed to slow to a crawl for Lincoln. He took in the well-dressed figure before him. There was something that he was sure that this city-bred fool didn't know—that very few knew, though Lincoln had made no effort to keep it a secret. When he was a young man back in the 30s, Abe Lincoln had been widely known as a wrestler. At county fairs, picnics, Independence Day celebrations, or random weekend nights in town, Lincoln had taken on local champions across Kentucky and had beaten virtually every last one of them. In over four hundred matches—he'd lost the exact count many years ago—he had never been defeated. Oh, there had been a draw or two, sure enough, but Lincoln had never lost once.

Flexing his legs beneath him, the champion wrestler of the state of Kentucky flung himself at the assassin.

The man grunted as Lincoln gripped his wrist. He slammed the hand holding the derringer against the roof of the carriage. The third time, it went off with a roar.

Lincoln grabbed the shoulders of the man's frock coat and yanked him toward him. The man struggled, entangled in Stanton's flailing legs. Lincoln slipped off the seat, dragging the man down with him. He struck him in the temple with his fist and then slammed his head against the front partition. The man let out a cry, half shock, half fear. Lincoln slugged him once again.

He felt a sharp pain in his arm. The fellow had a dagger, did he? Grabbing at that hand, Lincoln seized his little finger and twisted it backward as the man slashed him a second time. There was an audible crack followed by a high-pitched shriek.

The knife clattered against Lincoln on its way to the floor. The man was flailing against him, no longer attacking but simply trying to get away. The back of Lincoln's head hit the carriage door, knocking it open. He slid out, his head only inches above the rutted street.

He gripped the man by the throat and shook him like a man-sized rat. Pulling his arm back, he readied a solid final blow.

A lantern from a nearby shop illuminated the terrified face above him. Lincoln paused as he stared in shock.

John Wilkes Booth?

Dean backed away from the carriage. Around him people were screaming as they fled from the gunfire. He looked to the rear of the carriage. Jessup and Hillyard were still firing. He couldn't catch sight of the remaining guards. Sid was nowhere to be seen.

Hillyard, trying to reload, suddenly folded up against the fence to his rear. Jessup squatted down and continued firing. He had a pistol himself now, with the shotgun lying at his feet.

There was a roar from within the carriage. Dean took a step forward, then raced over and clambered into the driver's seat. It took him what seemed an eternity to find the reins. "I know where to go," he muttered as he took them in hand. "I know . . ."

Booth took the opportunity to strike Lincoln twice in the face. Dropping his elbow, Lincoln gave him a full shot in the eye. Booth slumped against the partition and let out a moan.

Lincoln kicked at him, trying to get himself untangled. A little too hard, it seemed—he found himself sliding right out of the carriage onto the street.

He lay there stunned a moment before raising his head. The carriage was moving away. Booth appeared in the open door, gazing wide-eyed at Lincoln. He raised his hands. He was holding the derringer, trying to reload it. Then the carriage jolted as a wheel passed over a body lying in the street and the gun fell from his hands. Booth stared at it in perplexity before once more lifting his eyes to meet Lincoln's.

A young fellow leapt onto the carriage and climbed next to the driver. A man wearing a ragged coat ran past Lincoln and jumped onto the baggage platform in the rear, hanging on for dear life.

Lincoln felt a hand on his shoulder. "Mr. President, are you all right?"

Nodding silently, Lincoln started to get to his feet. A soldier appeared beside him, aiming a carbine at the carriage.

"No!" Lincoln shouted. "Stanton's still aboard!"

"That's right." It was Hammond, this month's commander of the guard. "Cease fire . . . everyone."

Lincoln looked about him. Two troopers lay unmoving in the street. Another was moaning a few feet to the rear. Against a fence, a ragged man lay, a pistol at his feet. Two of Hammond's men were searching him.

Now that the gunfire had stopped, the crowd was returning. A woman pointed at Lincoln and let out a shriek. "Oh my God, he's bleeding!"

"Sir, you've been hurt."

"So I have," Lincoln agreed. "It's not that bad."

"All the same, sir, you need a doctor."

"Yes—at the White House."

"Sir—we can return to General—"

"No, Major, the White House."

The officer hesitated. "Yes, sir."

A large mass of cavalrymen had appeared from the direction of the battle line. They were shouting at the crowd to move aside.

Lincoln looked westward along the street. There was no sign of the carriage. They would never run it down now.

"John Wilkes Booth," Lincoln said to himself. It could not be denied that this life was full of surprises.

"What was that, sir?"

Lincoln shook his head. A man appeared before him, holding the ruin of his stovepipe. The president took it from him. It was torn and flattened almost beyond recognition. "My thanks," he said.

Cassie sat with one finger resting on a page of a McGuffey Reader, trying to make out the words in the dim light of a lantern hanging from a tree branch. Beale, one of her students, was working his way through the same passage in a loud but melodic voice.

She had a larger class than she had seen for the past few weeks. All of them had wanted to ask her about Mariah, and many had remained to be schooled. At the other side of the campfire, some of the older men were playing cards. Lemuel was among them, showing more facility with a card deck than Cassie thought strictly appropriate for a boy his age.

Her father had sent Lemuel and Scooter, their other hired boy, after her on muleback. At first she'd thought they intended to take her back home, but it seemed they were actually only tasked with keeping an eye on her.

Scooter, a free colored boy who made his living as kind of a freelance farrier and reins repairman, sat a few yards beyond them, playing his mouth organ for a small group of listeners. It was a strange, stirring type of music, unlike any she'd before heard, wailing notes that didn't quite sound right but called to mind thoughts of cold winds in a bleak, twilit landscape.

"Noise," she told Beale, who was stumbling over the word.

"That's right," he said. The rest of her students burst out in laughter. Hadrian, watching the card game, looked over at them. He had greeted her gruffly today. He'd visited Mariah once at the house, staying only a few minutes before leaving in a visible rage, not even stopping for the food Cassie had prepared for him. His expression at the moment spoke volumes. Woe betide any Copperheads who stumbled into his path this night.

Cassie had found the group in a better state than she'd feared after her several days of enforced absence. Some local farm women had dropped off food for them—guilty conscience over the attack on Mariah, perhaps? They'd scarcely been aware of the battle. The campground was just a little too far for most of the noise to carry. All she'd heard since she'd arrived was the occasional distant rumble of cannon. They were surprised to hear of the Rebel attack, and pleased to learn that it was going nowhere.

"Ol' Abe, he'll take care of that right quick," Toby had said.

The words had raised an image in Cassie's mind of Abraham Lincoln, the Railsplitter, waving an axe and chasing off masses of butternut-clad men. If it were only that easy.

A sudden clatter in the darkness caught her ear. She got to her feet, along with most of the blacks. All of them thinking about poor Mariah, no doubt.

A carriage was approaching out of the night, from the direction of Washington. Cassie set down her copy of the Reader. Looking about her, she saw that most of the men had slipped off into the night. Something that Hadrian had worked out, she would guess.

The carriage had approached close enough so that she could make out a single man sitting in the driver's seat. He raised a hand in greeting. The blacks muttered uneasily among themselves.

"Cassie!" the man called out.

She stared a moment in pure shock, then closed her eyes. *Richard,* she thought. It was Richard Dean, and none other. What could that silly man possibly want here?

The carriage drew to a halt. Richard hopped down and stood gazing at her, hands on his hips. The door to the carriage opened and another man got out, this one well-dressed. From the other side, two more appeared, a handsome young man and a greasy-looking figure that Cassie might have taken for a tramp. Reaching the door on this side, they half-hauled, half-helped an older man out of the carriage.

The ill-assorted group came toward them. Richard was smirking in a fashion that called up nothing good in the way of memories. The older man was staggering, scarcely able to keep on his feet. Cassie gasped as she saw his face, masked by a curtain of blood.

The well-dressed man in the lead wasn't in much better shape. In truth, he looked as if he had been mauled by a bear. His right eye was almost closed, his face swollen and turning purple all around it. He seemed slightly familiar to Cassie, though she couldn't quite place him.

They came to a halt about ten feet short of Cassie's group. The older man sank to his knees. Richard gestured at him. "Cassie," he said. "May I introduce you to Mr. Edward St—"

'That's enough, Dick." The well-dressed man's voice was audibly slurred.

"But . . ."

"Shut up, Dean," the ragged man said. The younger man, his face striking in the firelight, looked on as if none of it had any connection to him.

"Miss . . ." the well-dressed man said. "We need to get to Virginia. Your colored here will know of a safe route . . ."

"I hate to contradict you, sir, but you are mistaken if you believe that any of these people . . ."

"Goddammit." Reaching into his coat, the man pulled out a pistol. Behind him, the ragged figure did the same.

There was a high shriek from one of the girls behind Cassie, followed by a quick gabble of voices.

"Oh lawd above, he got a gun . . ."

"Momma, Momma, I's afraid . . ."

"Please mister—put that thing down . . ."

The man gritted his teeth and glared at the women. He made a theatrical gesture with the gun, and immediately Cassie saw an image of him clean-shaven, in a Roman toga, declaiming the words of the great William Shakespeare.

She blinked a moment, feeling as if the entire world had stopped making sense, as if everything she'd ever taken as true had been thrown into doubt by the appearance of this one man. She cast her eyes at Richard Dean, who was taking in the scene with an expression of infinite dullness.

What on earth is Richard doing with John Wilkes Booth?

"You quiet these women down, miss!"

In response, the gabble grew even louder. Cassie turned to shush them but something about their tone and expressions halted her. They were doing this with deliberation, not out of fear at all. They were clearly out to confuse these ruffians. She swung back to Booth. "Put your guns away."

"To hell with that," the ragged man shouted. "You get your niggers in hand!"

Booth raised a finger, a gesture she recalled from the stage. The ragged man took a step forward, lifted his gun and fired a single shot in the air.

The shot was immediately echoed by a dozen or more from the bushes to Cassie's right. She moved back involuntarily, raising her hands to cover her face, an image of the men being struck down burned upon her mind.

When she lowered her hands, they lay scattered before her, Booth, his ragged crony, and the handsome boy. Richard was nowhere to be seen. Beyond them, the injured older man held out a hand to her. She went to him, carefully stepping around the corpses.

She gasped as he drew near to him. She knew this man as well. Her father himself had introduced her to him no more than three months ago. "Mr. Stanton!"

"Yes, my dear . . ." She couldn't tell if he had actually recognized her, but that didn't matter.

Several of Hadrian's men were examining the carriage. Others were searching the bodies behind her. The women, led by Tabitha, had joined Cassie.

"Lord help us," Tabitha said. "Get this poor man some water."

"And a blanket," Cassie said.

One of the younger girls spoke. "He was a captive, wasn't he?"

"Yes," Stanton whispered. "Booth . . . That Booth is a fiend from Hell."

Someone handed Tabitha a bowl of water. She carefully gave Stanton a drink, and then the others lowered him onto a blanket.

Cassie got to her feet and turned. Toby and Seph were eying the bodies. "That mustache fella looked like he was set to speechify."

Seph, a heavy-set younger man, shook his head. "White folk."

Hadrian stood to one side, a shotgun under his arm. "All right. Load up the wagons and the mules. We got to be a distance from here by sunrise . . . ."

Cassie went to him. "Hadrian . . . what are you talking about?"

He gazed at her as if at a confused child. "Miss Cassandra . . ." he sighed. "We just shot three white men. Do you have any idea what will happen now?"

"Hadrian . . ." She pointed to where Stanton lay, his face being cleaned by Tabitha. "That is Edward Stanton, Abraham Lincoln's secretary of war. These men kidnapped him. They were going to take him down south, to the Confederates . . ." She turned back to him. "Nobody is going to blame you for this. Quite the contrary."

Hadrian stood gazing at Stanton, a slight frown on his face, as if for the first time in his life he had encountered something that he could not immediately grasp. He licked his lips. The men around him gazed at each other wordlessly.

At last Hadrian spoke. "I see."

Another moment passed in silence. Hadrian swung toward the men. "Toby, you take one of the mules, ride down the crossroads where the soldiers are at. Tell them Abe Lincoln's secretary is here and he needs doctoring."

Toby shook his head. "I don't know them soldiers gonna listen to me, Hadrian."

"I'll go with you," Cassie told him.

She headed for the buckboard while Toby went for the mule. On her way she collected Lemuel and Scooter and got them saddled up. While she waited for them, she thought again of Richard. There had been no sign of him. Had he been hit? Was he out there now, bleeding in the darkness?

Cassandra, you are such a ninny. She took hold of herself. Look what he had done. Look who he had been involved with.

Toby rode up on the mule and they started out. A group of men was carrying Stanton in the blanket closer to the fire. Tabitha held his hand, praying softly.

They left the firelight behind for the dark country road. Despite herself, she once again thought of Richard. Was he out there now, staring at her as she passed? She shivered and concentrated on the road.

★ CHAPTER 19 ★

"Who goes there?"

Steven Thorne pulled in his reins and raised an arm. The men behind him came to a halt.

"This is Major Thorne and the 6th Indiana Mounted."

"What's the password?" The voice had the clear tones of New England.

Thorne growled in his throat. They had been on horseback since late afternoon and now it was past midnight. He was in no mood for this. "How the hell do I know?"

Voices conferred in the darkness up ahead. "Well, he's certainly no Reb, that much is for sure."

"All right, come on ahead."

He rode a few more yards and came to a halt. An officer stood beside the road at the head of a small group of men. To the other side at least a dozen more gazed at him from shallow trenches. Beyond them stood a small-caliber cannon covering the road.

Thorne raised his head at the sound of distant gunfire. They'd been hearing that off and on for the past fifteen minutes.

"You're who again?"

"6th Indiana, under orders to report to General Wallace."

"I see. Well, that would be a neat trick, now wouldn't it?" One of them men beside him chuckled.

"Why is that?"

"Well, General Wallace and everybody else is scattered from here halfway to Baltimore."

Thorne pulled off his hat and rubbed his scalp. He was tired, aching, hungry, and had no clear idea of what he was doing. The little patience he had remaining was dissipating quickly. "You want to give me an explanation?"

"Sure. We're out chasing Jubal Early."

"Early." The last Thorne had heard, he was still engaged around Washington.

"That's right," the second man said. "We found out he was coming up the Baltimore Turnpike and set up an ambuscade north of Germantown."

". . . Wallace's brigade, the Oneida County regiment, and the 10th New Jersey."

"He came prancing up that road as bold as you please. No flankers or nothing."

"We opened up and tore them apart. Must have lost a tenth of his men in that first fusillade."

"The rest of them scattered to the four winds. We've been running them down ever since."

Thorne frowned. A night attack? From a general as cautious as Lew Wallace? That didn't make any sense. "Wallace ordered this?"

"Ayeh. Orders from U.S. Grant."

"From here on in, we hit the Rebels every chance we get. No matter how many there may be. Never give them a moment's peace."

Now that made sense to Thorne. He'd heard all sorts of things about Grant, some of it complimentary, much of it not. But one thing all agreed on: he wasn't afraid of closing with the Rebs.

"All right. Now who do I report to?'

The officer rubbed his chin. "Now there's a problem. You can't go riding around here in the pitch black. You'll be taken for Rebels."

Another far-off clatter of gunfire rang out. Wouldn't that be a grand climax to his military career? Shot down as a Rebel by Bostonians. "Well, what are we supposed to do?" he demanded, perhaps a little sharply.

"Francis, would you care to ride down to the colonel and see if there's anything for these fellows to do?"

"My pleasure, sir."

Thorne told the men to dismount and take a break. He and Archie Willis walked around, shaking the stiffness out of their legs. The officer—Thorne still had no idea of his name or rank—followed them around giving a detailed description of Jubal Early's bad fortune.

He was on the third or fourth distinct version of it when Thorne stopped him. "One minute . . . how could you be with the guns now when you were with the New York infantry a minute ago?"

"I wasn't there at all," the officer said huffily. "I've been here all the livelong night. I'm just telling you what I heard."

At that point, the other officer, Francis, rode up. "Major—if you want to follow me . . ."

They got saddled up and headed down the road. After about a mile they turned off into a hilly area. Several bonfires appeared ahead. A number of troops were standing guard. In the middle, between the fires, sat about a hundred men, dressed in butternut or gray.

An officer walked up to meet them and Francis explained the situation.

"All right, Major. This is the prisoner collection point. You'll be getting new groups the rest of the night. Just keep an eye on them and make sure none of them run off. You'll be told what do with them in the morning."

Thorne fought a sinking feeling as he got off his horse. "Very well."

Willis came up to him. "Is this what we rode forty-odd miles for? To guard prisoners?"

"That's what it looks like."

Willis shook his head in disgust. Thorne told him to put some men on the hilltops, put the rest out in a perimeter, and to place the horses at a good long distance from the prisoners with plenty of guards around them.

The troops who had originally been on guard vanished onto the darkened road. The Rebels glared at the 6th Indiana and muttered among themselves. "Fuckin' Yankees," one of them said, just loud enough to be heard. Thorne began a slow inspection of the area while he tried to figure out some kind of schedule.

Things hadn't changed much when the next draft of prisoners showed up. A small number—no more than two dozen, many of them in officer's gray, the rear being brought up by several enlisted men carrying someone in what appeared to be an officer's coat.

The prisoners already present got to their feet. A number of them rushed to meet the newcomers.

"Stand fast!" Thorne shouted.

The Union officer in charge rode up to him. "Let them go, Major." He nodded toward the burdened group. "That's General Early."

The soldiers set down the body. It was immediately surrounded by men. One after the other, they doffed their hats. One of them started sobbing aloud.

"Shot dead during an affray on the road," the Union officer told Thorne. "They refused to leave him."

"So I see."

Several of the men walked aimlessly back to where they had been originally sitting. Others immediately took their place. Thorne could hear them speaking.

"I'm sorry, sir."

"Oh God, I hate this war."

Someone else was murmuring a prayer.

Thorne signed a receipt for the officer and watched him and his men ride off. When he turned back, a Confederate captain was standing a few feet away, one of Thorne's men right behind him.

"Major, may I trouble you for a blanket?"

"Certainly, sir."

He directed one of the men to get a clean blanket. The officer accepted it with a nod and turned back to where Early lay. Thorne followed him.

The Confederate officer edged through the group surrounding Early's body, and with a series of soft gestures, as if he was tucking in a small child, lay the blanket over him.

"That's better," one of the watching men said.

Thorne found himself removing his hat almost without thinking about it.

A few of the men turned and went back to the main group of prisoners. Several others walked up to where the body lay and stood gazing at it. The captain walked from the group and halted a few feet from Thorne.

"He was not a great commander," he said after a moment had passed. "He was impetuous, excitable, and wild in the saddle. But he was *my* commander."

"I understand," Thorne said.

The man turned to him. "I think you do."

Thorne put his hat back on.

"Ever lose a commander yourself?"

"Not yet. We came close though. He lost a leg."

"Ahh. Well, I hope you don't."

"I thank you for that."

A burst of distant gunfire caught their attention. It went on for some time as they both listened in silence.

"Somebody else is getting cut down out there."

"Too goddamn many." The officer turned away and went back to the main group. Thorne didn't catch sight of him again before dawn.

The army messenger bowed to the President and left the room.

Lincoln looked about him. "Well, Edward's on his way to the hospital—that's a burden off our minds."

Seward nodded. A rumble of agreement went through the group gathered in the Red Room. It consisted of General Heintzelman, House Speaker Schuyler Colfax, Vice President Hamlin, the President, not to forget his wife, and Seward himself. It was well after midnight, but the lights were still burning throughout the White House and the place was alive with messengers, troops, staff, and officials. Outside, the crowd could be heard, a low, unceasing rumble with occasional voices shouting for the President.

Seward considered the report for a moment. Stanton seriously injured—no one knew how badly yet. Three of the kidnappers dead, another on the run. The thing brought to a head by a group of freedmen, no less.

"So it *was* Booth," Hamlin said.

"Did you doubt me, Hannibal?" Lincoln sat back with his long legs sprawled before him. His waistcoat was open and his shirtsleeves were rolled back. His upper right arm was bandaged, the cloth lightly speckled with blood.

"No, not at all. It's just . . ."

Seward leaned forward in his seat. "I think we were all taken aback, Mr. President."

"He's been a southern sympathizer for some time," General Heintzelman said. "We were well aware of that."

"Then why didn't you arrest him?"

Seward turned to where Mary Lincoln sat on a couch at the far end of the room. She was glaring at General Heintzelman as if he was her worst enemy. He gazed back at her nonplussed, at a complete loss for words.

She had nearly lost her mind when Lincoln had returned, screaming aloud at the sight of his injured arm. She had been taken upstairs but almost immediately found her way back down again, remaining at Lincoln's side as he was bandaged and refusing to let him out of her sight. At odd moments, she would begin sobbing quietly to herself, her eyes fixed on the President. He would quiet her with a few words, as he did now.

"Now Mary, we can't go about arresting everyone."

"Why not? You're the *President*."

"They'll be picking them up now, Mrs. Lincoln," Colfax assured her.

"That's so," said Lincoln. "We need to make certain that the Secret Service doesn't get out of hand. This is not Rome under the Caesars."

"The Pinkertons are the ones to worry about."

"Very true." Lincoln turned to his secretary, young Adams, who was hovering behind his chair. "Remind me to inquire into that tomorrow."

The speaker was staring off into space. "I wonder what got into his head. Booth."

"Oh, he played Macbeth too many times," Lincoln said.

The group laughed at the President's words, more than the line merited. Seward glanced at Mrs. Lincoln. Not as much as a smile marked that round little face.

A roar came from outside.

"I wonder if they know yet?" Seward pondered.

"Rumors, at best."

"And since we've bagged the perpetrators," Lincoln bent over and put a hand on his knee. "They need to be told. And I'm the one to tell them."

Seward could not but agree. The stories were running wild throughout Washington. He'd heard a half-dozen on his way over to the White House. The President was dead. He was on his deathbed. He'd been crippled. The kidnap plot had succeeded, and Lincoln was halfway to Richmond by now. No doubt they had grown even more baroque and wild eyed in the hours since. They needed to be put to rest for good and all. What better figure to do that than the president himself?

He was opening his mouth to voice his agreement when he was silenced by a sudden shriek from the sofa.

Mary Lincoln was on her feet, her mouth twisted, her small hands clenched as she stepped toward Lincoln. "No, Papa . . . You can't go out there. There are terrible people waiting for you . . ."

Lincoln got to his feet and went to her. "Now, Mary . . ."

Seward dropped his eyes. Usually there was a hint of the comic in the sight of the two of them together, that extraordinary stork-legged figure towering over his plump, childlike wife, but there was none of that tonight.

"I have to speak to them, Mother. They're worried. They've heard all sorts of wild tales. They need to know what happened. They need to see me, so they know that I'm all right."

The men glanced uncomfortably at each other as the President spoke soothingly to her. General Heintzelman bent forward. "I doubt you'll find any Copperheads on the streets tonight."

"Oh no," Hamlin agreed.

"That crowd would tear them limb from limb."

". . . why don't you come to the door and watch over me?"

Mary Lincoln was gazing away from him, her pudgy jaw set firmly. Seward chose that moment to get to his feet. "Perhaps it would best if the First Lady accompanied you."

The President looked inquiringly at him. He turned back to his wife. "What do you think of that? No one would bother us if you were there."

"Quite so, Mrs. Lincoln."

"Oh, I can't go out in front of all those people."

"Of course you can."

"Well . . ." Seward could almost see that healthy little ego working.

"All right, it's decided then." Adams appeared with Lincoln's coat. "If you'll help me get this on, Henry . . ."

"No . . ." Seward took a step toward him. "No coat."

Lincoln eyed him a moment, then glanced down at the bandage. He relinquished the coat to Adams.

"Abraham . . ." It was Mary. "You're going out there without a *coat*?"

Lincoln lifted one hand to her, then turned toward the door. The rest of the men in the room were on their feet. General Heintzelman was already headed into the hall to oversee the troops out in front.

They followed Lincoln into the hall, soldiers coming to attention to either side. At the front door Lincoln paused to talk it over with Seward and Hamlin. He decided to say a few words first, after which his wife would join him. Lincoln struck Seward as looking very weary. He'd lain down to rest after his wounds had been attended to, but had simply been too charged up to remain in bed.

Lincoln went to the door. Seward took a place beside Mary, wondering what he should do if she panicked. He smiled down at her. "It'll be fine, you'll see." A corporal stepped forward and opened the door for Lincoln.

There was a sudden mass intake of breath from the crowd as the door swung wide, suddenly transformed into a near howl as Lincoln emerged. A woman in front rank screamed and fell to her knees. A young man attempted to rush to Lincoln only to be shoved back by a soldier's musket.

They're like children, Seward thought to himself as he inspected the nearest faces, some clearly glistening with tears. *Children witnessing the return of a father whom they'd been told was lost forever*. He glanced at Lincoln, standing with his arms held high. He couldn't say that he didn't understand that.

Lincoln lowered his arms, then flexed the right one stiffly. "A fine night in Washington, my friends. Though a little more exciting than I might have wished."

The crowd burst into laughter, with a touch of hysteria remaining.

"This reminds me of a fellow I knew in Kentucky, a mountain man. He decided to move west, and in doing so came to a disagreement with the Blackfoot. Well, they scalped him and left him for dead. But then he came to. He reached up and felt the top of his head, then felt his chin, and said to himself, 'At least they left me my beard.'"

The laughter was louder this time.

"You'll be happy to learn that Mr. Stanton has been rescued, and that the gang behind this sordid act has been dispatched."

The crowd roared. It was a good stretch before they went silent again.

". . . and this was accomplished by a group of our colored brethren
. . ."

This roar more than matched the first one.

". . . only recently escaped from bondage. The Good Lord chooses
his tools carefully, his purposes to achieve."

Lincoln smiled as he waited out the uproar.

"And now you must allow me to retire for what remains of the
night. My arm grows stiff and I must rest. Tomorrow is another day,
and we have a war to be won. But first . . ." he half turned. "Mrs.
Lincoln would like to bid you good night."

Seward touched her elbow. The crowd roared again. Someone
inevitably shouted "Hip hip . . ."

Mary Lincoln made a little curtsy to the crowd. They cheered once
more as the President put his arm around her.

The crowd began to sing. A new song, one that Seward had only
heard snatches of, here and there. He believed it was called "Battle Cry
of Freedom". It was a catchy melody, and he began humming it to
himself, wishing he knew the words as well as they did.

> *The Union forever, hurrah, boys, hurrah!*
> *Down with the traitor, up with the star.*
> *While we rally 'round the flag, boys, rally once again,*
> *Shouting the battle cry of freedom.*

Smiling despite himself, Seward watched the faces of the crowd,
the president waving, his First Lady resting her head against his arm.

Someone nudged him. He turned to see the sergeant who had
delivered the message earlier. He bent close to hear what he had to say.

"Mr. Seward . . . if you could inform the President that Jubal Early
has been killed in battle . . ."

"Sergeant, I will be happy to do so."

Seward stepped out of the doorway and walked toward the
President. *By God*, he thought, for the first time since the fighting
had begun two years ago and more. *By God, we're going to win this
thing . . .*

★ CHAPTER 20 ★

Blandon took care in approaching the settlement, using a blind spot well covered by trees. They had watched the place for nearly two hours and still weren't sure what was going on. There was plenty of activity, lots of people and animals moving around, but who those people might be . . . That was the question on their minds. Giddens had insisted that there were no menfolk about, only women, ancients, and children. Several of the others disagreed. Blandon was of two minds himself until one of the distant figures they'd been taking for a "man" walked up to one of the women and proved to scarcely reach her shoulders. "That's either a kid or a dwarf," Blandon had said. "Come on."

Pickings had been pretty slim over the past couple weeks. The Yankees hereabouts had started to smarten up, hiding their valuables and in some cases even fortifying their settlements. Blandon's crew had been chased off with gunfire from one such about twenty miles northwest of here.

Even worse were several towns populated by some kind of folk that Blandon had never heard tell of, who all dressed alike and spoke some language he didn't recognize, though McCutcheon said it sounded to him like German. They simply ignored Blandon and his men, refusing to answer them, gathering together, gripping each other's arms and singing what sounded like hymns in that outlandish tongue of theirs. They failed to shut up even when Blandon separated one of them and treated him to a good beating. At last they simply rode off in disgust, cursing the farmers still singing behind them.

They'd had to depend on isolated farmsteads for food. But it just wasn't enough. The men were growing impatient, and Blandon couldn't blame them.

They paused at the rear of one of the farmhouses. "Now, I want y'all to behave." A couple of them had gotten out of hand during the last raid, beating a farmer who had merely been a little slow at handing over his watch. "No rough stuff, you hear?"

They all nodded and muttered agreement. Raising his pistol, Blandon led them around the house at a quick trot.

A woman with a basket of washing, likely headed for that very house, came to a dead halt and shrieked at the sight of them. Two other women swung around and stared. Spurring his horse, Blandon fired his pistol in the air. There was a shout from within one of the houses.

"We're Bobby Lee's boys," Blandon shouted. "You act right, nothing at all will happen."

His men quickly ushered all the women to the open area in front of the houses. A flagpole stood there, a union flag flapping from it. The men fired several shots at it before Benton cut it down and threw it into the dirt.

Giddens had been right. There were no men around. All women and boys, the oldest in their early teens. Blandon rode up to the clustered women. "Where your menfolk at?"

He pointed his pistol at one woman in particular, a skinny thing wearing a gingham dress. She refused to meet his eyes. "They're at a . . . meeting."

"Meeting? What kind of meeting?"

She licked her lips. "Business," one of the other women said.

"That's right," a third said. "Business."

"The hell they are . . ." one of the men said. "Militia."

There was a shout followed by laughter from one of the buildings. He turned to see two of his men chasing a graybeard off the porch. He stumbled and fell at the last step. "He had this here." Smathers waved an old fowling piece. "Gonna chase us off, he was. I reckon this must be General Meade."

Blandon waited for the laughter to die down. "We are from the

Army of Northern Virginia, sent out to requisition supplies. We intend to carry out our mission here as ordered, and we will brook no interference."

"Nothing but bandits," one older woman said.

Looking her straight in the eye. Blandon pulled out his gun and fired it once in the air. The woman started and looked away. "Now there'll be no more of that kind of talk. You keep quiet, stay out of our way, and we'll be gone before you know it . . ." His eye fell on one particular woman standing next to a couple of young boys. Blonde, shapely, and young. ". . . and ya'll can go back to your washing."

He holstered his gun and got off the horse. The men were already looting the houses. They'd done that enough times so that needed no direction from him. Behind him someone called out. He looked back to see Giddens emerging from a farmhouse waving a jug. "Look what I got here!"

He took a swig and handed it on. Blandon eyed the jug speculatively. A little bit of that wouldn't hurt.

He cast his eyes at the woman he'd noticed a moment before. Corn-colored hair gathered into a braid and wrapped around her head, big blue eyes, pretty round face. A fine-looking woman. A little young, but all woman for that regardless. The farthest thing in the world from those black bondwoman sluts he'd had to settle for.

He approached her through the cluster of women. They moved out of his way. He halted in front of the blonde girl. She glared at him as if in challenge.

He touched his hat. "Right fine day, miss."

She said nothing in response. She was wearing a cameo at the throat of her dress. He reached for it. "Now, that's pretty little thing there . . ."

She slapped his hand away. An older woman beside her said, "Abby, don't . . ."

Blandon took a step forward and loomed over her. She didn't retreat an inch. "That's right. Why you got to be that way? I just asked you . . ." He gestured toward the cameo.

With no warning, the girl slapped his face. "Get away from me, you smelly Rebel."

The older woman gripped her arm and pulled her away. "Sir, she didn't mean anything by that . . . She's too young. She doesn't know . . ."

A boy with the same color hair appeared before him. "You keep your filthy Dixie hands off her."

Without so much as shifting his weight, Blandon struck him twice in the face. The boy dropped to the ground. Blandon gave him a good, sharp kick in the ribs.

With a shriek, the girl threw herself at him, slapping him twice. He felt a sting.

"Ooh, she got you," McCutcheon called out. "You're bleedin', man."

He touched his cheek and looked down at the blood. The girl was staring at him wide eyed. Her mother stood paralyzed, her mouth wide open.

"You clawed me, you little bitch . . ."

He backhanded her. She fell back a step. Her mother made an abrupt move toward Blandon. He shoved her aside.

Gripping the girl by the elbow, Blandon propelled her toward the nearest house. "You need some learnin'," he told her. "And I aim to give it to you."

She started struggling again as he kicked the door in. He slammed her head against the doorjamb and pushed her onward. Kicking the living room furniture aside, he swung her to a halt on a rug in the center of the room. She stared at him dazed, her cheeks red, her mouth slightly open.

Stripping off his belt, Blandon wrapped it around his fist and took a step toward her. He struck her once, then again. She started screaming as he pulled back his fist a third time.

He gazed down at her, collapsed atop the rug. Outside, voices were gabbling madly with one wailing voice riding high above them all.

He pulled his knife. Crouching down, he grabbed the fabric of her dress and cut through it from hem to throat with scarcely more than a single stroke. He sliced her up some but that didn't matter. He stared down at her. That was it, that was what he was here for.

She shook her head slowly and let out a small moan. Blandon liked that.

He unbuttoned himself and then he was upon her. Her moans grew louder. She struggled beneath him, tried to bite the side of his face. He reared up and backhanded her, then slammed her head twice against the floor. They were always like this. Young or old . . . They had to be tamed, the nasty bitches. So prim and proper but underneath, nothing but animals. He knew how to deal with an animal. . . .

Then he was lost within her. He thrust wildly, grunting to himself. She made a few noises and then went still.

He spent himself and collapsed atop her. A moment passed before he realized that she wasn't breathing.

There was a shriek from behind him. He scrambled off the girl to see the girl's mother staring at him wild eyed, her arms spread wide. Skinner appeared in the doorway behind her. He made a grab for her, but she broke away, running directly toward Blandon.

Blandon swung wildly, knocking her to the floor. He stepped past her, fumbling with the buttons of his pants. He slipped his belt back on. Behind him the woman crawled across the floor, sobbing rhythmically as she went. He looked up to find Skinner gazing past him, his eyes squinting as if he found it difficult to believe what he was seeing.

The sobs burst into a full-throated wail. He looked back to see the older woman poised over her daughter. Blood was dripping from her chin. As he watched, she gathered the dress and tried to cover the girl up.

When he turned back Skinner was staring at him. "That weren't a Christian thing," he said.

Blandon pushed past him, still slipping his belt though the loops. "I done warned you about this," Skinner called out to his back, "I say, you listenin' to me . . . ?"

Outside they were all staring at him, his men and the Yankee women both. The women in open fear, the men in something like expectation. One of them lifted the jug to his lips. The liquor was doing its work. Blandon stood wordless, looking from one to the other.

Skinner walked past him. "Gid," he called to his somewhat dimwitted brother. "Get your horse. We've got to ride."

Gripping his confused brother by the arm, he pushed him toward the horses. "Come along. We're leaving this godless bunch behind."

McCutcheon, sitting atop a pile of loot, got to his feet. "Well," he said. "Well now . . ."

He shot toward the women, gripping the arm of the one in blue gingham who had spoken up earlier. She let out a brief scream as he yanked her out of the crowd, then shouted, "No . . . no . . . no . . ." as he dragged into the house across the way.

The others were already among the rest of the women, giving off frenzied hoots and yells as they made their choices. The shrieking women were dragged or carried into the houses, nearby barns, and even into the tall grass to the rear of the buildings. In a moment all that was left was the beaten old man, lying on his side with his hands over his face, a few older women clutching each other as they wept, and a handful of Blandon's men who looked at each other, shook their heads and walked away amid the screams and howls echoing from the buildings.

The liquor jug was lying where someone had dropped it. Descending the steps, Blandon picked it up. The whisky burned as he swallowed it.

"Goddamn you, goddamn you . . ."

It was the boy he had struck earlier, staring at him from a swollen and bloody face. "Goddamn you," he repeated. And then again, "Goddamn you . . ."

Swinging the jug, Blandon went on his way.

★ CHAPTER 21 ★

The Volunteers were just breaking camp when a staff officer rode up to Wade and told him to gather his men together and follow him. Speaking in low, terse sentences, he explained the situation to Wade as they headed down the road past the marshes and low brush.

". . . pretty much the entire Union army, as far as we can tell, along with reinforcements up from Pipe Creek. They'll be coming along in an hour or less."

Behind him Mayfield and the others began talking excitedly among themselves. Wade raised a hand to quiet them.

". . . marching straight down this highway, looking for a fight."

"Well, sir, that is what they will find."

"Right up here," the lieutenant colonel gestured to his left and led them up a low ridge that overlooked the road. When they reached the top, he cantered on for about five hundred yards before coming to a halt. "Remain here, and dig in."

"Dig in?"

"That's right, Colonel. Dig in. And kindly don't tell me that southern cavaliers don't do any such thing."

Wade raised his hands. "I understand. We will do as ordered."

"Fine. I'll find someone to put there on your left."

He saluted and rode off. Wade descended from his horse and started to give orders. The men bellyached about the digging, but got down to it. Noticing some trees to the rear, he sent out several enlisted men to do some cutting so as to build an abatis in front of their trenchline.

The ridge looked good. Very much the same situation as at Gettysburg, but with the sides reversed this time. It was the Confederates holding the high ground now. If anything, it looked even better than Seminary Ridge.

Along the crest he could see other units appearing—horses, artillery, the infantry bringing up the rear. As always before a battle, he felt a sense of breathless excitement, a stirring deep within, like nothing else he had ever experienced. He glanced down the road stretching east, still hazy under the morning sun. *Come ahead, you bluebellies. Come and be whipped.*

Thorne was never to learn, then or later, whether he had been the first to report the Rebel position. But he certainly been one of the earliest.

He halted his horse as the ridge came into sight, raising his German binoculars—a gift from Colonel Baird—and examined the ridgeline. He ignored the low voices of the men behind him. At last he lowered the glasses.

"Looks like we found 'em," Willis said.

"Unless there are two Rebel armies hereabouts, I would have to agree."

He called Corporal Eisele over. ". . . find General Grant, and tell him we have spotted the Army of Northern Virginia. They are holding a ridgeline about five miles east of York. They appear to have blocked the road. They have cavalry, foot, guns . . . Hell, tell him it's the whole goddamn Reb army."

Eisele nodded studiously above the notebook he was writing in.

"Get to him as quick as you can. Don't stop for anything." He gestured to the men. "Meyer and uhhh . . . Coughlin, there. You follow Eisele. Warn all the units you come across. Tell the commanders exactly what we've got here. Go."

Eisele was already on his way. The other two swung about and headed after him.

Thorne followed them with his eyes before turning back to the ridge. "Well," he said at last. "Let's go take a look . . ."

★ ★ ★

John Rawlins listened closely to the young man from the 6th Indiana. He quickly ran his eyes across the note the corporal had given him. "Thank you, Corporal. Wait right here."

Rawlins turned and rode to where General Grant waited on horseback. "We've found them."

Grant nodded to himself. He was chewing on an unlit cigar, one of an endless number sent to him by admirers, even though he'd never previously smoked cigars.

"About five miles east of town—that would be three miles ahead—on a low ridge overlooking the highway . . ."

"High ground."

"That's right, sir."

"How many?"

Rawlins glanced down at the sheet. "It says, 'the whole goddamn Rebel army.'"

Grant smiled, a rare expression coming from him. He removed the cigar and studied it for a moment. "Let's ride up there and take a look."

"Do you need the corporal . . . ?"

Grant shook his head. He raised his hand to the young man, who saluted and rode off. "Get word to the corps and divisional commanders. Tell Smith and Butler to get a leg on. Butler in particular. I expect them to be on the line in no more than an hour."

"Yes, General."

Grant bit down on the cigar once more. He glanced around at his staff. "Well—we're going to find out what General Lee is actually made of. Let's move along."

Wade was out in front arranging the abatis to his satisfaction when no less than General Hardee himself appeared. He had removed his coat and was sharpening the branches of a fallen tree. He looked up to see Hardee gazing down at him from the saddle.

"Where's your commanding officer, son?"

"That would be me, sir." He gave the general a good sharp salute. "Colonel Corey Wade."

Hardee urged the horse closer to get a better look at the wall of sharpened tree branches. Two of his staff followed him closely.

He nodded his approval. "Excellent thinking, Colonel. These have served defenders well since the days of the Romans, if not earlier."

"They'll work just fine today, sir."

"Let us hope so." Hardee straightened up. "have you spotted any of our Yankee friends yet?"

"A few horsemen, sir, no more than that." They'd driven them off with a handful of shots a few minutes previously. No losses to either side. It was scarcely worth mentioning. He glanced over his shoulder, squinting into the sun. "They're still out there somewhere."

"Scouts, no doubt." Hardee glanced to Wade's left. "Ah, here we are . . ."

Swinging around, Wade saw an infantry brigade taking up the position leading down to the road.

"That's the 3rd Arkansas. You need not worry about your flank, sir."

Wade raised his eyebrows. The Barefoot Brigade themselves—though they looked well-shod enough from what he could see. "I have no doubt about that, General."

"Doubt is not something that should enter our minds, Colonel." Hardee raised his voice so as to be heard by all the men. "Any more than I have doubts about you men. The Tennessee Volunteer Cavalry has done great things in the past, I'm sure you will add to your laurels today."

The men responded with a loud cheer. Something meant to pass for a smile appeared on Hardee's face. "So let's chase those Yankees back to . . . well, Maryland, I guess it would have to be."

The men laughed aloud. "Not a lot of other choices apart from the Atlantic," someone shouted.

"And that's how we like it." With a salute for Wade, Hardee started off for the Arkansas brigade. Wade gazed after him, feeling better than he had in weeks.

Thorne let out a burst of breath and descended from his horse. "Close one," he said to Willis, who nodded and got down himself.

"That whole line must have opened up on us."

"Lousy shots."

Glancing back at the ridgeline, Thorne stepped over to the staff officer waiting for him, easily identified by the perfect turnout of his uniform. Another lieutenant colonel—Thorne gave him a salute. "A bit of scouting."

"Yes sir." A reply to Washington would have to wait. Rawlins swung his horse about and cantered toward the waiting couriers.

Thorne was speaking to Colonel O'Kane of the 69th Pennsylvania when the Rebel artillery started targeting them. The marching infantry immediately panicked, pouring off the road and straight into the 6th Indiana's men and horses.

He spent the next several minutes getting the mess cleared up and the men down the slope toward the stream, where they'd be covered by the descending ground and concealed by the brush. There weren't many rounds fired in their direction—five or six at most. But that was enough—he could hear screams and wailing above the explosions, the shouting of men, and the neighing of horses.

Looking out over the road, he saw at least a dozen men down. He found himself hoping despite himself that they were Pennsylvanians. He glanced up at the ridge. The Rebs had a nasty habit of pausing their barrages and then opening up again when you started to relax.

He hadn't seen O'Kane, the 69th's commander, since the firing started. He assumed that the colonel was preoccupied in looking after his men. He recalled what he'd been saying when the shelling started: "I'll be happy to sit this one out right here. We've had enough. Let somebody else attack. It's their turn now."

The guns seemed to be concentrating on the treeline at the far side of the field. Thorne got up and brushed at his knees. "Let's go," he told the men around him. Many of them seemed to be Pennsylvanians.

Most of the men lying in the road were beyond any form of help. He lingered a moment over one boy who had the back of his head blown straight off before going on to a soldier who was still breathing. He was an older man with a graying mustache, staring off into space with a rosary clutched against his chest. Thorne hadn't had anything good to say about Catholics before the war—had scarcely known any, for that matter. He thought much better of the ones he'd seen in the army.

He had the wounded men carried off the road and into the brush. He doubted they'd live long enough to see a field station. The bodies would have to wait. He glanced over them, feeling more despondent than he could recall. He had seen worse than this. But then . . . there wasn't anything worse for the men lying here. There would never be anything, good, bad, or indifferent, ever again.

He raised his eyes. It just got worse. Everyone said you'd get used to it. Everyone lied.

There were figures capering atop the ridge. The Rebels seemed pretty pleased with themselves. They really looked to Thorne as if they were mocking the dead.

Another round of firing began. This time, the shells were rising from the treeline toward the Confederate lines. Better late than never.

A Yankee shell exploded to the left of their line. Wade shifted his feet to retain his balance, fighting an impulse to leap back into the trench. He had to look his best before the men. He gripped his hat as he was splattered with chunks of earth.

The Yankee guns were giving the line a good pasting. It was their habit to cover an entire line before an assault. They could afford to—they had the shot and powder to waste.

"Corey, why don't you get down from there?"

"Yeah, Colonel."

"That's just plumb foolishness."

"In a minute," he told them. It was good to show a touch of fearlessness now and again. There was nothing like it to give the men an impression—

The next round struck even closer, the force of it nearly knocking Wade into the trench. He dropped back in even as the dirt and gravel rained over him.

"Now if that ain't—"

Mayfield's voice was cut off by another blast to their rear. Two more shells followed before the guns shifted to give the Arkansas boys a taste.

There were no casualties, apart from a few cuts and bruises. Some of the horses had panicked and run off. He sent a squad out to bring them back. He gazed out over the field. The trees at the far side were now half-obscured by smoke.

"There is nothing so exhilarating as being shot at without issue." Who had said that? He couldn't recall. He would have to look it up. That was a good line. He'd have to put it into his next letter to Mother.

Grant stood looking out over the Rebel lines. His forces were as ready as they'd ever be. Not as much as they'd have been out west, but there was no helping that. The Army of the Potomac might be a fine spectacle in their perfectly turned-out uniforms, but they still lacked that indefinable something that made for a truly effective fighting force, something that the western armies, ragged as they might be, had in abundance. The easterners could never have carried out what Sherman had accomplished this past week—marching an entire corps through the almost trackless Kentucky high country and on into Virginia. The effort would have petered out and collapsed within days. But for the Ohio and Wisconsin troops, it was just another day's work. No different than that bold thrust of Grant's across the Mississippi last spring that had left Pendleton and Johnston flailing around looking to cut supply lines that didn't exist. They'd been thoroughly flummoxed right up to the very moment that Vicksburg had surrendered.

Rawlins ran his eyes across the smoke-shrouded Rebel lines. The southerners probably thought that Gettysburg had been the important battle that week.

They still believed in the decisive battle, the Armageddon that would decide the issue fully and finally. Grant did not. Rawlins himself could not encompass his commander's thinking completely, but this he knew: to Ulysses Grant, battles were simply the tools he utilized to create his strategy. Defeat or victory, neither mattered as much as the simple fact of pushing the overall plan forward. It was a new method of war, one that the southerners did not yet grasp. They would soon, and to their sorrow.

He pulled out his watch. "Five minutes."

Grant nodded and took another long look across the battlefield. Then he turned and walked back toward a fallen tree lying amid all the others. He halted halfway there and bent down to pick up one stick, then another. By the time he reached the trunk he had a small armload. He let them fall into a pile and sat down atop the trunk. He began peeling the bark off the sticks, one after the other.

Rawlins started coughing once more. It took him a moment to get it under control. It was always worse just before a battle. He could feel the aching, just below his ribs. At least there was no blood.

The guns built up to a crescendo and tapered off. There was a low shout that seemed to echo all along the line. Then the troops emerged from the treeline into the open. Rawlins took a single step forward, eyes fixed on that mass of blue, the flags and guidons streaming at their head. He muttered something that had the Deity in it.

He glanced back at Grant. The general was following the troops with his eyes. After a moment he reached into his jacket and pulled out a penknife. He opened it with a savage gesture. Picking up a stick, he began slicing off strips of wood with long, quick strokes.

Rawlins lingered for one more glimpse of the troops, then went to join Grant.

Wade was concentrating so much on his front that he almost missed the beginning of the Yankee advance. His men started shouting, and his eyes shot to his left to see the blue-clad troops emerge from beneath the trees. They looked magnificent at this distance. There must ten thousand or more in that mass. It was enough to take your breath away.

And all futile. They were attacking the center, the strongest point on the whole line. Hey diddle diddle, straight up the middle. You'd think they'd learn. Sharpsburg, Fredericksburg . . . not to mention Gettysburg.

At least they weren't headed toward him, he thought guiltily.

A shell burst within their ranks, scattering troops in all directions. Along the front line, others were beginning to fall from rifle fire. Wade shook his head. It was a pity, really.

Thorne lowered his binoculars, unwilling to watch any longer. He handed them to Willis. "Be my guest."

He turned and took a few steps toward the stream. He'd seen enough. Men were dying en masse over there, within shouting distance of where he stood. Dying of gunshot, dying of explosions, dying trampled down into the dirt by the boots of the still-living. Men in their prime, young boys scarcely able to raise a beard, older men who ought to be anywhere else but here. Yankees, Irishmen, German immigrants scarcely able to speak a word of English.

He eyed the sunlight glimmering on the ripples of the stream. It looked like summer. It truly did, even with the autumn chill in the air. It was as if he could throw his coat off and plunge right in.

He'd felt the same sense of disgust at Gettysburg, watching Longstreet's men get chewed up making that vast wild charge on the third day. That fool with the hat—who had that been, he wondered? Waving it on the end of his sword, as if to say, shoot me, shoot me, shoot me . . .

Well, they'd shot him all right. The very Pennsylvania boys that were seated around him right now. Along with a few thousand others. And for what, exactly? Here they were, only months later, doing the same damned thing. That's what this war was turning into—one side marches into the maelstrom, gets torn to pieces, and then the other takes its turn. Keep it up until there's nobody left.

A groan rose from the men around him. He looked over his shoulder to see that the blue tide had broken. The troops were streaming back toward the treeline, leaving behind a carpet of wounded and dying men.

He walked back to Archie Willis, who handed him the binoculars. "Pretty bad," Willis said under his breath.

The last of the Union troops were vanishing into the trees while the Rebels hooted and hollered from the ridgetop. "So I see," Thorne said.

"Casualties?"

"Heavy," Rawlins told Grant.

With a harsh slash, the general sliced off a long sliver of wood. For a moment Grant stared blankly ahead. "Sedgwick," he said at last. "As we discussed."

"Attempt to flank Lee's left."

Grant nodded wordlessly. Rawlins turned away. Behind him, Grant peeled off two more slices and then broke what remained of the stick over his knee.

Wade saw that the next attack was going to strike the far left of the line. That too, was a hopeless gesture. Longstreet was commanding that end, and it would take a lot more than a gaggle of Yankees to chase him off.

He listened for a moment to the distant shouting, the nearer roaring of the guns.

"We may have an easy day of it," Mayfield said.

Wade looked down at him. "Don't you jinx us now."

"Look there," Willis said.

Thorne nodded. "I see them."

About four hundred yards into the field, someone was crawling toward them. There was an object on his back that might have been an oversize knapsack, but a glance through the binoculars told Thorne that it was another man. "There's two of them."

"I'll go out there," Willis told him.

"Hold on a second . . ."

"I'm going, Steve."

He moved off, selected three volunteers, and headed out into the field. Thorne glanced at the ridge. He doubted that anyone would take a shot at them, but you never knew with the Rebs.

They reached the two men. Thorne watched through the glasses as one trooper, an oversized country boy, threw the topmost man over his shoulders. The other two picked up the man who had been crawling and slung him between them. The made slow progress across the field, the distant battle roaring behind them. Thorne glanced once again at the Confederate line. They seemed to be watching. Nobody had opened fire. Good for them.

At last they crossed the road. The two soldiers set the one man down while Willis helped the big lad with the other. Thorne crouched in front of the first man. "You made it."

"So we did," he gasped. Someone handed him a canteen and he gulped half the contents down. He'd been hit in the arm just above the elbow. It looked pretty bad to Thorne. He glanced at the other man. Willis was just then rising to his feet. He looked over at Thorne and shook his head.

The man before him squeezed his eyes shut. For a moment it looked as if he was about to collapse and Thorne reached out to steady him. But then he opened his eyes once again and gave him as beatific a smile as any he'd ever seen. "Least I brought my brother back. That's what counts."

Across the distant field, the bluecoated troops began to fall back, pursued by gunfire and cannon shells.

Rawlins was turning back to Grant to report that the second charge had failed when he saw the reporter. He was approaching Grant from behind, a notepad clutched in his hand. He was wearing a cheap checked suit and a derby hat.

Rawlins quickened his pace. He'd told those people to keep their distance. How had this man been allowed to reach Grant in the first place? Everyone was too enrapt in the battle, evidently.

The man bent confidentially over the trunk and said something in a low voice. Grant gave no sign that he had heard.

"Sir," Rawlins called out. "If you please . . . We're in the midst of a battle here . . ."

The reporter ignored Rawlins. "Well, it seems that you're having something of a bad day."

Grant gave a last slash at the stick in his hand and tossed it away.

"How about some kind of explanation?"

Rawlins paused beside the reporter. He smelled of some kind of pomade. "Sir . . ." Rawlins said.

The man ignored him. "General McClellan doesn't think much of you. He says you're a butcher. Seems to me he's right."

Stepping forward to take hold of the reporter, Rawlins gestured to two of junior officers. "Let's go . . ."

The man shook him off. "Who the hell are you . . . ?"

The two lieutenants gripped him from behind and started to drag him off. The man dropped his notepad and pencil as he struggled against them. "What the devil . . ." He tried to go slack but he didn't help him any. "Hey, Grant," he shouted. "How does it feel to be whipped by Bobby Lee?"

Rawlins picked up the pencil and pad and tossed them after him. The man was lucky it hadn't been General Sherman. He loathed reporters worse than a preacher did sin. He turned back to Grant. The general sliced at yet another stick, totally unconcerned.

"Sedgwick's attack has been repulsed."

Grant nodded.

"They did give the Rebels some rough handling before they repelled the flanking effort."

"Good." Grant was silent for a moment. His knife and the half-carved stick rested on either knee. "The right," he said at last. "We need that road open."

Rawlins nodded and turned away.

The barrage lasted considerably longer this time. Wade spent at least fifteen minutes with his nose pressed into the damp soil of the trench, hands over his ears as the shells burst around him. Someone started howling right in the middle of it, wordless shrieks that went on without pause or variation. The voice continued for several seconds after the last explosion.

Wade hoisted himself up, shaking off dust and clumps of earth. To his right two troopers were helping a man dig himself out of a collapsed stretch of trench. Past them he could see another with his hands over his face, blood trickling through the fingers. A soldier slid into the trench beside him, carrying a damp cloth.

He turned to the front, knowing what he'd see. He was just in time to catch sight of the first Union troops emerging from the trees. He watched them in silence for a long moment as their numbers grew, a blue mass that seemed to spring out of the earth itself, coming from nowhere and having no end. He swallowed deeply and shook himself.

"Well, you were right."

He smiled at Mayfield. "So I was. That's why they put me in command, Junior." He nodded toward the right-hand end of the trench. "Head down there and take charge, Alex. Keep 'em braced up. I don't want us embarrassed in front of those Arkansas boys."

"Yes, sir." He paused a moment. "Don't let no mules kick you, Corey." He was gone before Wade could reply.

He turned to face the field. The mass of troops seemed to be heading straight for his stretch of trench and no other. A burst of smoke erupted as one of them took a wild, unaimed shot. He thought of his college history readings—the campaigns of the great Khans, the Golden Horde roaring across Asia with none to stand against it.

But that was nonsense. These were nothing more than Yankee peddlers and office clerks, not a single Mongol warrior among them.

"All right," he shouted. "Everybody hold your fire until I give the order. Don't waste your powder and shot, understood?" The answers were no more than mutters. All eyes were on the approaching troops. He glanced back at them. A shell exploded, too far to the rear. "I know they look fierce, but you know something? Half of 'em are from Ireland, and the rest from Massachusetts."

That got a response—shouts, laughter, one hat thrown in the air. Wade smiled. The bluecoats had reached the halfway point. Another shell, better aimed this time, struck amongst them, cutting a large hole in that mass.

Wade pulled out his Colt and checked the cylinders. Fully loaded. He glanced skyward. The sun was high. It looked to be well after the noon hour, as difficult as that was to believe. He took out his watch. Yes—it was one-thirty. He studied the tinted Melainotype of his mother on the inside of the cover and then clicked it shut. He shifted to make himself a little more comfortable. It was uncanny how swiftly time passed on occasions like this.

They stood straight and unmoving as they watched the advance, even though some of Rebel shells were landing uncomfortably close. There weren't many of them anyway. Thorne supposed that they were running short of powder.

The troops were only a couple of hundred yards away, almost close enough to make out their faccs. Beyond them, the ridge appeared to be gigantic, a great, looming wall stretching to the far horizon.

They looked on in silence, a mixture of his own horsemen and the infantry. No one was cheering or waving their arms, or saying so much as a word. They just stood staring, as at a massive natural catastrophe unfolding at some vast distance, with blazing lightning and roaring thunder denoting forces no man could control. An act of God, beyond reckoning or comprehension.

He clenched his fists as the first line of troops reached the foot of the ridge. It seemed impossible they could ever break through to the top. Just a short ridge, that you could climb in matter of minutes on an ordinary day. But today, it looked taller than the Matterhorn.

They climbed it all the same. Falling one by one and in clusters, the banners and guidons that led them disappearing and then rising back into sight as they were transferred from dying hands to those still living, if only for a moment more. Thorne took an involuntary step forward as they reached the top.

He ran his gaze across the line. The battle was general, one single ribbon of fighting men at the crest of the ridge. His eyes were arrested at one particular point, where the men in blue seemed to be entangled in a stretch of brush. His raised his glasses for a closer look. No—it was some kind of obstacle made out of tree branches. He'd heard of it—an aba something. He watched the men struggling amid those branches and then falling one after the other as long as he could stand it, then let the glasses fall.

A shell went off no more than forty yards away. Not a single man moved as the earth and rocks pelted among them.

Wade gave the order to fire when the Yankees were about fifty yards short of the ridge. The first fusillade took down most of leading line. It slowed the rest of them not at all. They kept coming, a few stumbling over the bodies of those who had fallen.

Around him the men were reloading. "Fire again," he shouted, unnecessarily. They were lifting the carbines to their shoulders and firing as soon as they were ready.

The Yankees seemed to pause at the foot of the ridge as if to gather their forces, then threw themselves at the slope at as close to a dead run as they could manage. Their mouths were wide open, but Wade couldn't hear a thing.

Wade raised his pistol. He hadn't fired a single round yet. He was going to wait until he could make it count. He spotted a man wearing a broad-brimmed hat. An officer, more than likely. Taking careful aim, he fired. The Yankee clutched his shoulder and fell on one knee.

Then the fever was on him. He fired the next rounds without thinking about it. They were about halfway up and closing fast. Most of them had fired their muskets already, although a few rounds hissed over the trench here and there.

The hammer clicked on an empty chamber. He set the hammer at half cock and reached into his ammunition pouch, grabbed the horn and quickly powdered up the cylinders. Looking out over the trench he saw that they were fifteen yards down, if that. "Keep firing," he shouted at the men.

He grabbed a handful of wads, dropping several, but that wasn't unheard of. He shoved them into the cylinders, followed by the balls. He levered them in, one, two, three, then jammed the caps in place with his thumbnail. He looked up just a Yankee trooper gripped a tree branch and tried to haul himself over the top. Wade shot him in the chest.

Around him the men rose from the trench to shoot down into the mass of men entangled amid the branches. A few of the Yankees made it to the top, only to be shot down or beaten back with clubbed guns. There was no time to reload. After a moment, the gunfire stopped, and all he could hear was the cries and shrieks of men, the thud and clatter of weapons.

He found the highest spot he could to get above the fog of gunsmoke. To his left a Yankee grappled with one of his men, trying to pull away his carbine. Wade fired at him. The man pitched back into the mass trying to break through the branches.

The abatis was holding . . . But there, to his right . . . The bluecoats had pulled apart the trees to create a gap. Two of them climbed through it, the man in the lead gripping the throat of the soldier at the edge of the trench.

Wade dropped down into the trench and ran toward them, leaping over a man in butternut clutching a bloody arm. The Yankee soldier had been dragged back into the trench and was being beaten to the ground with musket butts. Behind him rose another, holding a gun tipped with a bayonet. Wade raised his pistol and fired. He wasn't sure that he hit him, but the Yankee fell back all the same, brushing against another trooper who dropped out of sight.

A shriek arose above the rumble of battle. Wade pulled himself to the lip of the trench. Below him, the fallen Yankee was impaled on one of the sharpened branches. Wade had a clear view of his face. He was clean-shaven, wearing glasses, his mouth gaping in agony.

Wade lifted the pistol and fired. The smoke cleared, revealing that face still howling. He fired again, unable to control himself, and went on pulling the trigger until all he heard was clicking.

Someone touched his arm. "He's dead, sir."

Wade looked over at the man, not recognizing the face. He nodded wordlessly before finding any words to say. "Yes . . . yes, so he is."

He looked up the trenchline. Everything seemed to be holding together. No other breakthroughs or weak points that he could see. The Yankees . . . Well, what do you know . . . As he watched they began falling back. First the odd man, then in twos and threes, then whole masses of men turning to race back down the slope.

He watched them go, pistol resting on his shoulder, glorying in the fierceness of his expression. He was about to call out to his men when a mass groan arose farther down the line.

He looked to his right. The 3rd Arkansas had begun to collapse.

Thorne shook his head as he saw that the attack was being thrown back. Beside him, Willis shouted and pointed. He shifted his gaze to the see blue-clad troops breaking through the nearest point of the

Confederate line, on the slope stretching down to the road. He lifted the glasses, but could not keep them steady. He let them fall against his chest. He could see it clearly enough—the men in butternut had broken, half of them racing up the slope while the rest were overwhelmed by the federal troops.

A sudden uproar drew his attention. To his right, a dozen or more of the infantry, Pennsylvanians from their tight jackets and *chasseur* trousers, had broken out and were racing toward the ridge, shouting to beat the devil. Their commander stood staring after them, mouth wide open.

Thorne shook his head. Damn fools—it was over a thousand yards to that ridgetop; they'd never get there in time to do any good.

He bit his lip as he regarded the unfolding fracas atop the ridge. But mounted men . . . Mounted men could.

Without another thought he turned toward his men. "6th Indiana," he shouted. Saddle up!"

They gazed back at him for a moment before letting out a shout that drowned out the roar of battle, then broke for their horses. It took Thorne a moment to find his mount amid the brush. He swung himself into the saddle, checked his pistol and carbine, then trotted out into the open where the men were gathering. He swung his horse around to face them and was about to speak when someone gripped his arm.

He turned to see the impeccably turned-out officer he had spoken to this morning.

Wade raced down the slope toward the melee, not looking back to see if his men were following. He instinctively grabbed for his sword, clean forgetting that he'd left it with his horse. His mouth was open in a long wordless howl.

He was lost in the fighting, surrounded by brawling men. He turned to wave his troops on. They roared past him, guns held high. He took a step forward. A man in blue was gaping at him. Wade shot him down where he stood.

Two wild-looking figures in butternut tried to make their way past him toward the rear. He grabbed the nearest and shoved him into the other one. "Get your asses back there! Now!"

A gun roared just behind him, nearly deafening him. He swung around. No shooter was evident, but there . . . Three steps away, a bluebelly was beating a man with his musket. Wade raised his gun and pulled the trigger. The Colt misfired. He clubbed the pistol and stepped toward the Yankee, but just then a butternut trooper appeared and ran him through with his bayonet. Wade recognized one of this own men.

Someone barged into him, nearly knocking him off his feet. "Excuse me, sir," a voice said.

Looking around him, Wade could see nothing but butternut and gray. He ran a few more yards and found a clear view of the slope. There they were, the men in blue, running down the slope to the road below. Wade raised his gun, but heard only a click. He swung the cylinder open. By the time he cleared it, the Yankees were all well out of pistol range.

Around him, men were cheering and hollering. He felt a hand on his shoulder and turned to see Mayfield.

"Lotta Yankees, Colonel."

Wade eyed him. "No mules, though."

They were laughing like a pair of fools when an officer in gray appeared. It was the 3rd Alabama's commander—Wade didn't catch the name. He spoke in an accent so thick that Wade could scarcely follow a word he said.

"I thankee yer cumin to th' brigade's hep, Cunnel."

He turned to regard the troops pulling themselves together around him. The line was bent nearly ninety degrees. The Arkansas boys couldn't reoccupy the original trenches with the Yankees on their flank. "Dunno what the devil got into these heah boys. Nevuh done happen afore."

"It happens to everybody, Colonel."

The colonel shook his head fiercely. "Not th' 3rd Arkansawr, it don't." He paused to examine the road below. "I'm a'thinkin' we could clear that theah highway no trubba tall."

"I'm with you, Colonel."

The colonel frowned at him. "Say gin?"

Wade didn't answer. He eyes were fixed on the road, where a large group of horsemen—several hundred or more—were emerging from the Yankee lines.

★ ★ ★

Thorne led the brigade, moving at a fast gallop. The staff officer had told him to advance and reinforce the troops holding the road. The Pennsylvania infantry would follow. They were to hold that position on the flank of the Confederate line until they received further orders.

A few scattered shots greeted him as he arrived, but nothing to worry about. He got off his horse and looked things over. The slope suddenly plunged as it reached the road, providing excellent cover. Union troops reclined on the slope, occasionally letting off a shot or two. Well over a thousand of them, as far he could see.

An enlisted man rode up beside him. "Get some men and take the horses into those trees. I want them out of sight."

The boy saluted and took the reins from him. Thorne ran over to join the men on the slope. A junior officer saluted him. "Sir . . . I'll locate our commander."

"Do that." Around him, his men were dismounting and moving toward the slope. "6th Indiana," he called out. "Let's notify Johnny that we've arrived."

The volley cleared the slope immediately. The few figures in butternut visible at the top of the ridge vanished. Thorne got to his feet for a clearer look. His stomach went hollow at the sight of all the blue-clad troops scattered across the slope. There must be hundreds of them.

From where he stood, he could see the field leading up to the ridge. Even more lay in front of the slope. He was looking at a thousand dead men. Men who had been alive and talking and thinking only moments ago.

And for what? They hadn't even broken the line. Only bent it a little.

He shook his head in disgust. So much for Grant. He was just as bad as the rest. Another Hooker, another Burnside. One more inept killer, efficient only at sending men to early deaths. Good for nothing at all else.

"Excuse me, Major . . ."

He realized someone had spoken to him several times. He turned to the officer beside him, evidently this unit's commander. A captain. Sweet Jesus, were they down to that?

The officer saluted him. "Glad you're here, sir."

Thorne returned the salute. "Glad to be here."

They pulled back a few yards to get out of the line of sight of the Union cavalrymen. Wade was discussing their options with Mayfield when suddenly the Arkansas commander went wide eyed, shot to his feet, and straightened out his tunic. He strode past Wade without a word.

Wade looked over his shoulder to see no less than General Robert E. Lee himself approaching, accompanied by two staff officers. Wade got up, brushed off his jacket and followed the Arkansas colonel.

Lee saluted them and listened closely to the report. "Excellent," he said at last. He looked between the two of them. "You've done magnificently well this day. The Army of Northern Virginia is grateful. *I* am grateful."

Wade nodded, nearly overcome. "Thank you, sir."

"Now, how does the situation stand?"

They led the general over to the crest, warning him not to go too far. As he was looking out over the road, a rider drew up behind them. General Longstreet dismounted and walked toward them. He gave Wade a sharp look but said nothing.

"Well, General," Lee said. "I believe we may have taken General Grant's measure."

Longstreet nodded agreement. "He's a pounder, nothing more. I can't imagine why Joe Johnston couldn't handle him."

"General Johnston was dealt a bad hand." Lee gestured down the slope. "Here's something of a postscript for us."

"I see." Longstreet glanced at the troops around him. "We'll have Hardee reinforce these boys and then clean 'em off the road."

"Yes." Lee nodded. "Let's give the men a rest first. They're exhausted. It's been a harsh and harrowing day."

"That it has."

"There's plenty of time." Lee grimaced at the federal troops. "Those poor boys aren't going anywhere."

Longstreet seemed about to agree when he paused and swung to his left. Lee followed his gaze. For a moment both were silent. Then Lee spoke:

"What the devil is this?"

Thorne had told the captain to prepare his men for a fighting withdrawal back to the lines. They couldn't remain hanging here—not with God alone knew how many thousands of Rebels peering down at them. The officer deferred completely. He seemed to be in way over his head, and overwhelmed by the events of the day.

Thorne sat back on his haunches. Yet another withdrawal, leading to an overall retreat. Back to Lancaster, at least, maybe even back to Maryland. The newspapers would howl, Congress would whine, Lincoln would give one more brave speech. And then what? A new general, perhaps. And then another campaign . . . next spring, at the earliest. This year was shot. There was no point attempting to mount a campaign this late in the season. This war was going to stretch on for another year, perhaps even into 1865, with all the misery and death and suffering that entailed . . .

God Almighty, how he was going to take it . . . ?

Someone shouted; he looked up to see a trooper pointing back toward their lines. Thorne looked over his shoulder. Down the road, at just about the spot where they had waited out the battle, a large group of cavalrymen was riding toward them. And beyond them, visible amid the road's curves, marched thousands of infantrymen.

"Who does this fellow think he is?"

Lee swung around to face Longstreet. "He's behaving as if he hasn't been soundly whipped."

"Just have to whip him again."

"Indeed we will." Lee gestured toward the north, in the direction where the federal troops were vanishing behind the trees. "We can intercept him before he reaches York, take him in the flank . . ."

"All marshes and streams, almost all the way into town."

"And he knew that." Lee gazed across the fields to the trees which hid his adversary. "Damn the man!"

Longstreet looked at him quizzically. Lee never spoke in that fashion about his opponents.

Wade stepped forward. "Sir . . . General Lee. I volunteer to take my brigade and assault the Yankee line of march . . ."

Lee turned toward him and smiled. "No, son . . . we need to save you and your men for a better day."

"He's headed for Harrisburg," Longstreet said. "Our supplies and powder."

"Yes he is. We'll have to outmarch him."

"I'll have Porter Alexander bring up a few guns. He's got enough shot left to slow up these . . ."

A sudden roar cut Longstreet short. They turned as one to look out across the field. A line of cannon had appeared just within the trees. A shell arced overhead and burst a hundred yards past them.

They all ducked involuntarily. Even Lee reached up to clutch his hat.

"Look there," Longstreet said as they straightened up. Along the road below them several cannon were being deployed.

"They'll have this end of the ridge enfiladed in about five minutes," Longstreet said.

Lee turned toward Wade. "Pull your men back whatever distance may be necessary." To his staff he said, "Inform Hardee, Hill, and Anderson to prepare to march."

As they turned toward the horses, Longstreet said, "I'll alert Harrisburg to start entrenching."

"Yes, do that."

Another shell exploded, this one even closer. Wade moved to gather up to his men. It was going to be a long afternoon.

★ CHAPTER 22 ★

Father was smoking a cheroot as he went through the day's postal deliveries, which he was allowed to do only in his study, and with the door closed. He prepared and smoked it with such extraordinary relish that Cassandra was convinced that he actually didn't care much for tobacco at all.

She was in the study, bent over her embroidery, to keep him company. She had made an effort to be kind since their confrontation in the hall.

"Now this," he raised a sheet of paper. "Is a surprise—a letter from Edwin Booth."

"Truly?" Somehow, the thought of Booth's family had not occurred to her. It was overwhelming enough to contemplate the fact that one of the great thespians of the era had been involved in such an atrocious scheme against the President himself.

"Yes. He deplores his brother's actions, and offers his most abject apologies."

"Ah."

"He offers his particular regards to, and I quote, "your daughter Cassandra, whom I hope was not unduly discomfited or unsettled by my wretched brother's depredations.""

"He didn't!"

"He did indeed. Read for yourself."

"Yes—put it there. I'll read it as soon as I finish with this."

"He asked about Hadrian as well." Father sank back in his chair. "What a figure of a man that Hadrian is."

He'd been going on like that about Hadrian ever since he'd met him shortly after Booth was killed—and he was not alone. Reporters, officials, busybody old women, all of them, who would have crossed the street if they'd caught sight of Hadrian approaching before last week, now could not get enough of him. His people had benefited. They had been overwhelmed with offerings of food, some of it rich stuff of a like they had never before encountered. Cassie had intercepted some of the deliveries and had them sent to other freedmen encampments— Hadrian's group was far from alone. They had also been given use of a building, which now served both as classrooms and sleeping quarters.

But as for Hadrian himself—he had little use for rewards and none at all for praise. He had attended one abolitionist meeting called to celebrate his feat, wearing a suit that Cassandra had selected for him. But he had remained only a minimum amount of time, and had soon returned to his encampment and his accustomed well-worn clothes. He had gently discouraged Cassie from any further excursions of the sort, though the invitations had poured in.

"He is better than what this world has to offer him," she said.

"That is unquestionably the case. Were his skin white, he would have the world at his feet. Nothing at all would be beyond him."

"We really must do something for him."

Her father took a contemplative puff of his cheroot. "Yes. I've been thinking the same."

"You have?"

"Yes. He requires something that would fit his abilities, provide him with a decent livelihood, but not be beneath him."

"Exactly." Cassie said after a moment. She was somewhat surprised that the direct and blunt Colonel Baird was displaying such depth of insight.

"It presents a challenge. But we must come up with something."

Cassie eyed her father, wondering if the time had come to bring up her plan. He was relaxed, undistracted, and in a good mood, a conjunction of qualities that was rare at best. She would probably have no better opportunity to put forth her thoughts on the matter. "You know, Father, the best way to do something for Hadrian would be to do something for his people."

Her father eyed her, fingers curled around the cheroot.

"They are in a predicament. They can never return to the South, but where is there a place for them in the northern states?"

He grunted agreement. "Sadly true."

"But . . . it occurred to me that the north and south are not all that exists of the United States."

"'Course not. There's the frontier."

"Yes. The far west."

"Plenty of room out there. An agricultural way of life, with which they have long experience . . ."

"And no large cities, for which they are not well prepared."

Her father squinted over his cheroot. "So—what would be required for this venture? Seed. Tools. Horses, supplies, wagons, wood, firearms . . . It doesn't seem like much."

"Land."

"Land! Yes . . ." Leaping from the chair as lightly as she'd seen him do since he'd lost his leg, her father went over to the map above the desk. "Plenty of land in the Dakotas. Especially with the Sioux acting up."

For the past year the Indians had been sweeping out of the Dakota territories, attacking settlers in Minnesota. It seemed that they had informed knowledge of the civil war going on between the white men and were taking full advantage of it.

"Yes . . . a lot of settlers are afraid to set foot there now. The freedmen would have no competition for land."

"And there's the President's Homestead Act . . ."

He snapped his fingers. "An amendment putting aside a certain percentage of frontier homesteads for freed blacks. Of course. That would work out very well."

"It would, Father. It would give them a place to stand. A place where they can build their lives as they see fit. These society women are cooing over them now, but in a month or two it will be something else. They are what this war is all about. They shouldn't be forgotten."

He was still studying the map, his eyes intent, as if seeing something invisible to herself or any others. She relaxed. She recognized that expression. "The abolitionists will be good for some funds. They're at loose ends since the Proclamation. The churches will certainly open their purses for this . . ."

"And don't forget your business friends either, Father."

"Hmm. I'll put a bug in Cooke's ear. Talk to Greeley and get him behind it. Bring in Mr. Douglass as well, he'll have sound advice . . ."

He was pacing the room, as if he had two flesh-and-blood legs carrying him. Cassie said nothing. Unlike many young women her age, she had a clear notion of when it was best not to speak.

". . . and you, young lady, you now have a subject for the talk you're giving at that women's gathering next week."

Cassie smiled. She already had an outline written. "Well, Father. Let's get this on paper, while it's fresh in our minds."

"Indeed."

She examined her embroidery. It was not quite finished as yet, but the rest would wait.

"And what is this you're working on?"

"It's a sash. She turned it around and displayed it to him. "For Steven. This yellow will go nicely with the blue uniform. And this is the emblem of the 6th Indiana."

"Ahh." He nodded as he admired it. "My dear, you are lady of considerable talents."

More than you might guess, Father, she thought, as he set the sash down and went to the desk for paper and a pen.

Without even realizing it, Dean found himself in the midst of a battlefield.

He'd been smelling the stink for some time without realizing what it must be. It was only when he nearly stepped on a body in the tall grass that he became aware of what he'd stumbled into.

He stopped and looked around him. He hadn't known there had been fighting here. He thought he was still in Maryland. Or had he reached Pennsylvania already?

A few steps on, he spotted a knapsack and raced over to it. He yanked it open, letting out an inarticulate sound when he saw there was food inside it. Hard tack, a bit of dried fruit. He dropped into a crouch and wolfed it down. He was starving. He'd been avoiding people since he fled Washington. Cassie Baird had no doubt informed the authorities. He was certain a description had been sent out. They'd be scouring the landscape for him. The last time he'd eaten was a couple of handfuls of grain he'd found in a barn. Had that been yesterday?

The knapsack dangling from his hand, he moved on, looking around him carefully. He spotted a few more bodies, a dead horse. Then he caught sight of something dangling from a clump of brush closer to the road and walked over to it. It was an officer's greatcoat, hanging from a branch as if on display. Good, heavy wool, well tailored, with a fine red satin lining. He thanked God as he pulled it on. The last couple of mornings had been freezing. It was a little large, but not too bad.

With greater confidence, he headed north. He'd been keeping to the fields to avoid being seen, but now, if he was in fact near to Confederate-held Pennsylvania, it wouldn't hurt to use the roads. If any of the locals saw him wearing Confederate gray, they'd just turn around and run off anyway.

He wondered what was going on back in Washington. Booth was dead, no question about that. Those niggers had killed him. He'd dropped like a sack when they opened fire. And who had given them guns in the first place? But Booth had been a silly ass anyway. Way too impetuous, too inclined to go off at a half-cock. Actors were like that. Look at how he'd tried to bag Lincoln. Jessup had been right. There hadn't been enough planning. Instinct, Booth had said, as if that was the answer to everything. Well, he'd learned how that had worked out. If he'd listened more closely to Richard Dean, he'd have been better off.

He thought of Mary—her warmth, her softness. She'd been about the best girl he'd ever had, even considering that she was Italian and a little overpadded. A lot more lively than Cassandra Baird, that was for sure. That dried-up old spinster. She'd regret turning her back on him, that much was certain.

But forget about Baltimore and Washington. That was the past. The future lay up ahead, with the Army of Northern Virginia. He wondered how they would honor him for his attempt on Lincoln. He wouldn't tell them about it, wouldn't even mention it—not until he was brought before General Lee. Oh, he'd let them know who he was, of course. Just tell them, "Name's Dean. I was with Booth." That would be plenty. That would tell them all they needed to know. Then he would be presented to Robert E. Lee. He could picture Lee rising to his feet, saluting him, that same as he would a soldier . . . No; an officer, that was even better.

Would there be a medal in it for him? He couldn't see why not. Maybe they'd send him down to Richmond, to advise Jefferson Davis himself. He could tell them the best way to make another attempt on Lincoln. They might even put him in charge. Who better?

He walked on, light of step. Apart from a few figures in distant fields, he saw no one. It was late afternoon when at last he caught sight of a group of horsemen coming down the road.

He could see clearly that the lead riders were in gray. Letting the knapsack drop to his feet, he waved wildly, making no effort to conceal himself.

The horsemen sped up. Their expressions turned quizzical as they drew closer.

"What the hell are you?" the lead rider asked as he came to a halt. He was a husky man, broad-faced and with a ginger beard.

"Well," Richard began. "I was with Booth . . ."

"A Yankee," a smaller, blond-bearded rider said.

"He done stole that coat," another man said.

The husky rider dismounted and approached Richard, never taking his eyes off Dean's face. He gripped the lapel of the coat. "Yessir—that's an officer's coat. Where'd you get that?"

The blond man was now standing beside Richard. "Stripped it off a dead man, dincha?"

"No . . . no, he wasn't dead . . ."

"He wasn't *what*?"

"You took this coat from a wounded man," the husky man said. "If that don't beat all."

He yanked the coat open, spotted the pistol in Dean's belt and pulled it free.

"That's an army Colt," the blond man said.

"So it is. He stole that too."

Richard raised both hands. "No! Listen to me . . ." He tried to draw away from them. Something struck him in the head.

"Fuckin' Yankees. By God, I hate them so much . . ."

"No southron ever do a thing like that."

In a moment they had stripped the coat off him and his hands were tied behind his back. "I want to see General Lee!"

"Oh, you'll see General Lee, all right," the husky man said. "You'll see General Lee, and Julius Caesar, and all the prophets."

A rope was lowered around his neck and then tightened. A mass of hands half-lifted, half-pushed him atop a horse.

"I was with Booth," he said desperately. "Down in Washington. We ambushed Lincoln . . ."

The blond man scratched his beard. "Think maybe we got some kind of mooncalf here, Albert."

"Too late now," the husky man said. He glanced up at Richard. "You made your peace there, sonny? Then you'd best be off."

He slapped the horse on the rump. "I was with Boottthhh . . ." Richard screamed, as he felt the horse's flanks slide out from underneath him.

The riders stood watching Dean's legs kick at the empty air. A couple of them were fighting over the coat, each insisting that it would fit him better.

The blond man considered Dean's quivering form. "I wonder who this Booth might be?"

The husky man turned away. "How the hell do I know?"

"He lost over four thousand men in this misbegotten attack."

Salmon P. Chase picked up a telegram from the tabletop and waved it at the rest of the Cabinet.

"Over four thousand. That's only the dead. The wounded, we have no idea."

Lincoln watched him with no expression. Halleck was studying the tabletop. Edward Bates sat aloofly. Gideon Welles was nodding as if in silent agreement.

William Denniston, the new secretary of war, said nothing. He had been in office only for a matter of days and was still finding his feet. They were awaiting the final word on Stanton, but there wasn't much hope. He had caught pneumonia in Seminary Hospital, and had been sinking for over a week. Lincoln had visited him there yesterday and had been appalled at how poorly he looked. He was not even certain that Edward had known he was there, though at one point he had gripped Lincoln's hand and grimaced in what might have been a smile.

That was likely the last Lincoln would ever see of him. The doctors had given him only a matter of hours.

". . . and then to top it off, he broke down and wept like an old woman when it was all over."

"At least we kept that out of the press," Halleck said.

"Small mercies."

"Drunk as a lord, no doubt," Bates said in a low voice.

"Either that, or mad as a hatter."

None of them were looking at Lincoln. None of them wanted to go as far as a direct challenge. But they were more than happy to make their opinions known . . . as long as everyone else was doing it.

"It's the same as ever," Chase went on. "We've seen this before. Remember Fredericksburg? No difference at all. Now, we will retreat until Grant is good and ready to try it again, which, this being autumn, means not until April or May, while General Lee lords it over the free state of Pennsylvania as if over his own personal domain."

Lincoln glanced from one of them to the next. "Is this then the consensus?"

Without waiting for an answer, he picked up a sheet lying before him. "While you were examining telegrams, you might have taken a look at this one. It reads, 'Heading north on the Harrisburg Pike. Flanking Lee's forces. I mean to continue on this course if it takes me into next Spring.'"

He set down the sheet. "Signed, General U.S. Grant."

"What . . ."

"You mean, he's *advancing* . . . ?'

"After a defeat such as that?"

Lincoln nodded. "I'm not at all certain that General Grant views the encounter at York as any sort of defeat."

Several of the cabinet turned toward General Halleck. "Don't look at me," he said. "I have no idea."

"Nor do I," Lincoln said. "And that is the very point. None of us have any idea. You see, gentlemen, this is a new kind of war. This is not a war being fought to seize land, or to establish a dynasty, or for plunder, as in ancient days. It's something else, it's a kind of war possibly never before encountered in history, certainly not on our continent.

"It's a war of ideas, of concepts, of notions as to what the world is, and how we should live in it. That's what we're fighting here. Not our southern neighbors. Not General Lee and his army. But an *idea*—the notion, ghastly to us, as it would be to all free men, that some men were born wearing saddles and others with spurs and whips to ride them.

"How do we fight such a thing? How do we kill an idea? Is it impossible to accomplish that without killing every last man who holds the idea in his head? That may be. General Grant told me that one of his officers believes that is the key. That we are fighting a would-be aristocracy and that every last member of that aristocracy must be killed before peace, and the Union, are restored.

"I don't know if that's true. I hope and pray that it is not. But I do believe this:

"I believe that General Grant has some inkling as to how it can be done. How an idea must be slain. That he has a clue as to how this war must be fought. That he is working his way toward a strategy, a method of doing this. But he is like a Columbus or a Magellan, facing a vast unmapped and unknown territory. He has to make his way blindly, and in doing that there will be mistakes, and there will be losses. These losses may be such as to beggar the imagination of a Khan or a Napoleon. The 4,000 at York may only be a down payment.

"Grant understands this. I don't think anyone else does."

Lincoln fell silent, taken by a sudden vision of a vast portal swinging wide. What would be revealed could well be a horror past bearing, in light of which all previous horrors faded into nothingness. But he knew without a shadow of doubt that the portal had been opened.

He became aware of his Cabinet staring at him, Chase with his mouth hanging slightly open, the others with widened eyes. Only Seward regarded him with equanimity, and yes, perhaps a touch of sympathy as well.

The secretary of state leaned forward. "If I were burdened with such an understanding, I too would weep."

The Cabinet glanced among themselves, but said nothing.

Lincoln forced a smile. "Well, gentlemen, let's move on."

Secretary of War Denniston cleared his throat. "General Grant . . ." His eyes flicked toward Lincoln for a moment. "Has evidently taken possession of twenty of something called . . . 'coffee-mill' guns at a thousand dollars apiece . . ."

"No, that was me," Lincoln said.

Denniston eyed him a moment. "I see," he said at last.

Blandon paused just below the crest of the hilltop. There were sounds coming from the other side, the distant voices of men along with an odd creaking noise he couldn't place.

He glanced back at his men. They gazed dumbly at him, saying nothing. There were only nine of them now. The others had drifted off in the days since that business in the farm village. He was no longer surprised to see another one missing when he awoke in the morning.

"Let me take a look," he told them. He got off the horse and headed toward the crest.

They were being careful, particularly after running into that patrol the other day. On spotting the riders and assuring himself that they were wearing gray, Blandon had waved his hat and shouted a greeting. But instead of approaching, the lead rider pulled his horse to a halt and conferred with the others.

"Howdy," Blandon said as he drew near. He saw that the other rider was a captain and gave him a quick salute.

"How are you, Sergeant?"

"Could be better. Tell you the truth, we're lost. We're with the Tennessee Volunteer Cavalry." No point in lying about that. "We were on patrol and got ourselves turned around somehow. You wouldn't know where the Volunteers are at, would you?"

"I'm afraid not." The captain chewed the end of his mustache. "Your name wouldn't be Blandon, would it?"

Blandon's spine prickled. He glanced back at Giddens and the others. "Can't say it is, Captain."

The captain bent over his horse's neck. "Well, that's a good thing."

"How's that?"

"This Blandon raped and killed a fourteen-year-old girl. The rest of his unit worked over some older women. We were told to keep an eye open."

"Is that so?"

"Indeed it is . . . what you say your name was, Sergeant?"

The officer had that educated tone that Blandon didn't like. "Johnston. Hiram Johnston."

"You haven't come across this Blandon, have you?"

"Sorry to say I haven't, sir. But I will keep it in mind."

The other horsemen were gazing at Blandon with no expression at all. The captain flicked his eyes across Blandon's men. There were ten of them, and he had four. He looked back at Blandon. "The locals did not approve. They're all riled up now. Nothing but ambuscades and bushwhacking for the last three days."

"We'll watch out for that too."

The captain nodded. "Well, we're bivouacked just a few miles from here. You'd be more than welcome to drop by for a meal."

"Thank you kindly, but I think we'll go on looking for our unit."

"Up to you." The captain touched his hat and spurred his horse. "Best of luck."

The riders didn't take their eyes off Blandon's men until they were well down the road. As soon as they were out of sight, Blandon led his men across the countryside. They didn't pause for several hours.

He halted at the crest. He had decided it was time to head south. Get back to Virginia and then he'd figure things out. Volunteer for another unit, maybe, or even head west, to Arkansas or Texas. Make a whole new start—that might be best. But first they had to get across the river.

He stepped to the bushes and pulled them apart. Downhill lay the Potomac, little more than a lazy, meandering stream this far west. Shallow and easily forded, as Bobby Lee had demonstrated to the Yankees time after time.

This was one of the fords, a nice, shallow spot that would enable them to cross while scarcely getting their britches wet.

But there was a problem, an obstacle the like of which he hadn't encountered before. Below him he saw a goodly number of Yankees on the river. They were winching a large boat over a shallow spot. On the bank lay a scattering of items they'd taken off the boat, apparently to lighten it. A number of heavy chains, some items he couldn't identify, and two large-caliber cannons.

Blandon recognized that vessel. He seen similar on the James a year and a half ago, during the Seven Days battles before Richmond. It was a Yankee gunboat. This was a later model, and it was fully ironclad, but the basic setup was familiar. The shaded conning tower, the two turrets that held the cannons.

As he watched, the boat suddenly jerked forward and floated free into deeper water. The workmen around it cheered.

"What the devil?"

Giddens was peering through the brush beside him. "That's a Yankee gunboat."

"So it is."

McCutcheon came up behind Giddens. "Jonah, there's another one over there," Giddens said.

Blandon squinted in that direction. There it was, about a quarter mile upstream, shaded by overhanging trees. The nearer gunboat swung close to the bank and let down a ramp. The workmen began to wrestle the cannon and other materials back on board.

Blandon straightened up. "Well, we'll have to find another ford. There's one about three miles west of here, ain't there . . . ."

"Holy shit."

Blandon looked to where McCutcheon was pointing. A squadron of bluebelly horsemen had appeared from behind a clump of trees. They were riding hell for leather, and aimed straight for the hill on which Blandon stood.

"Come on, y'all," Blandon said. "Let's get movin'."

"How'd they know we was here?" Giddens asked as they loped toward the horses.

"Somebody seen us," Blandon told him.

They were halfway down the hill when they spotted another Yankee patrol headed in their direction from the northeast. They sped up to a gallop when they caught sight of the butternut horsemen. Blandon led his men to the west. They managed to shake off the federals easily enough, but had gone no more than five miles when they came across a roadblock that sent yet another group of cavalry after them. They went cross-country once again, ending up in a marshy area, keeping the horses quiet as they listened to the Yankees hallooing to each other in the distance.

They didn't emerge until nearly sundown to slowly make their way north away from the river. Encountering a farm boy returning from a day's work in the fields, Blandon asked him if he'd seen a lot of cavalry hereabouts.

Yessir, the kid had answered, they were out and about by the hundreds, all up and down the river from Seneca to Brunswick. They weren't letting anybody at all within a mile of the Potomac.

". . . and they'll catch your Reb asses too," he assured Blandon before abruptly vanishing into the brush beside the road.

Blandon gazed after him, a curse on his breath, and then continued north.

Later that evening, he thought his way through it as he sat beside a fire carefully placed in a copse between two hills so it wouldn't be seen from a distance.

They wouldn't be heading south anytime soon. The Yankees were crawling all over this whole area. Of course, they could go farther west, thirty, forty miles to where the river was too shallow to float a gunboat, but then he might well run into his own people and he didn't want to do that either. Not with this rape story floating around.

But what were the Yankees up to? Where there were two gunboats, it was likely you'd find more. Blandon could think of several ways they could be used this far upriver, none of them to the benefit of the Army of Northern Virginia.

So did the army know about it? He had reason to doubt that. That captain had said nothing. They hadn't heard a thing while riding around south central Pennsylvania. Blandon would be willing to bet silver money that Bobby Lee and all his staff had no idea the Yankees were moving heavily armed gunboats into his rear. They would no doubt be quite pleased with the man who appeared with that information.

So—he'd return to division . . . or rather, go straight to headquarters, to Bobby Lee himself, and let them know what the Yankees were about. He felt a sense of excitement. It was just like his warning before Hanover, only better. That would make up for a lot in the way of mistakes. How could they punish a man who had warned them about a threat like this? Particularly if all his men swore they'd been nowhere near that peapatch of a farming village. He wasn't sure what the bluecoats were up to, but it couldn't be anything good.

He lay back on the blanket, hands behind his head. That would work out just fine.

Wade sat in the barn they had commandeered on the northeast side of Harrisburg. He had a board balanced on his knees and was writing his mother. Around him the men were relaxing—smoking, playing cards, shaving, and seeing to their uniforms. Several were at the creek out back washing up. He planned to join them shortly, as soon as he was finished writing the letter. It had been a few days since they'd had any time to themselves.

He was pleased that he had good news for her. The Tennessee Volunteers had come out of the latest battle well. They'd withstood three full assaults by the Yankees and hadn't given an inch. Why, General Hardee himself had complimented him in person over their steadfastness. Best of all, they hadn't lost a man. A half-dozen injured, that was all. And the ground in front of them had been carpeted with blue-clad troops.

Of course, he wouldn't tell her that part. He made a point of keeping the bloodshed out of it when he wrote her. There were some things that she just shouldn't know about.

"Corey?" It was Mayfield. "There's an officer from General Longstreet outside to see you."

Wade looked past him to see a pair of unfamiliar faces waiting just outside the entrance. Putting the letter aside, he got to his feet. He looked around for his uniform jacket, but remembered that Corporal Sennett had taken it to give it a good brushing and otherwise spruce it up.

He saluted the officer—a major—as he drew near. What could this be about? The major's expression did not promise good news.

"Colonel Wade, I am Major Prentiss. I have been dispatched from General Longstreet's headquarters."

Prentiss had a Tidewater accent, and was as perfectly turned out as an officer could be—cavalry boots, a feathered hat, a sash, a short cape over his jacket. His face was framed by a carefully barbered van dyke that Wade would never be foolish enough to attempt to grow. Wade felt like a coal miner standing before him, wearing only a shirt with no jacket. He buttoned the top of his shirt, feeling ashamed as he did.

"Would you care to take a seat, Major?"

Prentiss glanced into the barn and shook his head. "No thank you. This won't take long." He crossed his gloved hands in front of him. "Do you have any idea where this man Blandon is? Jonah Blandon."

So it was Blandon. He might have guessed. "I'm afraid not."

"I see."

"At this point, it would be best to consider him a deserter."

"Uh-huh. Did you notify the provost marshal as to that fact?"

"No I have not."

Prentiss looked around him. "You've been in combat in recent days."

"Yes—that's right."

"I understand. Now, you have no idea what Blandon has been up to?"

Wade shook his head.

"Let me explain. He raped and murdered a young girl in a farming village about forty miles southwest of here. His men proceeded to violate just about every other woman in the place. A travesty, sir. A hideous crime in the eyes of God and man both."

"Good lord," Wade said. "That was Blandon?"

"So you've heard this story?"

"It's been making the rounds. How do you know this?"

"One of his men reported it. An Elijah Skinner. Do you recall him?"

Wade remembered him vaguely: few teeth, eyes a little close together, and a massive beard.

"Skinner, and his simpleminded younger brother, fled rather than join in. They encountered a cavalry scout in trying to locate your unit, and were sent on to headquarters."

"Where is he now?"

"He has been court-martialed and punished."

"For desertion?"

"No, sir. He was technically not a deserter, was he? But he was carrying a substantial amount of currency, so we got him for that. He is now serving a sentence of hard labor, digging the fortifications around this very city. As for his brother . . . well, one does not punish the simple for being simple."

"I see."

"It's good of you to show concern for your enlisted men." Prentiss gave him a wintry smile. "I admire that."

Wade said nothing in response. He had nothing much to say.

"Now, here's the thing. We've been suffering serious resistance from the locals hereabouts over the past few days . . ."

"I'm aware of that."

"Very good." Prentiss nodded. "The farming community that was victimized is called Holland Farms. Yesterday, a few miles away from there, a foraging party was ambushed by civilians. One man escaped. The rest were found hanging from tree branches. The corporal's body had a sign attached, reading, 'For Holland Farms.'"

Wade stared at him.

"So you see, sir. This is not simply your problem any longer. It is the army's problem."

He eyed Wade for a moment before continuing. "Do you have any idea where Blandon is? Was he operating under your orders? Does he have any friends in your unit? Took them with him. I see. Any relatives? Would anyone here have any information as to his whereabouts?"

Wade simply shook his head.

Prentiss glanced over at the sergeant, as if they'd discussed it in detail on the ride over. "Colonel, is there anything you can tell me?"

He shook his head once again.

"I was afraid of this." Prentiss raised both gloved hands. "It's all the same in this godforsaken army. Nobody knows anything. Don't be offended, Wade. No disrespect intended. It's not just you. It's . . . everybody."

He looked Wade up and down before speaking. "Now, you need to look into this. You need to talk to your people. Somebody may have heard something. If they did . . ."

"If anybody knows anything . . . Then I'll goddamn well take care of it myself."

"That, sir, would be one solution." Prentiss took one precise step back and saluted him. "We will speak on this further."

Wade watched them ride off before he turned back to the barn. The men were looking at him quizzically. He said nothing as he went back inside.

One hand giveth, and the other hand taketh away. That was life for you. There couldn't be a single moment's triumph without a double portion of misery to wash it clean away. You couldn't get ahead—there was always worse around every corner. He was no longer Colonel Corey Wade, the man who had stood up to the Yankees at York, the officer complimented by General Lee himself. No—he was Wade the fool, Wade the incompetent, the man who had sheltered a vile killer, like a viper in his own bosom. The man who has set the Yankee civilians ablaze, the man who was getting his own people killed. The man who had helped disgrace the South and its cause.

He could picture General Longstreet himself: *Wade, that damnable young fool, what the devil is he good for?*

And General Lee—did General Lee know about this?

"Here you go, sir."

It was Corporal Sennett, returned with his jacket. Wade got to his feet. "Thank you, Corporal."

"My pleasure, sir. A great officer needs a good-looking coat."

Wade sat back down, gazing at the three stars on the shoulders. He raised his eyes to the board on which the letter to his mother awaited. Reaching for the sheet, he crumpled it and tossed it aside.

★ CHAPTER 23 ★

Jefferson Davis had decided once again to greet the British envoy alone. This time it was because he couldn't trust certain members of his Cabinet not to embarrass both the Confederacy and themselves.

"Well, they do have a point, Mr. President."

Davis turned to Vice President Stephens. "I understand their point, sir."

"Gentleman," Judah Benjamin turned from his post at the window. "Let's concentrate on the issue at hand."

"Yes," Davis sat back. "Quite so." Still, he would have expected Stephens to be a little accepting of the agreement, considering how much hopeless effort he had put into a negotiated end to the war.

He was sick of talking about it. Did these backcountry fools think that the British Empire was going to put itself on the line for nothing? There were risks involved. What if that fanatic abolitionist Lincoln refused to back down? Anything was possible from that madhouse on the Potomac. Consider those newspaper stories about Lincoln's attempted "kidnapping" by some imaginary Confederate cabal. And who had the ringleader of this conspiracy been? Why, John Wilkes Booth, a no-account actor. What lunacy!

"It's not at all a bad deal," Benjamin said. "They could have asked for more."

"I'm not saying it is," Stephens replied.

Yes, they could have asked for more. If Stephens only knew . . . As it stood, the offer was straightforward. The British wanted a base. The base needed to be on the Chesapeake. And that meant the James Peninsula. There was no real alternative. The fact that any such base would be a mere stone's throw from Yorktown, where the British had been seen off only eighty years before, really shouldn't factor into it. But it did all the same.

"But still . . . they do have a point."

"I heard you the first time, Alex," Davis said, more loudly than he had perhaps intended. "And I understand it."

He did understand it. That was the simple truth. But look at what the British were offering! A fleet was already being prepared on the Nore. Within a month, six weeks at the most, it would set sail for Virginia. A dozen or more men-of-war, fifty- to ninety-gun steamers unmatched by any vessel in the Western hemisphere. Dozens of support vessels. Several thousand Royal Army troops to garrison the new base. Let's see what Mr. Lincoln's popinjay gunboats would do against an armada like that.

From that moment it would be over. No more blockade, no more bloodshed. He would not have to gaze any longer on the hungry faces of the children of Richmond, hear the complaints of bankrupt businessmen. See, over and over, the black crepe bands on the sleeves of the men in the street, the black dresses of the women. The South would be independent and free, its people able to live as they saw fit.

Wasn't that good enough? Wasn't that what they had been working toward these past two years and more? What more did they want?

There were men in the Senate who had actually crossed arms with the British. Men who as youths had fought beside Jackson at New Orleans in 1815. Their attitudes toward the British were conditioned by old brutal memories, honed and sharpened over the years. That was the cost of Tennessee being part of the Confederacy, Davis supposed. Old Hickory had a lot to answer for.

But they would change their tune. Once the war was over. Once the South was back on its feet. Then would come the time to reveal the rest of it—that other base in Florida that the British desired. The long-term discount on cotton exports to the Midlands. The "observers," as they were carefully termed to be, that they wished to send to the Rio Grande, to keep an eye on French activity in Mexico. Several thousand of them. The trade concessions for British bottoms calling at southern ports . . .

And so on. They drove a hard bargain, the British. At several points in the discussions Davis had begun to believe that he knew precisely how a Hindoo prince must feel when confronted by representatives of the Lady King.

"A carriage approaches," Benjamin said. He swung away from the window.

"That's him."

Davis nodded, suddenly overcome with an infinite sense of weariness. These past few minutes were supposed to have been devoted to a discussion of how he might deal with the new British envoy, carefully dispatched across the Virginia lines from their Washington embassy. But they had simply not gotten around to that.

Stephens got to his feet. "We'll be waiting."

"And do keep them calm." The envoy was evidently an heir to nobility, of a type that most of his government had no idea existed. He'd had to distribute printed cards to inform them as to how he was to be addressed. That had not gone over well.

He heard footsteps in the hall. Straightening his jacket, he turned toward the door. Once again he thought of the princes of India, the potentates of Asia, all under the thumb of Britain. He recalled the words he'd once heard spoken by old Andrew Jackson himself: "Once the Redcoats are in, they never leave unless thrust out with the bayonet."

The door swung open. The man who walked in was, once again, younger than Davis would have preferred. He was wearing a sash laden with decorations. On seeing Davis, he paused for a moment, then bowed magnanimously.

And what if they don't leave here?

Davis stepped toward him, smiling broadly. "Marquesse Henry . . . welcome to the Confederate States of America."

"Jonah . . . Jonah, hold up."

Blandon looked over his shoulder. Giddens was giving him that sullen look he'd seen all too often the past few days.

"We're nearly back to that town where . . . y'know . . ."

Blandon reined his horse in. That hadn't occurred to him. He was so eager to return to the army with his information that he hadn't really been thinking straight. He wanted to get word to them as soon as possible, so they could act on it. He'd taken the most direct route he could think of.

But what difference did it make? So they were headed for that one particular little backwoods village. So what. Bunch of farmers couldn't even rightly protect their womenfolk. What kind of threat could they be?

"I ain't riding through there again," one of the men said. Mutters of agreement followed.

Blandon gritted his teeth. All right. They'd just detour before they reached the village itself. Turn north, ride across the fields until they got to the next high road.

They could do that any time. This minute, if he wanted. But instead Blandon rode on. He had to show them who was boss. They'd all been a little uppity the past few days. Giddens, for one, didn't seem very taken with his idea of heading for Lee's headquarters.

He smelled a familiar stench, plain even in the cool breeze. Two dead horses lay beside the road up ahead, bellies bloated and flies buzzing above them. Somebody had gone to the trouble of dragging them off the road. Blandon spotted a gap in the brush on the other side of the road. That made it three. No saddles or harness to reveal whether they were Confederate, Yankee, or from local farms.

There was another outburst of muttering from behind him. He listened for a moment, straining to make sense of the words. "All right, y'all," he said at last. "We'll cut across the fields in just a minute."

"Let's turn now."

"No! Y'all just calm down now. Actin' like a bunch of old women . . ."

"Hold on!"

He looked back. Giddens had stopped his horse and was looking wildly about him at the woods lining the road. "There's somebody out there," he said. "We gotta turn back."

"What you talkin' about?"

Giddens stared at him as if at a simpleton. "There ain't no birds singin'!"

The first wave of gunfire swept Giddens off his horse. Blandon was reaching for his carbine when he felt a blow to his side. The screaming horse reared and he found himself lying stunned in the dirt.

He turned his head to see the others down, either alone or with their horses. Two stood with their hands held high. Only one man—Duber?—had escaped, and was galloping down the road. He got about twenty yards before another blast of gunfire from the brush caught him. He went over the horse's head. It collapsed on top of him.

Blandon tried to rise, but a sharp pain from his leg dropped him onto the road again. He touched the wound in his side. It didn't seem that bad.

There was a gunshot from behind. Somebody was being finished off.

"None of that," a voice said. "No—we'll keep them for the army."

Someone stepped around his horse. A face appeared above him. Blandon recognized him despite his black eyes and the still-swollen features. The boy's eyes went wide. "Pa!" he called out. "Pa—it's him."

The boy was replaced by an older, bearded version of himself. The farmer stared expressionlessly down at Blandon. "Are you sure, son?"

"As God is my judge, Pa."

The farmer was joined by other stern Yankee faces, each regarding Blandon with dispassion. At last the farmer spoke.

"You defiled a virgin." His voice was soft, as if he was making a point in a friendly disagreement.

She wasn't no fourteen, Blandon said to himself.

One of the farmers called out, "Go ahead and finish the rest."

More gunshots rang out. Blandon felt rough hands grip his shoulders.

The farmer reached for the knife at his belt. "Look away, son," he said softly. He bent over. Blandon was screaming before he even got to work.

★ CHAPTER 24 ★

Thorne raised his glasses for yet another look at Harrisburg.

They had been camped outside the city for the past two days. The Rebs had tried to burn down the bridge across the Susquehanna, but succeeded only in damaging it. It had taken the engineers only three hours to fix up the span enough to allow infantry and cavalry to cross. But the delay in getting artillery over the river had enabled the Confederates to dig in. They were now snug behind their fortifications, hooting and jeering at the Army of the Potomac while safely protected by trenches, barricades, and those infernal abatis.

He lowered the glasses. So why didn't he see anybody over there now? He hadn't caught sight of a single Johnny Reb for the past hour. There had been a sudden surge of activity around one or so, but after that, nothing. He got to his feet in plain view of the other side. Ordinarily that would have gotten him some kind of response up to and including a ball fired in his direction. But today there was nothing.

He was morally convinced that the line was deserted. He decided to go over and take a look.

He was turning to holler to Archie Willis to bring over a couple of horses when he saw three men riding toward him. He came to attention and saluted as he spotted the stars on the lead rider's jacket.

"Something of interest, Colonel?" the general called out as he dismounted.

"Yes, sir." Thorne stared at him, more than a little startled. He'd received notice of his brevet promotion only after arriving at Harrisburg and was still wearing his major's insignia. He handed the general his glasses. "Why don't you take a look?"

The general paused to remove his kid gloves, then took the glasses and peered through them. He made some odd noises as he ran them across the line. His aides came to a halt just behind him, saying nothing.

"They've got trenches in front of that low structure right there . . ."

The general lowered the glasses slightly. "Clostermann's. It's a warehouse."

Thorne eyed him a moment. "Yes . . . well, it was crawling with butternut troops not an hour ago. But now . . ."

"Yes, I see. Vanished in a trice. Poof! And no more." He handed the binoculars back to Thorne. "A splendid set of glasses there, young man."

"Yes, sir, they're from Hamburg."

"Ahh." He nodded avidly, as if that was the best thing he'd heard all day. Thorne noticed that he was slightly walleyed, along with being rather short and slight of build. As for his uniform . . . Well, if the standard in the Army of Potomac was high, this officer easily surpassed it with his sash and knee boots, not to mention the gloves, which he was now in the process of pulling back on.

He raised one hand. "Dabney . . . the horses, if you will." He turned back to Thorne. "Let's take a look, shall we?"

They crossed the field at a slow trot, the general, his two aides, and Thorne along with Willis. Halfway across, Thorne pulled out his pistol and checked it. Willis did the same. Neither the general nor his aides reacted.

The trenches were in clear view before they reached the buildings. They were absolutely empty, not a single sign that anyone had been inhabiting them—not a rifle, not a backpack, nothing.

The general shook his head. "Oh my."

They moved on about thirty feet. Just before the unpaved street ended, there was a set of tracks that looked as if a cannon had been trundled off. The general made a sound as if he was disappointed in a silly error by a small child.

They halted at the end of the street. It was empty as far down as they could see, not a single person, horse, or even a dog in sight.

Thorne glanced over at the building the general had identified as a warehouse. There was a faded sign over the door: CLOSTERMANN'S.

"We'll go down as far as the Quaker meeting house. That's about three blocks or so," he assured Thorne.

As his horse began to move, Willis rode up beside Thorne. "Is he from around here?"

"Got me. I don't even know who he is."

"Oh, that's Warren."

General Gouverneur Warren, chief of the army's engineers. Well, that made sense. He probably had maps of every town in the state.

Reaching the third block, they halted once more. General Warren let out a sigh. "Dear me. I don't see any Rebels." He swung toward Thorne. "Do you, Colonel?"

"No, sir, I do not."

There was a sound from a house on the north side of the street. The shutters on an upstairs window swung open. Thorne raised his pistol but let the barrel fall as a young girl poked her head out.

"Hello!" she called. "Are you looking for the soldiers?"

Warren swept off his hat. "Indeed we are, my dear. What can you tell us?"

"They all marched away."

"Ahh. When was this. An hour ago? I see."

A smaller girl appeared in the window. She waved and Warren swung his hat with a flourish. Thorne smiled despite himself.

"Are you going to make them stay away?"

"I promise we shall do our best." Warren replaced his hat. "Now we must be off. But we shall be back, my dears, with many more men." He raised his reins, and then paused. "Oh, and girls, please remain inside. It may get very noisy out here."

They started back down the street at a fast trot. Warren said nothing further until they passed the trench. "A common error," he called to Thorne. "A single order miswritten or misinterpreted. Perhaps not written at all, but passed by word of mouth. Have you ever played the parlor game where a simple message is passed by whispers from ear to ear, Colonel? You should. The results would amuse you." He gestured to the aide called Dabney, who swung up beside him. "But we must move before they realize their error."

Thorne noticed that Dabney already had a notepad out. "To

General Grant: We have discovered a significant gap in the Confederate lines at the town's southern extreme. We are striking through the gap at once. Advise an immediate assault on the Rebel center left, along the line of Derry Street. We will be in the direct rear, with as many troops as we can collect. Now read it back."

Dabney read it back quickly. Warren nodded. "Get it to headquarters immediately. Off with you, young sir!"

The aide galloped off at a diagonal toward the Union lines. In a moment he was out of sight.

The men of the battalion meandered over to meet them. "I'll get them saddled up."

"Do that, if you please." Without slowing down, Warren rode past them. Thorne was puzzled until he spotted an infantry unit marching down the road about a half mile away.

He was getting the men lined up when another officer rode in, looked around and turned toward him. "Gambee, 55th Ohio," he called out.

"Proud to meet you."

Gambee got down off his horse. "Now, Auntie Warren says there's a hole in the Reb line here?"

Behind him, his troops were approaching at double time. "That's right," Thorne told him. "We were just over there. Not a Johnny in sight."

Gambee nodded. "Auntie's good at sniffing those weak spots out. Like a Comanche searching for a water hole."

Thorne listened quietly. While there might be more to it, there wasn't much point in bringing it up.

"It was Auntie who spotted the Little Round Top at Gettysburg."

"Was it now?"

"That's right. Sent Chamberlain and Strong Vincent up there to fortify. Damn good thing he did . . ."

Gambee's men were arriving. He turned to oversee them. Behind them, Thorne could see a good-sized group of cavalry approaching. One horseman broke from the rest. He recognized Warren.

"Any sign of our friends, Colonel?"

Thorne shook his head. "No, sir, not a peep."

Warren gave a satisfied nod to the abandoned Rebel line and rode off to consult with Gambee and the cavalry commander. He was turning back to Thorne when Dabney suddenly appeared, riding a visibly exhausted horse. He halted beside Warren and spoke to him in a low voice.

Warren clapped both gloved hands together. "Excellent!" He swung his horse to face the waiting troops. "Gentlemen! It is our intention to sneak into the waiting city, confront our unwelcome guests, and cause utter *havoc*!"

He smiled as if delighted by the prospect, pulled a watch from his pocket and snapped it open. "Are we ready, then?" He smiled again at the loud response and clicked the watch shut. "Then let's be about it. Quick-quick, now."

They crossed the open field at a slow trot, the infantry at double time behind them. As they approached the built-up area Warren gestured to Thorne. "About three blocks past our little girlfriends' house we turn right," he said loud enough for all the officers to hear. "Two blocks over there's an open space, a park, I believe, featuring a gazebo or bandshell. We will pause there until we hear the advance commencing. Then we will strike."

Warren got an odd look or two, but no questions. They passed the trench, then Clostermann's, and proceeded down the empty street. The shutters were closed at the girls' house.

Two blocks on, they paused for the infantry to catch up. Turning the corner, they spotted two men in butternut a half block down. Both of them came to a dead halt, muskets held high. Thorne drew his pistol and swept it between the two. "Drop your guns, boys," he shouted.

At least two other cavalrymen had spoken at the same instant, but the two men got the message all right. They laid their guns in the dusty street and stood up with hands high.

While two of the riders dismounted to take their guns. Warren confronted the pair. "What are you lads up to?" he said, with the tone of a schoolmaster interrogating a pair of truants.

"We're looking for our people," the shorter one said.

"Your people? And where are they?"

"Well . . . they're around."

"Around? Around where?"

One of the cavalrymen had extracted a bottle from the taller one's pack.

"Around town somewhere."

"I see," Warren said. "Well, tie their hands. Not too tight. No point in being nasty."

They moved on down the street. A few small houses, a Presbyterian church, and then the park. It came into view, revealing the gazebo, the ornamental bushes, the carefully placed trees, and beyond all that, the several hundred men in butternut marching diagonally toward them across the well-cut grass.

The Confederates halted. They gazed at the Union troops in dead silence. Then a single gray-clad officer stepped forward, and with a shout, pulled out his sword.

Thorne drew his pistol and fired without aiming at any one of them in particular. He was accompanied by a dozen other shots. The butternut mass broke toward them, the troops howling like so many demons. The Union horsemen charged. They met about halfway across the open space, and the city of Harrisburg began its transformation into Hell on earth.

★ CHAPTER 25 ★

Wade was working on his third attempt at a note to General Lee when the gunfire started.

He was trying not so much to explain or excuse himself, but to apologize for the dishonor he had brought upon his unit, the Army of Northern Virginia, and the Confederacy as a whole. He had thought he had the words clear in his mind, but every time he tried to get them down, they seemed to fade away. When he looked over what he had written, it came across as gibberish.

He raised his head as the shots rang out, a handful at first, followed by a deluge. "Colonel Wade . . ." someone called. "I hear 'em," he answered. Getting up, he threw on his jacket and grabbed his sword belt, then headed for the door. He turned around for his hat and caught sight of the two crumpled sheets and the new one lying atop the board. Picking them up, he tossed them into the stove.

The Volunteers were saddling up as he emerged. Their current role was to act as a mobile reserve to back up any line unit that needed assistance in case the Yankees attacked. He would have to check in at headquarters to find out where they should go.

He'd just gotten his sword belt cinched when something about the sound of guns registered. "That's not coming from the front."

"No sir. That's coming from town."

"What the devil . . ."

"Don't tell me them Yanks snuck in somehow . . ."

Wade cut off the speculation with a raised hand. "Let's get some speed on, boys."

They rode at a near-gallop through the empty streets. As they approached downtown, where General Lee had his headquarters in the statehouse, they encountered a lone rider. He pulled up as Wade waved to him.

"Where's the fighting at?"

"Your guess is as good as mine, Colonel."

"Anybody at headquarters?"

"General Lee's not there. He was conferring with A.P. Hill. I'd say just ride for the guns."

"Always good advice." Wade turned to wave the men on. Somewhere to the east, cannon started roaring.

Thorne paused to reload his pistol. He looked behind him. There was Willis, maybe a dozen other Indianans, and a lesser number of infantrymen who might be from Ohio or might be from the moon, for all he knew. No sign of Warren, or Gambee, or anybody else.

They'd gotten separated while driving the Confederates back across the park. Thorne had no clear idea where everybody else had gone, or, for that matter, where he was now.

He finished reloading and holstered the gun. Willis was bandaging the arm of Private Crowley. Thorne swung his horse toward them. "You all right, Crowley?"

Crowley nodded. He gestured toward his arm. "It just kind of . . . y'know . . ."

Thorne raised his head at a burst of gunfire. He wasn't at all sure how many they'd lost at the park. He had a feeling it was pretty bad.

He got down from the horse and gestured the others to do the same. They were merely larger targets mounted on these nags. They would be infantry as long as they were fighting in these streets.

He spotted some kind of fenced enclosure a half-block away. He didn't know if it was a corral or what, but it would do. He told Crowley to take the horses there and sent Lutton, who claimed that he was eighteen though Thorne had his doubts, along with him.

He was walking over to Archie Willis when a roar came from his right—the Union artillery, at long last.

"Well, here we are . . ." Willis fell silent as a shell appeared over the rooftops and landed somewhere east of them. Within seconds, it was followed by two more.

"What the hell . . ." Thorne heard himself saying.

"Jesus, Mary, and Joseph," one of the infantrymen said. "They're bombarding the houses."

Another round fell no more than two blocks away, shaking the earth beneath their feet. Smoke was pouring into the sky from the direction where the first shell had landed.

"Somebody needs to . . ." Willis started to say.

There was movement in the corner of Thorne's eye. He swung around to see a dozen butternuts turning onto the street. Drawing his revolver, he opened fire.

"Good God, they're firing on their own town."

"So I see." Some of the men had speculated that the Yankees would never attack one of their own state capitals. So much for that. Wade flinched involuntarily as another shell blew up only a block or so away. Something was burning in that direction, sending thick black smoke up into the afternoon sky.

The roar of battle was coming from the east side, where the trench lines were. The nearby musket fire had died out, leaving them with no clear idea of where the fighting in the city was occurring. Wade assumed that the city was filled with groups just like his, both Confederate and Yankee, making their way carefully along the deserted streets.

As they crossed an intersection he glanced down a side street. A nice residential area, fine houses with plenty of trees. It reminded him of—

Abruptly he caught sight of movement, a flash of dark blue . . .

"Yankees!" he shouted as he pulled out his Colt.

He started down the street, nearly colliding with Mayfield. The street was narrow enough to make it difficult riding two abreast. Reaching the spot where he'd seen the Yankee troops, he pulled up short and looked around him. There was nothing in sight.

He turned to see half a dozen of his men stopped behind him while the others trotted to join them in a line reaching back to the intersection. He raised the pistol. "Now, be careful . . ."

A blast of gunfire burst from behind the houses to his right. Sewell pitched face-first off his horse nearly at Wade's feet. He raised his gun and fired in the space between the buildings, aiming at nothing in particular. The rest of the men opened up as well, shooting in all directions. Around Wade the windows began shattering.

Thorne crouched low as he headed for the railroad embankment up ahead. They'd driven off that last group of Rebs in short order, but that had left them even more disoriented. All he knew was that a large-scale battle was unfolding somewhere to his front. The problem was getting to it.

The artillery barrage had stopped at last, but not before setting fires in several different areas of the city. He could see smoke rising from all quarters of the compass. It seemed to be spreading.

He reached the embankment and went to earth behind it. The rest of the men joined him. Raising his head, he ran his eyes over the area in front of them. He had a good view of several streets branching off from the one paralleling the rail line. And there, down the middle one . . .

"Look there," Willis said.

"I see 'em," he ducked down behind then embankment and glanced at the men around him. "You there . . . what's your name. Private? get that damnfool barrel down."

". . . sorry, sir . . . Private Emmet."

"All right," he told them. "Check your firearms. We'll wait till they get close and then give 'em hell."

"They infantry or cavalry?"

"I didn't see any horses," Willis said.

Thorne motioned for quiet. He thought he could hear someone speaking. He chanced another quick glance and saw that they were roughly a half-block away. Looked to be about two dozen of them. Dropping back down, he waited a long moment. There: somebody had just said something. He could almost hear that southern lilt in the voice.

"All right," he said. "Let's give 'em a hotfoot."

They rose smoothly from the embankment and fired almost simultaneously. The approaching Rebels didn't see a thing until the guns opened up. Five of them fell immediately, sprawled lifeless across the dirt street. The others scattered.

Thorne and the Indianans kept their heads down with pistol and repeater fire while the others reloaded their '61s. Return fire was weak and sporadic.

"Watch that bush," Willis said. He fired his Spencer and somebody at the other side cried out. A moment later the men rose to give them another volley.

"Retreat!" a Rebel officer shouted.

"Must be fifty of 'em over there . . ."

Squatting shapes began running awkwardly down the street. Thorne fired his last round. One of the Ohio boys, late at reloading, sent a shot after them.

The men got to their feet, laughing among themselves. "Fifty, huh? Where'd the other twenty-eight of us get to?" somebody said.

Thorne smiled and sat atop the rail to reload.

"Having a pretty good day here . . ." Willis was saying.

A gunshot sounded, knocking Wittfield off his feet. Thorne swung around to see a much larger force of Rebels racing down the railway toward them. As he watched, they began screeching that noxious battle cry of theirs.

Turning back to his gun, he shoved in one more cartridge. Only four rounds, but they'd have to serve. "Back to the street . . . let's go!"

One of the musketeers got a shot off just as Thorne opened fire. A couple of the Rebels dropped to their knees to fire back. The rest just kept coming. They were less than a hundred yards away.

Two of the men had picked Wittfield up and were carrying him with his arms slung over their shoulders. Thorne covered them, backing up slowly and taking slow, deliberate shots. In a moment they were back among the shelter of the houses.

Several of the Indianans finished loading their Spencers and opened up on the Rebels. "There's one down," one of them said.

Thorne went over to where Wittfield rested against a tree. His entire jacket front was soaked in blood. Thorne couldn't even make out where the wound was. His mouth was working and a trail of blood dripped from one corner.

Thorne leaned close to him. "Steady, Francis," he said. Wittfield was new, scarcely six months in harness. He'd left college to join up.

The carbines roared behind him. "That stopped 'em," somebody said at last.

Wittfield's lips contorted again. His mouth fell open and blood gushed out in what seemed be a steady stream. He said something that Thorne didn't catch. He leaned closer. "What's that?"

"I didn't know it would be like this . . ."

Thorne moved back, trying to think of something to say, anything at all that would serve as an answer. He was still thinking when Wittfield suddenly contorted and collapsed against the tree.

"Oh, Christ," somebody said.

Thorne got to his feet. A sound caught his attention, the clatter of feet from the next street over. The Rebs were trying to flank them.

"All right, let's go," Thorne said.

Someone gestured toward Wittfield.

"Leave him."

Wade led his horse up the middle of the street. He was holding his pistol in his other hand, cocked and ready to fire. The air was hazy with smoke—he could see clearly little more than a block ahead. Somebody said it smelled like coal smoke. There was a coalyard not too far from here.

The horses were nervous, whinnying and stamping their hooves. He told the men to dismount after that affray with the bluebellies just now. They were too easy to see on horseback. Where the Yankees had gone, he had no idea. He doubted that they'd hit any of them. They'd sure as hell chewed up those houses, though. Somebody had been crying inside one of them as they'd left the street.

Shapes were moving onto the street up ahead. He raised the pistol, but let it drop as the figures became clear: Yankee civilians.

There were dozens of them, all of them coming from the direction of the thickest smoke. Many of them were carrying various items—keepsakes or family treasures that they wished most to save from the flames, most likely. A few of the women had children in their arms.

The ones in the lead came to a halt as they caught sight of Wade and his men. A few of them lowered their heads and walked on, keeping as far away from the troops as they could. "Let 'em pass," Wade called back.

The others pushed on when they saw the first ones pass Wade's cavalrymen unmolested. By now they nearly filled the street from one curb to the other. They walked past quickly, saying nothing. Many of them were stained by smoke. A few had suffered what looked to Wade like burns.

A woman—a young one—came rushing up the street faster than the rest. Her hair was disheveled, and a sack of some sort slung over one shoulder was heavy enough to bow her down toward the street. She was heading straight for Wade. He realized too late that she didn't even know he was there.

"Miss . . ." he called out as she collided with him. She started to fall and he gripped one of her arms to help her keep her feet. As she caught her balance she looked up at him. Her eyes widened and she let out a high-pitched scream.

He raised a hand to ward off the fists beating at his chest. He let her go, but she kept on flailing at him all the same. At last he reached out gave the sack a sharp shove to move her on her way.

Two civilians stood glaring at him. They turned and resumed walking. He glanced over his shoulder to see the girl dragging the sack down the street. She looked back at him, her lips quivering. Somebody shouted, "God damn you Rebels."

He turned away. What had she been thinking, anyway? What had she taken him for? He thought of Blandon, what he'd done in that farm village. She couldn't have thought *that*. That couldn't have been it, could it?

A sense of unbearable shame shot through him. Up ahead they were still coming, looming like wraiths out of the thickening smoke. Waving to the men behind him, he started pushing through them.

The butternuts had stuck to them like bone glue. They fought a running gun battle for a good three-four blocks until Thorne led the men into the smoke-covered section of town. Now they'd lost the Rebs at last—at least he hoped so.

He gave his arm a shake. His sleeve was soaked with Wittfield's blood. It was starting to get tacky. It really bothered him. Cold as it was, he was considering taking the jacket off and dumping it.

Shapes appeared in the smoke up ahead. He lifted the pistol, paused with it halfway raised. There was something about them . . . .

Around him the men opened fire. The shapes began to drop. At least some of them were wearing skirts.

Thorne raised his hand. "Cease fire!" The shots continued. "Goddammit, I said cease fire!"

He swung toward them. Emmet was staring ahead of him, his face contorted. Thorne reached out and seized his carbine barrel. It burned his hand. Emmet had already fired.

Beyond him someone else fired. Thorne opened his mouth to shout but Archie Willis had already laid hands on him.

"Oh my God," Emmet said.

Thorne pulled his hand back, squeezed his burned palm. Turning, he saw several of the civilians standing in confusion, gesturing at the bodies at their feet. A woman was sobbing loudly.

"Come on," he told the men. He was finishing his first step in the direction of civilians when dimmer shapes appeared in the smoke beyond them. Flashes pierced the smoke, and the remaining civilians began to drop.

"Rebels," Thorne shouted. He raised his pistol and started firing.

Firing burst out very close by, no more than a block away. Wade swung in that direction, hand instinctively falling on his pistol butt. A man grabbed two children by the arms and rushed them past him.

The firing died down, but then returned louder than ever. Wade drew his pistol. Around him he could sense his men doing the same. A woman ran by, one hand stifling sobs.

His horse suddenly neighed and rose slightly on its rear legs. Wade awkwardly reached over to pat its neck with his left hand. It dropped back and shook its head fiercely.

The firing died down once again. After a moment, Wade let himself relax. "Steady," he said to no one in particular.

Thorne stood alone in the smoke. He could see no one around him. Any nearby sound was drowned out by the constant firing in the distance.

"6th Indiana," he called out. There was no answer.

He turned and went back to where the civilians had stood. No one stood there now. Whoever had been left alive had fled, leaving behind five bodies lying on the dirt street.

He paused above one girl wearing a blue dress. Even though she was lying face down, he could see that she was young. That much he could tell. No older than Cassie, if that. He crouched over her and, gripping her shoulder, turned her over.

He recoiled, nearly falling over backward. She had no face. It was just blood and bone, not a face anymore at all.

He let out a sound, gripped the pistol with both hands, as if to rip the barrel from the frame. He tore his eyes away, but immediately turned back to the ruined face. He heard a voice, speaking as if into his ear at this very moment:

"I didn't know it would be like this."

He gazed down at the pistol, its cylinder empty. He hadn't fired it at these people. Or had he? He was almost sure he hadn't. Almost sure. He thought back over it again, trying to pin the moment down. Dear God, he had to know he hadn't done this. . . .

He made a gesture as if to throw the pistol aside, instead resting the barrel on the ground. He reached up and rubbed his face. He could smell the spent powder on his hand.

He heard a sound and looked up. Amid the smoke, a man was aiming a pistol at him. At last, he raised the barrel. "Sorry, sir."

Thorne got his feet. The man came forward. "Captain O'Doinn, 69th New York."

"I'm Thorne. 6th Indiana. I've lost track of my men." He gestured toward the Confederate corpses to his left. "We had a gunfight here . . ."

"I heard it. There's some Midwesterners up the way by my people."

"Very well." He glanced once again at the girl, wishing he had something to cover her with. The officer followed his gaze. "Poor lass."

"What a madhouse," Thorne said as they stepped over the butternut corpses.

"Sure and it is," O'Doinn told him. "Shouldn't have been this way. It's a true thing that Baldy Smith paused during the advance to dress his lines. That allowed the Rebels to get in behind Sedgwick's troops." He smiled crookedly at Thorne. "Which is to say ourselves. It's been like this ever since."

Thorne didn't answer immediately. He was thinking of that girl back there. He wondered what her name had been. Had she been a beauty? Had she been admired by the men of her circle? Did she have a beau? Or had she been married, and had children, children who would wonder why mother had gone away never to return . . . Oh dear

God, he had to stop thinking of this. He would lose his mind if he didn't stop. "Well . . . what can you say about a general nicknamed Baldy?"

Several shapes appeared in the smoke up ahead. A voice called out, *"Go bhfuil tú, Captaen?"*

"Mar sin, tá sé," O'Doinn answered.

They paused among O'Doinn's troops. Thorne realized that he was still holding his Colt. He instinctively opened the cylinder to find it empty. Rummaging inside his cartridge case, he found nothing there either. "I'm out of ammunition," he muttered.

O'Doinn broke off from speaking with his men in whatever language they were using to point up the street. "He won't be needing his."

Thorne walked over to see a southern officer sprawled on his back. Under his gray overcoat he saw a cartridge case. Crouching down, Thorne reached for it only for his fingers to jerk back as they brushed against the body.

There was a roar from somewhere behind him as he rubbed his hands together. "There goes another house," somebody shouted.

Thorne flipped open the cartridge case, His hands shook as scrabbled at the balls and wads inside it. He became aware that somebody was speaking to him. He looked up to see Archie Willis gazing down at him.

"Steve . . . are you all right?"

Behind him a man appeared leading a horse. "All you men follow me," he called out. "We've got the Rebels on the run!"

". . . we've got the bluebellies on the run," the officer shouted at Wade. He was on horseback, and it didn't seem to bother him that Wade and his men had nearly opened up on him just now.

"General Longstreet is organizing a charge," he went on. "You boys go on up there and join him."

He continued on past them. "Where's he at, exactly?" Wade called out.

"Just go on ahead, you'll find him."

Thorne crouched at the far side of the intersection. He was not at all sure what he was facing, who was in command, or much of anything else. Around him a hundred or more troops waited behind bushes and trees. Not a single organized unit among them—they were all just as mixed as his own troops.

Willis scrambled up beside him. "Talked to a major from Sedgwick's staff," he said breathlessly. "There's supposed to be a lot of Rebels in these next few blocks. They think they're coming together somewhere around here. We need to bust 'em up."

Thorne gazed at him, unable to collect his thoughts. He started at a nearby crashing sound.

"There goes another goddamn building," somebody said.

"All right," Thorne said. "Let's run over there, take a quick look."

"Okay. Weber, Emmet . . ."

Thorne had taken no more than three steps out from under the trees when a sudden burst of gunfire from down the street drove him back.

"There's somebody up in that church steeple there," Emmet said. "I just saw him move."

Thorne looked in that direction. While the smoke here was not quite as thick as it was elsewhere, the steeple, a block and a half down, was still little more than a silhouette in the dimness. He pulled out his glasses. That was a little better . . . Yessir, somebody was up there, all right. "Did he fire at us?"

"Don't think so," Emmet said.

"He's spotting, that what he's doing."

Thorne nodded. "We need a sharpshooter."

Willis called out. A second later, a short, clean-shaven trooper approached. He saluted. "Sergeant Bauer, sir."

"Sergeant . . . that steeple over there . . ."

"Ja . . . I see him." Without another word, he shouldered his rifle, a very expensive model, and fired. Thorne looked at the steeple just in time to see a shape fall out and slide over the edge of the roof.

The sergeant set his rifle down and turned to the troops behind him. "A '61, bitte. Rifle loaded, ja?"

Taking the gun, he put it to his shoulder and fired in one smooth motion, then studied the steeple for a second. "Another Johnny in there. Gone now. Not sure if I hit him."

Thorne squinted at the church. "You actually saw somebody in there?"

"That I did." He nodded. "Sir."

"Why don't you stick with us?"

"My pleasure, sir. Can't find my unit, anyway."

A figure appeared behind them. "Start moving forward in five minutes," he said. He was gone before Thorne had time to answer.

Wade stopped and raised one hand. The men came to a halt behind him.

He studied the street ahead, examining it as closely as the smoke allowed. There had been gunfire in this direction a moment ago, one furious burst followed by two distinct shots. Now it was quiet, the street empty. There weren't even any civilians in sight.

He ran his gaze across the empty intersection and on to the church to the right. He couldn't say what he was looking for, but something up there had him spooked. It was the kind of thing you picked up after being in battle but could never explain to anybody who hadn't seen the elephant.

"What is it, Colonel?"

"I don't know. It's something, though."

"I reckon."

"You feel it?"

"That I do."

"All right. Let's saddle up." He got his foot in the stirrup and hoisted himself onto the horse. He looked back. The rest of the regiment was doing the same. "Pass this on," he told Mayfield. We're going to take this at a gallop. You see anything, just open fire. Don't wait or hesitate."

He waited until he was sure they'd all heard. Nodding at nobody in particular, he raised the reins and started down the street.

Waving the men on, Thorne looked across the street. He saw no sign that anyone was over there. He'd led them around the backs of the houses facing the church. Any Rebels awaiting them would expect them to come across the intersection. He wanted as much in the way of surprise as they could get.

He slipped out his watch. It seemed as if a lot more than five minutes had passed, but it was right on the nose.

Guns started firing somewhere to their left as he put the watch away. "Let's go."

He set off at a lope past the side of the house and on toward the street. There were bushes up in front, enough to mask their movement. There was no response at all as they poured into the front yard.

He was moving out into the street when he heard just about the last sound he'd ever have expected: horses approaching at a gallop.

Spotting them emerging from the smoke from the corner of his eye, Thorne threw himself across the street just as the gunfire started. He returned fire, not even bothering to aim. Behind him the men lurched backward out of the street. One of them wasn't quick enough. His musket went clattering as a horse knocked him over.

His men began firing, and a horseman stiffened and fell. The man behind him attempted to dodge but barged into another horse and went down. The second man slipped from the saddle but somehow managed to hang on as he was dragged down the street.

A ball splintered the church steps beside Thorne and he missed the next few moments. When he again looked up, the soldier who had been knocked down was struggling under the hooves of a horse. The rider was gazing down at him. It looked as if he was trampling him deliberately.

Thorne shouted and fired. He couldn't tell if he'd hit him, but the rider slumped and, after a moment, went over. The horse reared wildly before racing off after the others.

Getting to his feet, Thorne fired at the oncoming riders. His mouth was wide as he howled wordlessly. He realized that he was empty just as something knocked him off his feet. When he raised his head the last of riders were disappearing into the dust and smoke.

He forced himself to his feet. They'd gotten four of them. A few of the men were down as well but . . . they'd gotten four of the bastards, and half a block back a horse was shrieking as it attempted to rise from the street.

The Rebel who had fallen began moving his arms. The Union soldier he had trampled lay unmoving a few feet away. Two troopers walked over. The man grunted as they began kicking him. Willis walked up behind them, his pistol dangling from his hand.

Thorne strode across the street. Without a word he took the pistol from Willis, took one more step and then shot the bleeding Rebel in the face.

★ ★ ★

Wade didn't have time to check on their losses or anything else. He reined in as he became aware that they were among friendly troops, and turned to watch the men following him in. An officer came over and said, "Hey there, fella—we nearly opened up on you—" Then the Yankees attacked.

He instinctively ducked as the gunfire whistled overhead. His .45 was empty. He stuck it in his holster and was reaching for his carbine when a howling mass of men burst around the building to his front. Half of them went to their knees and opened fire. He could scarcely imagine how they missed him.

An officer ran past shouting, "Pull back." He was followed by a dozen or more wide-eyed butternuts. Wade turned to tell his men to retreat but they were already well on their way. He started off himself, grabbing the reins to pull the horse around. A moment later it was dragging him.

They ran into no opposition until they were two blocks past the church—the Rebels who had shot at them earlier had apparently retreated.

They overran the first Confederate position without either side knowing it until one of the Ohio boys looked over his shoulder, shouted, and opened fire at the barricade halfway down an alley. The butternuts, evidently engrossed in the firing a few blocks away, swung around with barrels still lowered. Only one or two got off a shot before they dropped.

One of them was still moving. A trooper ran up and fired into the prone body. Thorne went closer. The boy looked no older than fourteen.

"Let's . . ." Thorne called out. "Let's keep an eye open."

The next batch of Rebels up the block were a lot more alert.

Although Wade tried to brace up the men to make a stand, they were steadily driven at least four blocks before they got a chance to pull themselves together. The bluebellies had brought along a small cannon—maybe more than one—and every time the Confederates turned toward them, they'd drag it up and start blasting away with it. Where was *their* artillery, he wondered?

At last they found themselves among a large number of their own men. They reached a sheltered spot and Wade bent over to clutch his knees while taking deep breaths. His horse jerked at the rein, nearly pulling him off balance. They really needed someplace to put these beasts . . .

He got the men sorted out. Around them, they could hear the sounds of the battle—gunshots, cannon fire, some kind of banging noise like a blacksmith hitting an anvil that he couldn't place. The area they'd reached—a part of town new to him—was slowly filling up with gray- and butternut-clad troops.

He noticed a particular clump of men beside a brick building that looked like a school. Leaving his horse, he walked over. As he'd thought, it was the staff group. He paused as he caught sight of the major he'd spoken to yesterday, but then forced himself onward. The major didn't appear quite as well turned-out as he had then.

He recognized Longstreet's voice before he caught sight of him. ". . . behind us, between us and the river? Well, that damn well tears that, then."

Longstreet was reclining against a tree, which struck Wade as somewhat odd until he got a clear view of the blood-soaked bandage below the general's knee. Wade shot a glance at the officer with the thick eyeglasses kneeling beside him. Obviously an army surgeon.

"Who have we got to send over there?"

"These men here are about it, sir."

Longstreet ran his gaze across the men before him. Wade straightened up as his eyes fell on him.

"All right, get them organized and . . ."

"We'll have nobody to hold this area, General. The Yankees are forming up to continue their assault."

Longstreet let out a sigh and gripped his beard as if to pull it out by the roots. A much younger man pushed his way through the group. He saluted Longstreet and held out a folded sheet.

"From General Lee?" Longstreet bent forward, suddenly gritting his teeth as he shifted his injured leg. "Just read it to me."

Taking a minute to catch his breath, the courier leaned close. "General Longstreet . . . you may withdraw as you find necessary . . . enemy forces have divided our corps, penetrated nearly to the river . . . I am withdrawing our forces from the southern end of the city. . . ."

A sudden flurry of shots erupted behind them. The Yankees were making their move.

"All right," Longstreet said. "Pull 'em all back. Get 'em started down that main street there . . . Have Hudgins handle the rear guard . . ."

Drawing his sword, Wade took a step forward. "Sir . . . I would like to volunteer my regiment for an all-out attack on those advancing Yankees. That will give you enough time to organize—"

Longstreet shook his head. "No point. No point to it. The army is pulling out. We have our orders . . ."

"Sir . . ." Wade raised his voice. "Begging your pardon, but I am asking for an opportunity to recover the honor of my regiment, and secondarily, that of myself . . ."

"What . . . ? What are you talking about?"

Wade took a deep breath. "It concerns Blandon, sir."

Longstreet looked confused for a moment. "Blandon . . . what? Wait . . . Wade, isn't it? Step closer, Colonel."

The general winced again as he leaned toward Wade. "Forget about that bandit. He'll end up in a ditch or at the end of a rope. You, sir, have other things to worry about. Your men, first of all." He fixed Wade with his eyes. "Son, you are a good soldier. Look out for your men, and you will be a great one. Now, you've been told what to do. Go and do it."

Wade straightened up and saluted. The major was nodding in approval. Returning his sword to his scabbard, Wade turned on his heel and stepped away.

Behind him, he heard Longstreet responding to someone. ". . . be a long time before I ride a horse again. I'm not going anywhere. Surgeon tells me this leg has to come off . . . No, Walter, the army needs you. Go on, and my regards to General Lee . . ."

Then the voice was lost behind the gunfire. Wade walked on toward his men.

Thorne warily climbed the steps of the next house. Going to the door, he paused to one side. The men clustered opposite him. He examined the door closely. No sign of any break-in. He nodded at the big Ohioan facing him, who took a single step before raising his foot to the kick the door in. The men raced inside, '61s held high. Thorne followed them.

Inside they raced from room to room. Two of them made their way carefully up to the second floor. Going to the kitchen, Thorne pushed open the cellar door. Coal chute, a few boxes, some rubbish.

Emmet poked his head into the kitchen. "We're clear here."

Thorne nodded and headed for the front of house.

"All empty upstairs," a voice called out.

He stepped out onto the porch. Across the street, Willis emerged from a house and signaled that one was clear as well.

Two blocks back they had been fired on from a house after they'd passed it. They'd lost five men before they figured out where the fire was coming from. The Rebels snuck out the back to get away, but Thorne had foreseen that and sent men around to intercept them. They'd gotten three of them.

Now they were checking each house as they came to it. They'd found no butternuts yet, just a few old people and women with small children. Thorne had told them to stay put—it didn't look as if the fire would get this far and it wouldn't do for them to go wandering around in the middle of a battle.

"I say we just shoot the goddamn Rebs," one of the troopers was saying. "Just shoot 'em. Don't let 'em surrender, nothin'. It's bushwackin' I tell you."

"Keep it down, soldier."

"Sir."

They were coming out of the next house when one of the soldiers, a younger man unfamiliar to Thorne, paused before moving on. Without turning, he said in a low voice. "Sir—there was movement in the window of that house up there. Third one up."

"With the chestnut tree in front."

"That's it, sir."

"All right." He led them past a row of bushes. A platoon was making its way up the street. He gestured them over. "Go to the end of the bushes, and just stand there. Like you're waiting. There's somebody in that house there, and we're going to take them."

The platoon sergeant, a good man named Fisk, nodded. Thorne glanced around until he caught sight of Willis on a porch across the street. Thorne gestured at him. Willis shook his head and for a moment it seemed that he was about to cross the street, but at last he nodded and ducked back into the house.

Leading his squad behind the house they'd just cleared, Thorne headed up the street. He was relieved to see few windows on this side of their target. In the back they found a simple frame door. He tried it to find that it was locked.

"It's loose," the young soldier who had spotted the movement said. Gripping the doorknob with both hands, he pulled it toward himself. The door shifted and opened with scarcely a squeak.

The inside doorway led to the kitchen. It didn't seem as if anybody was in there. Thorne pushed it wide and stepped inside. The distant sounds of the ongoing battle drowned out any noise they were making. Somebody spoke in the front room.

There were two doors leading into the front. Three of his troopers glided across the floor to the one on the far side of the room. Thorne led the others to the nearest one.

He took a deep breath, then swung past the doorjamb. Three men in butternut were crouched together looking out the window. A fourth squatted beside them. He was looking at something in one hand. He was just raising his head when Thorne shot him.

The guns roared and the others fell beside him. Upstairs someone scrabbled across the floor. Thorne gestured, and two men started up the stairs.

The Rebel had dropped whatever he was looking at. Thorne picked it up. It was a cameo, containing a daguerreotype of a seated young woman in crinolines. On either side of her stood two young children. They were smiling.

He let it drop as he heard a sound behind him. A door stood closed at the far end of the living room. He walked over, keeping to one side, and kicked it open.

Guns roared upstairs. Inside the room, someone screamed. A vicious-looking figure with glaring, demonic eyes stood across the room. Thorne raised his gun and the figure did the same.

The woman screamed once more. Thorne lowered his gun. In a settee at the right side of the room a white-haired woman was cowering against a bearded man as aged as she. He was stroking her hair and making soothing sounds. His eyes never left Thorne's face.

Thorne glanced once again at the mirror on the far wall. The maddened eyes, the smoke-blackened skin . . . He couldn't blame them.

"Just shoot 'em all," a voice said. "No surrender."

Thorne turned and walked out of the room.

"Burn 'em," the officer was shouting. "Burn every last son of a bitch down!"

Around him men were kicking in windows, pouring in some kind of fluid, and then tossing in flaming brands. The houses exploded into flame behind them as they leapt off the porches. They'd been at it for some time—houses were ablaze for at least three blocks down.

Wade considered saying something, but then he realized that the officer was a colonel like himself, so he just rode on.

They might be retreating, but it didn't feel like a retreat to Wade. His heart was too light for even that to darken it. He was a good soldier. James Longstreet himself had said so. That was nearly as good as hearing the words from Robert E. Lee himself.

He felt as if he was beginning a new journey. The bleak days were ended. Ahead he sensed glory and triumph. He felt better than he had since he'd first ridden out with the army as young lieutenant. Nothing—not their apparent defeat, not the burning houses, not the endless bodies—could touch that.

They had reached the edge of town. A long, low building burned beside the road. He glanced at the sign. "Clostermann's."

Across the field ahead he could see masses of Confederate troops under the trees. Raising his hand, he broke into a trot.

★ CHAPTER 26 ★

A pile of dead men lay beside the road. They had been killed and then positioned so that they would easily be seen by anyone riding past. They were obviously civilians.

A young staffer suddenly appeared on horseback between Lee and the bodies. He saluted and breathlessly began speaking. "General Lee, sir. Colonel Taylor asked me to inform you that . . . . Uh . . . we're still inquiring as to the exact number of lost artillery pieces . . ."

Lee nodded wordlessly. By the time the young man was finished, the bodies were well behind them. "Thank you, Lieutenant." Lee said as he ran down. "Carry on."

He reached forward and patted Traveler's neck. Those men had clearly been shot, and just as clearly shot by men of his army. It certainly hadn't been done by the Federals. Another thing that his staff thought it best he not know about. Like that gang of deserters that had violated a village full of good, honest farm women a few days ago.

He shook his head. His proud army, an army established to fight for independence and state's rights, was collapsing into a barbarian horde around him.

He turned to look behind him. The smoke from Harrisburg was still visible. The place would probably be burning for days. He had yet to encompass what had happened back there. But of one thing he was sure: it was not war.

This war was turning into something he could no longer recognize. Oh, it wasn't simply that it was inglorious. He had no illusions about that. How could he, after Sharpsburg and Fredericksburg? There was no such thing as a clean war, and no such thing as a clean victory. He thought of the Boy Soldiers, who had died defending the Chapultepec castle in Mexico City. No, he had no illusions. There was always a leaven of shame to it, no matter what the outcome. But still . . .

He wished he could talk it over with Longstreet, with his firm, common-sense point of view. But Longstreet had been terribly injured and was presumed captured. General Hill had not yet been heard from. General Hampton had been forced north and was making a wide circle to rejoin the army. He might not return for a day or longer. Their casualties were unknown but heavy. Just as bad, they had left behind most of their supplies and a still uncertain number of artillery pieces. General Alexander was going to report to him on the exact number later in the day.

The army was now stretched out for ten miles or more, across half a dozen different roads and highways. He had no clear idea as yet where some of his units were. There had been no helping it, withdrawing piecemeal as they had from the city, and crossing the Susquehanna before light.

He needed to get the army across the Potomac as soon as possible. He couldn't bank on the memory of Meade's defeat on the river to keep the Yankees at a distance. This Grant was in no way a typical Northern commander. There was no telling what he'd do.

Lee was still uncertain whether they had held out long enough. He had not heard from Richmond, and that worried him. President Davis had just been about to meet with the British. What had they decided? He should have heard by now. Had the message been intercepted? If the South remained free, he would be able to live with it. Even with the death of Harrisburg. Even, God help him, with the massacre of innocent civilians.

He noticed a small group beside the road. It was a family—a husband, wife, and two small children, their belongings at their feet. Refugees from the city, he supposed. They looked as miserable and lost as so many churchmice.

As Lee drew near, the man sat up straight, staring directly at him. Getting to his feet, he took one step forward, then another. His wife got up and gripped his shoulders, whispering fiercely into his ear. She glanced at Lee, her eyes wide with terror.

Lee had nearly reached them when one of his officers thrust his horse ahead of him. He swung a riding crop high. "Get back there, you son of a bitch . . ."

"Leave them be," Lee called out.

The officer turned back to him. He touched the brim of his hat. "Yes sir."

The officer rode on. Lee nodded to the couple. They failed to respond, instead simply turning to follow him as he rode past, the woman cowering, the man grinding his teeth.

Is that what he was to become? A figure of black legend, a Cromwell or a Tamerlane, a nightmare creature to frighten children with?

He glanced once more at the smoke of Harrisburg. He thought of Cain, forced to wander the earth forever without rest. For the first time in his life, he believed that he understood that story.

". . . yes sir, not two hours past. Robert E. Lee, as proud as Satan."

The man was unshaven, his eyes wide and bloodshot. Behind him stood his wife, hands clasped before her. At her feet huddled two small children.

"You're sure it was Lee," Thorne said.

"Oh, it was Lee, all right. On that gray horse of his. They were all bowing and deferring to him."

Thorne glanced down the road. Two hours . . . that meant the Rebels' main body was not that far ahead. He'd have to send word back to Grant. He swung once again to the man. "My thanks."

"Don't let him get away this time, Captain."

"We won't . . . Could you use some food, by the way? For the children?"

The woman cocked her head in a mixture of supplication and relief. "Some food and water for these people," Thorne called out. "And, uh . . . a couple of blankets."

"Thank you, sir." The man removed his hat. "As close as you are now, he was. Proud as the Devil."

Thorne buttoned his jacket up. The cold always cut deeper when you were tired, and right now he was exhausted. He had scarcely slept at all last night. Every time he nodded off, he saw that girl with her face blown clean away, the Rebel's head exploding as he pulled the trigger. At one point he'd jerked awake thinking that he ought to arrange a court-martial for the man who had done that. Then he remembered.

He'd scarcely eaten either. A handful of hard tack washed down with stale water from the canteen. Not that he could actually claim to be hungry.

They had been called together just after dawn, all the mounted troops. A cavalry colonel—an odd-looking fellow who seemed more like a Mexican or a Chinese than anything else in Thorne's experience—had ridden amongst them, barking the orders of the day.

"You are to pursue the Rebel army and harass it . . . Every available unit. Every last horse, every last trooper . . . Follow them, harry them, tear at them . . . Avoid full-scale battles . . . The Rebels are not to reach the Potomac as a coherent, organized force."

He paused at last to gesture at the still-blazing ruins of Harrisburg. "You see what those animals did to an American city . . ." He eyed it for a moment, and then turned back to them. "From here to Richmond, the only good Rebel is a dead Rebel."

The rest of them had cheered.

He heard more of the like from up ahead. After a moment, a group of farmers came into sight. They were holding shotguns and standing over a dead butternut as if he was a prize buck. The infantry was waving their caps as they marched past.

Thorne looked around to see what Willis made of it, but couldn't find him. They'd argued earlier this morning, when Archie had told him he didn't think that horseman had trampled the Ohio trooper deliberately.

He rode on, dozing now and again. He straightened up as he heard more shouting ahead. A group of men were seated atop a fence, calling out to the passing troops. They were well into Maryland by now— Copperhead country.

"You boys slow down now. You don't want to catch up with Bobby Lee," a fat man was shouting. "End up just like the last time . . ."

His friends were laughing and egging him on. That ceased as a half-dozen soldiers broke from the road toward them. The one in the lead knocked the fat man off the fence with a swing of his musket butt. The other troops hauled the rest of them off their perches and began working them over.

The troops started cheering. Thorne turned his head and rode on.

After a moment he shook himself, then raised a hand and sped up to a quick trot. Lee's army wasn't that far ahead.

"Close it up," Wade called out. "let's get those horses moving."

The artillery teamsters gave him dirty looks, but did what they were told. Nobody wanted to be caught by the Yankees, much as he doubted they were in any shape for pursuit after what had happened at Harrisburg.

He'd set out this morning to sweep the eastern flank of the line of march, but instead had been ordered to help pull together the army, which was strung out for miles. It wasn't easy.

There was a lot of defeatism in this army. A swift change in fortunes would do that. Many of the men still had not gotten over what had occurred in Harrisburg yesterday. Wade could understand that, but all the same, if the Army of Northern Virginia was apt to give up after a setback, they'd have never made it as far as Bull Run.

He noticed a group of horsemen approaching with that particular air of command. Yep—it was General Porter Alexander, completing his inspection of the guns. Wade saluted sharply as they rode past. He didn't look worried.

He thought of Longstreet and a pang of emotion gripped him, half regret, half gratitude. He wondered where the general was now, and what had befallen him. But they still had General Lee, and any army that had that man was, in Wade's book, well-nigh invincible.

He spurred his horse and rode on. "Come on now—close it up . . ."

Thorne didn't lay eyes on a single person as they rode through Frederick. Perhaps they'd sensed the mood of the army, or, more likely, they'd heard what had happened to Harrisburg.

They were only a short distance beyond town when a scout appeared, riding hard. He came to a halt before Thorne. It took him a moment to catch his breath, as if it had been he and not the horse who had been galloping. ". . . Rebel column, about three miles on."

Thorne led the regiment down the road at a near gallop. They had gone about two miles when they were diverted off the highway to a farmer's track. Thorne was assured that it ran parallel to the highway for at least five miles.

A little way in, they passed a wagon stacked high with ammunition boxes and towing what looked like a couple of pieces of equipment torn right off the counter of a general store.

"What the hell are those?" a trooper asked.

"Ager guns," the officer riding next to the wagon told him.

"How do they work?"

"They work real good."

Only a short distance past that, a soldier waved them toward a copse of trees with a lot of horses within it. The soldiers tending them gestured for quiet as they rode in. One pointed to a ridge a few hundred yards to the west. "Highway's just past there."

"Rebels?"

"Aplenty, sir."

The wagon with those strange coffee-grinder shaped guns pulled in as Thorne led the men to the ridge. "How many ammunition boxes do we take?" a corporal asked the officer.

"All of 'em."

The corporal nodded and turned to a group of soldiers marching in. "Spare privates, come unto me."

Thorne made his way to the ridge and climbed to the top. There were already a few troops present. Thorne went past them for a look through the brush, thin and faded this late in the season. There was the highway, there were the butternuts, and there were as many guns as he'd ever seen in one place, trundling slowly down the road.

A group of officers sat together on the rear side of ridge. Thorne went over to join them.

"Gentlemen," a luxuriantly whiskered officer was saying. "I know that we're all the same rank, but I am regular army, so it seems to me that implies seniority . . ."

"I don't give a shit about that," Thorne told him.

The officer opened his mouth to respond, but then looked him over and thought better of it. The other officers glanced toward him and shifted uncomfortably.

"I'm taking my men to cut off the head of this artillery column. Don't any of you open fire until I do."

They looked between themselves but said nothing. Thorne turned away without another word.

He descended the ridge to find that Willis had gathered the men together. Thorne nodded to him. "All right," he told the men. "We're heading down this ridge. Emmet and Kellogg, I want you to climb up there and tell me when you spot the front of the Reb column." He started to turn and paused halfway. "Make sure your guns aren't loaded."

As they started off, he noticed that the peculiar guns were already well ahead of them, trailing a train of soldiers burdened down with ammunition cases. Thorne had no idea how they'd ever fire that many rounds. In a few moments they had caught up with them. Thorne said nothing as they passed.

They went through several copses of trees and across one creek before he saw Emmet waving to them. He quickly climbed the ridge. Looking over the crest, he saw the first caisson of the column approaching, followed by several cannon.

He backed away. "Sharpshooters," he whispered. As the word passed he spotted the gun crew pulling their weapon up a shallow slope of the ridge.

"Sir." The German sergeant saluted him. He had two men with him, both armed with rifles. They seemed to defer to Bauer as if he was some kind of prophet. "These two, very good."

"Excellent." He gestured them to the crest. "Now—I want you to knock down the lead horses."

"Ja."

"Then wait until the next one tries to get around . . ."

"And shoot them too. Block them off."

"That's right." The far side of the highway was rough ground, gullied and scattered with rocks. He doubted anyone could get a wagon across it. "Then start on the officers. Anybody wearing gray."

Bauer nodded and turned to the two men. "We've got it, Otto," the older man said, not even sparing a glance for Thorne.

He left them to finish preparing and went to crouch beside Willis. "We're going in. As soon as the highway is blocked. Leave only a platoon up here to secure the ridge."

Willis nodded. Thorne looked back down at the highway. There was at least a regiment of Rebels in sight, both horse and foot, with perhaps a full division within easy supporting distance. He hesitated. "Archie, why don't you stay up here on the ridge? You don't have to . . ."

"You're talking nonsense, Steve."

Thorne opened his mouth to speak again. Willis raised a hand. "No."

Thorne nodded at last in response. Willis smiled and went to give the men their orders.

Wade rode to a low knoll and looked things over. The line of march was sloppy, but much better than it had been. They'd closed it up considerably since this morning. That was about as much as could be expected, under the circumstances.

He ran his eyes across the ridge that overlooked the highway. Next on the list was riding out to check that flank. He had an uncomfortable feeling that nobody was covering that side of the highway. He could see that the ridge dipped about a mile or so ahead. He'd take the regiment over and ride a few miles north, just to be sure.

Spurring the horse back to level ground, he set out to look for Mayfield.

Thorne was thinking about that sash that Cassie was sewing for him. He wished he'd had a chance to wear it at least once. He wished he was wearing it now.

He looked around him. The men were quiet. A few of them were leafing through their Bibles, others were looking at pictures. Most of them simply stared expressionlessly into space, lost in reverie. They knew the odds. They knew full well what was waiting down there.

Below him, the lead wagon, pulled by four horses, had just come level to them. He glanced to where Sergeant Bauer crouched with his rifle over one knee. The wagon began pulling ahead. He turned to Bauer just in time to see the rifle rise and speak in one smooth motion, as if he'd practiced this shot a hundred times.

The lead horse collapsed. The other three began flailing wildly, neighing and leaping on their hind legs, hopelessly tangling the harness. The driver rose, frantically yanking at the reins.

For a moment that was all. The other wagons and guns continued onward as if nothing had happened. Then all at once, every man down there, teamsters, soldiers, and officers, turned to look up the at the ridge. So compelling was their gaze that Thorne involuntarily took a step back.

"Hyah!"

The third wagon pulled out onto the grassy edge of the road as the driver harshly clapped the reins. A moment later, the second wagon made the same move, turning directly into the path of the third. The third wagon's horses collided with the rear of the wagon ahead, collapsing into a shrieking mass.

The driver of the second wagon didn't even look back. He kept clapping his reins right up to the moment that Bauer shot his lead horse down.

The road was now well and truly blocked. Thorne turned to the other two sharpshooters. "The officers . . ." he said, his voice harsh. They opened fire even as he spoke.

An officer on horseback riding toward the disabled wagons suddenly jerked erect and fell from his horse. Another, wearing a gray caped greatcoat, was pulling back on the reins when he was hit. He slumped over the neck of his horse.

"Good," Thorne whispered. Up and down the highway, butternut troops were firing wildly at the ridge at targets they couldn't see. The Union troops began cutting them down.

Below him the Rebels were retreating behind the wagons and caissons. A few, realizing that many of them were filled with barrels of black powder, kept going, to vanish into the brush on the far side. Thorne wondered how long the rest would remain.

He pulled out his Colt and lifted it high. Around him he sensed the men rising from the brush. He tried to bring Cassie's face to mind. He failed. He paused to concentrate, but with a roar, the Indianans carried him down the slope.

Wade had just gotten the men organized when the first shot rang out. For a moment he couldn't figure out where it had come from, but then a disturbance up at the front of the column caught his eye. He watched two wagons pull out, collide, and come to a halt as more gunshots sounded.

"Yankees," someone shouted.

"None other," Wade said. He raised a hand to urge the Volunteers on and was turning to shout orders when there was massive thump against his chest. The next moment he was falling.

★ ★ ★

Thorne nearly lost his balance as he reached level ground. He stumbled a few feet from the slope toward the second wagon that Bauer had stopped. The canvas in the back was loose and he could see that it was loaded with cannon balls.

A figure moved behind it. He opened fire at the same moment as the men around him. The Rebel dropped.

He waved toward the rest of the wagons but the men were already running in that direction. He saw the Rebels breaking, racing for the brush on the other side, some of them going so far as to toss their muskets aside. The men continued firing at them. He saw several drop, shot in the back.

"That's for Harrisburg, you sons of bitches . . ."

He opened his mouth to tell them to cease fire, but he couldn't find his voice. Best to ignore it. Ignore it, and it would end eventually. He could think of no other way to get through this. To get to the end, to the other side where none of this would be happening any longer. If such a thing as another side existed.

He could see soldiers in blue attacking all the way up the column. He took a few steps in that direction. His eyes fell on a pair of cannon being dragged in a circle by a pair of terrified horses. "The guns," he called out. "The guns . . . cut the horse's tackle . . . Turn the cannon over. Find some axes. Smash the wheels . . ."

Knock out the guns. That was important thing. Every one lost now was one less that Lee would have later. Thorne knew that Grant would be arriving with the main column, but he had no idea how soon that would be. One thing he was sure of was that the Rebels would counterattack well before then, and in numbers they would not be able to withstand. The Rebs had better find their guns wrecked.

Around him the men began hammering and chopping at the cannon wheels. He could see troops in blue doing the same thing up the highway. It looked as if some of them were setting the caissons ablaze as well. He was about to turn away when he spotted a mass of men, butternut and gray, emerging from behind a curve in the road farther up. The yell they gave out sounded as loud as the trump of doom.

It took a moment for Wade to pull himself together. He was sitting with his back against a wagon wheel. He looked around him. A man in gray was lying only a few feet away, his face half turned, and it took a second glance for him to see that it was Cummins, from Murfreesboro. Cummins was a good fellow. Never complained, always carried out his orders.

He tried to gather his feet beneath him, but that got him nowhere. He grimaced against the metallic taste that filled his mouth, the leaden feeling in his chest. He looked down to find that the front of his jacket was soaked with blood. Someone had unbuttoned it and shoved in some bandages, but they didn't seem to be doing much. It looked bad. It looked very bad.

He rested his head against the spokes, his mind a blank. At last he scrabbled at his waist, finding the chain and pulling out the watch. He opened it up and gazed at the picture within. He favored his mother. That's what everyone had always said.

He reached into his case and drew out the inkbottle, his pen, and then the writing pad. He kept them well away from his chest so they wouldn't get stained. There were things that she should know, about how it had gone with him. That Robert E. Lee had praised him. That James Longstreet had said he was a good soldier.

He set the bottle down, got it open and carefully dipped the pen inside. Gunfire had broken out again at some unnoticed moment, making it hard to think. He let his head drop back. He would rest a little while, and then the words would come.

Thorne got the men moving back toward the ridge. The other units were doing the same all up and down the road, stopping to fire as they clambered back up the ridgeline. The Rebels kept on coming, as implacable as the tide.

Thorne looked around. Twenty yards away a trooper was trying to set a caisson ablaze. He lit it, ran off a few steps, then halted and ran back, flicking another locofoco and sticking it into the straw piled beneath the caisson. Thorne was about to call to him when Willis appeared.

"Start the men back up the ridge."

Willis nodded and ran off shouting to the men. Another howl from the Rebels drew Thorne's attention. They were climbing the ridge in pursuit of the Union troops. He could see men falling as they were shot, a few hand-to-hand affrays at the ridgeline. The rest of them kept on coming.

The men were all headed toward the ridge. He followed them. That caisson had apparently caught—he could hear the hiss of burning powder.

At the foot of the ridge he came to a halt. "Indianans, to me . . . . Load up and stand ready." He checked his Colt and quickly reloaded three cylinders. When he looked up the Rebels were a lot closer. At least they were moving too fast to do any accurate shooting.

They were well within range. "All right," he shouted. "Let's give 'em something to think about." He levelled the pistol. "Fire!"

Around him, the muskets roared. A few of the front rank of butternuts fell. Not enough, of course, but he hadn't been expecting that.

"Let's go," he said to the men. They started up the slope. Once up there, they'd give the Rebs another round, then descend the other side and go straight for the horses. Leave a rear guard to slow the Rebs down. Pick them up with the horses and then head north for the main column and . . .

He was turning to the slope when a godawful hammering started. It sparked a sense of recognition, as if it was something he'd heard once before, though he couldn't recall where. It was loud and relentless, a hellish sound, like a dozen devils pounding on anvils. He turned to look for the source, but his gaze became fixed on the enemy troops.

The Rebel soldiers were . . . melting. That was the only word he could think of. The entire front rank was falling, not one after the other, but in a single wave that seemed to move steadily along the line. Infantry, cavalry, horses, all collapsed soundlessly as the earth around them exploded in small bursts. Thorne gaped at the sight without a thought in his head, unable to grasp what it was he was seeing.

The riders began pulling their horses to a halt. Someone was attempting to shout orders over the pounding. That wave of death reached the end of the front rank began to move in the opposite direction, sweeping the second rank down as the hammering continued.

"Colonel, get up here . . ."

The pounding suddenly fell silent. Thorne moved his head. Atop the ridge about twenty yards down he saw a cloud of powder smoke. A banging sound began, and someone shouted a curse.

"Steve . . ."

The Rebel troops stood as if fixed in place, staring at the mounds of the dead lying before them. One of the cavalrymen pointed at the smoke atop the ridge. Someone gave an order. Then the pounding started again.

It tore into the middle of the Confederate ranks, carving a widening hole among the butternut-clad troops, the officers in gray. They withstood it only for seconds before they broke, heading in any direction that promised safety. The gunfire followed them, knocking down fleeing men by the dozen. From the ridgeline came a cry of triumph.

"Goddammit, Steve . . ."

Thorne was turning toward the slope when an explosion flung him face-first into the brush.

He was nowhere near the ridge when he awoke. He was lost amid a pall of dust and smoke. Was this . . . Harrisburg? Is that where he was? It couldn't be anywhere else, could it?

He thought of the girl with no face, saw her clearly for just a moment. She would be here. He could feel her, somewhere close. He swung around, looking in all directions. Somehow he missed her. But she was there, waiting. Waiting to tell him something that he would rather die than hear.

He realized he was still holding his pistol. He moved to slip it back into the holster. It took him several tries.

There was a clattering sound from behind him. He looked over his shoulder. A wagon appeared in the smoke, pulled by two terrified horses. He stood staring as it rattled past him.

He became conscious of the sound of gunfire, somewhere in the near distance. There was fighting going on. No question about it.

And he had lost his unit. He tried to remember the name, but for some reason it wouldn't come. He could see their faces, especially all the dead ones, he could remember clearly where they had all died—Gettysburg, York, Harrisburg—but the name of the unit. That was lost to him.

He took a few steps in the direction of the gunfire. He had to find his unit.

A few horsemen appeared within the smoke, followed by foot soldiers. They were headed in the same direction as he. Catching sight of him, one them rode toward Thorne. He gave him a salute as he drew near. "Major . . . can we be of assistance?" he asked in the tones of the state of Maine.

Thorne gazed at him a moment before answering. "I . . . I need to find my unit."

Another officer approached, a tired-looking man with a ginger mustache.

"And what unit is that, sir?"

"The . . . the . . . the 6th Indiana." He let a laugh at how simple it had been to say it.

"Well . . . I think we could spare you a horse . . ."

The mustached officer spoke for the first time. "I believe the major needs some rest."

The younger officer eyed Thorne for a long moment. "I think you're right."

Someone gave him a full canteen. Someone else rolled him a cigarette. They sat him down on a wrecked wagon, telling him to remain there. They would send back someone from the 6th as soon as they came across them. He watched them march off, savoring the cool water.

He didn't use tobacco, but he enjoyed the cigarette all the same. It made him feel a lot better, despite occasional bouts of coughing. By time he was finished, the dust and smoke had started to clear, and the sound of gunfire had become much more distinct. He got up and started walking toward it. He had to find his unit.

A few steps on, he came across a man sitting up against a wagon wheel. He was all in gray, but that didn't matter. A man couldn't help where he was raised. He had a writing pad on one knee and was holding a pen in his hand. He was gazing off into the distance, as if thinking of what to write next.

Thorne squatted before him. As he was about to speak an explosion came, shaking the ground beneath them. "Hell of a day, my friend."

He noticed an expensive watch lying in the officer's lap. He snapped it shut and slipped in into the man's greatcoat pocket. "Better hide that," he said. "There's vagabonds everywhere you look."

There was something sticky on his coat. Thorne wiped his fingers clean, then reached for the writing pad. It read:

To my Dearest Moth

He picked up the pen. An ink bottle sat beside the man's hand. He carefully inked the pen. "Now," he said. "Just tell me what you want to write, and I'll put it down for you."

The officer simply stared, saying nothing.

"Just tell me. Tell me what you want to write."

The pen shook over the white paper. Someone started sobbing very loudly.

Lee urged Traveler into a fast trot when the cannon fire began up ahead, followed by the rattle of musketry. That didn't sound good. A few moments ago they had heard a number of large explosions to their rear. There was still no explanation as to the cause. And now this . . .

He slowed down as he came to the crest of the hill. As he had guessed, it overlooked the Potomac. The river flowed directly below him, less than half a mile distant. On it—he frowned in puzzlement—floated what appeared to be a barge, piled high with hay bales. On the near shore, perhaps a hundred yards from the canal running parallel to the river, a unit of his cavalry was deployed. He saw that a number of them lay on the ground, along with several horses. A little to their rear, a large group in butternut milled in confusion. As he watched, several of them levelled their guns at the barge and opened fire.

Aboard the barge, a hay bale was pushed aside and the snout of a cannon appeared. With a roar, the cannon belched flame. Almost immediately the shell exploded between the cavalry and foot soldiers. The men below him scattered as shrapnel swept through their ranks, dropping several of them to the ground.

Aboard the barge, a figure rose at the top of the bales. He defiantly waved a rammer before ducking back into shelter as the troops opened fire.

Behind Lee, one of his staff shouted. Looking to his right, Lee saw a black beast of a vessel belching smoke as it appeared from behind a curve of the river. Lee knew it for what it was: Yankee gunboats much like this one had stolen a victory from him after Malvern Hill. As he watched, the forward turret swung around and the huge cannon within opened fire. The shell exploded among the infantry below him, tossing several men into the air. The troops ran wildly toward the shelter of a nearby wood as the rear turret began swinging in their direction. The cavalry were right behind them.

Lee raised his eyes as the second cannon fired. There was another line of smoke well behind the gunboat, growing larger as he watched. He turned to look eastward, and saw a hint of yet another gunboat there as well.

There was a muttering from behind him. Hundreds of troops had climbed the hilltop to witness the bombardment. As he watched, a group of them parted to allow a man on horseback through.

"Ah," Lee cried. "General Alexander—you are the man of the hour. Bring forward your artillery to sweep aside these vessels, if you will."

Porter Alexander's head dropped as he rode toward Lee. He sat a moment in silence, his shoulders slumped. Lee could have sworn that he heard the words before Alexander actually spoke them:

"General Lee . . . I have no artillery."

Lee listened to the details with only half an ear. A Yankee ambush, large numbers of guns and their ammunition destroyed or captured, the rest scattered across the Maryland countryside. It would take hours to gather any of them together, and the Army of Northern Virginia didn't have hours.

Porter Alexander sat with his face in his hands. Lee nudged Traveler beside him and gripped his arm. "General . . . you did what you could."

He turned away and rode back over the crest of the hill. To his right some brave unit had rolled a small gun, a regimental piece firing a two- or three-pound ball, out onto the flat ground. The gun spat fire. For a moment it seemed as if the ironclad hadn't even noticed it. Then the turret swung and the mammoth cannon opened fire, the flames and smoke nearly reaching to where the small cannon stood. Had stood, rather—nothing remained but a scattered pile of bodies. Of the gun itself there was no sign.

Lee raised a hand. "Order them back," he called out. "There's no purpose to that. No purpose . . ."

He stared out over the field, as he sifted the possibilities through his mind. To turn back and confront Grant would be suicide, with his back against the river, without adequate guns and with the army as scattered as it was. To move east would be just as bad. He would be caught between Baltimore and Washington and Grant would cut him off and attack at his leisure.

That left a movement to the northwest, where the river would be too shallow for any sort of ironclad. March past the Sharpsburg battlefield and cross the river there . . . to be cornered in the mountains of northwest Virginia between Grant and Sherman emerging out of the Shenandoah Valley.

He paused as he considered the magnitude of the trap that had been set for him. Caught between a lunatic and a drunkard. He pushed the thought aside even as it arose.

The monitor fired once again, the shell exploding close to the hill.

"General Lee . . ." Someone called out. The voice was echoed by a chorus of other voices behind him.

Lee bent forward and stroked Traveler's mane. He went through the alternatives once again, searching for something he might have overlooked, for any possibility whatsoever, knowing that he would find nothing. Aware at last that the moment had come. The moment that, deep down, he had always known must come, despite all the effort, all the plans, all the heroism, all the courage.

A wild thought occurred to him: to take the men behind him and lead them into one last charge against the metal beasts below. They would follow him, as they had followed him into certain death before. They would do it once more, even in the grip of madness.

The ironclad had nearly reached the barge. At the bend of the river, the second one was now visible. A cannon fired and the shot exploded at the foot of the hill, splattering him with clods of earth.

. . . but he was a Lee, and the Lees never took the easy road.

He sensed a presence beside him. "General Lee, please . . ."

He reached out to stroke Traveler's mane one more time. He raised his eyes to the sky. "Thy will be done."

Turning the horse, he nodded to the young man alongside him and rode toward where his staff awaited. It took him a moment to find his voice. "Gentlemen . . . it is time for me to speak to General Grant."

★ EPILOGUE ★

As they entered Capitol Square, a man nearly blundered into their path before catching himself. He was reaching to tip his hat to Cassie when his face went cold and he turned abruptly away.

Steven gripped her arm tighter. He wasn't the first of the type that they'd encountered this morning. Yankees were less than welcome in Richmond this Inauguration Day.

Most of the crowd awaiting them in the square were northerners. At least she assumed that the few hundred standing to the left were from the South, quiet and sullen as they seemed. A wide space divided them from the bulk of the crowd, who appeared much more cheerful and animated. And there, far to the right, stood a small group of freedmen, all very merry and wearing their best.

The sight of them brought Hadrian to mind. She thought of him often, wondering how he was doing on the Dakota frontier. He had set out last summer, the original core group of his people expanded to nearly a thousand. She had seen them off at the station, as they boarded the train that would take them to the Great Lakes on the first leg of their voyage. Toby bowing with his hat to his chest, the women weeping as they hugged her, Mariah the last of them, not daring to look back at her as she fled with her eyes filled with tears. At last only Hadrian remained, dressed in a frontiersman's buckskin jacket that suited him well. He had gazed at her in silence, then had taken her hand for one long moment, before turning away without a word. It was the only time they had ever touched.

They climbed the slope toward Thomas Jefferson's Capitol, gleaming white in the morning sun. Dignitaries were already sitting on the platform in the front. She could clearly make out General Longstreet, his crutches leaning against the back of his chair. Beside him sat Mr. Seward and Chief Justice Chase, and she thought she saw Vice President Conkling seated next to him. Neither Grant, Sherman, nor any other northern commanders were visible. It was thought best that they not appear.

In front of the stand stood hundreds of blue-clad troops, their weapons grounded but ready. There had been rumors of an attempt on the President's life, to be carried out in the name of John Wilkes Booth, of all people.

Others were visible atop the Capitol itself, sharpshooters prepared for any attempt on the President. Steven knew one of them. The best shot he'd ever seen, he said.

She glanced up at him, unconsciously looking for a sign of the darkness that he had brought back from the battlefields. But she saw nothing. His good friend Archie Willis, who had accompanied him home, had warned her that Steven was not truly himself. And he'd had some very bad days. Days when he had wandered the roads alone, speaking to no one. Days when she had found him weeping in a darkened room. And sleepless nights haunted by a faceless figure that he would not describe to her.

But that was over. The beginning of their wedded life seemed to have put a seal on the invisible wounds he had suffered.

They came to a halt. On the platform, Mr. Seward was alternately haranguing Longstreet and Conkling. Cassie understood that it had been Seward's idea to hold the inauguration, against seventy years of tradition, in Richmond, the former capitol of the Confederacy. A necessary gesture of reconciliation, as he put it. Lincoln had approved, as did many others, including Steven and most of the war veterans.

But not everyone did. The more wild-eyed Republicans were calling it "treason," and some of the most radical had gone so far as to call for Lincoln's impeachment, directly after an election that had given him the largest majority since George Washington. The New York papers were dead-set against it. Cassie had seen a cartoon in Mr. Greeley's paper showing an elongated Lincoln, his head in the clouds and encircled by cuckoos and fairies, being stalked by dwarfish Rebels with daggers led by a deformed Robert E. Lee.

In fact, that was the reason her father had not accompanied them to Richmond today. He too thought that Lincoln had turned weak with the end of the war.

If the war could be said to have actually ended. The resounding blows of the final weeks had not been enough to stifle the spirit of southern rebellion. Grant had taken the defenseless Richmond two weeks before Christmas, as "a gift to the President of the United States." The Confederate government had fled to Atlanta, but had lasted only a few months longer before Joseph Johnston, surrounded by Grant, Sherman, and Thomas, had been forced to surrender. The captured Jefferson Davis was being held under house arrest at the Soldiers' Home in Washington —another thing that annoyed the radicals, who demanded that he be locked up in prison to await trial for treason.

But even that resounding victory hadn't completely ended the bloodshed. There were still irregulars fighting in the mountains of Tennessee, the Carolina Piedmont, and in east Texas. Farther west, John Bell Hood had revived the Texas Republic at El Paso. The most recent news was that he had taken his "army"—if that was the word for a force smaller than a division—across the river into Mexico to drive out the French. Nothing further had been heard for months, and it was likely that the poor deranged Hood and his misguided followers had left their bones somewhere on the Mexican high plains.

Steven believed that the fighting would not end completely until Robert E. Lee made his intentions known. None of his army, the Army of Northern Virginia, were involved in the continuing fighting. They had all gone home after Grant offered them parole. Apparently some had been greeted as "cowards," while their commander had been attacked as a traitor. Duels had taken place and riots had occurred over the name of "Lee." All the same, Steven still believed that he was the only man who could pull the South together.

But no one knew where Lee was. He was in isolation, overcome by shame, the southern hotheads said, by fear, said the Republican radicals. He had gone west. He had accompanied Hood to his final reckoning. The strangest story was that he had fled the country with the huge British fleet that had sailed into Halifax in late January, remained for two weeks, and then returned to England as mysteriously as it had come.

She stood up on tiptoe as a tall shape appeared from within the Capitol. The Northern section of the crowd burst into cheers, drowning out the few boos and catcalls from the southerners. Steven pointed toward the freedmen's corner. They were no less than ecstatic. One coffee-colored woman was blowing kisses to Lincoln with both hands. Cassie looked up at Steven to see him smiling broadly.

On the platform, Lincoln said a few words to the seated men before stepping to the podium. The crowd fell silent. He looked out at them for a moment, his gaze lingering on the southerners, before he began to speak.

"At this second appearing to take the oath of the Presidential office there is somewhat more occasion for an extended address than there was at the first . . ."

There was a catcall from her left. She couldn't catch the meaning, but a large number of the men laughed nastily. The crowd over there had grown a little larger in the past few minutes, as more people arrived. She glanced up at Steven, who looked down at her and shrugged.

Lincoln did not seem to have noticed. He went on smoothly, his tone of voice remaining unchanged.

"On the occasion corresponding to this four years ago all thoughts were anxiously directed to an impending civil war. All dreaded it, all sought to avert it . . ."

A rumble of agreement arose from the northerners, drowning out belligerent remarks from the southern crowd.

"Both parties deprecated war, but one of them would *make* war rather than let the nation survive, and the other would *accept* war rather than let it perish, and the war came."

The sounds coming from her left were abruptly cut short. Cassie looked over at a sudden wave of movement among the southerners. They were turning as one to look at a man on horseback riding toward the Capitol.

She was a little too short to make out any details. Then Steven let out a gasp and gripped her arm fiercely enough to cause pain.

On the platform Lincoln glanced in that direction, and seemed to rise even taller. With a quick gesture, he swept the papers before him to one side. After a moment's pause, he began speaking once again, in the tone of a man in the midst of a friendly argument. "It was for us— all of us gathered here, and all within our great commonwealth, that fourscore and nine years ago, our forefathers brought forth on this continent, a new nation, conceived in Liberty, and dedicated to the proposition that all men are created equal . . ."

The man of horseback dismounted and walked toward the platform. The troops surrounding it parted to create a path for him, the soldiers raising their muskets in salute before them.

"It is rather for us to be here dedicated to the great task remaining before us—that from the honored dead we take increased devotion to the nation for which they gave the last full measure of devotion . . ."

Upon reaching the platform, he paused for a moment, as if uncertain of his welcome. Then, doffing his hat, he climbed up the short set of steps. At the top he paused, as if listening.

". . . we here must highly resolve that those dead shall not have died in vain—that this nation, under God, shall have a new birth of freedom, and that government of the people, by the people, for the people, shall not perish from this earth."

Turning from the podium, Lincoln regarded the man awaiting him. When they began walking toward each other, it was at the same moment.

The sun did not break through the clouds—it had been sunny all morning—and the church bells did not ring—that came later. But a roar began growing from everyone present, and Cassie reached down to rest a hand on her swollen belly and think, *Yes, darling—you too were here with us. We were all three of us together at that moment that America became a nation once again.*

The roar of the crowd peaked as Abraham Lincoln shook hands with Robert E. Lee.

★ AFTERWARD ★

J.R. Dunn

There's something almost godlike about writing alternate history—seizing on the bare clay of the historical record itself and transforming it either to right historical wrongs or thrust it further into nightmare.

But there are some elements that can't be changed—the motives, personalities, and characters of the participants above all. However much you may alter the historical circumstances, the individuals (particularly those that the critical literature calls "icons"—the actual historical actors) must remain the same, their personalities, foibles, weaknesses, and habits all unchanged. If you want to remain honest to your premises and your art, these must stand as they were, as far as you can grasp what they actually were in the first place.

What this means is that their actions will also tend to remain the same, given the change in the circumstances facing them. Lee is not going to turn into a vicious brigand. Meade is not going to be transformed into a wild-eyed gambler. Events will follow a pattern not completely different from those in the base timeline due to the limitations (and possibilities) inherent in character and psychology.

Therefore, any campaign featuring Lee, Longstreet, Meade, Grant and their subordinates will have unquestionable similarities to the one that we are familiar with. Not in the form of a blueprint as much as in echoes—the same themes being played in a different key.

It's often overlooked that Grant's overall war plan for 1864, encompassing not only the eastern theater but also Georgia and the

Gulf Coast, was comprised of a series of massive pincer movements— possibly the largest ever contemplated up to that time. (If we take Rurik/Rorik's simultaneous attack on Byzantium from the Mediterranean and Kiev as being more legend than anything else.)

With Sherman boring into Georgia, Nathaniel Banks was ordered to seize Mobile, while Grant advanced on Richmond across northern Virginia. Such a three-pronged attack would have created insoluble strategic problems for the Confederacy. Lee had been dealing with superior northern numbers by using railroads to shift units from quiet areas to trouble spots along interior lines, in the hope of curtailing northern advances on one front while the others remained quiescent. Grant's plan was to deny Lee use of this strategy by hitting Confederate forces on three fronts at once.

But instead Henry Halleck, always eager to meddle, ordered Banks, a barely competent political general, up the Red River to attack Texas in imitation of Grant's Mississippi campaign, though to no purpose whatsoever (Union control of the Mississippi had pretty much denied Texas any further role in the war). He was swiftly beaten by Richard Taylor and forced back into Louisiana, and took no substantial part in operations thereafter.

Grant proceeded to Richmond, to be foiled by yet another nitwit, "Baldy" Smith, who arrived at the city ahead of everybody else (including Robert E. Lee), but refused to seize the town because he was afraid that Rebels might be in there. This misjudgment resulted in a stalemate lasting the better part of a year.

But Grant was able to deny any reinforcement of Confederate forces outside the Virginia theater, enabling Sherman to seize Atlanta and march on to Savannah.

I have chosen a minor-key duplicate of this strategy, aimed at the destruction of Lee's forces, rather than the Confederacy as a whole. Grant confronts the Army of Northern Virginia in Pennsylvania, harrying it constantly, just as he did in the Overland campaign. At the same time, Sherman marches a force over the mountains of Kentucky and into the Shenandoah Valley, rendezvousing with reinforcements from Washington as he pushes north up the valley towards Lee's rear.

The full ramifications don't become apparent until it's far too late for the Army of Northern Virginia.

In a number of cases, I've duplicated or followed the pattern of engagements in our timeline. Jubal Early's harrying of Washington is a near-duplicate of his actual raid (though the outcome is very different). The ending of the Battle of York, where Grant simply ignores his "defeat" and continues advancing past Lee, is drawn from the Battle of the Wilderness. Union forces passing a Rebel force too exhausted to gather itself for an attack is patterned on the aftermath of the Battle of Franklin, where a complete Union army marched through the Confederate position with the butternuts simply too played out to do anything more than watch.

As with battles and strategies, so with words. Surely, the words spoken in our timeline would have echoes in any other, emerging as they do from the same hearts and minds. By this means, I was able to preserve one of the greatest addresses ever given on this continent, the climactic words of which could serve as a better motto for the United States than the one we already have.

There are few episodes of American history that cause more controversy, by its very nature, than the American Civil War. At times, it seems that there's not a single element of that conflict not subject to dispute. I expect the same response here and look forward to it.

Finally, a word about Robert Conroy. I never met the man, and yet I knew him all the same. Better, in some ways, than some people I have known for years. I served as copyeditor for his last half-dozen books. The work always reflects the man. Like his many other readers, I grew to appreciate his knowledge, his common sense, his high respect for women, his faith in the American experiment (Conroy was the beau ideal of the serious patriot), and above all, his sense of decency.

I am honored to have taken part in the production of this, the final expression of Bob Conroy's vision.

Vale, frater.